Also in this series:

Cracked
Book One of the Soul-Eater Series

ELIZA CREWE

CRUSHED

Book Two of the Soul-Eater Series

Cover Art by Dominic Harman

ISBN-13: 978-1502945853
ISBN-10: 1502945851

For my fans, for believing. This one's for you.

ONE

Like most things, fun is better when it's stolen. A fortunate coincidence, considering that's probably the only kind I'll ever have again. Stupid Crusaders with their stupid rules. For a homicidal group, they're appallingly restrictive.

No, Meda, you can't leave campus.

No, Meda, you know we have a curfew.

No, Meda, you can't eat that guy.

But as they're the only thing standing between me and the demon army that wants me dead, I have no choice but to obey – or at least, like tonight, not get caught disobeying.

I flex my fingers and suppress a giddy laugh as I leap the fence into my victim's backyard. One silent bound and I'm over, landing lightly on the balls of my feet, my knees bending until my bottom almost hits the ground. The unkempt bungalow is old, and sad. It appears to be the type of place that's swallowed a great many happy children and spat out discontented adults, and the work left it tired. It squats in the moonlight, dark but for the bluish flash of a TV in the living room. It's 2am.

He didn't leave a light on for me. But then, I'm hardly expected.

I snake up to the nearest window, cicadas humming an accompaniment to my movements. Hot summer air kisses my skin and I can't help but relish the freedom from all those rules. All those eyes. But this freedom comes with a price: Jo's gonna be pissed.

I wince. No one else will know I snuck out, but her stellar bullshit-o-meter always knows when I'm up to no good. Granted, that's most of the time, but still. She was suspicious today, catching escaped rays of my giddy excitement as I force-trudged through my dull day. I bet anything she'll check up on me, and when she does… I cringe, then shake it away. The consequences will come whether I let worry spoil my fun or not.

And nothing's going to spoil my fun.

I let out a long breath, and, as if it knows what's coming, the Hunger stirs. It writhes and swells, and I don't care about rules, or Jo, or wrecked friendships.

I'm Hungry.

I peer in the window, and let out an excited gasp when I see him, unconscious in his recliner. His face is slack, his mouth hanging open, but I remember that face. I remember how it looked, awake and vicious, lit with a sick light, even though it's been months. His stained white undershirt stretches over his middle-aged paunch, the dingy white somehow still appearing bright next to his dark skin. I press my hands to the window pane, like a child overcome with avarice for the latest toy.

"Annabel," I call, singsong, into the night. The silvery light on my hands lets me know the ghost's beside me before I turn. I haven't seen her since March, not since that night in the motel with Uri when I made my promise. It's taken forever to coordinate my escape, to lull the Crusaders into lowering their guard.

Despite the months that have passed, Annabel is exactly as I remember, damned to the perpetual sameness of the dead. She was only a little girl when her life ended, when her stepfather, the man in the chair, took it from her. She still wears the nightgown she had on that night; her hair's still twisted into little braids. I imagine if she were corporeal, the beads at the end of them would clack. They, like her, are silenced forever.

Her eyes are where mine were, on the man sleeping like the innocent he's not. While I'm all delighted joy, she's angry revenge, which is pretty adorable on a six year-old, even a dead one – like a wet kitten.

"It's time, Annabel." I say it softly, but not without a knife-sharp edge. It's not directed at her, but the violence filling me can't help but seep through every available conduit.

She turns to me and her hard face softens. Her new expression is a combination of gratitude and hope underlain with a crushing sadness. A face that knows it's had something precious stolen, something that even vengeance can't return.

I'll try anyway. I smile at her and the ugliness of what I intend perks her up.

My eyes return to the man in the chair. Colton is his name, though she called him Daddy. I curve my fingers under the crack of the window, and it slides up with the rough scrape of long neglect. Colton sleeps on, but I'm so close now it wouldn't matter if he did wake. Ten feet and not a thing between us. His life is already in my hands, so close I can taste it. The Hunger roars in my ears, and my fingers tighten on the window frame until it cracks.

It's been too long since I've eaten. Far too long. Damn those Crusaders.

I brace my hands on the windowsill and pop myself up. But just as I jump, I'm flooded with a jolt of extra power. My push ends up being too hard and I smack my head into the windowsill. I bite back a curse and let go, falling into the bushes.

Shit, shit, shit.

Hot power surges under my skin, a pulsing, swelling heat that sends me crouching lower and my eyes flying to the nearby shadows. It can only mean one thing:

Demons. Nearby.

And I'm all alone.

TWO

I WAIT, BUT the swell of power doesn't increase. It stays a steady, low burn. Not demons, just *a* demon. One. I let out a long exhale, and my lips curve in a little smile. Thanks to my Templar-amped demon powers, one demon's not really a challenge.

I stay low in the bushes, watching for movement, but nothing stirs. Nothing but heavy, hot air, buzzing bugs, and a faint snore – Colton, still asleep – but I know the demon hasn't left. I can feel him, throbbing under my skin, just as he can surely sense me. What's his game? He has no reason to assume I'm someone to fear. The chances of him running into me, the only non-demon being in the universe he'd sense this way, are pretty slim. Still, he doesn't move.

Screw it, I don't have time to mess around. I have to be back in prison before dawn or my jailors will drag me back. And I'm not leaving till I have a nice long chat with Colton. A little shiver of anticipation tickles my spine.

I slide the window back down, then step from the bushes. "Come out, come out, whoever you are," I call quietly.

There's a hesitation, then a rustle to my left, and a body bounds over the fence. It's a guy, about my age, maybe a year or so older. In the darkness, I can't make out much of his face except for very white teeth displayed in a wide smile.

"Well, if it isn't the delectable Meda Melange." The heavy French accent makes it sound like delec-ta-aahble. "I thought that was you." The white smile stretches wider as he strolls forward and I realize I recognize it. Well, really I recognize the French accent first, but the smile confirms it. You don't forget a guy that hot, even if you didn't meet him on the most intense day of your life.

Like the last time I saw him, he is dressed entirely in black. As he's a half-demon and agent of evil, I can only assume it's his standard uniform. His dark eyes are the kind that should smoulder from the cover of a romance novel, but they aren't smoldering now – they're laughing. His name isn't nearly as memorable as his face, so I just gasp, "You!" Rude, maybe, but I figure "half-demon-boy-from-the-demon-dungeon" would really give my ignorance away.

"Happy to see me?" His tone is more suggestive than our relationship – inadvertent prison-mates – really warrants.

"Surprised," I respond. My tone is amiable, but my stance is not. "I thought you were dead." Last I saw him, he was locked in a cell, a sitting duck for the Crusaders invading the demon headquarters. Leave it to the Crusaders to drop the ball. Ah well, no rest for the wicked and all that. I'll just have to kill him myself.

Like he's reading my mind, his eyebrow quirks in challenge, as if to say, "You can try." And that sends my smile stretching because I would love, love, love to. Colton, delightful though our game will be, won't really be a challenge.

My muscles coil, filling with energy. I take a couple of paces to the left, and he counters with a couple to my right, keeping the distance between us the same. He moves with an athletic playfulness, almost dancing out of the way. Even though I'm far stronger and faster than he is, as a half-demon, he's still got some super-abilities.

"So how did you escape?"

He shrugs, and, while he's off-guard, I make a quick feint forward. He slides nimbly to the right.

He's quick. Real quick.

He grins at my test. It's clear he's not taking me seriously. His mistake.

"I was released once the fighting started. I'm sure my boss intended for me to join the fight, a Crusader would have, no doubt." His eyes spark naughtily. "But that's the thing about being a bad guy – I rarely feel compelled to do as I should." He grins. "Hell assumes

I'm dead, so for the moment I'm free. I can do anything I want."

Free? A sigh of pure envy slips out.

"So you see, Meda," he emphasizes my name, probably to point out that I don't know his. Ass. "We don't actually have to fight here." He straightens out of his half-crouch.

I stay in attack mode. "Maybe I just want to."

He puts a hand to his heart. "Don't say that, Meda." With his accent, my name sounds like Mee-da. "If you don't have to kill me, and I don't have to kill you, what other possible barrier could there be to our friendship?"

I don't respond and he drops his arm, the teasing expression fading. "There are maybe a hundred creatures in the entire world that could possibly understand us." He shakes his head. "It seems a pity to waste one." He cocks his head and grins too big. "And anyway, I knew the minute we met, we were meant to be friends."

When we met, we were locked in a demon dungeon, awaiting my execution. He either had a great deal of faith in my ability to escape (fair enough, I do rock), or he's full of shit – sadly, that's the more likely option. As if he can read my mind, he answers my unasked question.

"I thought you'd pick our side over dying."

Those were the options I was given, side with the demons or die. I came up with option three – kick ass and take names (alright, so maybe there was some *slight* intervention by the invading Crusader army on my behalf). But I wouldn't have chosen the demons anyway. One reason I didn't was because I refused to kill my best friends, Jo and Chi.

But the other… Uri. His name is a donkey kick to the chest, even after all these months. He was with us when we were captured. He wasn't when we escaped.

My thoughts must show on my face because the guy says, softly, "I'm sorry about your friend." His voice pulls me from my thoughts. I'm glad; they aren't a place I like to dwell.

This guy – blast, what is his name? – was locked in the cell next to me for disciplinary problems. Apparently he takes orders about as well as I do.

"So anyway, I'm not really on Hell's side." He shrugs. "Not for the moment, anyway."

"For the moment?"

"Eh, I'll probably go back eventually. After three months on my own, it's a little…" He catches himself before he finishes the sentence, so I do it for him. *Lonely.*

He shrugs. "Honestly, I was planning to turn myself in, so when I felt a demon nearby, I figured I might as well do it now. Then I realized it was you, which is way better." His impish grin is back. "All the camaraderie, none of the torture."

"Torture?"

He winces, rubbing his palm against the back of his neck. "The demons will, uh, have some questions about where I've been the last few months."

I study him. He looks sincere, but demons are tricky. I've only met one other half-demon (me) and I can attest that they aren't much better. It'd be better to kill him, but…

I shake myself. I should kill him.

He nods toward the house. "After someone special tonight?" He feigns casual interest, but I can see the light in his eyes, the way he rolls slightly up on his toes as he eyes the house.

Colton. The delicious shiver returns just at the thought of him. Something special indeed.

"Ever tag-team?" he asks.

Ha. No. "I don't have a lot of friends into human homicide."

"Aw, come on Meda." The guy – did it start with an R? An A? It was something foreign – cuts into my thoughts. "I'll let you eat him," he offers. "I'm still plugged in." Plugged in, meaning he's still getting false-life from Hell and doesn't have to eat the life of humans. Don't get me wrong, even plugged in demons still like to kill, but as anyone can tell you, doing something because you want to is way better than doing something because you have to.

I, on the other hand, am not plugged in and have to eat human life regularly to survive – something the Crusaders are not exactly comfortable with. They nearly starve me in their long slow deliberations on the state of my diet. I'm at the four-and-a-half-week mark and already about to lose my mind.

"Come on," the handsome half-boy cajoles. His smile stretches, beautifully, wickedly wide. "Please? It'll be fun."

It *does* sound fun. What I have planned for Colton is a game, after all. A surge of rash excitement brings my own lips curling up. I have to force down a giddy laugh and my feet tug me gently toward the house. I force the wicked things to stop before they can take a step, however, and bite my lip.

No, I should kill him. He said himself he would eventually go back to the demons.

But he turns long-lashed eyes on me, full of entreaty, as if he were saying: please, please let me come murder the molester with you. How do you say "no" to eyes like those? They are a magical combination of sex and puppy.

Better than it sounds, I promise.

Then he adds something so obvious, I should have thought of it myself. "You can always kill me after." A smile plays at the corners of his mouth as he makes the suggestion.

He thinks he's teasing, but I think it's a fine option. A little fun with someone who doesn't hate me for it – though he'll probably hate me for what happens after. Ah, well, you can't win them all.

I let my smile break full across my face and he smiles brilliantly in return. I get ready to run, nodding toward the house. "First one there gets first blood!"

He grins and we sprint. He doesn't stand a chance against me, but then, that's why I made the bet.

As I said – half-demons are tricky.

THREE

I BEAT THE guy – Arnold? Nah, doesn't suit him – into the house. We stand over the quietly sleeping Colton, not two feet away.

"Follow my lead," I mouth and he grins back. Then the Hunger creeps back to the fore, taking over, swallowing any smiles, crunching my good humor between its jagged teeth.

Colton lets out a soft snore. Wakey, wakey, sleeping beauty. My foot snaps out and kicks the recliner over, dumping the slob onto the carpet.

"Gaah," he grunts, disoriented, and struggles from under the recliner. He rolls onto his back, blinking blearily. He doesn't notice us at first, standing as still as statues, and it's not until he's shoving himself to his feet that he becomes aware he's no longer alone. He gasps, falling back on his butt, and blinks.

"Who the hell are you?" he demands when blinking hasn't erased us.

I don't look directly at him, but continue to stare at the space above his head. "Play with us," I sing-song.

"What the hell?" He stumbles to his feet and squints at the clock. 2.12am.

"Play with us," I repeat, and this time Raynold? (nah, that's not it, either), clever lad, joins me.

"Play with us." The guy uses the same childish pitch, the same sing-song intonation. From the corner of my eye I see that he, too, stands perfectly still as he chants our creepy chorus.

Colton's gaze shifts from me to the boy and back again. His fear blossoms like a flower, dumping its spicy scent into the air. I can't stop my mouth from dropping open to better pull it across my tongue. Colton suspects we're not just children, that we are, in fact, the terrifying things that go bump in the night. But, no, that's wrong. Not things that *bump*. Bumps are clumsy and inelegant. They are sounds made by creatures not at home in the darkness. I don't bump. I crunch in the night. I crack; I splatter; I splash. But I never, ever bump.

Colton's spicy scent says he knows it.

And yet, he tries to bluster through. "Get the hell out of my house." He lifts a shaking arm to point at the door, but doesn't come any closer. He puffs his chest. "Get out of my house! Or–"

I fly forward before the words can leave his mouth and the shock of my speed sends him stumbling. "Or what, Colton?" At the sound of his name his eyes bulge. His mouth opens and closes noiselessly. "Or

me, and I realize I'm being selfish. I point at him. "Or him!" I shout. "Touch me or him and you can leave!"

Colton spins and launches himself at the guy just as I give Colton a shove from behind. He goes flying, face first, toward the boy. At the very last second, the boy sidesteps smoothly. Colton hits the ground with a *whump*, and slides across the carpet on his bulging belly before hitting the wall.

Blood perfumes the air, just a little, from his carpet burns. The smell makes me gasp, and I have to fight down the beast. I'm not ready for the game to end. The Hunger burbles and laughs, receding a tiny bit. It can be very sporting.

Colton lumbers to his feet. He rallies and, with a war cry, comes for me again. The half-demon boy snakes out a foot, and again Colton goes flying. With the added speed from his fall, Colton almost gets me, but I kick away from the wall and dive back toward the main part of the room. I prepare to tuck and roll, but the boy swoops down, catching me about the waist and pulling me to him with a delighted laugh. We're smashed chest-to-chest and in his terrible and beautiful face I see wild excitement and delight and Hunger and wonder and *fun*. I can't help but laugh with him.

Colton comes barrelling at us – ah, right, we're in the middle of something – and the boy swings me out of the way. Our game becomes a dance. If we'd choreographed it, we couldn't cooperate more smoothly. He spins me, I toss him. The cheeky lad even manages to fit in a full-on Hollywood dip.

Colton's movements become more frantic and he starts flailing and screaming like a madman. Then, with a wild yell, Colton throws the last of what he has at me, just as my partner shoves him between his shoulder blades. I dodge and Colton slams into the wall, a cut opening on his head. The scent of his blood sends the Hunger screaming through my veins and I'm not alone – my wicked companion's nostrils flare. He grins at me and I grin at him, two Cheshire smiles brilliant in the dim and dingy living room, and I know in that moment we are thinking the exact same thing.

It hits me like a lightning bolt. "Armand," I say, and his grin stretches wider, a new light in his eye. We stand transfixed, caught in a shared moment, caught in each other, the air scented with the blood of a dying man.

The thud of Colton's knees hitting the carpet pulls my attention back to him. He faces away from us, his hands and head resting against the wall as he pants. The Hunger surges and pulses; it cares not for friendships. A smear of red runs down the wall from where Colton's forehead pressed against it, a brilliant, beautiful streak of color against beige. I let Colton have this break, this moment to collect himself. Our little game is reaching its climactic conclusion. When Colton gets back up, the gloves come off.

The claws come out.

The minute passes. For me, it happens slowly, but

for Colton I suspect it speeds by, fleeing like it wants to be gone from this reality as much as he does. Then I say it. Softly, sweetly. As genuinely as Annabel said it to him all those months ago. "Play with me."

Colton jerks. I hope it's in recognition.

"Please," he gasps out. "Why–" He begins a question, but he's sobbing too hard to finish it so reverts back to, "Please." He slumps down further, until he's face-down in the carpet.

"I will let you go, if you just touch me," I say, my voice hard. Then I pull another line from Annabel's memory. "Just touch me real quick, and you can leave."

Colton, on his knees, stills at my words, then wails into the carpet.

Does he recognize it?

He mumbles something I can't make out, something mangled by his sobs. I take a step closer. He gasps gibberish into the shag.

"What did you say?" I ask, creeping closer.

Again he keens wild words I can't make out. I hear "murder." I smile and dive forward, flipping him by the shoulder. He lets out a wild triumphant laugh and grabs my arm.

"I'm touching you!" He screams, his eyes rolling, wild with happiness. "I win." I hear Armand chuckle. It *was* rather clever.

I don't let Colton go, but rather keep holding him, waiting for him to calm down, waiting for him to notice the pitying look on my face. It's not real, of course. My pity is rare enough; it's not to be wasted on the Coltons of the world. But I want him to guess what I'm about to say, before I say it.

He does. Oh, he does. His laughter chokes to a halt and horror replaces happiness. His eyes widen and tear up, his mouth falls open, and his head jerks back and forth in a tiny little "no". He stares at my mouth, begging my lips with his eyes not to make the shapes he knows are coming. They do anyway.

"Too bad it doesn't matter," I say, almost gently.

He shakes his head. "But... but, you said I could leave if I touched you!" His voice raises an octave and he clutches at my arm, his hands smearing sweat and blood. "I'm touching you! I'm touching you!" he screams.

I smile and sway my head smoothly, weaving it like a snake as I stare him down. "Doesn't that sound at all familiar?" I drop my voice low and husky. "Just touch me and you can leave…"

His hands become rigid on my forearm and his breath comes in little gasps. "No." But he's not disagreeing with me. His eyes tell me he knows, and that he knows I know. He's disagreeing with the situation. He's saying "no" to the fact that this can happen, "no" to my knowledge, "no" to his imminent demise.

There's really only one thing I can say to that. "Oh, yes. You said that to sweet little Annabel, didn't you?" My voice becomes lyrical, a hymn to the dying.

"I–"

"Didn't you, Colton?" I nod as I say it, moving in as I do, threatening him with my nearness until he nods along. "But you didn't, did you? You didn't let her go." Now I shake my head until he shakes his with me.

He trembles and tears and blood and snot run down his face in a gooey mess. It doesn't matter if his tears are for himself or for Annabel. Any pity for her has come far too late. He made her a mere memory so he could have a filthy memory of his own. And I'm stuck with that memory as well, courtesy of Annabel. But I don't fault her. I would want revenge as well.

She will have it.

Any pretence of quiet sweetness is gone, and I let him see the full range of my fury. "Did you?" I roar.

He can't form a response, but shakes his head wildly, as if his sudden honesty can save him. I lock eyes with him and the moment gets longer and longer, and I just let it hang there, suspended. Finally he can take it no longer. "Please," he manages, a bare whisper.

I reach up slowly and stroke his face as he screams in terror, and I hear a chorus of other screams in my head. Annabel's and the Hunger's. It's time.

I pull back my arm. Slowly, so slowly, so Colton can watch its progress. My palm is open, but my fingers are curved, so it will be my metallic, razor-sharp nails that hit him first.

I shake my head. "Sorry, Colton," I say, but I'm not. "Karma, not unlike myself, is a bitch."

But before I can swing, a force slams into my side and I go flying.

FOUR

DAMN DEMON. WHAT the hell was I thinking, trusting that boy?

I hit the wall with enough force to break through the plasterboard. I yank myself out of it, but pull too hard and stumble a little. I twist, snarling, to attack.

But it's not Armand. Turns out, I'm no longer the only bitch in the room. Typical Jo, I hear her before I see her. *"What the hell, Meda?"*

"Jo?" Her arrival is shock enough, but her appearance is even more dumbfounding. Under her leather motorcycle jacket, she wears only a night-shirt that barely reaches mid-thigh. Her twisted and knotted leg, bare but for its metal leg brace, sticks out below. Her battered backpack hangs from her shoulder and her hair is an unmitigated disaster – even more violent than her expression, if you can believe it. She must have left the instant she realized I was gone, which, given that we're some distance from the school – must not have been long after I snuck out.

"What. The. Hell. Meda!" she repeats. Her tone says she's not done wanting to hit me. I flinch, then rally. A prisoner owes her jailor no apologies for trying to escape.

"How'd you find me?" I ask.

"That's all you can say?" She sputters, nodding around the disaster of the room, the trembling and blood-soaked Colton cowering in the corner.

He picks his face up from the floor. "Thank you," he sobs.

"Shut up, Colton," I order, and he whimpers. "Yes, how?"

"The Beacon Map, you idiot."

Huh, I am an idiot. The Beacon Map is a skull that displays a map on its surface kinda like Google Earth on an iPad. Beacons, people marked by God as good for mankind, show up on it like little lights. As it's the Crusaders' mission to protect Beacons from demons, the map is a handy tool to let them know where to find them.

Us. To find *us*, now. Somehow I got tagged. It doesn't mean I'm good, just that I may possibly *do* something really good. An important distinction, and one I hear a lot around Templar HQ, believe me.

The Crusaders are protective of the map. The demons got a hold of it like a hundred years or so ago and slaughtered dozens of Beacons, starting the Hemo-clysm – the bloodiest period in world history: world wars, mass genocide, concentration camps, atomic bombs, and the like. So when I couldn't find it in the underground vault with the other artifacts (I checked – I'm not that dumb), I assumed it'd been relocated – away from where I could get my wicked little claws on it.

But obviously they must have hidden it. Trust my obnoxiously clever best friend to figure that out – and find it.

"And if I found you that way, that means anyone could have." Fury makes her voice shake and her hand grips the strap of her backpack. "Do you know what would happen if the Crusaders notice you've gone? Do you?" It ends on a squeaky scream that makes me concerned for her – and my – health.

"Gee, let me think – they wouldn't trust me? Oh wait…" I say. "Or maybe they'd send me to bed without my supper?"

She blanches, just slightly, at that. She's had a front row seat to the agony the Crusaders' restricted diet has put me through.

"Or maybe, just maybe, they'd accuse me of betraying them?" Again, a near daily occurrence at Chateau Shithole.

"Well, haven't you?" she snaps. "You snuck out to murder someone!" She jabs a finger in Colton's direction and he wails.

"Shut up, Colton!" I snarl, and his cry shrivels to a whimper.

And still, Jo lectures. "The Crusaders will bring you someone soon. You're–"

"–supposed to accept my meals trussed up and delivered unconscious? I have news for you, I'm not the Crusaders' pet tiger."

"It works doesn't it?" she bites back. "But no, you have to have it your way. You can't even try to get along."

I can only sputter for a full twenty seconds. "Haven't tried? I haven't ripped the face from a single one of those preachy, sanctimonious little pricks. They're the ones who aren't trying."

"Oh yeah? What about Isaiah–"

"Isaiah had it coming." So maybe I *almost* ripped the face off one measly sanctimonious little prick. But only just almost – and that was weeks ago. "He's out to get me."

"Isaiah's a jerk–"

"What do you know? Something we can still agree on!"

"–but he isn't 'out to get you.'" She makes obnoxious little quotation marks with her hands.

It was good while it lasted.

"Did it occur to you when you planned this little adventure, that there are demons who really *are* after you? Like maybe a whole bloody-damn army of them? You could have delivered yourself right to them with this stupid stunt."

Speaking of which – crap – Armand. My eyes

skitter until I spot him stashed in a coat closet. The door's open about three inches so I can see him, but it blocks Jo's view. He puts a finger to his lips in the universal "shhhhh" motion, then winks.

The wink takes me right back to five minutes ago. The dance, the fun.

The blood.

I shiver and he smiles impishly. I can't help but appreciate his warmth in the face of Jo's frigid disapproval.

"Meda, are you even listening to me?" Jo's acerbic tone snaps me back to the present. Thank God Armand had the foresight to hide. I can't imagine how Jo would react to finding me hanging around with another half-demon. Probably drag me back for execution herself.

While I was searching for Armand, Colton took advantage of my distraction to crawl toward Jo. He reaches out a trembling hand, but stops short of touching her boot. "Bless you, miss!" he sobs. "Bless you."

She curls her lip as she regards him. "Come on, Meda, let's go."

"Go?"

"Back to school before they notice we're missing." She says it slowly as if to a dense toddler.

I reply in kind. "I'm not going anywhere till I'm finished."

Colton wails again, but this time I'm too busy facing off with Jo.

"You *are* finished. So far, you've only just snuck out, but if the Crusaders find out you murdered some guy…" she trails off, shaking her head like she doesn't want to think about it.

The Hunger roars and howls. It burns along my nerve endings screaming that it won't be denied. I shake my head. "You know what he did, Jo. He deserves it."

Her eyes narrow. "I don't care about him, only about you. The Crusaders will feed you soon, they have to. One more week, maybe two. You don't need him." The "him" in question squeals in terror at the mention of "feeding."

But I do need him. His soul, his blood, his death. The freedom he represents. Well, maybe not so much that *he* represents – I can't think of anyone less "free" than him at this moment. Rather, the freedom his *death* represents. I need what it says to the Crusaders, even if they never get the message. I am what I am and I am not ashamed.

"Meda," Jo's voice has softened, and I hear her take a step towards me. I take a step back. In the state I'm in, it's better if there's some space between us. I drag my eyes away from Colton and notice that she has uncrossed her arms and is fiddling with her necklace – a cheap metal half-heart long since turned green. On her face is a very un-Jo-like expression.

"Please, Meda. Just let him go." She's not begging – she's still Jo after all – but she sounds… plaintive.

A tone she uses so rarely, I can remember exactly the last time I heard it – the night we watched the movie. The night I wished there was something I could do to relieve some of the strain that seems to be ripping her apart, the stress that made her actually admit she wished she were *normal*. My hand goes to the other half of the necklace, hanging from my own throat.

Here I am, not a week later, having reduced her to the Jo equivalent of begging.

I close my eyes and take a breath.

I force the Hunger down a little, pulling it back, inch by inch. The red drains from the world.

"Bless you, miss!" Colton grovels, still on his knees. "Bless you!"

This time Jo handles it. "Shut *up*, Colton."

He whimpers, and I try to block the Hunger's roaring response to the sound. Sweat breaks on my forehead.

I take another breath. One more week, I tell myself. Two at most. I stretch my neck first left, then right, popping it. You can wait.

I can wait.

But when I open my eyes, it's no longer Jo I see in front of me. Between us is another girl, a little girl whose life was brutally ended. Her dollish face is rigid. She's stricken, too shocked, too horrified to cry, though the tears shine in her eyes. She shakes her head, like she can't believe what's happening. "No," she mouths. She looks at Colton, who's pulling himself from his knees, sensing the sudden improvement in his fortune. She turns back to me. "No," she mouths again, then "no, no, no," frantically.

I open my mouth. To what? Apologize? What good would that do?

"Meda?" Jo senses something is happening, though she can't see ghosts.

"Meda?" the little ghost girl mouths.

"It's *her* isn't it?" Jo asks. I don't have to say yes. "Just ignore her. It's not your job to–"

A tear wells over Annabel's lower lid and rolls down her cheek. It's fat, swollen with broken promises.

Hell. "Sorry, Jo." I exhale. The Hunger snaps back to attention. "He's got to die."

Colton screams.

"Damn you, Meda. He does not!" All pleading is gone and she's back to pissed. "I won't let you!"

"You can't stop me," I snarl. And she can't. We train together regularly because she and Chi are the only people I'm trusted not to kill. She's good, real good, mostly because she knows how I think.

But no one's that good.

"The Crusaders could stop you," she threatens. "I should call them and let them deal with you!" She throws her hands in the air. "Dammit Meda, don't do this."

But it's decided. I couldn't call the Hunger back a second time if I wanted to, and I definitely don't want to. "You can leave, or watch." Then, stupidly, I suggest,

"Or you can help." My eyes slide to Armand's hiding place.

She doesn't try to hide her disgust.

"Then get out, Jo. Because it's happening."

"Meda–"

"Get. Out," I snarl.

Jo clenches her jaw to hold back a scream of pure frustrated fury. When she speaks, her voice is still thick with it. "Damn you, Meda."

Colton breaks for the hallway and I dive for him. I catch him by the heel and he slams into the floor. As I drag him back he starts screaming, high, girlish wails that echo around the room and fill my blood with pulsing excitement.

And yet, over it all, I still hear Jo's final, soft "damn you" before the front door closes with a click.

FIVE

COLTON DOESN'T SURVIVE as long as I would like. Partly because he'd already bled out quite a bit while Jo and I argued, and partly because I'm too pissed to be careful. But then the soul-drunk hits, the bubbling high that follows the devouring of a person's life, and I don't care.

I stand, near-giggling over the destroyed corpse, surrounded by the sweet scent of blood and revenge. Worries float away, like they're tagged to the tail of balloons caught in a hot, happy updraft.

I barely react as Annabel coalesces in front of me. She blanches as she looks at the corpse, but composes herself before she turns to me. Her expression is sadly solemn as she regards me. Then slowly she lifts her hand to her mouth and presses her cocked pinky to her lips, signifying I fulfilled my promise. We didn't actually pinky swear, but there's no arguing with ghosts. Or children.

I kiss my own pinky in return. She smiles slightly, and then freezes, as suddenly still as if she were a photograph. Her image becomes pixelated and grainy, dissolving into a girl made of glitter. Then she dissipates, swirled away by an unnatural wind to the places dead people go.

I'm left alone, standing among the wreckage that set her free. I'll never see her again.

I don't jump when Armand steps from the closet. I never forgot he was there; his approving presence was like a warm hum in the back of my mind. I may have shown off a little.

"Meda," he says. I twist, gently, slowly, to look at him. His eyes gleam in the dim light. The reckless abandon of the slaughter spills into everything, drowning my inhibitions in a wave of who-can-care, and my feet draw me to him. "That was magnificent."

I smile at him, aglow.

He opens his mouth like he wants to say something, but then closes it. Then his jaw flexes and he grabs my hand. I gasp as a wave of electricity rushes over my too-sensitive nerves. I want more and twine my fingers through his, sliding our palms together, revelling in the sensation.

"Don't go back," he says. "Not right away. Come with me." His eyes dance, and I see a world of wonderfully wicked things there. Beautiful eyes, deep and dark, like caves full of nightmares. "Let's go find another one."

I lean into the words until only a few inches separate our faces. The Hunger burbles happily at his suggestion of more. It's content, but never, ever satisfied.

Why shouldn't I go with Armand? We could play in the dark, doing what we do best. Why follow Jo home, to sit in my prison? It seems a ridiculous idea, given how the night calls.

I smile at Armand and his eyes shine.

A hard banging makes Armand jump, but I'm too relaxed.

"You done yet?" Jo demands through the door. Her voice radiates fury – and yet she waited for me. The realization hits me like a splash of cold water. "Meda, come *on*."

I turn back to Armand, and see he's looking toward the door as well. His lips compress into a thin line. He catches me noticing, and his mouth relaxes, his lips restored to their plump sensuousness. They're a little damp, the slight shine almost mesmerizing. Then they bend into a smile. He knows what I'm thinking, but I don't care.

"Meda!" Jo calls, like an ice bucket. "Come on, Meda. I'm…" Long pause. The taut desperation creeps back in. "Let's go home."

It's no home to me. What waits there but a strait-jacket of restriction?

"Please, Meda," Jo says. Her voice is heavy, and I wish I could share with her my life-sucked effervescence. I wish I could tie her worries to my happy balloons and send them floating away. Friends should be able to do that. I can't, but there is something I can do, one worry I can lift away. Armand's eyes are on my neck watching the way I toy with my necklace. The metal feels slick from the blood on my hands.

"Bye, Armand," I say, releasing him and drifting toward the door. "It's been fun."

He grabs my hand. I tug, but not hard enough to pull it away, though of course I could. He couldn't hold me if I wanted to go. His grip tightens for a half-second, but then he gives a wry smile and lets go.

"*Au revoir*, Meda," he says, and backs out of line-of-sight of the door.

A nagging nibble tugs at a balloon string, and I pause. "Don't tell anyone you saw me." It's a threat, but I'm too mellow to force any heat into my words. Somehow I don't think I need to, that he already knows me well enough to understand my threat isn't empty. "Or I'll come find you." I turn my back to him and put my hand on the knob.

"Is that a promise?" he murmurs, his accent drawing the softly-spoken syllables together.

I don't answer and I don't turn around.

But I do smile.

***

When I emerge, Jo's waiting. She gives me a withering look, then pulls a package of baby wipes from her bag and tosses (hurls) them at me to clean up with – how like Jo to come prepared – then climbs stiffly onto her motorcycle. I'm definitely not forgiven for sneaking out, but because we're in a hurry, Jo's forced to bite back her bitch-out for later. Her rage is confined to huffy looks and moody lane-shifts.

Unlike booze-drunk, the soul-drunk only increases my reflexes – the better with which to go on murderous rampages, my dear – so it's safe enough for me to drive my own motorcycle. The hot air skims over my skin, the songs of the night sing in my ears, the stars are so bright I can almost feel them for the suns they are, shining down, bathing me in warmth.

I replay the night in my head, pulling out each detail to savor in Technicolor detail. The expression in Colton's eyes when he knew it was the end, the rush of power as I controlled him, the rush of justice when I crushed him.

And Armand. His eyes hot on my skin; his smile, so wicked. The way we moved in concert. How different it felt to share it with someone who understands. I've only ever shared my… gifts with my victims.

Needless to say, they don't really appreciate them.

I keep hoping the clever sun will pop over the horizon, calling us to class and curtailing Jo's waiting lecture, but apparently it's feeling rather dull this morning, and slow. The road passes too quickly while time crawls too slowly. It's not quite dawn when we reach the Templar community and Crusader home base.

After the demons destroyed the last Templar community in their attempt to kidnap me, the Templars relocated to the mountains of West Virginia. It's a little valley as far away from everywhere as they could manage while still being able to procure electricity and wide enough roads to bring in the trailers.

Yes, I said trailers. The Crusaders take their vows of poverty seriously, or at least this branch does. Just my luck to get the Harley-riding, trailer-living clan.

Jo and I stash our bikes under their tarps and re-hide the keys before starting the trek back toward our valley. Hidden escape vehicles, along with the rings of sentries we have to sneak past, are just a few of the new measures the Crusaders implemented after the demon attack in March. The improved security of the new school is something I appreciate most of the time, seeing as the whole host of Hell wants me dead, but it does make it tricky to sneak out for a midnight snack.

The school is housed in a hastily renovated timber mill, an enormous building made of crumbling brick that climbs up the mountainside from the river in a set of stair-steps. The mill was built about a hundred (million) years ago and has been abandoned for at least half that time, so is not quite up to snuff – what with the giant holes in the rotten floor, the crumbling brick, partially collapsed roof, etc. But when your kids train their whole lives to fight demons and have super-healing capabilities, minor things like collapsing buildings are ignored – extra-curricular survival training, really.

Eventually the school will be moved into the new, high-ly fortified stronghold the Crusaders are constructing in the center of the valley, but, as yet, it's only partially completed.

Jo's and my rooms are with the seniors on the top and most decrepit floor of the old mill, at the very end to isolate me somewhat from the other students. I reach the side of our building, and start scaling it. The crumbling brick is both helpful for providing hand-holds, and not so helpful, for obvious reasons.

I'm about ten feet up when I realize Jo doesn't follow. I twist and look down. She waves me on and points around the side of the building, where there's a door.

Ah. Not such a big deal if the Crusader kid is caught out of bed in the early morning. But the half-demon? Clearly up to no good.

Our windows are barred, pointless really, given the Swiss-cheese nature of the rest of the building, but they were here before us. I climb past my room and heave myself up to the shingled roof. Then I creep along to a busted eave and slip into an attic Jo, Chi and I claimed as ours back when we actually hung out. Then there's only the trick of tiptoeing between rotten boards, then skipping down the steps to my room.

I pause outside Jo's room, but don't hear any movement.

Sweet. If it takes her too long to make it back, there'll be no time for a lecture. I hum a little as I sweep into my room – then stutter to a stop.

"Took you long enough."

Crap. Damn those Crusaders, and their refusal to let us put locks on our doors. "Darkness cannot live where the light shines," I was told, which is a self-righteous way to say they don't trust us.

My happy hum turns to a groan. My buzz has long abandoned me to face her alone. The door knob is still in my hand and I'm tempted just to slip right back out.

"Don't even think about it," she threatens, shoving to her feet.

I hide my wince by turning towards the door as I close it, then give her an affronted face that says "I would never!" before creeping over to drop into my plastic desk chair. I brace myself for the coming lecture. I don't have to wait long. The three hour drive did nothing to lessen her rage. If anything, it gave it time to build.

"What the *hell* were you *thinking?*" Jo demands, hands on her hips. Her face is already flushed and working itself up to a magnificent shade of red. "*How could you?*"

Murder Colton? Happily and with pleasure. But I do *not* say so. Jo-lectures are quicker and less painful if I keep my mouth shut.

Yeah, no, this is definitely not my first. I'm becoming a bit of an expert.

She rants and raves and punches the air, while

I fight the urge to make gabby hands every time she turns her back.

It's not that I don't want to be good – I do. For my mom, for Uri, for Jo (when I don't want to kill her). Not to mention, the Crusaders are the only thing standing between me and the demon hordes who want me dead. It's just Jo's and my definitions of "good" are about as similar as an Eskimo's and a Jamaican's definitions of "cold."

She rounds on me. "Well?" she demands, hands on hips. "Do you have anything to say for yourself?" She looks at me expectantly.

"Gee you're pretty when you're angry." I duck just in time to avoid the pencil sharpener she hurls at my head. I hold my hands up before she can launch another missile. "I'm kidding, I'm kidding!"

She clenches her fists.

"You actually get really, really red and kind of blotch–"

She makes an enraged roar that sounds like it was supposed to be my name and dives for me.

I scramble towards the bed, but she manages to grab my ankle and I land face down. Something hard digs into my stomach, and I reach under and haul out a DVD. *Titanic*. I didn't put it there.

At the sight of it Jo pauses in her attempted homicide.

Oh.

Oh, crap.

The events of the evening all become clear.

She must have snuck over to watch the movie once everyone was in bed – about the same time I was waiting to make my escape. Then she found me gone.

She's almost always busy these days. Off with Chi, or squeezing in extra training, or in the infirmary because she destroyed her leg in practice. It doesn't exactly help our relationship as the only time I see her is when she pulls herself away to lecture me.

Except, of course, the last time we watched a movie.

"Ta-da!" she says. I take that as my cue and open my eyes. Dominating the top of my dresser is a boxy television, and sitting next to it is a real, honest-to-goodness DVD player.

I hug it. It is my squishy and my squishy it will be.

Jo laughs. I look at her like the miracle worker she is.

"I thought you might like it," she says with satisfaction. "I explained to Headmaster Reinhardt how you stay in your room in the evenings in order to keep a low profile…"

Blatantly untrue, which she knows. I stay in my room because I haven't anything better to do.

"…and he agreed that maybe you should have something to pass the time." Then her nose wrinkles, and she grabs a flat DVD case off the top of the TV, looking at it. "All the movies we watch have to be approved, but it's better than nothing." She shrugs.

I grin. It's way better than nothing.

She grins back, and points to my desk. "And of course – popcorn."

Jo slips the movie in and we settle down. The movie's pretty terrible, some kind of rom-com with a perky heroine dumber than any extra in a horror flick. It's still better than nothing, and, anyway, I laugh at the main character as if it were all comedy.

After a while, I notice that Jo's not laughing with me. She's not really watching the TV and the bowl of popcorn sits nearly untouched on her lap. She catches me looking. She forces a half-smile and makes an effort to watch the movie. But she has that strained look in her eye that always seems to sit there these days.

"What?" I ask her.

She shrugs like it's nothing, but I don't turn away.

"Do you ever…" Jo starts, then shakes her head. "Never mind, it's stupid."

"Do I ever what?"

She doesn't answer, so I pause the movie and try to look encouraging. Not my best expression, but it seems to work.

"Do you ever wonder what it's like to be…" She nods at the TV. "Like them?"

I try to keep it light. "Like trashy BFF's fighting over the same guy? Nope – you know Chi's not my type." She glares. Of course I know what she really means: normal. Do I ever wonder what it's like to be normal. She doesn't say the word, like she doesn't want to admit out loud that we're not normal. That worries me more than the rest of the question.

"You know… kids whose biggest problem is the mean girls at school." She points her face toward the TV where the pretty brunette is awkwardly frozen with her mouth open.

"Jo," I tease, "we are the mean girls at school."

She doesn't smile. "Forget it." She sets the popcorn on my desk with more force than necessary. She grabs a pillow and plumps it like it's the enemy. "It's stupid."

It is stupid. We aren't normal. Not even close. And no, I haven't ever thought about it, not once. But it occurs to me – Jo could be. Had she been born somewhere else, to people who weren't Templars – or even who just didn't know they were Templars. She would fit into a normal family and a normal high school (though I've no doubt she'd still be a mean girl).

But I'm not that way. My different-ness is more than a matter of upbringing, it's in my DNA. It's not even just that I eat people; it's that I want to. I revel in my strength, my speed, my superiority. I delight in things no normal person would – or should. I can barely wrap my mind around the idea of wanting to give that up.

It makes me sad. Not that I've never thought

about it, but that Jo has.

She still isn't looking at me, her stiff face is pointed deliberately toward the TV. In the glow of the television, she looks... fragile. No, that's the wrong word, even now. Jo's not fragile. Rather, she looks brittle – still strong, but like the wrong hit could send her splitting in two. I don't know what to say, so I hide in humor. "Ohhh," I say, as if I suddenly understand. "You mean if we didn't have armies of demons hunting our every move."

"I said forget it," Jo mutters.

"Or maybe," I nudge her with my elbow. "You want a BFF who's only a man-stealing monster, instead of a man-eating one."

She rolls her eyes and smothers the world's smallest smile. "Yeah, that's it."

"Oh no, I know what you want." I rise a little in my seat, as if making a pronouncement. "You want to live in a society where premarital sex is only barely frowned-upon."

That earns me the expected smack in the face with the pillow. I may have needled her about it a few (million) times. "Jerk."

I slide up onto the metal railing at the foot of my bed – out of range – before adding, "Ah, well, I won't take that attack personally. I've heard sexual frustration can do that to a person."

I grin, bracing myself for a shove. But I miscalculated. Instead of diving at me, she grabs my feet and flips me backwards. I land on my back in a big whoosh of breath.

Jo might not like being a monster-fighting hero, but she does have a knack for it.

She leans over the rail I just fell from and smirks at me.

I groan. "Ah, I get it now. I, for one, would definitely take a life where people aren't constantly trying to kill me."

The smirk disappears from Jo's face so fast, it's hard to remember it was ever there. She falls back onto the bed, and I pull myself back up to my feet. She slides back over to her spot and faces the TV again.

"Jo, I was kidding."

She looks at me. Dead serious and a little pale. "Are you?"

Well no, not really. Monster though I am, I really don't like people trying to kill me. Who would?

Jo doesn't wait for me to answer and turns back to the TV. After a long moment, very softly she says, "I just wonder what it would be like to have the kind of life where everyone goes to work in the morning, then, at the end of the day, comes home."

We spend a quiet second thinking of all the people who never came home. Her list is much longer than mine. Her face shrinks back to its tense misery.

I clear my throat. "Boring, I think."

She looks at me sharply. "Do you really mean that?" She studies my face, looking for proof. "Really?"

"Yes," I say. And I do. "I can barely make it through the movie. God, what if that was my life? The horror!" I make an exaggerated face. She doesn't respond. "Boring," I say again, firmly.

She turns back toward the movie, and lets out a little sound. In a normal person I would say it's a sigh, but this is Jo. She's too tough for that. The only sigh-like noises she makes are in frustration – usually at me.

"Yeah," she finally agrees. "Boring."

We sit through the rest of the movie in silence.

My eyes flick from the DVD back to Jo. She doesn't look nearly as pissed off and actually smiles wryly. "I promised that in the next movie lots of people would die."

I can't help it, I laugh. "Because the boat sinks." I roll my eyes. "Not exactly what I had in mind."

"Yeah, well, for some reason, the admins weren't comfortable with *Bloodspill VI*," Jo says dryly and scoots up to a sitting position. "Seriously though, Meda. I need you to behave." She holds up a hand to forestall my inevitable whinging. "I know it's not easy, but it'll get easier, I promise. They're just testing you right now, to prove that you can be trusted. You just have to sit tight a little longer."

I pick up the DVD case and fiddle with it, popping it open and clicking it closed as if considering it, but I already know I'm going to cave. Once again I'll grin and bear it.

"If you had any idea all the things I wanted to do, and didn't, you'd give me some credit," I grumble. Alright, maybe more sulk and bear it. But still.

Jo, sensing her victory, pushes her advantage. "I need you to try harder. No fights, no sneaking out, *especially* not to murder anyone."

She locks her eyes on me, but I'm not ready to give in quite yet. "I really don't see what the big deal is," I grumble. "We made it back fine. No one will ever know."

And that, of course, is when the sirens begin to wail.

SIX

JO PALES AND our eyes meet.

"It's not about us," I say with false bravado. "No one saw us."

"What if we left some sign?" Her eyes frantically flick back and forth as she tries to think. "Or were caught on a camera?"

My mind flies back along our trail. I close my eyes so I can picture it, trying to remember if we went by any cameras. I open them. "Jo, we didn't–"

"Shhhhh–" she flaps her hand at me. The siren reaches the end of its wail, then the beeping begins. It's a Morse-like code to let everyone know what type of situation we're in. We both hold our breath.

Long-long-long.

I let out a breath. It's not a breach. If it were about us, it'd be long-short-short. But then Jo grabs my arm, and I realize it's not good either.

Long-long-long means "in-coming." There's a

large group coming up the mountain – and we've got to get into position.

In the event of an attack, all the students are to consolidate in the partially completed school. At its center is basically a bunker, a heavily fortified building that contains the headquarters, the infirmary, and stairs into the escape routes below. This is the only part that is actually complete. Surrounding that are the half-built cement walls that are going to be rings of maze-like hallways. When the school is complete, if it's ever attacked, the Crusaders will be able to retreat, ring by ring, into tighter, more defensible spaces. It's layered like an onion, and ugly enough to make the artist in me cry.

In the distance, I hear the pounding of feet as the other students race to the meeting point. I start off to join them, but Jo's hand on my arm stops me.

"What?" I ask. She pointedly looks at my blood-stained clothes.

Oh. "Good catch." I whip off my pants and shirt, shoving them in the single trunk I was issued to serve as All Things Storage, and grab a pair of sweat pants and a white tank-top. I also toss a pair of pants to Jo, as there are probably kids in our hallway. She's taller and has more curves, so they're cropped and slightly booty-licious, but better than being pantless. Jo dodges into her room to strap on her favorite sword and knife. Students weren't originally allowed weapons before they graduated but the slaughter in North Carolina changed all that. I'm the only exception, which is fine by me. Demons physically can't use weapons, and though I can, I find them distasteful. And unnecessary.

We merge with the rest of the students as we reach the exit and spill into the field on the way to the new school. The headmaster hasn't sounded the red alert, so we're not in immediate danger. Still I, along with everyone else, watch the hills as we run toward the bunker. We're silent but for the soft pant-pant of our breath as we strain our ears for trouble.

Chi, Jo's boyfriend, paces outside the entrance to the maze, pushing his hair out of his face. Tall, buff, and blond, he's a good-natured guy who favors comfortable clothes and difficult women. He exhales when he sees us and smiles in spite of the tense situation. It takes more than the threat of an invading army to dim his sunshine. Jo doesn't smile back, but she relaxes a little.

"Ladies," Chi says, overly formal as he falls in next to us.

"Mr Dupaynes," I reply with a regal head-nod.

Jo snorts. He nudges her with his elbow and she wrinkles her nose at him.

Chi sticks with us as we jog with the crowd through the maze of half walls. When we get close to the central building, though, he gives us a funny little salute and peels off. As an upperclassman with all his limbs in working order, his position is in the second to last ring. Jo has to prove herself in classes before she can be added to the roster as a combatant, and I'm not to be trusted.

Instead Jo and I continue into the main floor of the bunker, which, along with the second floor, make up the infirmary. The polished white floors and walls seem to glow, despite the hordes of quasi-dirty children cluttering up the place. Instead of the giggles and whispers that interrupt the evacuation drills, the students are tense and silent but for the occasional whimper of a younger child. In their wide eyes and clenched hands I see the memory of the last time they had to flee from their school. "Jo, do you think–" I turn to face her, but she's no longer behind me. "Jo?" I twist, searching the crowd, then find her wild mess of hair on the other side of the room, moving with purpose. I put up my hand, to call her over.

Then I realize that purpose isn't to find me.

Jo works her way to the edge of the room and, with a furtive look, slips out into a hallway.

No choice for it, really – I slide around the room and into the hallway after her.

I'm not familiar with this building, but Jo spends a lot of time in the infirmary. She walks briskly down narrow hallways and I creep after her, keeping on my toes and trying to match my gait to her uneven one, so the sound of her steps mask my own.

The *bam* of a slamming door ahead brings us both to a frozen halt. There's no mistaking the sound of boots coming this way.

It occurs to me, maybe too late, that if it does turn out to be a demon attack, the half-demon caught skulking would not look good.

Jo spins and, spotting me not ten feet behind her, starts. She glares, swear words forming silently on her lips as she limps quickly toward me.

Ah, yeah, it probably occurred to Jo as well.

She doesn't stop when she reaches me, but grabs my arm and shoves me backwards. We go a half dozen feet, then she wrenches open the door to a storage closet and shoves me in, wedging herself in after me.

"Where are you going?" I barely breathe the words, and still they earn me an elbowed *hush* in the ribs.

When the coast is clear, she slides back into the hallway, me close on her heels. I try again. "Where are we–" I whisper, but she cuts me off with evil eyes and a mouthed "Shhh."

This time we don't run into anyone, and Jo pulls me into another stairwell.

It's dusty and doesn't have a railing, and I try to imagine the layout in my head. If I'm right – and I'm nearly always right – this one actually goes nowhere. I shoot Jo a questioning look, which she ignores, and we continue up one more story. When we turn the corner to the last leg of stairs, Jo's plan becomes clear in the shape of a small, mesh-enforced window. The window is over our head, but there's a handy crate filled with construction garbage shoved in the corner. Jo drags it under the window and we each balance on a skinny edge.

On the other side of the valley we see the dull shine of cars, about ten of them, as they come down the road, surrounded by a motorcycle escort. The shine disappears behind some trees as the road curves. Below us, lined in front of the bunker is our army of Crusaders. About two hundred adults stand at the ready and, behind them, a ring of motorcycles. As we wait, the riders kick-start their engines, and they burst to life with an angry roar. I know more Crusaders are hidden out of sight, ready to ambush the visitors if it becomes necessary.

The cavalcade keeps coming, undaunted by our welcoming party. The cars are silver and expensive, BMWs I'd guess, with darkly tinted windows. The motorcycles aren't the chrome-covered Harleys our people ride, but sleek little machines that keep the rider bent forward toward the handle bars. As the cars approach, our motorcyclists arch around our army to circle alongside and behind the incoming vehicles.

When the cars are a mere ten feet from our army they roll to a stop. There's a quiet minute, when nothing moves. Jo's forehead is wrinkled, but more in thought than terror.

"Jo—"

She shushes me with a hand, then points out the window. A door in the first car opens. A man in a suit, the same grey as the car, steps out. He says something, but we can't hear. Jo scans the crowd below, but all eyes are on the drama unfolding, and she eases up the window.

The Sarge steps out of the crowd. "Hello, Art." She talks loudly enough for the assembled Crusaders, and, coincidentally, us, to hear. At the name, Jo draws in a breath.

"Who–?" I ask.

"Arthur Graff. The Sergeant of the Northern Chapter," comes the quick reply.

So, expensive cars and suits notwithstanding, they must be Crusaders. But why are they here?

I shift uneasily on the crate, and I look again to Jo for the answers. Again she ignores me, her focus out the window, where Graff is speaking.

"Thank you, Lizzie." Dear God! *Lizzie?* The Sarge's name is Lizzie? "I'm sorry to drop in on you unannounced, but I was in the area and thought we needed to get some... things settled."

What things? I flash a look at Jo, but she's still fixated out the window.

Graff doesn't say more, and I see that The Sarge has her hand up as if to stop him. She walks toward our guest, but stops with five feet still separating them. "On Tuesday morning, what did I tell you I would be having for lunch?" she asks him.

"Tuna on wheat. With relish," Art answers, promptly.

The Sarge smiles and strides forward to shake his

hand. Apparently it was a test to make sure he wasn't a demon in disguise. Everyone assembled lets out a collective breath. The angry grumbling of the motorcycles dies as they're cut off and helmets come off their riders. Hands are shaken and backs slapped all around. Apparently we're happy to see these guests of ours.

Or at least most of us are. Jo's mouth has compressed to a thin line and the eyes she turns to me are so filled with worry, it seeps out and contaminates her whole face. It even spreads to me.

"Who are they, Jo?"

"The Northern Chapter," she murmurs deep in thought. So deep in thought she's forgotten to be pissed at me. I break out in a tiny sweat. "Our parent chapter," she adds.

I comb my memory for what I know about them. There was some disagreement between the founder of Mountain Park and the Northerners, and so when the Mountain Park founder rescued the Beacon Map from the demons, he leveraged that into an opportunity to start his own chapter. Theirs is still the largest and most powerful, however, and they like to throw their weight around.

Which, judging from the look Jo's wearing, does not bode well for this little monster.

After my true nature was revealed, a steady parade of representatives from the different Crusader branches showed up to debate what to do with me. I'm half-demon, which, combined with my Crusader abilities, means I'm physically more powerful than anyone on either side – demon or Crusader. Basically, I'm the single most powerful weapon on earth. Or at least, I could be, if I were trained to my full potential.

I try not to let it go to my head.

But because of all the lies I've told and the whole people-eating thing, my reputation isn't exactly stellar. Many Crusaders think they can't afford to risk training me in case I end up giving in to my darker side (or already have and this is all just a clever ruse). On the other hand, with the way the Templars are losing to the demons, many Crusaders (and myself, naturally) wonder – can they really afford not to train me?

And then, just to keep things complicated, I'm also a Beacon, which means one day I will have the opportunity to do some great good, a good so great as to change the course of human history. But the *potential* to do good and choosing to actually do it, are two very different things. Apparently a lot Beacons turn out to be duds, rendering questionable the value of my Beacon-ness. After all, if human Beacons fail to choose good over evil, what hope does a half-monster stand?

It's a lot for the Crusaders to work through.

Call me self-centered, but I'm a little worried this en masse arrival of the Northerners has something to do with me.

Jo's thoughts must be running along the same route as mine; her fingers clamp onto my arm. "Meda, promise me you'll be good."

"I already promised." I try to pull my arm away, but she only grips harder as she stares me down.

"Promise me, again."

I eye her. "Jo, do you know something you're not telling me?"

She releases me quickly – maybe a little too quickly?

"No, of course not," she says easily.

Too easily?

"It's just… the Corps are not as–"

"Corps?"

"Corporates." She jerks her head back from where we just came. "That's what we call those up-tight suits."

Heh, I like it.

"Anyway, they aren't as… flexible as other branches. Meda, you *must* try to be good. Actually…" She shoots me a look. "It's more than that. You need to try to blend in."

"Jo, you're not listening. I *am* trying."

She jerks to a halt and turns to face me. "No, Meda, you're not. Not really. When you hid with us the last time, when you thought we would kill you if we found out you were a half-demon, you did a much better job."

I think back. Maybe she's right, but there's a fundamental difference – back then I was only trying to *seem* good, this time I'm actually trying to *be* good. The latter is much harder, and it smarts that she prefers the former.

Jo's still talking. "So, Meda, I want you to try like you did last time. Try like your life depends on it." Her hands are crushing mine. "I believe you that you're trying, but not that you've tried your hardest. That you've given everything you thought you had, and then some more." She releases my hands. "That's what I want to see from you." She looks at me, and the worry and weariness is all over her face. "Please?" she adds.

I groan in defeat. "Alright, Jo. I'll try."

She relaxes enough to release my hands, and we melt back into the flood of students leaving the infirmary. By the time we make it back to our rooms, we have just enough time to get ready for breakfast. Jo disappears to get dressed and I pull on my usual uniform of black jeans and a dark T-shirt scored from the local thrift store. The Crusaders take vows of poverty and though I've done no such thing, the fact that I'm broke and unemployed keeps me in the style to which they've become accustomed. Today's shirt is an uber-soft and slightly bleach-stained black and red one proclaiming me to be an employee of "Romanello's Pizza, Pasta & Subs." I added some artistically located tears.

Jo tromps into the hallway a minute later but stops when she sees my outfit. "You said you'd try to fit in."

I look down. "It's jeans and a T-shirt. What could possibly be wrong with jeans and a T-shirt?"

She shakes her head. "You need to try harder. Try to look..." she fumbles for the word, "cheerful."

I can see why she had trouble finding that one. I

don't think it would naturally jump to the tongue of anyone describing me. "Cheerful," I repeat dubiously.

"Yes, and happy. And…" She hesitates, again fumbling. When she says it, I see why. "Sweet."

"*Sweet?*" The Temps aren't the smartest people I've come across, and I do have mad-skills in the manipulation department… but *sweet?* Everyone has limits.

Her lips compress into a narrow little line. "Sweet," she repeats, then ducks back into her room. She comes back clutching something, which she holds out to me. "Like this."

It appears to be a T-shirt, but… "Jo," I say in dawning horror. "That's pink."

"Brilliant deduction, Watson," she says, stretching her arm out further.

I shake my head, holding my hands out and taking a step back. She approaches me, unfazed.

"Just wear it, Meda." Apparently, despite my promise to behave, I am not quite forgiven for last night's escapade. "You said you'd cooperate."

I knew I'd regret my promise, just not quite this soon. "*You* don't wear pink!"

"Yeah, well, no one thinks I'm in league with the devil." She shoves it into my chest.

I narrow my eyes. "I do."

SEVEN

MEALTIME AT THE Crusader school is a bit like stepping in front of a firing squad except they haven't any guns, much to their dismay. Most of the students can't forgive me for being a half-demon (which I can't help). Everyone hates me for being responsible for the demon attack on our last school (which I am), and a third of those believe I brought the demons on purpose (which I didn't).

I suppose it should bother me to be so hated but, without it, I wouldn't have the delight of torturing them with my presence. What can I say? My cheerful spirit can't help but spot silver linings.

I nod and wave to my enemies like Miss America, pausing to blow kisses at the worst of them as I work my way across the cafeteria with a plate loaded with horridly healthy food. While I was out satisfying one Hunger, I should have picked up some Cheetos to satisfy the other. Seriously, since when is broccoli a breakfast food?

Jo watches my production with sour-lemon lips. Apparently donning a pink shirt isn't enough to completely erase midnight homicide, either. Really, I think this particular shade should be worth at least two.

A small handful of students don't hate me. One is Mags, a redheaded mess of a girl who sided with me against a bully named Isaiah, back before anyone knew I was a half-demon. Once I was outed, she still stayed on my side, if uneasily. She makes a point of forcing herself to sit with me at meals. She's a convenient friend to have – hair like that makes her easy to spot in a full cafeteria. I head that way.

Another non-enemy is the jolly giant, Zebedee, or "Zee", as I haven't been invited to call her. She's a friendly and terrifyingly large girl who, as far as I can tell, doesn't hate anyone. If she did… well, I can only imagine it would be spectacular. She doesn't exactly love me either, however. She regards me the same way I would a cat – like I'm distasteful, occasionally entertaining, and not to be trusted not to pee on the rug. Which is completely unfair – I only thought about it once.

I had my reasons.

There's Chi, too, of course. And Jo, who doesn't hate me – just everything I do, think, or say. Oh, and how I dress, too, apparently.

And, lastly, there's a small pack of wide-eyed innocents in awe of my Beacon-ness who follow me around expecting me to perform a miracle any minute. Some-

times I screw up my face like I'm trying. Or constipat-
ed. They don't sit with us. I don't let them.

I plop in my usual seat across from Jo and next
to Mags. The redheaded girl can't help but jump at my
sudden arrival. She tries, poor thing, but just because
you believe a convict should be released doesn't mean
you're comfortable inviting her to tea. I don't give her
grief about it. Much.

Chi sits on Jo's left. He still looks happily surprised every time she sits next to him and always drapes
an arm around her. I suspect it's because he's too terrified to pinch her to make sure it's real. As much time
as they spend together, I would have thought the shock
would have worn off by now, but then, Chi's always
been a slow study. The time Jo spends not policing
me is spent in Chi's pocket. Or maybe it's more accu-
rate to say he's in hers. It's hard to tell – it's an Escher
painting of in-each-other's-pocketness. Had I foreseen
how she'd abandon me, maybe I wouldn't have tried so
hard to help them get together. Every evening they're
off together, and I'm in my room desperately wishing
for a TV with more than five channels. Or a computer.
Or any form of entertainment from the twenty-first
century.

I wonder if she told him about my activities last
night.

Chi looks at me, wide-eyed and too innocent.
"Sleep well last night, Meda?"

Of course she did.

Jo elbows Chi hard enough to make him "whoosh", and throws "shut up" eyes at me, before pointedly looking at Zee and Mags, in conversation next to us.

Hmmm… maybe I can toss Jo another victim to take my spot on her shitlist. I look at Chi angelically. "Why, yes, I did. Thank you, Chi." I look down demurely, like I have no idea what he's talking about. And like I love broccoli. For breakfast. Honestly, I think that's the bigger lie. I snatch a bite to complete my disguise, even though the dinosaurs haven't offered prayer yet.

Chi's never been much of a rule follower, plus he blindly trusts me, unlike Jo who's far too clever and who knows me too well. He would find my escape an adventure, not a disaster. Sometimes I think I picked the wrong BFF.

But I know I never picked her and she never picked me. The universe, God, or, I occasionally think, possibly the devil, picked us for each other. All I know is, whoever did it, has a phenomenal sense of humor.

As predicted, Chi can't let my ploy rest. His blue eyes sparkle. "Really? I heard you got hungry for a little midnight snack," he says slyly.

Jo elbows him again, hard enough to make him cough to cover his grunt. I crack and grin. Sometimes, I think the universe also has pretty good taste.

She turns on me and her eyebrows shoot up to her hairline. "What are you laughing at?"

Blast. Looks like the shitlist's got room for two. There are pros and cons to having a violent best friend with a ferocious temper: she's almost always entertaining, but sometimes she wants to kill me.

"Don't think I didn't notice your cute little act. Can't you even walk through the cafeteria without antagonizing anyone?" As if she's bloody-damn Mother Teresa. More like a mother hen – and I am severely hen-pecked.

I look to Chi for backup. His eyes go from Jo to me, back again, and then toward the ceiling.

"Coward," I hiss; at the same time Jo says, "*Chi.*"

"Err, ah." He looks at Jo and clears his throat. "Meda, look. Part of being a Crusader is getting along with other Crusaders, not just me and Jo." He warms a little to his subject, leaning in. "You're going to be living with us, working with us, putting your life in our hands." He doesn't seem to notice my blanch. "Joining the Crusaders basically means surrounding yourself with us till the day you die," he finishes cheerfully.

I look at him squinty-eyed. "I don't think you're making the point you think you are."

The room gets unusually quiet and I notice a line of adults making their way into the room. Most of the Crusaders prefer not to eat with the hundred or so students crammed into the cafeteria. There's usually only a few present for supervisory purposes, and old Crusader Crips who loves to give the prayer. Today however, Headmaster Reinhardt and The Sarge lead a mixed group of Mountain Park Crusaders and Corps.

I inspect Sergeant Graff. Despite his grey hair, he doesn't appear to be quite as old as the headmaster, who has a bit of a bend in his stance. He looks cool despite wearing a suit in a crowded, air-conditioning-less room – as if his pores wouldn't dare exude water without his express permission.

Jo's paying attention to the new arrivals, so I look to Chi for an explanation as to why they might be here, but he only shrugs. Once the adults take their places, there's a shuffling as everyone climbs to their feet for prayer. A throat clears. It's The Sarge's – another surprise. A brusque, warlike woman, she's not one to spend a lot of time with children, and I find it hard to believe she's suddenly offering to lead the morning prayer. I shoot an uneasy look at Jo and she trades a worried one back. The Sarge oversees the Crusaders in the field, and, after the attack at the last school, she's taken over security. As in, she stops demons from sneaking onto campus – or, more relevant to me, students from sneaking off it.

"Students, by now you can probably already guess what I'm here to talk about." The Sarge's laser-beam of an eye drifts over the crowd, the other long-replaced with a scar that twists half her face in a permanent grimace. Her gaze brushes over me but doesn't pause. I take that as a good sign. I look back at Jo and see her forehead scrunch, then smooth.

She can guess what's coming, and we're not

caught. I let out a breath.

The Sarge is speaking again. "As you may have heard from friends in the field, for the past several months the demon attacks have been increasing in number and ferocity, targeting not only Beacons, but the Crusaders assigned to guard them." Her words are clipped and business-like. Several heads bob around the room. "I see no need to sugarcoat," The Sarge says unnecessarily. As the broccoli on my plate evidences, they don't sugarcoat anything around here, not even breakfast. "We believe they are just practicing, feeling us out for a full-blown attack." She pauses half a breath, then, just in case we didn't get it, she clarifies, "War is coming."

My attention snaps back to The Sarge's grim face and I hear the babble of students around me. They may have predicted that The Sarge wanted to discuss the attacks, but apparently they did not predict this. War.

One group stays silent – mine. I look around my little group and none of them look surprised, just tense and ill. Jo looks white enough to faint. None of them meet my eyes. Somehow they all knew already, and no one told me.

"*War?*" I hiss at Jo. "I thought demons and Crusaders weren't supposed to fight each other directly." That was something I'd been taught in my Crusader History class. Demons and Crusaders are supposed to fight over neutral souls, not with out-and-out warfare.

"Things have changed," she says faintly without

turning.

Obviously. "But why now?" I ask. Seriously, am I just that unlucky? Centuries of little skirmishes, and I happen to show up when full-scale war breaks out. Before she has time to answer another thought cuts in. "And you knew!" I hiss. "Why didn't you tell me?"

She finally looks at me. "I didn't *know*, I *guessed*. The demons have been attacking us directly for months – war was the next logical step. Why did you think there have been so many wounded?"

There have been a large number of injured Crusaders winding up in our infirmary, but I didn't think anything of it. If anything, I chalked it up to us having a brand-new facility. "I don't know what's normal around here!"

Her mouth sets. "Not this," is all she says.

"But why now?" It comes out a bit like a whine.

She pauses, as if she's considering how much to tell me. The Sarge begins speaking before Jo can, apparently tired of waiting for us to shut up.

She doesn't waste any breath on reassurances, but instead jumps right into logistics: what the war is going to mean to us, how we will prepare, how we can help, how selected seniors may be drafted early.

At that, Jo's hand clamps on Chi's.

A year ago, even six months ago, a statement like that last would have earned an excited cheer from the students. Now, after the brutal battle at the school, they are not so naïve. Grim faces fill the hall.

The Sarge ends abruptly with a, "That is all." Despite her words, it takes a moment for the hall to realize she's finished. The headmaster takes over for his wife, introducing the Northerners – not that anyone cares at this point – and then leads the prayer. It's full of all the reassuring platitudes and inspiring nonsense that we didn't get from The Sarge. Finally he, and the rest of the hall with him, chants the Crusaders' motto: *dum spiro spero*; which means something along the lines of "in life, hope," then an obligatory "amen." The students explode into conversation before their butts even hit the seats.

"War? War?" I sputter, my gaze darting among my friends.

Zee's the first to answer. "Relax." I wait, bated-breath, for her to explain why, but the black girl only shrugs. I hate the stoic, hero types.

"She's right, Meda. You need to calm down," Jo says, but she looks barely calm herself. She picks up her fork but grips it so hard it's shaking in her hand. "You heard The Sarge, we're safe here." Then she looks at Chi and Zee, almost certain to be among the first drafted, and corrects herself. "*You're* safe here. They've worked really hard to keep the location of this school a secret."

That does calm me a little.

"And Meda, as far as you're concerned there's a silver lining." Her eyes move back and forth across her plate, as if they're keeping pace with her equally rapid thoughts. "With the war coming, I bet the headmaster can use the fact that this location is a secret to keep you here, under his custody."

If she meant to calm me, she failed. Spectacularly. "What do you mean? Where the hell else would I go?"

She sets her fork down carefully with a clack. She has that doctor-with-bad-news expression. "The Corporates, Meda." She takes a breath. "I think they're here for you."

"*What?*" It's more squeak than word. "But the war, they could just…"

But Jo's already shaking her head. "They wouldn't come here to discuss the war, they'd just call. We're not that important. Except for one thing: you."

"And the Beacon Map," Chi adds, and I look at him hopefully.

Jo taps her fork on her plate. "Maybe," she concedes but she doesn't look like she believes it. "But if anything, it's probably both."

"Can they just do that? Take me?"

"I don't know, but they've got a good argument. Think about it." She leans in a little. "They're the most important, most powerful chapter, while we're a tiny half-constructed outpost. They think they can keep you from the demons better than we can." Her face sours. "Plus, your mom was Mary Porter and you have friends here. They think we're biased on your behalf."

I sit back, trying to digest all the bad news I've just been fed. Suddenly there's no room for breakfast –

even if it wasn't broccoli.

"But they've been discussing me for months. Why now?" I look at the group of suits at the head table.

The answer is so obvious, Chi gives it. "The war, Meda. You're a greater asset now than ever."

I look to Jo to confirm. Her eyes are troubled. "And a greater threat."

EIGHT

I MANAGE NOT to faint. The others talk around me, but it's hard to hear their words over the buzzing in my head as I work through the bad news. The Corporates want to take over my custody. If the Crusaders here are considered biased *towards* me, I can't imagine what it'd be like at a chapter that's biased *against* me. Not good. Not good at all.

Then, on top of that, there's the minor issue of the good-versus-evil epic war about to be unleashed, and I'm stuck right in the middle of it.

Seriously not good.

I'm caught in my internal drama so it takes a minute before I realize my friends have grown quiet around me. I glance up, but none of them spare me a look. All their attention is spread out over the cafeteria. Jo sits upright with a "try me" expression, while Chi and Zee both lounge against the table while managing to look distinctly coiled. Mags's face is redder than usual and I

imagine the expression she's going for is tough, though
I have to say she doesn't quite hit the mark. They all
look ready for a fight – and that's when I notice they
aren't the only ones. The cafeteria is filled with fighty
expressions, most of them pointed at yours-truly – the
half-demon in a room full of Crusaders.

Crap. The war's not going to help with my popu-
larity. I wince. "Guess my dreams of being voted prom
queen are out," I murmur. No one laughs.

As soon as the bell announces the end of breakfast, I hop to my feet, figuring it's better to stay out of
the crowds as much as possible. Chi and Jo must have
the same idea as they also leap to their feet and walk
ahead of me, like a pair of bodyguards clearing the way.
We stride between tables of students collecting trays
and shuffling to their feet. Some glare as I go by, some
avert their eyes. It's going be a long day.

For most of my classes, I'm without friends or
even tolerating-acquaintances. Chi, Jo, and Zee are all
seniors, while I'm pretty horribly behind, even in the
non-Templar classes. The two years I spent on my own
before landing with the Templars were spent doing
whatever the hell I wanted – and, surprisingly, what
I wanted was not to study Western Civ or Advanced
Algebra. Mags, only a sophomore, should be in some
of my classes, but she apparently got brains instead of
beauty, and isn't. That leaves me alone in hostile territory for most of the day.

Usually not a position I'm opposed to, except that

I'm not allowed to eat anyone.

The only exceptions are the physical classes –
Combat Training and Strength and Conditioning – and
my first class today, English, which I share with Jo.

Me can read good.

Unfortunately it only barely counts, as the professor uses that cruel and unusual punishment known as
assigned seating. As we enter class Jo stops at the Bs
while I head back to the Ps, for Porter. I tried to explain my last name is Melange, but the Crusaders prefer
to pretend I spontaneously spawned from my mother.

The cramped classroom is packed with short,
two-person tables, crammed so close that the bulkier
kids need to twist sideways to fit between them. The
usual sleepy boredom of the class is replaced with a
buzzing energy brought by this morning's news – the
tiny confines seem almost too small to contain it all.

I work my way through the classroom, toward the
middle of the back row. Omar, one of Isaiah's cronies,
slides out a foot to trip me. I pretend not to notice,
then stomp on it.

Jo spins at the smothered yelp, and gives me the
"be-good" glare. Then her eyes flick to Omar, taking in
the way he's cupping his foot and puts it all together.

"Be-good" morphs to "Fine-but-no-more."

I smile.

She rolls her eyes.

I slide into my seat, ignoring the glare of my table-
mate, Eli. "If it's not the Loch Shit Monster," he says

nastily. "How's it hanging, Nessie?"

"Oh that wit!" I say as I drop into my seat. "Rapier sharp, I tell you! And here I thought it'd be as dull as the rest of you."

Professor Wendell, an angry woman who was young with the dinosaurs, chooses that moment to enter the room, but her arrival does nothing to halt Eli's whispered assault. She only operates at a bellow, either because she assumes we're as deaf as she is, or, I suspect, is trying to make us as deaf as she is under the whole misery-loves-company theory. Usually I'm grateful for my spot in the back row, as there are times when I see Jo visibly cringe when Crusader Wendell gets particularly worked up, but today it provides the perfect cover for Eli's snide comments.

I promised Jo I'd be good, so I clamp down my back teeth and I stare straight ahead. I try to block his words out, but they're right there, making a little hissing sound as they slip into my ear.

He grows bolder when I don't respond, and leans in even closer. From the corner of my eye I see a fat smirk stretch across his face and I can't help it, my hands think about how easy it would be to snatch that smirk right off his face. They creep onto the desk, dancing a little across its surface.

Down, girls!

I flatten my hands on the desk with a little more force than necessary. The nearby students turn around and, despite being all the way across the room, Jo turns around as well. I swear she has a special sixth-sense that warns her when I'm plotting. She sees how close Eli leans, and the way my wicked hands are already again waltzing across the surface of the desk. Her be-good glare is back.

I force my hands smooth again and she turns around. The instant she does, Eli starts in again.

Good, good, good. The word follows like a swarm of stinging bees. Breathe in, breathe out. I look at the clock. Forty-five minutes left to go.

Forty minutes.

They're just words, insults by an idiot. Not even particularly clever ones.

Breathe.

Thirty minutes.

Just words.

Eli elbows me *hard*. That's it. My chair squeaks as I shove back from the table and my hands curve into claws. Jo spins in her chair and catches my eye. She lifts her eyebrows in a way that uncannily resembles the way my mom used to do it. "Behave," they say.

I glare back a "no."

Her eyebrows go yet higher in a haughty "*yes.*"

I switch approaches. My eyebrows sweep down at the sides, in a "pleeeeeeeeeease."

My hands twitch and wiggle. Jo sees them, shakes her head and mouths, "Sit on your hands."

She can't be serious. As if my butt would stop my hands even if it could. Does she not realize it's in league with the rest of me?

But her expression says she's not kidding. Then she mouths, "You promised."

I sigh. I did, though it doesn't seem fair as that promise was made before the student body decided to declare war on me. Still, I sit on my hands like an obedient little monster, unwilling to threaten my and Jo's fragile peace. Think of something else, Meda. Ignore him. Go to your happy place. I close my eyes and expect to see my mom. But I don't.

I see Armand.

***

My second-to-last class on Monday is by far my favorite of the day and the only other one I share today with Jo – Strength and Conditioning. I duck into my room to change into gym clothes (though dutifully pulling the pink T-shirt back on over my sports bra), then wait in the hallway for Jo. She clomps out at the last minute in her gym clothes with her wild-woman hair bullied into a ponytail. She looks vaguely ill. She doesn't smile when she sees me, but this time I don't think it's my fault. While S and C is my favorite class, it's Jo's least.

Poor girl, it's the only one she doesn't excel at.

"Hi, Jo." I walk next to her down the hallway.

"Meda." Her gaze latches onto my vilely pink shirt and her expression sours. "Don't think I don't know what you're doing."

I bat innocent eyes. "I don't know what you mean."

"You thoroughly intend to ruin that shirt in gym so you can't wear it the rest of the day."

My shock at these baseless accusations stops me in my tracks. "Who, me? Scheme like that? Jo, I'm offended." I hold a hand to my heart.

She rolls her eyes and presses her lips together so they can't smile.

I continue. "Why, I'm just following orders!" I start walking again, shaking my head.

"Uh-huh." We clatter down the stairs and out into the sunshine. S and C is held in a hastily renovated warehouse on the other side of the valley from the school.

"I was told to wear this shirt, and I always do what my good buddy Jo tells me to."

I'm watching her out of the corner of my eye, so I notice when her smile turns a little mean. I realize I overplayed my hand just a hair before she confirms it. "Oh, good, I'm glad to hear it. I've got a whole stack in my room. Backups, just in case." Her evil cat's smirk stretches as she looks me over. "You know," she says thoughtfully. "I've always thought you'd look good in yellow. A bright, sunshiny yellow."

At the thought, I turn faintly green. "Yellow, Jo?" My voice is a tiny thing.

"Everyone looks happy and harmless in bright yellow."

"*Bright* yellow?"

"Or I have a pastel. The nursery-of-a-baby-of-un-specified-gender yellow."

I glare at her, and her grin gets more wicked. "I think it might even have a duck on it."

"I hate you."

She swings an arm around my shoulder and grins. I fake a tragic sigh, and she laughs.

Maybe I can live with yellow.

Then her arm stiffens on my shoulder and I look up. We're approaching the construction site of the new school. Jo slows and uses the arm wrapped around my shoulder to slow me as well.

The Sarge leads a parade of people into the new building. The group is mostly Corps, some Mountain Park officers and, oddly, Professor Puchard who sticks out like a geeky thumb in an otherwise ass-kicking fist. I haven't had much to do with him, as I'm not trusted enough to be trained to use any of the grimoires, but I recognize him as the Crusader who would have done my Inheritance ceremony had circumstances not made Jo be the one to do it.

We wait, watching, as they disappear into the maze, leaving one Crusader at the entrance to watch. There will be one stationed at each entrance, I know. They always do that when they meet to discuss me. They don't trust me not to spy. Which stings, as they started that *before* they caught me scaling the walls.

Once they're out of sight, Jo drops her arm from

around my shoulder.

"What are you thinking, Jo?"

Her face instantly smooths. "Nothing."

"Secrets don't make friends, Jo."

She rolls her eyes. "I just wish I knew what they were discussing, is all."

I study her suspiciously. I've been subjected to a thousand, maybe a million, Jo eye-rolls, and this one felt forced. She rolls her eyes again at my prolonged study (this one feels entirely natural) and starts toward class again. She doesn't wait for me when I hesitate before joining her, and I have to jog a few steps to catch up.

The bell rings and we pick up our pace to make it to S and C relatively on time. The ancient warehouse where class takes place was patched together so quickly you can still smell the sap in the new boards. One wall of the building had completely collapsed and was replaced with a large metal roller-door. It looks horribly out of place on the old brick-and-wood building but is a life-saver on hot days, like today, when it's left open. Class is organized in circuits and, with the door open, I can see that our classmates have already started breaking up into their randomly assigned groups. As we walk up to the assignment sheet Jo groans, then makes a face at my happy grin. I love S and C.

I've always been a badass, but thanks to the added strength and speed from the Inheritance ceremony, I impress even myself. Plus, after seven hours in hostile territory, I can't help but delight in ninety minutes in which I get to remind everyone they shouldn't mess with me. I'm Bruce Banner all day, but in S and C I get to remind everyone that I am, in fact, the Hulk. For ninety minutes I can turn it over to the beast. Footrace? Hulk, run! Hurdles? Hulk, jump! Punching bags? Hulk, smash! Weightlifting? Hulk is the strongest there is!

Actually, screw the Hulk. He only kicks ass when he's pissed. I take names all day.

Meda is the strongest there is!

I'm sent to beat the boxing bags (Meda, smash!), while Jo's off to weightlifting.

I square off with my canvas-covered foe and kick its ass in a flurry of fists and dust. I pause and notice the circle of kids around me, their mouths hanging slightly open.

It never gets old.

We cycle through our circuit, until we're on our last leg – wind sprints. Crusaders are fast, Olympic-record fast, but I usually lap them by one and a half. Or, if I'm really determined to sweat through a hideous pink shirt, two to one. Today it seems like it's more three to one, as I zip past Mark, a tallish kid with nice shoulders, for the third time, then the guy ahead of him, Saul.

Then I notice they're not paying attention to where they're going. Their heads are twisted away toward the other side of the gym. As I loop around the orange cone, I look for the distraction. My tiny heart makes a tiny splash as it sinks into my stomach.

Jo.

She's a third of the way up the rope climb and struggling visibly. Even the kids who haven't yet been granted the Inheritance can pull it off, but Jo hangs about eight feet up flailing, her legs swinging.

I'm reminded of just this morning when she opted not to scale the brick wall with me.

Jo tries to clamp her feet together on the rope, but her bad leg slips, jerking her down six more inches. She stares up the rope in fierce concentration, as if she can will her way to the top.

Or maybe she's trying hard not to hear the whispering going on below. I realize I've come to a stop, as have the other kids in my group. In fact all the kids in the room are now watching her humiliation.

"Jo," the professor says calmly but without any mercy. "This is basic conditioning."

As if Jo doesn't know.

"If you can't even climb a rope, how can you keep your Beacon safe?"

Where does her Beacon live? In a tree?

"Miss Beauregard, if you cannot climb this rope, I cannot recommend your continuation on probation."

Ouch. Back before I knew her, Jo was the head of her class; until she was attacked by demons. Both her parents died and her leg was ripped to shreds. She spent the last two years mostly bedridden. She was deemed a non-combatant and condemned to a future as a desk-knight.

I know. Jo the accountant. Or worse, Jo the school teacher. I just vomited a little in my mouth.

But after our battle royal with the demons a few months ago, Jo decided she wasn't going to accept her fate. After much arguing, the admin agreed to give her a trial period: if she could catch up before graduation, she could be back on the roster. She attacked physical therapy and came back to S and C with a bang, but recently she's regressed.

We don't discuss it. I pretend not to notice her failures and she pretends they didn't happen. She doesn't like to talk about it and I don't like emotions. It's why we're friends.

We're also friends because she doesn't have a choice. By the time we finish S and C, she always needs a friend to lean on as she limps out of class. Thanks to her association with the Monster-girl, and the fact that everyone thinks she's going to going to get the golden-boy Chi killed with her incompetence, there's not exactly a line of people waiting to help her.

Jo's face is already flushed with effort, but I swear it gets redder. She manages to get one hand over the other, and kind of half-assedly pulls herself up. She was holding her breath, and when she lets it out, she loses the tension in her biceps and dangles limply like a lure on a fishing line. I can see her labored breathing from here.

The whispers get less subtle, and I make my way into the thick of the watching crowd.

"She doesn't belong here," a voice to my left says.

"She's going to get someone killed."

I stop to glare at everyone within my line-of-sight and they shut up.

In the sudden quiet, a muttered "Demon-lover", by one of Isaiah's crew sounds exceptionally loud. It almost makes me laugh. Jo hates demons more than anyone I know. I haven't the puniest, most pathetic shred of doubt that, had I not met Jo back on that night in March, her single-minded hatred for demons would have made her my nemesis. Instead she's forced to defend me.

What a thing, to have your best friend also be your worst enemy.

I shove the jeering boy hard with my shoulder as I move past, to let him know I heard. Instead of the fear I want, he jerks up his chin.

Problematic, but I'll have to deal with that later. I hear something that pulls my attention away from the little dirtbag. Something I never thought I'd hear in a million years. At least not from Jo.

"I can't."

My head snaps around to where Jo still dangles, her arms visibly shaking. "I can't do it," she repeats, a little more firmly. Then softer, almost broken. "I think I need to go to the infirmary."

The professor doesn't look pleased by Jo's admission, but he doesn't look disappointed either. He looks… relieved. A failure here, on a stupid rope-climb, would bring her one step closer to admitting defeat. I want to deck him.

He opens his mouth to say something, but I cut him off. "Yes, you can." She's always harassing me to be better; it's only fair I return the favor. I push through the crowd, carelessly shoving kids out of the way (some with more force than others), until I'm at the bottom of the rope, looking up at Jo.

"Come on, Jo. Climb," I order.

Her reply hits me like a slap. "Stay out of this, Meda."

Some of the meaner kids snicker, and their nasty comments fill the air. I don't think they all hate Jo. I don't even think half do, but they all love Chi, and are frustrated by Jo's refusal to accept "God's will." If any of them bothered to ask Chi, they'd know he's not the least bit worried about being partnered with Jo. Even if he were, he'd rather die a dozen times than live without her. But no one asks Chi. Besides, it's honorable for him to sacrifice himself for her, but it's sinful for her to allow it.

I don't know what's going on with Jo, but unlike any of the other jerks in this room, I actually have fought demons with her. And she's good at it. Great even.

She just needs to remember that. "No," I tell her. "Now climb the damn rope."

"I. Said. I. Can't," she grits out.

"Yes. You. Can."

She *snarls* at me.

"Miss Porter," Crusader Keller places a hand on my shoulder. I manage to shrug it off rather than rip it that way. "I think Miss Beauregard knows the limits of her abilities." He stresses the word limits.

"She has no limits," I snap at him. "Dammit, Jo, climb *up*."

The laughter gets a little louder at the ridiculousness of the situation.

The professor steps in. "Miss Porter, I'm going to have to ask you to leave."

I turn on him. "It's Miss *Melange*," I glower. "And make me."

The class gasps, and I hear Jo's horrified "Meda!" above them all.

The professor and I stare at each other as he considers my challenge. Then he says to Jo, without taking his eyes off me, "It's alright, Miss Beauregard. If you would like to quit, you may come down."

Quit. Jo's no quitter.

To my horror she slides down without a word. She lands heavily at the bottom and stumbles a little, her weak leg giving out, and she grabs the rope for support. Someone snickers, but someone else, to their credit, elbows them in the gut before I figure out who. Jo sticks up her chin but doesn't make eye contact with any of the students. She looks only to Professor Keller when she says, "Permission to go to the infirmary, sir?"

"Of course." His voice is not without sympathy.

Jo stumbles again as she turns and I duck forward to take her arm, but she jerks it away. "I told you to *stay out of it*, Meda."

I hear a few more snickers as Jo limps off, and I whip around. Professor Keller steps between me and the rest of the assholish student body, filling my view. I try to look around him and he reaches out an arm as if to stop me. I snarl, finally looking at him. He doesn't back down, but he does drop his arm. I turn on my heel and stalk out.

***

Thanks to my early exit, I'm early to Western Civ. I drop into my seat in the empty classroom and glare stonily at the chalkboard (yes, chalk, none of those fancy-pantsy dry-erase boards here!) until the bell sounds (yes, a real, old-school bell), and the room starts to fill up.

A sly voice slithers into my pissy contemplations. "Hey, Meda."

My hands tighten on my pencil. Of the mountain of people whose shit I'm not currently equipped to take, Isaiah is at the top. "Not now, Isaiah," I growl, without looking at him. It's a struggle not to kill him when I'm in a good mood.

I am not in a good mood.

I hear a chair slide as he pulls it over and sits facing me. His tone drips Sweet-and-Low sympathy –

overly sweet and entirely fake. "Having a bad day?"

Even though he's not in S and C with us, it's pretty obvious he heard what happened. Not surprising. Scientists looking to break the light-speed barrier should study the speed of gossip in small-town high schools.

If Isaiah were clever, he'd know that now is a dangerous time to antagonize me, but I'm fairly certain no one has ever accused Isaiah of being clever.

He keeps talking. "In S and C, perhaps?"

The pencil snaps in my hands, I picture his spine. Be good, Meda. You promised. "Not now, Isaiah," I repeat, keeping my eyes carefully on the chalkboard on the front of the room.

"I think now's perfect." His tone oozes with smugness. "I heard your pussy, demon-loving friend's finally dropping out."

Beeeee gooood, the annoying words buzz.

"You heard wrong," I bite out.

"I don't think so," he says, and I don't turn my head. I can tell by his voice he's smirking and if I see it, I will rip it off his face. "I heard she wussed out on the rope climb. Dangled there like a six year-old crying for her mama."

I tense, seething. He'll be the one crying for his mama after I…

Good, the word stings.

He slides closer so he's talking nearly into my ear. His voice lowers. Not low enough that everyone avidly listening can't hear, just enough so it rumbles out nastily. "That incompetent bitch is gonna get someone killed."

"Keep talking, and you're going to get someone killed." It just slipped out!

He doesn't listen. "I heard that Chi wants to ditch her but he can't."

This is a new storyline. Curiosity turns my head. We're close – kissing-distance close. Or biting distance, in our case. He must realize this and pulls back slightly, but keeps his smirk. His eyes spark, like I suspect mine do right before I deliver a death-blow.

"Because the dumb slut slept with him, and he's too nice to–" WHAM, out of nowhere he nose-butts me in the fist!

Yeah, I don't think Jo's gonna believe that either.

I wince, imagining Jo's response. My arm's still outstretched from where it slammed into his face and I whip it back to my side. Isaiah's on the floor, blood bubbling from between the fingers clenched over his nose, the bags under his eyes already darkening. I look from him to the room full of dead-silent witnesses.

Screw it. In for a penny, in for a pound. As they say, if you're gonna do the time, you might as well enjoy the crime.

Suddenly my day is looking up.

I glare around the room, the ferocity I've been feeling all day displayed for anyone to see. A couple of kids gasp, and they all step back. "Anyone have any-thing else to say about Jo? Rope-climbing? Demons?" I snarl. I let a wicked smile curl up my lips. My eyes spark with challenge and I hope someone does. "No one?" I catch the eye of one wide-eyed sophomore and she actually shakes her head before she ducks it behind the girl next to her.

Isaiah makes a groaning noise as he shuffles around on the floor. He pulls himself up using a table, then moves to place it between us. He pulls his hand down from his nose, so he can shout at me. "You are screwed!" Blood still pours from his nose and runs over his mouth. It sprays as he screams. "When Crusader Grayland gets here–"

But I am not afraid of ancient Grayland. I am not afraid of Isaiah. I'm not afraid of anyone. But Isaiah should be very afraid of me. The wolfhound has slipped her leash.

I slam my hands down on the table between us with a loud *whack*, then throw it into the wall so hard it shatters. I fly at him, whip fast, and he stumbles backwards into another table. I grab a fistful of shirt so we're nose to bloody-nose. "I'd be careful if I were you Isaiah – he's not here yet." I use my creepy, lyrical tone. The one I reserve for people I'm about to peel apart limb by limb. Like almost everyone, he immediately recognizes it. He pales, white skin behind red blood. "And, as you pointed out, I'm already in trouble." I lean in, my cheek almost touching his neck, as I breathe into his ear. "I have nothing to lose." I pull back and bare my teeth. He glares back, but doesn't say anything.

I was wrong; maybe Isaiah is a bit clever. Because in that moment, suspended, enraged, and free, I can't say for certain what I would do if he did say something. Delightful options play through my mind in red-splashed tableaux. The vision makes my breath catch, and some of my thoughts must have played on my face, because Isaiah's breath catches too.

Then the classroom door opens, and the spell's broken.

"What the devil is going on here?" Crusader Grayland asks in his creaky voice. Then he gasps too. "Miss Porter! Release him at once."

I don't. I want the whole class to understand what I could do to Isaiah before Crusader Grayland – or any of them, really – could stop me. They have never seen me as I am, only the tamed, washed-out water-color Jo makes me be.

I want it to be an image they never forget.

The tension builds, until Crusader Grayland pops it with a "Miss Porter!" in a stern tone. I hear the cane-tap and shuffle of the old Crusader moving toward us.

With one more parting glare, I shove Isaiah away, hard enough for the table he slams into to fall over so he lands on the floor once more.

The class lets out a collective breath. "Miss Por-ter!" Crusader Grayland says again, this time in a tone that's half-relief, half-outrage. "This is unacceptable! Take yourself–"

I cut him off. "It's Melange. Miss *Melange*," I snarl.

"And I'm already going."

I grab my books and storm out, slamming the door so hard the glass shatters.

I smile savagely at the sound and take off down the hallway.

NINE

I'M SURE PROFESSOR Grayland intended me to go to the headmaster's office, but since he didn't actually say it, I don't feel inclined to obey. I turn the corner, intending to hide out in my and Jo's attic, and come face to face with Crusader Beck. She stops when she sees me, but when I move to step around her, she slides neatly in my way. Of course. I may be done with today, but today is clearly not done with me.

As if to confirm my suspicions, she speaks. "Miss Melange, come with me please." Her tone brooks no discussion. I gnash my teeth. Professor Grayland, clever old dodger, must have messaged ahead.

To my surprise she doesn't take me to the head-master's office, but instead down and out of the school. We're halfway to the new school before I realize our destination.

Now? Now the Corporates decide they want to grill me? Of course.

The middle-aged man guarding the door nods as we approach, expecting us. He and my escort are careful to box me out as they cast whatever spell is used to deactivate the locks. The Templar blood-activated locks used at the last school were abandoned, and it doesn't take a genius to figure out why. None of this is news to me; it's hardly the first time I've been hauled up in front of whatever visiting Crusader wanted to play one hundred questions with the Monster, but today I find it particularly irksome. The guard returns my disgusted glare impassively.

We cross the infirmary briskly then head up the stairwell to the top floor.

I hear Jo in my head trying to douse the fire in my heart. "Be good, Meda." Good, good, good, good, good. The word plays in a loop until it means nothing. I've been good and they refuse to feed me. I've been good and they won't train me. I've been good and they changed the locks. I've been good and they want to send me away.

So the Corporates think they want custody, do they? *Custody*. I'm not some big-eyed orphan begging, "*Please sir, may I have some more?*" or singing about how the sun will come out tomorrow. I'm not the foster kid who'll smile on the Christmas card in an ugly sweater matching my new mom's. Rather, I'm the kid in the back of the orphanage playing with a lighter and the head of the doll that belongs to the sobbing girl next to me – they just need to see it. We'll see who wants custody then.

Besides, what *good* would good behavior do once they find out I broke Isaiah's face? Actions speaking louder than words and all that. No, good is no *good*. In this case, bad is better.

My face must reveal some of what I plan because Crusader Beck eyes me suspiciously. My lips curl, but before she can say anything, my hand snaps out and slams the doors to the meeting room open. The tables in the room are arranged in a "U", and the house is packed. I pause until I have everyone's attention then I theatrically raise one arm over my head and one curled out from my body like a ballerina and enter the room in a series of twirls. The room is wide, but not particularly deep, so it's not many spins until I reach the middle.

"Ba, badda-ba ba!" I sing and break into a few tap-dance steps – or at least my mocking approximation of some tap-dance steps – jerking my arms back and forth like I'm holding a cane. Then I wrap it all up with a lunge and a clap.

"Ta-da," I sing. Oh, and add in some jazz hands, naturally.

Stunned silence greets my performance. I don't look around, but instead focus my eyes – and my snot-tastic sneer – front and center where The Sarge and Sergeant Graff are seated. At my energetic arrival the other Corps leapt to their feet, and even now stand with their weapons out, ready to spring.

I look the well-pressed soldiers up and down.

"Tough crowd," I mock. I look to The Sarge, the only unsurprised face in the house. Her lips are thinned to the point of nonexistence.

"What?" I ask innocently, then let some anger creep into my tone. "I assumed I was the entertainment for this little party."

The Sarge doesn't bat an eye. "I am not amused." The Sarge has this way of saying things, I don't know if it's her raspy growl or her one-eyed glare, or maybe just the knowledge that she knows more ways to kill someone than everyone on death row combined, that makes it really hard to disrespect her.

"Oh, I'm sorry, you were expecting a comedic routine?"

I said it's hard, not impossible. At least not for someone as gifted in the art as I.

I clear my throat and affect a stand-up demeanor. "A funny thing happened on the way to this meeting…"

The Sarge interrupts my joke with a lifted hand. It's probably better that way – me kicking Isaiah's ass is probably the kind of funny you had to be there for, anyway.

"Miss Melange," she says, all business. "We can play silly games all day, or we can get this over with in time for dinner."

She gave me too big an opening to pass up. There's one part of my nature no Crusader can, ah, *swallow* without disgust. Rude teens, they probably have.

Rude teens who eat people… What can I say? I'm one-of-a-nightmarish-kind.

"My kind of dinner or yours? Because I admit, I'm starving." I say the last bit lustily with a wide display of teeth. I cast eyes around the room. "I don't suppose anyone's brought any…" I pause deliberately, "*one* to eat?"

The Crusaders aren't a squeamish lot, but I still hear a sharp intake of breath on the last question, and a few shift in their seats and trade looks amongst them-selves. The reaction of the delegate I'm most interested in, Graff, is disappointing. He leans back in his cheap plastic chair. I can't see his hands, but his elbows are wide, so I'm guessing they are neatly folded on his lap. I lock eyes with him and raise my eyebrows defiantly, but still get no reaction. I decide to push it.

"I can't help but notice you're all arranged a bit like a buffet—"

"That's enough, Miss Porter," The Sarge cuts me off, her tone as bland as the expression on the Corp Sergeant's face.

"Melange."

She ignores me. "Your feeding is scheduled for a week from Thursday. You might be interested in knowing that Crusader Bergeron will be making the delivery." She emphasizes the name.

Luke Bergeron. He was my mother's best friend and fiancé before she was kidnapped and impregnated with yours-truly. After I was rescued from the demon headquarters, I learned that he and my mom had kept in touch over the years. I get the feeling he sees himself as a kind of stepfather to me, and I have to respect that kind of courage. After all, I murdered both my real parents. True, one was an accident.

But one wasn't.

I have a short supply of friends (granted, that's partially my fault), and an even shorter supply of parental units (entirely my fault), so it's always a treat to see him.

Delinquent-foster-kid-Meda shrugs like she doesn't care.

The Sarge doesn't wait for me to respond, but launches right into the meeting. She doesn't thank me for joining them, but wouldn't have even if I hadn't waltzed in like an ass. She's too military to bother pretending I had a choice.

"You remember the delegates from the Northern Chapter, who were introduced this morning." She indicates the Corporates. "Also joining us are representatives from some of the other chapters." She nods toward the far right, almost in the back corner and I twist to take a look. I can't help it, what I see causes my sneer to crack for a minute. Floating about two feet off the table are the heads and most of the shoulders of Crusaders I don't recognize. I'd heard of the communication spells the Crusaders use to talk to one another – it's how the Crusader kids talk to their parents – but I'd never seen it in person. The Crusaders like to limit my contact with magic.

The Sarge's no-nonsense voice clips into my shock and I slide my too-cool mask back in place before I turn to face her. Four are from the other major US branches, LA, Chicago, Miami, and Wisconsin, but the rest are from around the world.

These aren't the people who ask questions, they're the ones who make decisions. Big ones. It's the kind of thing you wish you knew before you walked into a room and showed your ass. Figuratively, of course – at least so far.

Hey, the day is young, it's a little too late to change paths now. I freshen my sneer.

"On to business," The Sarge says. "Before we start anything, I want to stress that everything that occurs here is to remain confidential." She looks around the room hard-eyed, then pauses on me. My expression is not exactly cooperative. "It's for your own safety. What we learn here today could affect how people view – and treat – you, and we don't want anyone to do anything rash." She looks back around the room. "Not until we decide how we want to handle it."

That makes me a little uncomfortable.

Satisfied, The Sarge continues. "The compounding of your Crusader and demon heritage has made you physically stronger than either alone. What we haven't explored is whether that same compounding affects your magical abilities."

My ears perk up at that. Crusaders all have different strengths when it comes to spell-casting, and the academic portion of it is quite challenging as well. I'm not going to lie, it has occurred to me (and Jo, of course) that my demon-Crusader heritage may have given me some extra abilities in the magic department, but there's no way to test the hypothesis without teaching me magic, which the Crusaders are reluctant to do. But maybe that's changed. I try to hide my glee. Meda the Magic Monster.

The Sarge shuffles some papers in front of her, and there's something about the small movement that makes me nervous. "With the war coming, we've been pushed into a faster time frame than we would have liked. There are Crusaders dying every day, entire Templar families being wiped out. There was a full scale attack on the Wisconsin community. We've lost twenty-two Beacons in the last two months. *Twenty-two.*"

The Sarge is known for a lot of things (most of them guaranteed to give a naughty demon nightmares) but explaining herself is not one of them. She shuffles her papers again and it occurs to me why I found the motion so disconcerting – The Sarge is uncomfortable. The *Sarge*. Uncomfortable. Explaining things to me. The woman is three-quarters stone, one-quarter kick-ass. Maybe they are going to teach me magic, but the rising hairs on the back of my neck seem to suggest no. I look around the room, trying to drag clues from the other faces. Several look away, unwilling to make eye contact.

"We," there's a bite to The Sarge's tone that suggests *we* didn't do anything, "think it's time to explore the effects your mixed heritage has had on your magical capabilities."

I look back to The Sarge. "What do you mean 'explore'? Are you teaching me magic?" It's pure optimism that makes me ask at this point.

The Sarge clears her throat, a surprisingly high-pitched sound for such a terrifying woman. "We believe we have a method of testing your abilities that won't make that necessary."

"Method." I get the distinct impression it's not something harmless like, say, magical litmus paper.

"Yes." She looks to Professor Puchard and gives him a little nod. That explains his presence as the resident magical expert.

Like most of the faculty, he's old. His speckled bald head reminds me of the brown eggs Mom used to buy when we lived in London. He pokes his glasses up onto the bridge of his nose before clasping his worn leather hands in front of him. "You are aware that the demons and Crusaders are mirror images of each other – equal opposites, so to speak. We're not exactly the same, of course."

"Yeah…" I had learned that in my classes, but I'm not sure how it's relevant here. Really, I'm not sure how relevant it is period. I mean, how the hell can they be "equal opposites" if one side gets to come back from the dead? A Crusader can kill demons all day, but unless they take the time to drain the false-life from them (a tricky thing in the middle of a battle), it doesn't do much good. But that's probably beside the point right now. "That's what they tell me." I force a little more sass back into my tone. I am trying to piss them off, after all.

Out of the corner of my eye, I see The Sarge's lips tighten, but she's not looking at me, she's looking at Graff. Professor Puchard taps his curled fingers on the table before continuing. "Yes, well, I'm sure you're aware there is one spell that the demons make quite a bit of use of that we, ah, don't."

I raise my eyebrows and glance around. The Sarge's lips are even tighter. Whatever's coming, she doesn't like it.

Professor Puchard's eyes shift sideways, but not to The Sarge – to Graff. That can't be good. "Ah, you see, free will is the basis of goodness."

What?

His tone becomes distinctly academic in nature. "Goodness is a choice, not an action." Professor Puchard misreads my confusion and hurries to explain. "A charitable donation, for example, on its face appears 'good', however, it alone does not determine the goodness of the donor. If the gift is given to gain a lucrative position on the charity's board, or for recognition by the community of the donor's 'goodness', then it's not 'good' because the intent is personal gain." He is more comfortable in his usual role of pontificator and seems content to continue.

"Possession, Miss Melange," Graff cuts in smoothly, and I'm almost grateful to him for getting to the point. "We Crusaders have our own version of demonic possession. We don't use it, because, as our esteemed colleague pointed out," he tilts his head at Professor Puchard, "it violates our belief that goodness is a choice to be made, not an action to be performed, but we do have the ability."

Possession… as in, possess *me*? Creep into my skin, take me over, control me? I take an involuntary step back, as if an extra eight inches will protect me. I shake my head, looking at The Sarge. "You can't be serious," I say, directly to her.

"It's the only way to see if you have additional magical powers without teaching you magic," The Sarge responds. She aims for her matter-of-fact tone, but it's off.

"*Then teach me magic*," I demand.

She doesn't respond to that, just clamps her mouth closed. Graff responds instead. "That's not possible."

"Why not?" I know the answer as well as he does, but no one wants to say it. "I'm here, aren't I? I'm following your rules. I eat who you say, on your schedule." With each of my points, my voice gets louder. "I gave up my freedom for you." Still no one says anything. "I chose dying over siding with the demons, is that not enough? When will it be enough?"

My voice echoes in the quiet room. The Sarge looks at Graff as if to say *you answer her*. He clears his throat. "Miss Melange, it's not that we don't trust you–"

"Bullshit," I snap.

"–it's simply a matter of risk management. We have the ability to test you without risk. Given that, it's foolish–"

"You mean, without any risk to *you*. You just said you never use this spell. Tell me, how many times have you cast it?"

"Professor Puchard is an expert in–"

"*How many times?*"

His jaw tightens and he looks to The Sarge as if to ask her to get me under control. She only shrugs. *Your plan, your problem.*

"Miss Melange–" he starts again, but I don't feel like letting him.

"How does it even work? What happens to me – my… me-ness while you're wearing my skin like a suit?" I demand of Professor Puchard, the resident "expert."

He blinks owlishly behind his lenses. "We believe you're still there. You'll just be," he looks for a word, "sharing an existence."

"Sharing an existence? What the hell does that mean?"

"Some possessed have compared it to having a roommate of sorts. Someone living in their mind that takes over the driver's seat."

"Living in their mind?" Oh shit. "As in, reading

my thoughts?"

"We assume there must be some information transfer as the demons are able to step into the lives–"

"*SOME* INFORMATION TRANSFER?"

"What does it matter? Do you have anything to hide?" Graff asks, his eyes sharp.

"Art," barks The Sarge, calling him back. She turns to me. "Every effort will be made to preserve your privacy." She turns back to Graff with her eyebrows raised. "I was assured." She holds the look until he nods curtly.

"Of course," he responds blandly.

"Every effort? You don't even know what you're doing." The frightening thoughts tumble through my brain like a waterfall. "I mean, are you sure you'll be able to get back out? Are you sure I'll come 'back' if you do? That I won't be left some kind of zombie?"

Professor Puchard jumps back in at this point. "Research indicates that you will most certainly come back. There are numerous reports of individuals throughout history coming back into their bodies and claiming possession. Why the Bible itself says–"

Research indicates. Not exactly the "of course" I'm looking for. Professor Puchard continues speaking, but my head is spinning. *Some information transfer.* What does that mean? Would they be able to read my mind? Could they probe into my memories? Would they see how I snuck out? How Jo knew? Would they know about Armand?

More importantly, would they be able to feel the parts of me I hide? The darkness I fight, the way I Hunger not just for the life of my victim, but also for their death. Goodness *is* a choice, and I make that choice (almost) every minute of every day. But would that be enough if they could see the darker parts of my heart?

"No," I say.

"No, what?" Graff looks genuinely surprised. The Sarge does not. She knows what they're asking is wrong. She also knows I'm not some blindly obedient Templar kid.

"No, I won't do it."

The room erupts into chatter, but it's The Sarge I'm looking at. She stands, but the table stops her from coming any closer. "Meda, we wouldn't do this if it weren't important," Sarge is explaining again. "The gravity of our situation—"

Graff feels no need to justify. "You don't have a choice." His authoritative tone cuts through the babble like a blade.

You don't have a choice. I hear footsteps close in behind me. *You don't have a choice.* We will slip in your mind, take over your body. We will steal your freewill; we could plunder your thoughts, your memories, your every private moment if we wanted.

You don't have a choice.

He stares directly at me, and I at him. The others in the room are just bystanders. They may ultimately agree with the decision to possess me, although with reservations. But not Graff. There's no remorse, just implacable determination.

He and I face off. I lean forward, my legs coiled like springs, my hands fisted at my side. He stands rigid, his head tilted just the tiniest bit back so he can look down his nose at me. He's comfortable in his power, wears it as easily as his beautiful suit.

There's only one person in this room who won't do as he wants – and she is used to a kind of power of her own.

You don't have a choice. My eyes slide to the left and right. Everyone is tense; the other Corps have come half out of their seats. I hear the movement of people behind me, slipping around to grab me if necessary. The Sarge looks pissed, but not enough to intervene. I'm outnumbered with no one to help me. It's true. I don't have a choice.

I straighten and force my fists to relax.

When I do, I see several others around the room relax as well. The tense moment has passed. Graff doesn't smile at my acquiescence, but I sense his satisfaction. "We will keep it as brief as possible." He waves at Professor Puchard. "Professor?" He reaches behind him for his chair, turning his back to me.

And here I thought they knew better than to trust me.

Two strides and a giant leap take me over the table. I slam into Graff and he, I, and his chair go flying into the wall. I smash my fist into his arrogant face, and smug satisfaction wells in me like the blood does from his broken nose – that makes twice today.

And here I thought it was going to be a bad day.

Sadly, I only have a moment to enjoy it. No, not even a whole moment, a half-moment, a quarter-moment – and I suspect I was only given that much because The Sarge was enjoying my punch as much as I was – before I'm hauled off him.

"There's *my* choice, *Art*," I snarl as I'm dragged away, gnashing my teeth in his face. Graff cups his hand over his nose then pulls it away to look at the blood pooling in his palm and rolling from between his fingers to stain the brilliant white cuff of his expensive shirt.

"Professor Puchard, *now*." He snaps through blood-stained teeth.

A Corp holds each of my arms, and someone I can't see grips me around my midsection. Whoever it is hauls me backwards off my feet. I flail, dragging my arms together in an attempt to shake the Crusaders off, and kick blindly behind me. It's mostly for show; even I know I can't take on a room full of Crusaders – at least, not without casualties. But I want there to be no doubt in their minds that I do not consent. I do not agree.

I have no choice, but that doesn't mean I'm going to make it easy on them.

My heel catches the Crusader behind me and he

releases his hold. I leap toward the Crusader holding my left arm, slamming into her like a bowling ball and pulling the guy attached to my right arm off-balance. I jerk my right arm free and slam my elbow into the gut of the woman still holding me. Free, I half dive, half scramble toward the door. I wrap my hands around the knob, but I don't pull.

I can't.

I'm frozen, locked in place by a thousand invisible hands. They're everywhere; every inch of my skin feels the pressure of fingers and palms I can't see. Some small and soft, others huge and leathery; all with a grip like iron. I try to jerk, to shake them off, to make my arm move, but the hands squeeze tighter and tighter, becoming bruising in their force. I stop fighting and the hands relax, their grip firm but not crushing.

Then a hand on my right arm starts to move, sliding up my wrist to my hand. It pinches my pointer finger in its steely grasp and peels it from the doorknob. I try to force my finger back down, but the invisible hand grips it too tightly. We battle, still and silent, until sweat breaks on my brow, until I feel the hot pop of my finger bone cracking. I release my hold.

Then my middle finger is gripped and peeled from the knob. Then the rest, one-by-one, as I stand there watching helplessly. Once I've released the knob, my hand is forced jerkily to my side. I can't stop it; the more I try, the more pressure the hands exert. And they're everywhere; I can't even open my mouth to curse.

My foot lifts, awkwardly, then the other, turning me in small, shuffling steps until I face the Crusaders again. Everyone watches, wide-eyed, as the puppet master makes me dance. Everyone but Professor Puchard. All I can see is the top of his speckled-egg head as he looks down at the grimoire open before him. He murmurs words I can't understand.

Then the hands on my face begin probing until they find the joint of my jaw. They dig in, trying to force my mouth open, as more hands pull back my lips and wedge themselves between my teeth. I fight it. I fight it until I'm sure my jaw is going to break. Finally the hands are too much, too strong. My muscles give and my mouth cracks open the tiniest bit. Before I can close it, a hand slides in, flat on my tongue, forcing it wider. I gag as the hand pushes into my throat, then choke as it pushes still further and I'm unable to get any air at all. I can't fight, can't flail, I can only stand there as the world turns grey. But I won't give in, I won't let *them* in. I will suffocate to death before I'll allow it.

Then, finally, suddenly, the hands release me. I bend, eyes closed and take huge ragged breaths. *Take that, assholes.*

But I'm wrong. So, so wrong. The hands ride my gasping breath like a wave and are now *inside*. I let out a gurgled scream and try to reach into my mouth to claw them out.

But I can't. They're deep inside, in my chest, my limbs, sliding along the inside of my skin, shoving and squeezing. Then they start… pushing me out. Or maybe pulling me.

I'm pulled from my own fingertips until I can't feel them anymore. I'm pulled from my toes, then my legs, and my body collapses onto the floor. I'm shoved up my neck and I hear my breathing stop, and I'm pulled from my vocal cords so I can't scream. I'm shoved up, up into a corner of my mind. I can still see through my eyes and I can hear. I still exist, but I'm a passenger. I control nothing.

"Professor, she can't breathe. Look at her! She can't breathe!" I hear The Sarge shout.

My mouth still hangs open, but with no one to control my lungs, no air is pulled into my lungs. I can't feel any part of my body, can't feel the floor under me, can't feel my lungs not move.

But I can feel myself die.

I can see the dark spots enter my vision, and I can feel the equally dark spots in my thoughts. But I can do nothing.

"Herman!" The Sarge shouts, and Professor Puchard blinks eyes made unnaturally big by his thick glasses. "She can't breathe!"

"Well of course not. She's not in control," he states like it's obvious. "Someone has to be in control. Who's going to possess her?"

I'm alive enough to think the situation deserves a

snarky comment, but not alive enough to come up with one. Not that I could say it aloud for anyone to appreciate anyway.

"You are!" Sarge snaps.

"I can't; I'm casting the spell," he states without nearly enough urgency, in my opinion. "Simply breathe into the mouth."

The Sarge growls but whips around. Before she can take a step in my direction, Graff leaps over the table, oddly reminiscent of how I had done not ten minutes before. He slides to his knees before me and breathes into my face. At first nothing happens and I see his eyes shift sideways toward Professor Puchard as if to ask "what now?"

Then my body arches. I can't feel it, but my view of the room changes. My eyes roll back and I see the pink of my eyelids, the black fringe of my eyelashes, the jerking movement of the walls before me as my body seizes, then arches, then seizes again.

And I can feel the heat of something foreign, something *wrong*, filling me. It squishes in next to me, packing me into my little corner of my consciousness. The pink of my lids darkens. I've been without air too long.

"What's happening?" demands The Sarge.

"He's in," Professor Puchard says. He sounds closer.

"Then why isn't she breathing?"

"I followed the spell." Professor Puchard sounds

both confused and defensive.

"*Then why isn't she breathing?* This was a mistake. It's over. Get him out," The Sarge orders.

"I'm telling you, there's no mistake."

"Get him out!"

Then We breathe. I don't feel it so much as hear it: a giant wheezy gasp. It sort of hitches and wobbles, as if the breather is new to the art and is still trying to get the hang of it. Then there's another gasping breath, and another. The breaths smooth out and the black in my vision lightens back to the pink of my lids.

Then Our eyes snap open.

The Sarge kneels over Us, Professor Puchard leans behind her, his wrinkly neck stretched like a vulture as he peers over her shoulder. The rest of the Crusaders surround Us, curious but unwilling to come within reach. A heavily-accented voice is demanding to know what is happening – one of the incorporeal visitors. Then the image of the room begins to waver, as if I were viewing it through a thick pane of old, distorted glass. Or water. The asshole has forgotten to blink. I try, I make the motion that for seventeen years has successfully closed my lids. I exaggerate it, trying to force the motion. Nothing.

"Meda?" The Sarge asks slowly, examining my face.

My eyelids finally slide closed, though they aren't really mine anymore. I refuse to call them *his*. Our eyelids. Then they open again and Our vision is clear. A rumble vibrates Our throat. It drags itself from a noise into a word. "Nnnnnnnnnnnnno."

"Arthur?"

Our head jerks in a wobbly nod. The Sarge involuntarily pulls back, then peers closer, as if searching for some physical difference.

Our body begins to twitch and move, one hand coming up, then another, Our legs bend, Our head moves side to side, then around in a circle. It's like the warm up of a puppeteer, seeing which strings pull which limbs, or maybe more like a driver testing out the controls and motions of a new car. Our motions become smoother and more controlled, and We sit up. He clears Our throat a few times, then says a few "mi, mi, mi, mis" like a singer preparing to go onstage. Everyone waits silently, except for the shouting incorporeal Frenchman who still can't see what's happening. Their expressions are blends of horror and fascination, depending on their personality.

We push awkwardly to Our feet, and The Sarge scrambles back and to her own feet in such an uncharacteristic manner that under other circumstances I would find it funny. But I wouldn't laugh now, even if I could. I'm too busy shoving against the hot, swollen foreignness that fills my body. It squishes in my mental fingers like some formless sponge, swelling to fill every available space, pushing me back, back into a tiny corner of my mind. I am nothing but a watcher, a prisoner in my own body. Merely an existence, trapped until he chooses to let me go. If he *can* let me go.

I don't hyperventilate, but only because it requires lungs.

"Sergeant Reinhardt," We say formally to The Sarge, tilting Our head. The words are stiff and deeper than if had I said them. He clears Our throat and wiggles Our jaw. When he speaks again it sounds more natural – more like me. "I believe we had better begin our experiments."

"Yes," The Sarge agrees, still studying my face. Then she seems to snap back into herself. "Yes, of course." She turns and addresses the crowd. "Move back. Give her – him – them some room." People shuffle back to their spaces behind the table, clearing room for Us to work. My body is still moving, jogging in place, then bouncing on the balls of Our feet, as Graff refines his control, and… I sense something from the Wrongness. Just a hint of a feeling, like catching a scent in the wind – of *delight*. I press my – existence, is the only way I can describe it – against the intruding pressure, following the "smell", and it grows stronger.

He's *enjoying* the possession. His body is old, worn down. Even at his peak, he never had the strength, the vitality that I do. For him, possessing me is like climbing out of a battered hoopty into a souped-up Maserati. He'd forgotten what it was like to move without pain, in joints still protected by cartilage, with lungs that still pack blood full of oxygen. He flexes my arms and notes how thin they look but how powerful they feel.

What would it be like to fight someone with these?

Oh shit. That wasn't the whiff of a feeling. That was a thought, a fully-formed thought. I CAN HEAR HIS THOUGHTS. Oh shit, does that mean he can hear mine?

Yes. The word swells out of the red-wrongness like a punch in the gut.

I shove away from "him", breaking the connection, pulling in all the pieces of my existence, trying to squeeze myself as small as possible. I pause, "listening" for his thoughts, but "hear" nothing. But does that mean he can't "hear" me? I can't know.

My body, meanwhile, is striding over to the table where Graff sat. We pick up a briefcase and withdraw a pair of bulky headphones. We slip them over our ears and the external world goes as silent as my internal one. I don't understand, but then someone slides a piece of paper in front of me covered in symbols I don't recognize. We look at it and start reciting words I don't understand, words that sound like gibberish. A hand enters Our field of vision holding a piece of chalk. We take it, then he focuses on the wall ahead of Us and I see our body sway and realize he's marking symbols on the floor. Symbols he doesn't want me to see.

It dawns on me – the whole reason I'm here. The spell. He's casting a spell and this is their solution to not teaching it to me. I can't hear what the others in the room are saying, can't read the spells, don't have a chance of memorizing the words as he says them and

I can't see the symbols he's writing. I can't listen to his thoughts, not without letting him listen to mine. I'm trapped, hidden in my own mind, unable to do anything.

In that moment, I hate them. I hate them all.

Everyone but The Sarge has returned to their places, though very few have sat back down. The Sarge remains on our side of the table, her disapproving eyes on my hands. Suddenly there's a blast of light and everyone in the room ducks away, even The Sarge. When she pulls her hands from her face, her expression is incredulous. Her lips move and, though I'm no expert at lip-reading, I'm fairly certain it's a swear word. Everyone I can see cowers behind their hands seconds before again the light flashes. The Sarge asks Us a question but Graff can't hear any better than I can, so The Sarge addresses her question to her left. I assume it's to Professor Puchard, him being the magical expert, but it's outside my field of view so I can't be certain.

Graff moves on to another spell, then another. A roaring wind sends furniture scattering. Strangers I don't know pop in and out of existence right in front of my face. The door and windows glow. We're surrounded in a bubble of light. I don't know how long I'm there, hours it feels like, as I cower in my own body. The sky outside the window turns navy, then black as, without me, my body performs spells I can't even name.

But while I don't know what the spells do, or how

to do them, I do learn one thing: I do them well. Terrifyingly well, if the expressions of my spectators are anything to go by.

Finally the spells wind to a close. The Sarge waves at Us and her lips move. We still have the headphones on, but her message is clear: she's ready for him to come out. That makes two of us. I unfurl just enough to scream at him. *Get the hell out.*

But We shake Our head.

The Sarge speaks again, more agitated. This time she enunciates so even I can figure out what she's saying. *Get out.*

Yes, get out. GET OUT. Our head shakes again and Our throat rumbles as we refuse. "If she can do this," We wave Our hands, "then we have to know…" he stops, catching himself. "The *other*," he finishes vaguely, but it's clear from her expression that the Sarge knows what he means. We turn to Professor Puchard so I can't see The Sarge's response. He looks thoughtful, rubbing his hand across his chin, then nods at us. The Sarge marches forward and jerks the headphones from Our head.

"That wasn't part of the plan," she says.

"The plan is to learn what we must about her abilities," Graff says in my voice.

"The plan was to ascertain whether her heritage impacts her magical aptitude. I'd say we can conclude it has."

"You know this is more than we could have

expected. We need to know what she's capable of." We sound so reasonable. "You know the council will agree with me on this." There are nods from around the room. "You would too, if you weren't so biased." He gives her a meaningful look. "We can either do it now or later."

Do what? But I'm too scared of what he'd learn if I tried to push into that red again.

Me, *too scared*.

"Would you rather we go through this all over again?" My mouth says to The Sarge.

Her lips tighten.

"You know I'm right."

"Do I?" Her tone is pure acid.

No, please no. Get him out.

Graff, through me, says nothing else, but he doesn't need to. The Sarge shoves the headphones back into Our arms, and waves towards a Crusader to hoist Graff's body.

Where are we going? But I can't ask. I can do nothing but brace for the ride.

We turn, and stride from the room, then down and out into the hot dusk. Our destination becomes clear all too quickly.

We're headed to the dungeon.

TEN

THE LOWEST FLOOR of the old mill, below the class-rooms for the youngest children, isn't used for classes. Partly because its rotting floor hangs over the swift mountain river, but also because the room is dominated by giant saws that once reduced trees to pieces before they were sent downstream. I speculate they'd work just as well on people.

If I had control of my body right now, I would find out.

The wall against the mountain has been disman-tled, and a dungeon has been carved into the rock behind. The iron bars are spelled against demons – and probably against me, too, as Jo pointed out when par-ticularly irritated. I don't care to find out if she's right. And besides, she always is. I try to slam on the brakes, but am powerless.

The guard at the entrance steps aside and we walk into the cool damp of the cave.

It takes a moment for Our eyes to adjust, so We feel them before We see them. The rush of power is unmistakable. Demons. Our body starts at the sudden jolt of power, then pauses. I hadn't told the Crusaders the effect nearby demons have on me. Minimizing my demonic traits seemed like a good idea at the time. I risk a mental probe to see what he's thinking.

Surprise, speculation, mistrust. Calculation and–

He feels my probing and tries to slam down the gates, cutting off communication, but he can't. Not completely. Not like I could. And I feel it. *Fear*.

"Visitors! So nice of you to join us," a voice languidly calls from the back of the caves. "Isn't it nice, Sasha?" A chubby middle-aged man in a too-tight suit climbs to his feet, his flabby features wildly at odds with the sensuality of his voice.

"Lovely," agrees a woman with a frizzy bob and spectacles. She doesn't get up from the cot, but leans forward, her eyes gleaming. The third demon, another man, this one Asian, does nothing, but remains lounging against the back wall of the cell, eyes closed with his legs stretched out before him.

Sasha looks us over slyly. "Coming to play?" She pouts. "You really should have called first. It's bad manners to–" Her eyes land on me and she cuts off with a hiss. "The mutt?"

Mutt? Grrrr.

The eyes of the demon on the floor pop open. "She's here?" He jumps to his feet and they all move closer to the bars. Once he gets a look at me, the whole perimeter of the cell flashes and we all blink and look away.

"Ah, ah," tsks a Crusader to my left. "You know you can't communicate to anyone outside these walls."

The demon growls and smacks the bars, then yelps and cups his hands to his chest.

"Let's get on with it," The Sarge clips.

"On with what?" Sasha asks, as if she read my mind.

The Sarge doesn't answer, but curtly nods at Us to proceed. Graff strides Us up to the cell, but The Sarge stops us.

"Wait. You can't touch the bars."

So Jo was right, they are spelled against me.

Instead, The Sarge orders a couple of Crusaders to pull a demon, the chubby one, from the cell. He looks more curious than frightened as they haul him out by his arms. You can't beat secrets out of a demon (it's literally impossible, as part of their contract with Hell) and the Crusaders aren't into recreational torture.

"Should we kill him first?" the guard on the left asks.

That gets the demon's attention. He starts struggling furiously. The Sarge jerks her chin in a "yes" to a Corp who pulls her sword.

"Wait," We say, with a raised arm. "Not yet. Let me try…"

The Sarge looks at Us curiously, but We don't say

more. I expect Graff to put on Our headphones, but he doesn't. Instead he moves Us forward until We're face to face with the panting demon, who's no longer struggling now that death is off the table. He watches warily, but doesn't fight when Graff stretches Our arm and places Our hand gently on the demon's shoulder.

Then the demon drops to his knees screaming.

We start but don't remove Our hand, which is now surrounded by inky black smoke that is pouring from the writhing demon.

"What's happening?" demands Sasha, nothing languid about her now. She smacks the bars and yelps. "What are you doing to him?" She already knows, but can't believe her eyes, just like I can't believe Ours. But the rush of brilliant pleasure pouring through my veins is unmistakable, a high that can only be caused by one thing. We're sucking the life out of the demon, *while he's still alive*.

The demon beneath Our hand jerks and spasms, then with a giant, frantic kick shoves himself out from beneath Our touch. We lunge after him but the contact is broken.

The spell is not. The life still streams from the demon in all its inky-black glory. Gasps surround Us. It shouldn't be possible. Still, the black smoke pours from the demon, pulled to Our hand like dust into a vacuum. Still, the false-life rockets along my nerve-endings, and the Hunger comes screaming to the surface.

It shouldn't be possible.

More. A silent voice calls, and I don't know if it's me or the Hunger or Graff. *More.* We fling out Our other arm toward the cell and Sasha lets out a violent scream of pure agony. We twist Our head to see the billowing blackness of her life pouring toward Us. The remaining demon jerks her away from the bars, scuttling with her as far from us as the tiny cell allows, but there's nowhere to go, nowhere to hide.

More power than I've ever experienced floods through me. It's Niagara Falls versus a mountain stream. It crashes, pounds, pulses. There's nothing like it. Nothing, nothing, nothing. A cackle of pure, delighted glee bubbles from my throat.

It's squelched by a wave of horror, and the stream of life suddenly stops. A wave of horror that's *not mine.* Caught in the moment, I'd dropped my guard.

Graff uses the opportunity to fling his swollen redness at me. I try to pull back, to slam the gates, but I'm too late. It's like trying to stop water with a chain link fence. He floods through, suffocating me, squashing me.

Shattered bits of my memories spark in my consciousness as we mentally battle.

A dead woman in black wellies. A ghost boy with angelic curls.

Shattered bits of the memories he's trying to steal.

A pool of blood on an expensive carpet. The stained ceiling of a cheap hotel room. The smell of popcorn.

I push harder, trying to shut him out.

My mother.

No! I scream and instead of trying to shut him out, I attack him for all I'm worth. I throw myself at him, push myself into his consciousness. I slash at the redness of him and bits of his memories rain down like candy from a pinata.

A demon in a dark alley; a boring meeting in a foreign language.

His wife, dead.

I feel him rear back, pulling away, and I'm vaguely aware of Our body collapsing with a strangled scream and the Crusaders swarming around us in a panic. But I'm not done, I slash at him, shoving and pushing into his memories with a force greater than he could have dreamed of attacking me with.

A baby boy; a corporate boardroom; a black 306 on a green motel door as we hug a broken, weeping record: "Oh, God, I failed. I'm sorry. Oh, God…" I hear her voice as if it was in my own ear.

He can't block me out, he can't fight me off. With vicious glee I grasp more and more memories, letting him feel my hot joy at turning the tables. I frolic in his memories as messily as I do in the corpses of my victims, tossing them, shredding them, dancing in the puddles they make on the floor.

His wedding. His daughter's death. A particularly good sandwich. I don't care, I play with them all, as he flails in horror, trying to ward me off. Then I scream, *Get out!* I slash further, deeper. *Get out!* The words echo in Our head.

"*Get out!*" I bellow again, and this time the words echo in the room. I swell to fill MY fingertips, reach out along MY legs. He's gone, thrown from my body by the force of my attack. I leap to my feet, snarling, and the Crusaders scramble back.

As well they should.

The demons, barely alive, writhe and whimper, and, oooh, how I wish I knew the equal-opposite of the spell Graff just cast on them. I would suck the life from every Crusader in this room if I did.

"Arthur?" asks oblivious Professor Puchard.

I don't have to answer; The Sarge already knows. "Meda," she says and reaches for my arm. I jerk it away.

"No," I snarl.

"Meda, what happened?"

"What do you think?" I sneer.

Her eyes widen, then her jaw hardens and she shoots a glance where Graff's body still lies limp, Professor Puchard hovering over it. "The agreement was—"

"Agreement? What agreement?" My voice has a hysterical edge. "*I* agreed to nothing."

"Meda—" She touches my arm. I swing and smash my fist into her face. She doesn't try to dodge and the force of my blow causes her to stumble back a few feet.

"No one touches me again. *Not ever.*" My throat is sore and the words rasp painfully.

She doesn't disagree. She doesn't try to touch me,

or even come any closer. She stays where she is and only her gaze touches mine. "No, Meda. They won't," she swears.

I don't know what to do with that. I don't know what to do with anything. I can't breathe. I can't breathe, I can't breathe. I shove past her, toward the exit.

I don't get more than a few paces when Graff jerks upright with a gasp. I stutter to a stop, frozen like a deer in headlights, but he doesn't look at me. He grips the hovering Professor Puchard by the shoulders, panting, "She threw me out." He jerks Professor Puchard closer. "*She threw me out.*"

"But that's impossible."

Graff doesn't get a chance to respond, because The Sarge grabs him by his fancy suit and slams him into the wall. I don't stay to watch. I can't. The walls are too tight, closing in. I turn my back on them and push my way toward the door. I don't get far before a Corp steps in my way with an apologetic expression. "You need to–"

Before I get a chance to show her exactly what I do need, The Sarge stops her from across the room. "It's alright, Eve. Let her go."

"With all due respect, Sergeant, we can't risk–"

"*Let her go*, Eve," The Sarge snaps. "She can't leave."

Eve's lips tighten but she steps out of the way as I shove past. Behind me I hear The Sarge's tone harden as she turns her attention back to Graff. "What the hell do you think you were doing?"

"What I had to." His voice is shaky but unapologetic. "It's the difference between the interests of one versus the whole world."

"No, it's the difference between right and wrong." She thumps him against the wall. "She's just a girl."

"Is she?" Softly.

"You son of a–" she begins, but apparently finishes her sentence with a punch. All hell breaks loose behind me, but I don't turn around. I shove out of the dungeon. Once free, I don't stop, but only move faster, running up the stairs, pounding a few of them hard enough with my feet that they crack under me. I reach the main floor and explode out of the school entirely.

The night air is hot after the cool dankness of the cave. Under the vast empty sky I can breathe again, but I don't stop. I don't ever want to stop. My legs pump and I push off the ground with enough violence that I'm more kicking the earth rather than running. I kick across the field, into the woods. Away from the dungeon. Away from the school, away from the Crusaders and their double standards. Away from their dominating control.

They take and take and take, the box they've put me in shrinking every day, the walls closing in. Naïvely I thought eventually they'd stop; they'd have too. There's only so much to take. But I was wrong.

Now they've taken me.

And I can't. I can't, I can't, I can't.

I only get a few dozen yards inside the woods when The Sarge's words hit me. *She can't leave.* My feet come to a stumbling stop. The silence in the woods is filled with The Sarge's words. *She can't leave.*

I gasp, the air hissing as I pull it over my teeth. Too much air to fit down my throat at once. I bend, trying to get it all in, but it won't. For the second time today, I can't breathe.

The Beacon Map. There's no escape. They would only find me like Jo did.

Jo. I need to see Jo. And like that, air pours into my lungs.

As fast as I sprinted into the woods, I sprint back out. My feet don't want to go back *there*, my body rebels, but I make it. I have no choice. *Jo, Jo, Jo*, my feet pound out. She'll know what to do. *Jo, Jo, Jo.*

I circle around the school to the wall I scaled not twenty-four hours earlier. There's no way in hell I'm going anywhere near the dungeon. I slip up onto the roof, then into my attic.

I can force the Crusaders out if they try to possess me again, I know that now, and The Sarge said they wouldn't. But can I trust her? Can I risk it? What's the alternative? The Crusaders are the only things protecting me from the demons. As my run in with Armand proved, it's too easy for them to find me. So what can I do? Jo will know. Jo has to know.

I jump down the stairs, taking them five, six at a

time. I land at the bottom and I feel almost in control of myself, the closer I get to Jo's room. But then all that comes crashing down and I break into a skittering halt.

For on my door is a shiny new lock.

They're going to lock me in my room.

My breathing freezes in my chest. They can't. No more. NO MORE. I force myself to breathe, forcing away the panic that makes it impossible to think. I welcome the rage that takes its place. I like rage. Rage I can handle. Rage is control.

No more.

Light shines through the crack beneath the door. They're waiting for me. Whoever did this is waiting. I shove the door open so hard it bounces off the inside wall with a crack. What I see I don't understand. Not right away.

Sitting inside are Jo and Chi – and Jo's holding the key.

ELEVEN

I SHAKE MY head, not wanting to believe it. Jo wouldn't do this to me; she wouldn't take away my last tiny shred of freedom. I have no doubt now that the Crusaders would. I expect it from them, expect anything of them at this point.

But I don't expect it from Jo.

"Tell me that's not what I think it is," I snarl.

She rises to her feet. "It is, Meda, but listen–"

"I'm done listening!" I advance on her. "I listen to you, I listen to the Crusaders. All I bloody do is listen, while you and your precious Crusaders lecture. And who listens to me?"

"Oh, don't be so melodramatic–"

"*Melodramatic*?" The word is barely recognizable, the way it comes from my lips.

"–it's just for a little while." Her words tumble out, trying to squeeze into the short time she has before I throw her out – if she's lucky, through the door. "Just to keep you out of trouble while Sergeant Graff is here. You don't know what they will do if–"

At the sound of his name I snap. "No, you're the one who doesn't know."

I'm in her face, but she doesn't back down. "Whether you believe it or not, it's for your own good."

"I'm beginning to think you're the last person who knows what's good for me."

"Meda, you snuck out last night. And then, I get hauled out of the infirmary to hear that you attacked Isaiah."

"I didn't *attack* him. I *punched* him. If you ever see me attack a classmate, believe me you'll know the difference," I growl dangerously.

"Are you threatening me?" She sounds more pissed than worried. "I'm your friend!" she shouts in a very unfriendly manner.

"Really?" I shout back. "*Friends* don't lock each other up."

"Yeah, well, friends don't break their promises, either. You promised me you'd be good. What happened to that? It lasted what – five hours? Six?" The shrink ray is back, but I am impervious – my rage is a shield.

"He deserved it."

"Why, Meda? What did he say that was so horrible that it was worth breaking your word to me?"

It'd serve her right if I told her the whole school thinks she's blackmailing Chi with sex, that everyone believes she's going to get him killed with her incompetence. I open my mouth to say it, but the words fizzle and die on my tongue. Dammit.

"Nothing? You have nothing to say?" she demands.

I clamp my mouth shut before I say something I'll regret, then switch tracks. "What can I say? I'm a fighter, not a lover," I jeer. Then I say pointedly, "I used to think you, of all people, would understand. But what can I expect from a girl defeated by a rope climb?"

Jo looks slapped.

"Meda!" Until now Chi had hung back, but at my attack he takes a step around Jo. "That's not fair. She–" Jo puts an arm up and stops him. He turns to her, "Jo, this is insane. You need to tell her."

Jo answers without taking her eyes off me, her face stony. "No, Chi. Let her think what she wants."

"Oh, so I'm still allowed to think without your permission? I didn't know."

Her voice is rock hard when she continues. "I don't care what you think – only what you do. And you aren't going to sneak out anymore. The door's spelled, so don't think you can break your way out. Headmaster gave me a key, so I can let you out–"

"Like I'm some kind of dog," I sneer.

She continues as if I haven't spoken. "–in the mornings without anyone noticing. We'll say the lock is yours, to keep any of your enemies from messing with you or your stuff."

I snort. "Great, so now I need protection from

pathetic children." Then I get an idea, a horrible one. "How long have you been planning this?" I knew she suspected I was up to something before she caught me sneaking out. "The movie. It was an excuse to keep an eye on me until they added the lock, wasn't it?"

I don't need her to answer, the guilt is written all over her face.

"Get out," I snarl.

"Meda, it's for your—"

I leap forward. Chi again moves to jump between us, but Jo stops him with an upraised arm. I stop inches from her face. "I swear that if you say it's for my own good one more time, I will rip your fucking head off." We hold each other's eyes. "And *that's* a promise to you I'll keep."

Her lips tighten, but she doesn't drop her gaze.

"Meda," Chi says, his voice calm and even. "Jo's your friend."

I snarl at him then turn away. "Get out!" They don't move for a long moment, then I hear shuffling steps towards the door. When they reach it, they stop.

The door opens. "Meda," Jo says softly.

"Get. Out." I bite off each word as if it were her head. The door closes.

I hold my breath, waiting to see if she turns the key in the lock. There's a long pause and my heart lifts a tiny bit. But then the lock slams home and my heart comes crashing down.

Hope, like Jo, is a sneaky bitch. I slam my hands

against the wall I share with her and let out a snarl. I pound it a few more times, making divots in the brick, sending little bits crumbling down.

Jo. My first and only friend. But she's not really my friend. She can't forgive me for being what I am. She tried, but she doesn't like me for me. She wants to change me. Like my mother did.

See how that worked out for *her.*

Jo wants me to be someone else. Someone who kisses ass and follows rules – a tamed tiger who sits and purrs until her handler shouts "attack" at her enemies. But I am not a pet.

And I won't be locked in a cage.

My hands tighten on the wall, my fingers bearing down, turning brick to dust. The idea of breaking through this wall flirts with my self-control. A minute stretches, filled with the soft rain of brick dust on wood floors.

Freedom, freedom, freedom, my heart beats.

She can't leave. The Sarge's words again.

A *tap, tap, tap* from behind me cuts into my thoughts. Jo, no doubt. Trying to explain again. Or get the last word, more likely. I don't respond.

Tap, tap, tap, the sound comes again.

"What?" I snarl, spinning. But no one answers and there's no key in the lock. Instead, again I hear the tapping. But the noise isn't coming from the door – it's coming from the window. I turn again, squinting into the striped darkness, dark bars against a dark night. But there's more than darkness, there's a person's shape. Someone's hanging from the bars. Grinning.

Twelve

ARMAND. I DO nothing but stare stupidly for a minute.

Tap, tap, tap. He makes a motion for me to open the window. He's dressed in a fitted black top and his hair is messily shoved behind his ears. Each of his hands wraps around a rusty metal bar outside my window and his biceps flex from the effort of holding himself up.

I shouldn't open the window. Jo wouldn't like it.

Whack. Up goes the window.

"Good evening, *Mademoiselle* Melange," he says, emphasizing his French accent.

"What are you doing here?" I hiss.

"I followed you." He's completely unrepentant. "It took a while to get past the guards, even with your excellent example."

Huh, yeah, that probably wasn't too clever of me. As much as I hate the Crusaders right now, they're better than the demons. For starters, the demons *do* believe in recreational torture. How could I have been so stupid?

"But *why*?"

He looks startled by my question. "I would think that would be obvious." He drops his eyelids seductively. *To see you*, they say. But his mouth responds, "To destroy the Crusaders, of course." Then he grins cheekily.

It almost makes me laugh. It's funny because it's probably true. It's not funny for the same reason.

"Get out of here, before I call the Crusaders on you."

"I'm kidding, I'm kidding. I'm on vacation, remember?"

"I remember that you *said* you're on vacation," I snap. Despite our fun with Colton, I don't trust him any further than I can throw him. Less, actually; he's lean – I'd probably have pretty good range.

He looks hurt. "Don't you trust me?"

I let my expression answer.

He pouts, a look that shouldn't look so appealing on a teenage boy. When he gets no reaction, his smile slides back. He shrugs, and since he's holding himself up on the bars, the movement ends up bouncing the rest of him as his arms stay stable. "Fair enough," he admits. "But, I'd like to point out that I can't trust you either and I'm on your turf. You could call an army down on me like *that*." He releases one hand from the bars to snap his fingers, and swings wildly. He scrambles to grab it again and pull himself back up. "So," he says with a slight grunt, as he re-settles himself against the bars, "it seems to me, of the two of us, I'm risking more for us to be together."

I make a face at the way he says "for us to be together", and cross my arms, unconvinced.

He lets out a puff of air, slightly exasperated. "If I were here to kill Crusaders, first, I'd have traded your location to my boss in order to get his forgiveness for my little disappearing act. Then, I would have snuck an army of demons through those woods with me." He tosses a look back at the woods behind him. "We would infiltrate the school, and take the children hostage, then trade them for adults." A darkness creeps into his expression, and a sharpness. Like a hound on the scent. My heart beats a little faster in response. He pulls himself closer to the bars, until his face is pressed against them. "The Crusaders aren't big on negotiating, but I doubt they'd be able to hold out if we had a few dozen children. Once we had the adults, we'd slaughter them. Then the children would be unprotected." His mood shifts suddenly and his lips quirk in a little smile, breaking the spell. "I'll tell you what I would not have done – stopped to tell the infamous Meda Melange what I was planning."

That would be the height of stupidity. On the other hand, I've learned never to underestimate people's capacity for stupidity. They always manage to surprise me. "Then what are you here for?"

"I'm bored," he complains. "I've been on my own

for months now."

"Go find one of your demon-buddies."

"Can't. They'd turn me in."

"Some friends," I say, but I know the feeling.

He shrugs again and his eyes twinkle mischievously. "You can never trust demons."

"Yeah, well, I kinda already guessed that, them being the embodiment of evil and all."

He laughs. "Come, Meda! Come out and play!" He swings from the bars again. "I promise I have no armies stashed in the woods." His energy is infectious. The way he smiles and laughs and swings from barred windows like he hasn't a care in the world. He even moves with a gleeful giddiness that is hard to resist. But I don't have a choice.

"I'm not in the mood," I lie, not wanting to admit I'm locked in.

Jo locked me in.

"Not for anything?" he asks plaintively. "You haven't even heard my suggestion, yet." His eyes are full of naughty promises.

But the reminder of Jo's betrayal kills any kindness I was feeling. And, despite his claims to innocence, well, as he said, you can never trust demons. I should turn him in before we're caught and they accuse me of being in league with him. I shudder at what the Crusaders would do then. "You know, now that you mention it, there is something I'm in the mood for." I cup my hands around my mouth, making it obvious I'm about to shout for the Crusaders.

Armand remains unconcerned. *Foolish boy, I'm not one to play chicken with even when I'm in the best of moods. And I'm most definitely not in the best of moods.*

I shrug and take a deep breath. I open my mouth and–

He whisks something out of his pocket and holds it up to the window. It gleams dully in the light from my bedside lamp.

The key.

I swallow my shout so hard I choke on it. I bend over, coughing and wheezing.

He grins at my discomfort. "I'm sorry, Meda? You were saying?"

I cough and point.

"Something about what you were in the mood for? Involving me?" His tone is all innocent suggestion.

"Is that what I think it is?" I gasp.

He looks at the key in his hand, as if considering. "Oh, I don't know." He slides a look at me, his teeth white in the dark. "But I suspect it's the key to your heart."

"Where did you get it?"

"I had some time to kill, waiting for you to come back to your room. I may have managed to sneak a copy."

"You've been hanging around all afternoon?" How is it possible that I didn't know? I would have felt the bump of power if he'd been anywhere nearby.

I should feel it now, actually.

Something's not right. I drop to a crouch, bending so my legs are springs, and glare at him.

His eyes widen. "Hold on, calm down." He scrambles for something around his neck, swinging again as he lets go of the bars with one arm. He grabs an amulet hanging from his neck and pulls it off. There's a familiar swell of power under my skin, electrifying my nerve endings. I barely catch myself from sighing at the pure pleasure born of the power boost. "I'm hiding from demons," he explains. "It'd be inconvenient if they could sense me every time I walked past one."

"You didn't have it last time," I accuse.

"I did, I just didn't wear it. I told you I was planning to turn myself in." He grins. "But instead I found you."

He did say that.

"Come on, please?" He wears a pleading look as well as any big-eyed puppy. It's tempting, so tempting. To beat the Crusaders, to slip their cage. The wake of my earlier rage leaves me feeling reckless, dangerous. Rebellious.

"Don't you trust me?" Armand tries to look angelic, and the expression so ill-fits his face it makes me laugh.

"No."

My response only makes him laugh. "Don't say the Great Meda Melange, Destroyer of Demons is scared to be alone with a measly little half-demon?" He tries to look harmless. He succeeds, because he is. I can handle Armand.

What *am* I worried about? And it hits me. I'm still worried what Jo would think. But on that front it seems like I no longer have anything to lose.

"Come on, Meda, it'll be fun."

"I can't. I'm not allowed," I say, but it's automatic.

"Aww, but that just makes it better. Fun is so much better when it's stolen."

My eyes snap to his. I shouldn't. It could be a demon trap. Or, even if it's not, if the Crusaders catch me sneaking around with the enemy, we're dead. It's risky, reckless, and wrong.

And yet, my mouth bends in a smile. "What did you have in mind?"

He grins. "Whatever you want." We lock eyes for a moment longer, then he breaks it. "Hold on," he says, then walks his hands up the bars. I get an eyeful of tight tee over tighter abs, as he hauls himself onto the roof.

I wait as he sneaks in to let me out of my prison. I start to have second thoughts, nibbling, nagging thoughts that buzz around with the Good bees. This isn't smart.

But then I hear the snap of the lock, and it startles the bees away. Armand eases open the door and holds out his hand. "Come on," he whispers.

I hesitate.

"We won't do anything bad," he says, piously. "I promise."

I slide my hand into his. My hand appears deceptively small encased by his large one, but I know I could crush his bones with a squeeze if I wanted to. I don't. Not now, at least, but the reminder that I can solidifies my intent. I look back up at him and he's watching the thoughts play across my face with a smothered smile.

His smile escapes, spreading full across his face. "But we won't do anything good, either."

Good. I'm awfully tired of *good*.

Thirteen

I LET ARMAND lead the way so I can keep an eye on him. He takes us up through my attic, putting his arms out and hopping playfully across the rotten spot in a way that reminds me of Uri. Then he levers himself out the window, turning around to stick an arm down for me. I ignore it and climb out myself. We start across the slanted roof, staying low. The night is heavy and dark, riddled with secrets.

"Where are we going?" I whisper.

"You'll see."

I stop in my tracks. He notices within a few steps and returns.

"I'm not in the habit of following my enemies to undisclosed locations for mysterious purposes."

"I'm not your enemy," he says, but I don't move. "Alright, fine." He runs his hand through his hair. "There's this guy I came across, not far from here. I thought we could, you know," he makes a short slashing motion across his neck. "He seems like the kinda guy you'd go for. In a homicidal way, I mean."

"You arranged a murder?" Awww, that's so sweet.

"Nothing elaborate, of course." He grins slyly. "Didn't want to overdo it on a first date."

And he ruins it.

"What else would we do?" He shrugs. "I thought the murder part would be obvious."

"Oh, the murder part is – the problem is that the obvious victim is *me*."

"How many times do I have to tell you? I am not here to kill you."

"You really expect me to take you at your word?" I point a finger at him. "Agent of evil, remember?"

He points right back at me. "Princess of Hell – remember? We belong on the same team."

"No, we don't. And we aren't."

"Not yet."

"And since when does Hell have royalty? I thought they were all bureaucrats."

"Oh, sweetie," he says, patronizing. "That's cute."

"What's cute?"

"That you think celebrity children of powerful people aren't royalty."

"Are you accusing me of being a Hilton?" I sputter. "Or a, a–" my head might explode, "Kardashian?"

"The Hellish equivalent." He pauses, then adds thoughtfully, "You know I don't think it needed the qualifier."

I growl at him.

He holds up his hands. "Kidding, kidding. Sort of. Your dad is more like a senator – high up but not quite at the top. Enough power to get you out of a DWI, but not quite enough to–"

But my brain stopped a while ago. "What do you mean 'is'?" I grab him by the throat. "What do you mean my dad *is* like a senator?"

He peels my hand off his throat, but keeps hold of it. He doesn't answer.

"He's still alive," I say. It's not a question. Those bloody damn demons and their bloody rebirth, it's not bloody damn fair. "Un-effing believable."

"Daddy issues?"

I glare at him.

"Oh come on, don't let it spoil our night."

"He wants to kill me."

He shrugs and points out the obvious. "A lot of people want to kill you."

"Are you trying to make me feel better?"

"I'm just saying, what difference does it make? He's not any more alive than he was a minute ago."

"But now I know."

"But that should just cheer you up," he says, teasingly, still trying to get lighten my mood. "Knowledge is power."

"Did you just quote a public service announcement at me?"

He sticks his nose piously in the air. "Just doing

my civic duty."

I point at him. "Agent. Of. Evil."

He grins.

But it did help actually, as he has a good point. Already my sneaking out has unintended benefits. I eye him.

The Crusaders know pathetically little about demons. The types of people who sell their souls are not known for loyalty and self-sacrifice – really, they're quite known for the opposite – so their pact with Hell includes a proscription against speaking of certain things – like Ariel selling her voice to the Sea Witch. Even under torture a demon can only reveal what Hell wants it to.

As someone who Hell wants dead, I find this lack of information disturbing. And here stands a boy who hasn't sold his soul, who knows a great deal about Hell.

And, as he said, knowledge is power.

My punishing grip on his hand loosens, but I don't let go. Instead I give it a little pet. "You're right," I allow. "It doesn't matter, not really." I shrug. "What's one more demon?" I flick a glance at him from under my lashes.

His eyebrows are a little high. My mood changed too quickly – he's on to me.

"But I'm still not going anywhere with you."

They come back down.

"Anyone ever tell you you have trust issues?" he says in a groan, then drops fluidly and pats the moonlit shingles next to him. "Here we stay then. Or is this too dangerous? There is a ledge like, oh, ten meters away."

"Keep it up and I'll let you decide," I say sweetly, but I sit.

My big exciting escape to… the roof. Wow, I'm a badass, let me tell you. I sure showed those Crusaders! I muffle a groan of self-loathing as I drop down next to him.

Armand sprawls back on the roof, leaning on his elbows, but I stay sitting up, my arms wrapped loosely around my knees. With the lack of light pollution up in the mountains, stars litter the sky like confetti in Times Square on New Year's Eve, hidden only by the occasional cloud. Stars like these are the type to hypnotize a girl. They make bad boys seem like good ideas. I slant a look at where he leans back on the roof. His thin, faded T-shirt is washed-a-thousand-times-soft and clings to his chest and abs. I swear to God, I can see the outline of muscles. Through the shirt. In the dark. Not that I'm looking.

Get him! my hormones scream.

Don't fall for it, my brain cautions.

Pretty! they whine. Stupid hormones.

Calm down, hormones. We are just pumping him – (really brain, you chose the word *pumping?*) *– for information. He is literally evil. We need to keep our distance.*

A pause.

Get him!

Sigh. I peel my eyes of him and look at the scenery instead.

In the moonlight, the trees are etched in soft silver, and even the cement-and-rebar mess of the half-constructed school looks somehow magical. It's pretty. Romantic, even, if I were another girl. But I'm not; my heart doesn't cling to moon-bright clouds or silver-traced trees. Mine revels in shadows. The dark places created by the contrast, places meant to sneak and hide. A pretty night, meant for ugly things.

I sneak another look at Armand from the corner of my eye. His expression suggests he might be thinking the same thing.

And yet we sit, tethered to this roof.

I shift my eyes back to the view. "So… how many amulets like yours do the demons have?" I ask. He doesn't answer immediately and I twist to see him looking at me, eyes slightly narrowed.

I need to be careful. Lying to a Crusader is like taking candy from a baby. I suspect, in the art of subterfuge, I'm the infantile one in this relationship.

Fortunately, I'm a bit of a child prodigy.

"What?" I ask. "You could have an army stashed in those woods for all I know. So, how many?"

He laughs quietly. "Not an army's worth, I assure you."

That's not an answer. I stare until I get one.

He groans. "You really don't like me, do you?"

"'Like' has nothing to do with it. I don't *trust* you."

"Oh, so you *do* like me." He grins.

Clever subject change, Monster boy. But not clever enough. "Answer the question."

He groans again and pats his pocket. "This is the only one. At least that I know of."

I study him for the lie. I can't tell, but I'm unwilling to beat the truth out of him. At least, not yet. I change the subject. "So what do you do for Hell, exactly?"

"What do you mean?" he asks, his voice a little too innocent.

"Surely they don't let you just muck about all day."

"Why do you say that?"

I roll my eyes. "You wouldn't have run away if that were the case."

He slants me a look, calculating. He opens his mouth, but I cut him off.

"Bullshit," I call.

He sits up. "I didn't even say anything." He wears outraged innocence well, and I take note of how he does it. It's a look I've yet to perfect, judging by how often Jo calls me on it. "How could it be bullshit?"

I just look at him knowingly. "It was, though, wasn't it?"

He holds the expression a second longer, then he relaxes back in his bad-boy slouch. "Caught."

"So what do you really do for Hell?"

He hesitates before answering, and his head tips back and forth, as if weighing the pros and cons. He clears his throat awkwardly and cuts me a side glance.

Finally he answers. "I'm, ah, an incubus in training."

"An *incubus*?" I burst out laughing. According to my Demonology professor, their purpose is to inflate Hell's ranks "naturally", AKA make half-demons like me. "You knock up girls for a living?" I snort. "No wonder you like fighting for Hell. Talk about an assignment."

He sticks his chin up in mock superiority. "I don't 'knock girls up.'" He quotes me, faking an American accent – or at least he tries. It's terrible. Then he levels his eyes at me, and his lids lower. His voice gets husky, his accent a little stronger. "I seduce."

Get hi– Oh for freak's sake, hormones!

His voice gets lighter again. "It's an art."

I laugh again, though there's a little catch in it. "I bet," I say dryly. Then something occurs to me. "So is that your plan, eh?" I nudge him obnoxiously with my elbow. "Work your incubi magic on me until I swear undying love?" I move into a falsetto. "Oh, Armand! You handsome piece of eye candy!" I flip over onto my hands and knees, straddling his long legs. "Whatever you want!" I crawl towards him, slowly up his body, until my face is inches from his. I look at him through my lashes. "Anything you want, like…" I let the word trail off softly and he swallows. "Kill Crusaders!" I perk and he barks a laugh.

"Rotten girl."

"Don't you forget it," I grin then resume my position next to him. "So you plan to charm me into spilling all my Crusader secrets, aye?"

"Not anymore," he says sourly.

"Aw, that's too bad," I tease. "I've never been seduced by a professional."

He rolls his eyes.

"So are there a lot of baby Armands running around?" I ask.

The question startles another laugh out of him. "No. Not that I know of." He shrugs. "Unlikely, really."

I raise a brow at him. "Bad at your job?"

He gets a wicked look in his eye, then his face softens, and he traps my eyes in his. He swallows and that muscle on the edge of his jaw flexes. I gulp. Then he raises his eyebrow, mirroring mine from a moment before. "What do you think?"

Sorry, what were we talking about?

He keeps talking, thank God. "Demons aren't very, ah, *potent*, being mostly dead and all. Neither are half-demons, generally."

Huh, good to know.

"And even if we manage to impregnate someone, there are few women strong enough to carry a baby to full-term, even if they wanted to – which most don't."

Makes sense. At best, it's an unplanned pregnancy, at worst – well, the dad *is* evil. Even if the mothers don't figure it all out, they probably notice enough to know it's not normal.

"And, really, we're forbidden to impregnate women anymore."

I look at him curiously. Kinda makes his job worthless.

"Too much medical intervention these days," he explains. "Too much about the fetus that needs to be hidden. Your mother knew enough to hide the truth from a doctor, but no normal woman would. It'd ruin our cover."

"Then what, exactly, do incubi do?"

He falls back on his back, staring at the stars. He's quiet for a long moment, then he answers softly. "I give a girl something she thinks she wants more than anything else in the world." There's another pause. "Then I take it away."

"Why?"

"For her soul." He shrugs, but it's stiff. "It's what we do."

"You steal their souls?"

"No," he says firmly. "I steal only their hearts. They trade their souls willingly to get them back."

Sounds like a pretty thin justification to me, but I leave him his lie. He's still looking at me, as if waiting for me to pronounce judgment. I do. "Sounds mean."

He looks away with a sharp laugh, wrapping his arms loosely around his knees. "I'm an agent of evil, remember?" He doesn't say anything more, but stares out at the moonlit nightscape.

I study his perfect features, the bad boy hair, the dark lashed eyes, the too-full lips. The sharp cheekbones and straight nose. The perfectly cut body. I have no doubt he's very good at his job – and a suspicion bubbles to the surface. "That's not how you really look, is it?"

His eyes widen a millimeter. "Why would you say that?" The fake innocence is back.

"Because no one looks like that." I look him up and down.

"What, this old thing?" He pulls up his shirt to show off his abs. "Like what you see?"

I narrow my eyes.

"No," he admits, dropping his shirt. "This isn't how I really look. I imagine I'm much plainer."

"Imagine?"

He laughs. "I grew up with demons – I was the ultimate dress-up doll as a child. I haven't looked like myself… ever, possibly. They've been messing with my appearance as long as I can remember." He says it lightly, but I detect an edge.

"So you can't change your own appearance?"

"Only full demons can, and they can only make the changes while in Hell, where their abilities are amplified," he explains. "Or in the Acheron." He catches my curious expression. "What you Crusaders call the demon headquarters." He waves his hand casually like he's stating the obvious. "But enough about me." He rocks his head toward me. "Your turn."

"No," I shake my head. "I don't think so." I'm learning more on this roof than I ever learned in Demonology.

"That's not very polite."

I shrug. "I'm not polite."

He laughs again. "Well, if you keep your secrets, I'll keep mine." He rolls his lips together and lies back on the roof.

Can't have that, it completely ruins my justification – err, I mean, legitimate reason – for fraternizing with the enemy. "Fine," I say. "What do you want to know?"

His eyes brighten, but he doesn't answer right away. Finally he asks. "Why did you punch that boy?"

He must have listened to my argument with Jo. Remembering the fight ruins my mood. "The other kids are pissed at Jo for letting Chi partner with her, when her leg is a liability. It's honorable for Chi to sacrifice himself to be with her, but not honorable for her to let him." I sneer. "Isaiah took it a step further and said Jo was sleeping with Chi to trap him. So, I punched him."

Armand's smile fades, and he tips his head, perplexed. "Wait, so you were fighting for her?"

"Yes."

"Then why not tell her? She can't get pissed about that. And the guilt…" he lets out a happy sigh, like he smells something delicious.

"Because not knowing everything totally pisses her off," I say grumpily.

An approving grin stretches his face.

But it's not true. And why am I lying? Not that I

have any compunction about lying, but I usually have a reason. Never say it's to impress this boy-man-monster? That's both embarrassing and probably pointless, as I'll most likely kill him before morning.

"That's not really it, just a side benefit. She's my best friend," I say simply. "And that's her worst fear: that Chi will die because of her. I won't throw that at her." My mouth twists. "A chair maybe, if she keeps it up, but not that."

He doesn't laugh. Instead he tips his head again, and studies me. A wrinkle puckers his forehead.

"What?" I ask, irritated.

"Nothing." He flops back down. "Your turn," he says, but his tone is thoughtful.

"If incubi aren't allowed to impregnate humans, how do you exist?"

He snorts. "I guess I should have figured holi-er-than-thou Crusader school wouldn't teach sex-ed."

They actually do, but I don't get the joke.

He takes on a patronizing tone. "We aren't allowed to impregnate *humans*…"

Ah, I get it. "Your mother was a demon?"

"…I'd be willing to show you the mechanics if you're interested."

"You wish."

"I do," he agrees, shamelessly. "But yes, *Maman* is a demon. It's rare. Being a mom requires a certain amount of… sacrifice that most demons aren't interested in."

I think of the sacrifices my own mother made and wince.

"Plus the whole half-dead thing makes them tough to – how did you say?" He looks at me, "*Knock up* to begin with. But it does happen occasionally."

"So how many halflings are there?"

He thinks about it. "A hundred or so."

"Have you met any?"

"Many."

"What are they like?"

He thinks about that. "Like me, I suppose." He smiles. "Hopeless reprobates, the lot of them."

Not what I want to hear. He seems to guess that. "Not like you," he says thoughtfully. "You're different." He pauses. "More human." His eyes fix on me.

I snort. "Let me guess, you like that about me, eh, incubi?"

He laughs. "Nah. Probably not."

I hit him. "Ass."

"All right, all right. Maybe I do for one night, but not in the long run. Humans can be so preachy, and boring. They waste shadow-filled nights on rooftops talking," he says with exaggerated disgust. I take another swing at him, but this time he catches my arm with a grin. Then the grin fades. "But it does make you interesting. Just because I can't share those softer traits, doesn't mean I can't appreciate them. Like a hunter who admires the beauty of the deer."

"Right before he takes it down," I say dryly.

He doesn't deny it. "Yes. But it doesn't make my envy any less real."

"Envy?"

"It's the nature of a demon, I suppose, to want what we can't have." His tone lightens. "Why do you think I find you so irresistible?" His eyes latch on my face.

"Oh, incubi, take an 'A' for effort." I laugh. "At this rate, you'll have me charmed into betrayal in no time."

He laughs, but his eyes stay on my face longer than is comfortable. He's still holding on to my arm, and he runs his thumb lightly over my wrist. I force back a shiver and tug it away. Breaking eye contact, I lie down on the roof, the grit that has flecked off the shingles rolling under me. A second later, he lies down next to me, resting his hands on his stomach.

"So what was it like, growing up with a demon as a mother?" I ask.

"Nope, it's my turn."

I sigh, but wave a hand for him to ask away.

"Why do you stay here? With them?"

Isn't that the million-dollar question? "The free food."

He gives me a look.

"Just kidding. The food's terrible. Oh, who wouldn't I kill for some Cheetos?"

"Be serious," he says, but he shakes with quiet laughter.

"I *was* being serious. The Crusaders completely ignore the neon-orange food group."

"A travesty. How can you live under these barbaric conditions?"

"Because I'm one of the good guys, obviously." My tone implies a "duh" at the end, and he snorts. "Besides, I couldn't leave if I wanted to." There's an edge of bitterness I can't quite hide.

"Oh?"

"Team demon wants me dead." For starters. I'm not about to tell him the whole I'm-a-Beacon thing.

"Present company excluded."

I send him a side-glance. "Maybe," I allow.

"I don't think the demons want you dead," he says, thoughtful.

I raise an eyebrow at him.

"Well, they do, if you don't join them," he clarifies. "But it doesn't fit their style. Demons almost always have an agenda, you just have to figure out how to use it to your advantage. Yours is easy. They wouldn't waste a weapon like you out of spite. If you joined them, they'd probably let you live."

"Probably? That's reassuring."

"I'm serious. They would take you in and protect you from the Crusaders." He rolls up on an elbow, leaning over me, and smiles mischievously. "Let me tell you, it's a lot more fun to play for the bad guys."

"I'm not going to sell my soul for a little fun." But after the last few months I can't say the idea isn't a little appealing.

"You don't have to. I haven't. You just have to work for them."

I eye him skeptically.

"Oh, they'll try to get your soul, believe me. And I don't know if you've noticed, but we can be very persuasive," he says seductively, and then ruins it with a shrug. "But it has to be willingly." He regards me. "And you don't seem like the kind of person who lets other people make up her mind."

"Then why are you trying to?"

He laughs. "Fair enough. I just want you to know you have options."

"They'd kill me before I got a chance to explain anyway."

He's quiet. Then, "Not if someone explains for you, first."

I look at him sharply, then away, hoping he didn't catch the rotten excitement I shouldn't feel.

I feign mild curiosity. "What happens when you sell your soul? The Crusaders say it erases your humanity, that you become just a beast, a being of evil."

He pauses, thinking it over. "It doesn't really erase your humanity. It's still there – whatever was there to begin with. It's just stripped of its pretenses."

"What do you mean?"

He pauses, as if thinking of the best way to explain. "Did you know that most people consider themselves to be good?" He looks at me and I shrug. "Well, they do," he confirms. "Studies have shown–"

"Studies? The demon boy is quoting studies at me?"

He laughs. "It's not all fun and games in Hell. We study humans. Psychology, sociology, anthropology – the behavioral sciences. What makes them tick, what influences their decisions." His mouth twists. "How to make them do what we want.

"Anyway, there was a study that showed that people, given a scale from 1–10, rank themselves at about a seven – at everything. IQ, work ethic, driving ability. People like to see themselves as 'good', no matter how messed up they are. That includes murderers, child molesters, rapists, robbers. It's amazing the way people can justify anything: 'It was just a mistake, it was the situation, my mommy didn't love me enough.' And those are *actions* that are explained away, it doesn't begin to cover the depraved *thoughts* people have, the horrible things they want to do, but don't. The terrible things they think." He shakes his head.

"When you sell your soul, all that ends. The pretenses are stripped away and you see yourself for what you are. You meet *Him*." The creeptastic way he says it needs no clarification; he's talking about the devil. "He can see into your soul, see every filthy thing you ever did, every thought you ever had. You can't hide what you are, you can't lie to yourself, you see what you really are. What you deserve." He turns dark, dark eyes on me. "And the people who sell their souls are not sevens.

Not even close."

He takes a deep breath. "So to answer your question, the humanity is still there, whatever there ever was. But they're free from it."

"Have you met Him?"

Armand shudders. "He doesn't exactly hang around. Only demons who sell their souls see Him."

It's obvious he doesn't want to talk about it anymore. "So what was it like growing up with a demon as a mother?"

He settles back and describes a childhood spent in the Acheron that could have taken place in a freshman dorm at a party school – all sin and fun. "There are very few rules in Hell," he wraps up. "We aren't allowed to kill each other, but short of that, the sky – or maybe I should say, the Pit – is the limit." He chuckles. "My every wicked whim was satisfied. No, not just satisfied, encouraged. I learned from the best. It's a kind of art there, pain, murder, seduction." He smiles at some memory. A dark smile filled with happiness only a monster could understand. I can't help but feel envious.

"Your turn. What was it like growing up among humans?"

"Ha. For every rule you didn't have, I had ten. I was hardly allowed to do anything, and ohhhhh, how I hated it." I let out a sharp laugh. "I don't think we could have more opposite upbringings. The fights I had with my mother." I shake my head.

"What was she like?" His question is soft.

"She was... patient. Kind. Usually exasperated," I smile at the memory. "Occasionally angry," I rock my head and give him a naughty smile, "but always with provocation." He grins back. It occurs to me now that, despite his funny, happy descriptions of growing up among the demons, he didn't mention his mom very often. At all, really. I think about my mom, an activity that's always a bit like licking sugar off asphalt – bitter, sweet, and rough. I picture her sunshine smile, her golden-brown, fly-away hair – not entirely unlike Jo's, actually. My creaky heart thuds the painful way it does. "She... loved easily, I think. She loved me in any case, and I was rarely easy."

"No wonder you seem so human, raised by someone like that." He doesn't look at me as he says it.

We're completely sprawled out on the roof now, and I feel relaxed for the first time in weeks. Maybe months. I make a mental note to grab the pillows and blankets from the attic cubby for next time.

Next time. I don't want to think of the implications of that.

"So why the sudden urge for a vacation?" I ask. "Sounds like living with the demons is one never-ending party."

"Ah, well, you know. Work is work, I guess," he answers vaguely.

"No," I say dryly. "It's not. You're a professional playboy for pity's sake."

I expect him to laugh, but he doesn't. He doesn't

say anything, either. I turn to study his profile. "So what's the problem?"

He plays with a small piece of broken shingle, spinning it between his fingers. He doesn't look at me. "There are plenty of bad people out there, or people on the edge, who need only the slightest nudge to send them spiralling downward." He chucks the piece of shingle off the roof, as if to illustrate his point. "But those aren't the ones I'm sent after. My job isn't to turn the mean ones, but the weak ones. Their only crime is loneliness.

"They aren't evil. They don't dream of money or power or bloody perversions in the dark." He pauses, and I wonder what images play in his head. "They dream of something beautiful," he says softly. Then his voice hardens. "And I use it to destroy them."

"So why do it?"

He shrugs and doesn't look at me. "I have no choice."

"You could *not* side with the demons."

At that, he does turn. "It's what I am," he says simply. "I've tried, like you, to be something else." His eyes are inscrutable, filled with a terrible nothingness. "It didn't work out." He blinks, and the shadows disappear. "Besides, it's not forever."

I look at him curiously. His mood shifts and his lips quirk up in a sneaky little smile. "You asked if I'm bad at my job? I am. Abysmal, really." He shakes his head tragically. "Right now, they're chalking it up to my being a rookie but," he shakes his head woefully, "I'm afraid I'm just not gifted in the art of seduction." He looks at me through his lashes.

Liar.

"They'll have no choice but to reassign me eventually. But for now, I need a break. So I'm taking a vacation."

"In the mountains of West Virginia. I would have picked Tahiti."

"I'm ready to leave when you are."

I laugh. "How exactly do you see this…" I wave between the two of us, unable to come up with a descriptor.

"Beautiful friendship?" he supplies with a devilish grin.

"…going?" I finish, ignoring him. "Us being mortal enemies and all."

"I prefer the term 'star-crossed lovers.'"

I snort. "Regardless, it can't end well."

"The best romances don't."

I roll my eyes then slant him a sideways look. "Eventually, I *am* going to have to kill you."

"Why do you say that?" He looks almost serious for once. Almost.

"For starters, you know too much. About this Crusader camp, about me."

He opens his mouth as if to somehow contradict me, but I keep going.

"Even if that wasn't the case, we're still on opposing sides in a war. You said yourself, you're going to go back eventually. What happens then?" I shake my head.

"Ah, well, don't worry about that," he says, resting back on his elbows. "I have a plan."

"A plan?" I ask dubiously.

"Oh yes," he assures me. "A quite clever one in which, I, the hero, daringly rescue our doomed love."

"Hero?" I roll my eyes. "You're an agent…"

"…of evil," he finishes. "I know, I know. But we're all the heroes in our own little dramas," he says smoothly.

I laugh. "And what role do I play in your little drama?"

"Unwitting dupe."

"Hm. Looks like I'm gonna kill you sooner than I thought."

He laughs, unconcerned.

He looks back over the horizon, and I'm startled to notice it's turned from navy to grey. He seems to notice at the same time, because he sits up with a quiet "Wow", and a stretch.

"Yeah," I say, doing the same, but neither of us stand, reluctant for the night to end. Finally, I have no choice. "I'd better get back, before Jo comes to unlock me." I make a face.

He groans and stands, then offers a hand to pull me up. This time, I let him. "Come on, jailbird."

Jailbird. So true. I wince.

He follows me as I creep back across the roof. I

sit to swing down from the roof and into the cracked gable, but then stop.

"What are you going to do today?" I want to ask if he's coming back, but he'd probably like that too much.

He shrugs. "Anything I want, I guess."

Must be nice.

A slow smile stretches his full mouth. "But I guess what I'll want is to be back here by midnight."

I don't let him see my smile as I swing down from the roof, but I suspect he knows it's there.

Fourteen

Loud banging wakes me. I rub my eyes and blearily
seek out my clock. 8.40. Jo must have unlocked my
door but not woken me. Coward. As a result, I slept
through breakfast and part of first period.

Devastated by this idea, I stretch languidly and
leisurely climb out of bed. Whoever's outside is still
banging. One of the many crappy things about board-
ing school is they always know where to find you if you
play hooky. I reach out and jerk the door open. A kid
from my first class, a short boy who's never done me
any harm, stands on the other side. Jaden, I think.

"Yo," I say, then yawn hugely. I don't cover my
mouth.

His arm's still up in the air, poised mid-knock.
"Uh," he swallows. "Headmaster wants to see you."

"So?"

I don't move and neither does he. Finally he adds,
"So you're supposed to come to his office."

I raise an eyebrow. "Are you supposed to make me?"

"Errr…" He shifts from one foot to the other. I don't think he wants to admit the answer is "yes." I sigh. It's not his fault. I throw him a bone.

"Hold on." I shut the door in his face. I throw on some clothes, tossing a sneer at the pile of cheerful options Jo had left for me yesterday. I pull on a tight black T-shirt with the silhouette of an attack dog on it, a pair of my holiest jeans, and sneakers. I shove my pre-lunch books in my backpack and glance in the mirror. My hair, short and evenly cut, stands up at the back in a spiky mess. I decide I like it, so leave it.

I jerk the door open again, making Jaden jump. He gives me a sheepish smile before leading the way down the hall.

I yawn again. Thank God I ate those demons yesterday. As many meals as I've been missing, I'd waste away. Still, my stomach rumbles. Jaden must have heard and digs in his backpack and passes me a granola bar with a tentative smile. It's smushed and twisted out of shape, but I take it and scarf it down in three bites, shoving the wrapper in my pocket.

It doesn't take long before Jaden deposits me at the headmaster's door. I gave him a "well-done soldier" and a mocking salute, which I'm amused to see he returns, before he jets down the stairs in an overabundance of energy.

The headmaster's office is located in one of

the center sections of our stair-step school, right in the middle between the high school classes and the younger kids. His door's open when I arrive, but he's facing away from me, leaning back in the battered chair behind his equally-battered desk. Probably into his seventies, he's compact and muscular, gnarled all over with a tangle of muscles and scars: a tough piece of gristle that death found too tough so spat back out. I used to find him quite scary, but after dealing with him and The Sarge, it's clear why he was the one chosen to deal with children.

I rap two knuckles on the door and he swivels to face me.

I wonder if The Sarge's demand for confidentiality on yesterday's events applies to herself, and study him carefully, searching for any tension. Or judgment.

"Miss Porter, glad you can make it," he says, dryly. "Imagine my surprise when I try to scold you for punching Isaiah, only to find you playing hooky."

Nope, just his usual amused tolerance. I relax and settle into our usual routine. "Miss Porter," he begins.

Melange, I silently amend.

"Violence is never the answer."

Fourth period Combat Training to the contrary.

"If you have a problem with a student, you should report it to a teacher."

After that, I tune in and out. Mostly out.

When his tone gets conclusive, I click back in for the sentencing. "It's clear you can't be in class with Mr

Hooper."

Wait? What? I'm out of Advanced Crusader History for good? This is better than I expected.

"But it's too far in the semester to bother sticking you anywhere else; you're behind enough as it is."

OH MY GOD! Free period!

"And there's too much going on right now." His face tightens and he rubs his temples. His thoughts drift away, and wherever they go, it's not a happy place. "We don't have the Crusaders available to watch you."

Free, free period? No, that's too good to believe. I eye him suspiciously.

"But I think I've found the perfect solution."

Perfect for who? Given the twinkle in his eye, I suspect not me.

"A place where you couldn't possibly get in trouble," he says, creaking to his feet.

"Where?" I ask distrustfully.

"You'll see." He leaves the office, and I have no choice but to follow. My mind races: no Crusader can watch me, no other class will have me… I'm half afraid he's going to lock me in the dungeon.

I clear my throat. "Headmaster?" I squeak.

He ignores me and we head further downward, through the middle grades, and into the elementary level.

Then we pass the doors out of the building, and still he keeps going.

He's taking me to the dungeon. I won't go down

there. Not again. My feet start to drag.

But then, just as we're about to reach the next flight of stairs he stops outside a door and I realize that what he has in mind is far, far worse.

"No, please," I say, true horror in my voice.

He shakes his head. "I'm sorry Meda, but you've brought this upon yourself."

No, it's too humiliating to contemplate. "I'll be good! I promise!" I plead. Oh God, the ridiculing I'll be subjected to once word gets out. "Please!" I beg shamelessly, but I can tell it's no good.

It's the smothered smile that tips me off.

"You'll report here during Crusader History and Western Civilization. I recommend you use this time to study for your other classes." His leashed smile breaks free. "Maybe you'll learn something about keeping your hands to yourself – I believe it's covered extensively in their curriculum." He pushes the door open, and I have no choice.

Every monster in the room turns to stare as I enter.

Kindergartners.

FIFTEEN

HEADMASTER REINHARDT CLOSES the door behind us with the wooden thunk of the trap door of a gallows.

"Come now, Miss Porter, it won't be so bad."

He must be joking. I'm a seventeen year-old in *kindergarten* – it's the script for a bad comedy. I can just picture Isaiah's smirk when he hears about this. Not to mention, my knowledge of children could fit comfortably in a thimble. I didn't even spend time with them when I was one.

My only day in preschool didn't end well. Especially for the other kid.

The very proportions of the room throw me off. Big room, short tables; big chalkboard, small chairs; big globe, small people. And there they are, thirty sets of too-big eyes set in midgety, largely dirty faces. They watch me with open curiosity. Well, most of them do; one is eating paper. Their teacher, a bent woman not much larger than her students, stands. For all she looks

like a stiff breeze could push her over, it's my guess no
kid ever has. I bet she sharpens her dentures on naughty children.

"This is the child?"

Child?

I twist to the headmaster, begging with my eyes.

"This is her," he answers, clapping me on the
shoulder.

It's time to get serious. "You can't trust me around
teenagers, but you'll throw these little children to me?"
I growl it in my most dangerous voice.

He doesn't blink. "I have it on very good authority
that you're rather fond of children."

Have it on good authority?

Jo.

That's it; I'm going to kill her. I knew she'd be
pissed about Isaiah, but to stick me in with kindergartners? And I AM NOT FOND OF CHILDREN! I
just have a rule about eating them. And they're vaguely
terrifying. And manipulative, and demanding, and cruel.

OK fine, I do like them. With traits like those,
how could I not? That doesn't mean I want to spend
hours with them. Oh God, the jokes I'd make if this
was anyone else come bubbling to my surface. It's so
humiliating *I* want to make fun of me. My nine-million
enemies are going to have a field day.

"Have a good day, Miss Porter." His laughing tone
suggests he knows how likely that is.

I glare in response. He leaves.

"Have a seat, Miss Porter." The old Crusader extends an arthritis-twisted finger toward a normal-sized table against the back wall. "You have some work, I presume?" Her drawn-on eyebrows brook no argument.

But I am angry.

They want me in kindergarten? Then I will be in kindergarten. I march over to a tiny chair and haul it out, then plop myself down with a challenging glare, shoving my legs under the short, round table.

The teacher doesn't flinch. If anything she appears amused. I break first and look at what the other kids are doing. Coloring.

Heh, that's actually not so bad.

I grab a sheet and slam it down loudly and grab a pencil.

I wait for the confrontation, but it doesn't come. Instead there's a placid, "Back to your assignments, children." The eyes that were all on me turn back to their papers. Unlike the older grades where we're at two-person tables, the kids here sit about eight to a round table. In the middle is a pile of paper, pencils, crayons, and markers. My tablemates are two boys and five girls. Most of them are ignoring me, now that the drama's over. The tongue of one little boy with blond curls sticks out of the corner of his mouth as he concentrates on his paper.

I sneak a peek at the other kids' papers – cheating already – and the assignment seems to be drawing some kind of monster. I see eyes and mouths, but the rest is largely unrecognizable.

I catch the girl on my left studying me. She's a little thing, and looks to be half-Asian. Her skin is a pretty ivory, and her wavy, not-quite-black hair is pulled back into pigtails. They no-doubt started the day tidy, but the adventures of the past hours have pulled them half out, and one sags almost to her shoulder. She studies me intently then turns to her drawing. Then back to me, then to her drawing.

If we're drawing monsters, I figure she's as good as any. I start sketching.

Fifteen minutes later I feel a tug on my shirt. The girl. She points proudly to her art, wiggling excitedly in her chair.

"What's that?" I ask.

She looks at me like I'm stupid. I must be stupid, because I keep looking at her. I should know better than to encourage them.

"That's you." She points at her drawing with her marker in a strange, backwards, twisty way as she squirms in her chair.

It's terrible. For starters, "I don't have three legs," I say.

She wrinkles her forehead and turns back to her picture. "There's two legs."

"Liar." I point at the third green (*green?*) stick coming from what could only be a torso.

She picks up her picture and holds it at arm's

length, tipping it to one side and her head to the other. Then she giggles, and rolls her eyes. "That's your tail."

"I don't have a tail." I check to be sure.

She giggles then regards her artwork with a wistful little sigh. "But wouldn't it be nice if you did?"

Hard to argue with that.

I show her my drawing of her. She doesn't approve.

"It's supposed to be your favorite Beacon," she scolds.

"Goody-goody," I accuse. "I'll draw that next."

She glares to let me know I'd better before turning back to my picture. It's far superior to her hunchbacked tripod – it has both her eyes on the same side of her head, for example. I even artistically neatened her hair. Still, I can't miss the disappointment on her face. She turns her enormous, chocolate-brown gimme-beams on me and I break as easily as Colton's bones.

I set down my masterpiece with a sigh and add a long curling monkey tail. The girl's so pleased she takes it from me and proceeds to deface it with a marker in the name of coloring.

I'm going to kill Jo.

***

When the bell rings, thirty tiny witnesses, the carrier monkeys of my humiliation, spread the story of my shame to the rest of the school.

My day tumbles downhill.

The jeers land fast and furious as I stomp my way through the day. Between classes, in class. I swear to God, even a teacher takes a swipe. By the time lunch rolls around, I am *seething*. I step into the cafeteria and find the originator of all my problems waiting by the door. I swear to God, if she thinks to pick a fight with me right now, *she will get one*.

"Meda?"

At the sound of her traitorous voice, it takes every last ounce of self-control that I have not to rip her freaking head off.

"Meda, wait." I hear her shuffling steps as she tries to keep up. I ignore her. Then she grabs my arm with a frustrated, "Meda!"

"What?" I round on her fast enough to make her stumble.

"I just… Where were you last night?"

I freeze. Armand. "Last night," I repeat slowly.

"Yeah. I just found out you didn't come to dinner."

It clicks. Not Armand, but when I was with the Crusaders. "So you weren't here either?" I ask. "Hm. Maybe *I* should be demanding answers from *you*." I jab her in the chest. "Since we're in the business of policing each other."

"*I* have nothing to hide," she grits out.

"Then where were you?"

"With the headmaster." She tries to leave it at that,

but I won't let her.

"Oh? Discussing my *fondness* for children, perhaps? Or maybe picking out the jewelry for my door?" My voice is violent silk.

"Talking about how to stop you from attacking your classmates," she snaps. "I was pulled out of the infirmary to find out you'd–" She catches herself and shakes her head. She forces her tone back to calm. "Anyway, I missed dinner. And they said… I heard you did, too."

"Worried I was out terrorizing the natives? Don't worry, *Mom*, the babysitters kept a sharp eye on me."

"That's not what I–"

"You can police my every action Jo, but don't expect me to help."

"I didn't mean…" She doesn't seem quite sure how to finish. I see an army of words muster on her tongue, but not a single one breaches her lips. She ends up pressing her mouth closed.

"Didn't mean to *what*, Jo? What part didn't you mean?" I step in to hiss. "To lock me in my room? To sit back and watch them starve me? *To make me the laughing stock of the school?*"

Pink tinges her cheeks. "I'm sorry about the kindergarten thing. It's just, I couldn't think of… and I was angry."

I bark a laugh. "Well, that makes it OK then. Good to know. Well, be warned, now I'm angry. Why don't you sit back and see what I do?"

Her eyes grow wide. "Meda, you can't. Don't do anything–" She cuts herself off. Too late.

"Stupid?" I growl.

"Meda, I–"

"Get. Out. Of. My. Face, Jo." I'm shaking. "Get out of my face, *right now*."

Jo's primary traits, cleverness and mulishness, battle for supremacy. Fortunately cleverness wins and she turns sharply on her heel and heads toward our usual table. I snatch up a tray and turn to get into line when Chi's voice stops me. I didn't realize he was behind me.

"You could give her a break, you know."

"Could I?" I snap. So, *so* not in the mood.

"Yeah, you could," he bites back, so uncharacteristically I have to stop. "She just got kicked off probation, did you know that? She won't graduate."

"What? Why?"

"The rope climb. Said they 'don't see the point.'"

Startled, I look for Jo, who sits staring at her empty tray. I force my gaze away.

"That's too bad."

Chi explodes. "'Too bad'? *Too bad*? That's all you can say?" The expression on Chi's face makes me wince. I almost *ate* him once and he didn't look at me like that. He waits, but I don't know what to say. "What do you want me to do about it? Give her a hug? I'd lose an arm – even if we were on speaking terms."

"Oh, I don't know," Chi says with a biting sarcasm I didn't think him capable of. "Maybe be nice to her?"

"Why don't you tell *her* to be nice to *me*?"

"You think I haven't?" He thrusts his hand through his hair and growls in frustration. "The two of you…" He shakes his head, then jabs a finger angrily toward my chest. "She is doing it all for you, whether you like it or not." He takes a step back, hands out. "All of it." He mutters and turns on his heel, not waiting for a response.

Great, even Chi's against me now. I don't know what I was expecting, of course he'd side with her. I toss the tray back down, having lost my appetite, and head back to my room. Thanks to them, I've missed yet another damn meal. I slam my door open and it makes a satisfying thwack against the wall.

I take a step into the room and stutter to a halt. A giant bag of Cheetos and an orange soda sit on my desk. They were placed so recently that condensation runs down the side of the still-icy beverage. I shoot glances around the room, but it's empty. I take a few slow steps forward and pick up the note propped against the bottle.

Cheers to the seventh food group.

Seventh? Oh, I get it. Neon-orange. Teehee.

I run my finger down the side of the bottle, delighting in its coldness in my air-conditioning-less room, then rip into the Cheetos. As I crunch the toxic orange Cheetos like they're the bones of my erstwhile best friends, a slow smile spreads across my face.

***

That night, when Armand unlocks the door, I'm waiting for him.

SIXTEEN

EVERY DAY CONSISTS of waiting for night. Usually I try to sleep after supper, but tonight I don't bother.

It's Tuesday, a week after Armand first arrived, and he's late. I watch the clock slowly tick past midnight, the same way I sat here since dinner and watched it crawl to midnight, and I can barely contain my fury. Not at Armand. At everyone else. The taunting by the student body has gotten worse, spearheaded by Isaiah and his besties. Jo tries to apologize, but I won't let her; not as long as she's locking my door each night. Chi and I are still on speaking terms, but he's not often at the school. As warned, he, along with Zee and some other seniors, were drafted into service covering Beacons nearby when their Crusaders are called elsewhere. He's in and out, and when he's in, he's with Jo.

Before, I was partially off-limits, thanks to my connection to Chi. Now, with my apparent break from them, the gloves have come off. Rumors that the nicer kids wouldn't believe seem suddenly plausible now that I'm shunned. Before, I could laugh off the shunning by the student body with Jo. Alone, it doesn't seem so funny.

But at least I have Armand. He's the escape valve on the pressure cooker of my rage. The longer he takes to get here, the more it builds. If he doesn't come soon, I'll explode.

Finally I hear a quiet creak in the hallway. It's so low, anyone listening less intently would miss it. But it's the sound I've been waiting for all day. When Armand slides the key in the lock and pushes the door open, I'm already there.

He sees the thundercloud roiling under my skin, feels my electric rage crackling in the air. In one look he knows what I'm feeling; in just one look I know he knows.

He takes in my thunderous expression, and doesn't offer me words. Instead, he reaches out his hand for mine and offers me what I really want: escape.

I take it.

We climb to the roof, and he doesn't hesitate before throwing a leg over the side of the building. His eyes spark when, this time, for the first time, I don't stop him, but follow him over the side. We move silently in the dark, sliding from shadow to shadow, as smoothly as pools of liquid, merging with the inky darkness. We work in concert, flowing across the school grounds. Guards are everywhere, but they're focused out, not in. We slip into the tree line, working from tree to tree, up the side of the mountain. Hot rebellion pumps through my blood, reckless and wild. A cool patch remains, a crisp voice in my head.

You can't trust him.

But you can't trust anyone. And if Armand betrays me, at least I can fight back; he's the enemy. I can't kill Isaiah, I won't kill Jo. I can't fight the whole school. But if need be, I can make Armand hurt as badly as he hurts me.

More so.

There's freedom in that – expecting nothing from someone and owing them nothing in return. Our time together is temporary. No, it's *stolen*. We both know how this is going to end. Oh, he may scheme otherwise, thinking he can stop me by making me like him. He's an incubus – manipulating through emotions is his stock in trade. He thinks that when the time comes, I won't have the heart.

He's part right.

We'll face each other in battle, and when that day comes, we will do our utmost to reduce the other to bloody pieces. And we will do it unapologetically.

We know what we are.

Just because our relationship has a bloody expiration-date doesn't mean I can't enjoy it while it lasts. Unlike the Crusaders, I can appreciate something for what it is, without demanding it be more. If anything, their scantiness makes our hours more precious.

I turn to him now. We crouch behind a giant spruce, and he's looking at his watch, waiting for the next gap in the guard rotation. He's been busy. I'm impressed.

As if he can feel my regard, his eyes rise to mine. Only inches separate us, and I'm hyper-aware of just how short those inches are. I'm overcome with another wave of rebellion, and my eyes move to his lips.

He tears his gaze back to his watch. "It's time," he mouths, and we're off again, fleeing as lightly as deer. We do this several more times as we make our way to freedom. Finally, we're on the last ring. Beyond lies open forest and freedom. We crouch, our muscles tense as we prepare to run. He watches his watch, and angles it toward me so I can watch as well.

10… 9… 8…

"Wait," Armand suddenly breathes, and reaches in his pocket. He pulls out the amulet and, to my surprise, he slips it over my head. His fingers trail along my neck and I shiver. "Just in case."

He grabs my hand. I let him.

…2… 1.

We're off, into the night.

Once we're past the last guard, we don't stop running. We run for miles. I'll be back before morning, before they notice I'm gone, before Jo lets me out of my cell, but for now I'm free. I pound the earth with my feet, taking my rage out on it as I kick harder and higher. I aim for branches, for logs, destroying them with my hard stomps and kicks. Armand is right beside me, delighting in my wild violence. We kick and crash and laugh and run. Two terrors, destroyers in the dark, letting off steam.

But the frantic destruction isn't enough. It will never be enough, because it isn't what I crave. Instead of calming me, the cracking of wood in my hands only serves to remind me what it is I truly want. I catch Armand's eye. "Where is *he*?"

The slow, wicked grin that stretches across his face says he needs no further explanation, and when he turns right, I follow. We run for miles and, though we're nowhere near a town or settlement, I know we're close when his ground-eating stomp is replaced with the silent lope of a jungle cat. He slows further and waits until I'm beside him. "I came across our... *friend* when I was scouting the area."

I peer into the darkness, but we're still deep in the wooded mountains, without the slightest hint of human habitation. "How do you know he's my type?"

Teeth flash in the dim wood. "Trust me. You'll see."

Presently the outline of a structure takes shape against the darker stripes of tree trunks. It's small, more shanty than house, really, and appears to be an unskilled man's DIY project. The house of a squatter, or an illegal hunting cabin more likely. Armand has a sneaky smile on his face as he gallantly bows for me to precede him. I trot toward the nearest – and potentially only –

window, obviously recycled from another structure.

I was right; it is a hunting cabin, complete with his trophies mounted on the wall. Only his prey isn't four-legged.

"Oh, Armand," I breathe. "He's *perfect*." My fingers stroke the glass, my nails making a rasping noise, as I pet the sleeping form rolled in his sleeping bag.

His eyes gleam. "I knew you'd like him."

I purr agreement, turning back to the peacefully sleeping man. *Tap, tap, tap*, I rap on the window, not unlike how Armand had done on mine, just a week ago. *Tap, tap, tap.*

Groggily the man's eyes open, and he finds my face in the window. He's not scared, merely curious, at the appearance of a young girl at his horrific little hut. I smile and he smiles back.

"Come out and play," I say in a voice that's mostly a sigh. I doubt he can hear me but he obeys anyway, scurrying toward the door with the eagerness of a mouse toward an apparently-unguarded piece of cheese. He stumbles but doesn't stop to turn on a light. He wouldn't want me to notice his trophies. Not yet. Not while I can still run.

He pushes open the door, my little rodent man, and I can't see him anymore, but I know he's coming.

He rounds the corner and upon seeing me, he hesitates. Just for a second, as a little suspicion niggles his ratty brain: "*What an odd place to find a piece of cheese…*" His eyes slide from side to side, but he's unable to find

Armand's shadow among the many.

He suspects, of course he does, the trap that's about to spring closed. But he can't resist. They can never resist.

"Come," I call, but I don't need to. He's already moving, furtively now as he ignores his better judgment. "Come out and play," I murmur, soft, sing-song. Again, the words are just the ones Armand said to me.

But what happens next isn't the same at all.

Snap.

Squeal.

***

Of all the virtues I lack, patience isn't one I've particularly missed – until now. Armand though... I shiver. He cats better than I, toying with our victim, drawing out the inevitable long after I would have given in. He draws us closer, closer to the knife's edge of satisfaction, until I think – as much as I can think at that point – that, now, *now* it must happen. But then he pulls back at the last second, pulls *me* back, leaving me trembling with Hunger. Shaky, dizzy with it.

Then he does it again.

Delaying our gratification over and over again, prolonging our joy, building the anticipation until I can't stand it, till I could climb the walls with it.

And he wants it. Oh, he wants it as badly as I do. Each movement is brutally controlled, vibrating with carefully controlled savagery. His eyes burn with it, but there, too, I can find a terrible, implacable patience, more frightening than the violence.

To me at least. Most likely our little rat would disagree. Would *have* disagreed, because the end did finally come; of course it did.

And. It. Was. Glorious.

Again I shiver, *shudder*, remembering, and lose my footing for the briefest moment. As if he knows what I'm thinking, Armand's eyes flare.

And there, just there, I see it again. That terrible patience. With a sweep of an eyelid, it's gone.

I shiver again and blink it away. Now isn't the time.

Soul-drunk we race toward the mountain lake, giddy, almost hysterical. High. I don't hesitate before I rip off my shirt and sweats, and dive into the water in my bra and undies. Likewise he strips to his boxers and follows with a splash.

"Race you!" I shout, and point to a mostly-rotted dock on the other side of the lake. He grins, shoves a huge wave of water in my face, and starts swimming. "Cheater!" I gasp, and take off after him. We splash through the water, swimming as hard as we can and snatching glances at each other between strokes. His head start wasn't nearly long enough, and I overtake him, reaching the platform with enough lead-time to work in a bored whistle as I wait. A pretty breathless whistle, but good enough for him to make a face as he pulls up panting beside me. I grin and leap at him, wrapping my hands over his shoulders and dunking him. His hands slide over the bare skin of my mid-section as he wraps his arms around me and pulls me under with him. We wrestle, dunking and diving, hands gliding over skin, intertwined under the water. There's a wildness to it, an edge to our play-fight, a sharpness to our laughs.

Finally, the rush of the soul-drunk slows to a trickle and we break away to tread water in the dark, moon-stained lake. Dark spikes of pines line the edges, like jagged teeth ripping at the star-freckled sky.

I kick off the platform and backstroke toward the rocky shore, hearing the rhythmic splashes of Armand following. We make our way leisurely this time with long, slow strokes until it's shallow enough to walk. I drop onto the beach. As Armand rises out of the water, it runs down his body in little rivulets.

I know it's fake. It's not his body. It's a demonic trick.

It doesn't make a damn bit of difference.

I force myself to look away. And to breathe.

He collapses next to me and we're quiet for a moment.

I remember one of the few (awkward, oh God, so, so awkward) sex-centered conversations I had with my mom. It was right before she… died, and she'd caught me checking out a guy while we waited in line at a store. She waited until we were driving down the highway before she said anything--probably so I wouldn't leap out of the car, clever woman. She started with a stiff ramble on responsible choices and prophylactics in a way that suggested she'd rehearsed. If I checked her browser history, I'd probably find a search for 'teen-aged daughter having The Talk.' Finally she trailed off, my stony demeanor perhaps suggesting that she wasn't getting through to me. When she spoke again, her tone was different. Edged.

"Don't ever… give yourself to someone you don't trust, Meda," Mom finally started.

I'm pretty sure I had a bratty comeback regarding the euphemism "give yourself." Probably paired with the classic snotty-shit eye roll I'd managed to perfect in my fourteen years on earth.

She ignored me like the brat I was, and kept talking. "When you sleep with someone, whether you know it or not, whether you want to or not, you give them a little piece of you they can break."

I had another dismissive comment on the tip of my tongue, but there was something in her voice that stopped me. Something dark and sad. Something that scared me enough to shut the hell up and just nod. She'd turned toward me. "You may think you're differ-ent, but you're not." Her eyes grew distant. "Trust me."

Having gotten to know him, I know Luke would never have broken my mother's heart, which means that look was put there by my father. Her expression, those words weren't from someone who was forced. They were from someone who'd made a decision. A bad one.

On the one hand, I want to shake her and say "Really, Mom? *Really?* You had to learn the hard way that sleeping with a demon was a bad idea?" On the other hand...well, sitting next to Armand's mostly-naked-spectacular-ness, I could see how it could happen.

But I won't be that girl. I won't follow in my mother's footsteps.

I eye his damp muscles and swallow.

Really.

"It's illegal, you know," he murmurs. "Stealing."

I clear my throat. "Stealing?"

"My heart. I could have you arrested."

I snort. "For that tiny thing? I'd get a misdemeanor at most."

"Ouch!"

"Ah, well, incubi, get outta here with that fake cheesiness."

"*Fake cheesiness?* That was one of my best lines!"

"The fakest. The cheese whiz of romance."

He chuckles and leans back. "Ah, well, I know how you love your neon-orange foods."

I laugh and my eyes meet his. Instead of humor diffusing the tension, it seems to only amplify it, and again I'm caught. Rotten boys with their rotten eyes with their ridiculous rotten eyelashes. They suck a girl in, a pair of Venus fly-traps. No, Venus *eye*-traps.

Can't... fight... must... lean... in... closer...

"*Never... give yourself to someone you can't trust, Meda.*"

Ah, rescued in the nick of time by the ice-cold water of my mother's memory. Always reliable to pop up any-time I'm about to have fun. But I'm grateful. I manage to pull back. To breathe.

"What?" asks Armand, blinking those eye-traps. I look away before they can get me again.

"Nothing." I wave her away. "Just... ghosts."

"Where?" He straightens and looks around.

"You can see ghosts?"

"Course."

"Yes, how foolish that I didn't realize."

He laughs. "Our job is to punish the wicked when they die. Kinda hard if you can't see them."

"And the memories? Can you see their memo-ries?" It occurs to me I may be giving away too much, but curiosity hurtles me forwards.

"How else would we know how to hit them where it hurts?"

I wait for an explanation.

"Hell isn't all about hot pokers and coals." He relaxes back, taking his eye-traps with him. "Or rath-er, not just about that." I hear a smile in his voice, but don't turn to see it. Too risky. "Physical torture is amateurish. Lazy." His accent gets thicker. "Real tor-ture isn't about the body, it's about the soul. In Hell, a demon can pull the memories from a person, ferret out their weakness, then use it against them."

I shiver at his tone, but it's not in fear. Never that. I don't say anything for a long moment, giving the shifting darkness time to settle.

He doesn't make it easy. "You could come, be a part of it, you know, instead of…" he waves his long fingers in the air, "this. I know today was bad, so why will you go back for more tomorrow?"

Why, why, why. He looks to me for answers, I look to the sky. We're both disappointed.

Armand props himself up on one elbow so he's leaning over me. He's close, real close. I can – and do – count the water droplets on his chest. "And you're not allowed to fight back at all? I mean, even if you do want to be good – which, I can't imagine why anyone would." He shoots me a wicked look from beneath thick lashes. I stick out my tongue. "You don't have to be a doormat to be good. Even good people are allowed self-defense."

"I know that."

"Then why the hell can't you defend yourself?"

I fake a Jo-lecture voice. "'The Crusaders want proof you've changed. It's all a test.'" I drop my voice into a threat. "'You have to pass.'"

A dark light brightens Armand's eyes. "So cheat."

"Cheat?"

"It's not that you can't get revenge, you just can't get *caught*." There's wicked delight in his eyes, the escaped rays of a bitten-back laugh. He slips his hand in his pocket and pulls out my room key. "And you couldn't possibly do anything – you've been locked up all night."

The light bulb that explodes in my head damn-near sets my brain on fire. It's so simple, so obvious. I'm embarrassed I didn't think of it myself.

But I know why I didn't. Because I've been trying to be good. I'm new to this, but I'm pretty sure revenge schemes aren't part of that.

But they so, so deserve it.

A part of me whispers that this is a mistake, the part where the memory of my mom lives, the part that houses the hive of the good bees. But that part grows smaller every day, eaten away in big bites of injustice. It's a glacier floating in a too-hot sea, warmed by the heat of my rage.

Memory Mom makes one last bid. *You won't win them over with hate.*

That's probably true.

But you don't have to be a doormat to be good. Armand's voice this time.

That makes sense, too.

I'm at a crossroads. One path is a slow, painful, righteous trudge uphill to a place where my nemeses see the light. The other is easy and fun, downhill and dark. Armand takes my hand.

I won't walk this path alone.

The grin that dances across his face finds a partner on mine.

Armand and I have a busy night.

SEVENTEEN

I'M THE FIRST one to breakfast the next morning; the puppet master needs time to set her stage. I pile my plate with props: scrambled egg whites (yolks being orange, I suppose, and therefore forbidden) and toast. Armand keeps me in junk food so I don't need it, but Meda the Innocent needs to be in character.

I choose my position carefully – downstage as we say in the biz – picking the table furthest from the door, but with a clear view when They come in.

As show time draws near, the audience files in to take their seats. The headmaster and the Northerners enter, though not The Sarge. I'd hoped their box would remain entirely empty for this morning's performance, but no matter. As they say, the show must go on.

Annnnnnnnnd… Action!

The curtains sweep wide for the opening act, banging as if they were lowly cafeteria doors slammed in a rage. The Schmuck Seven roar in, my leading man,

Isaiah, at the head. The entire cafeteria swivels at their dramatic arrival; their mouths drop open in amazement, a reaction guaranteed to warm any director's cold, dead heart.

One half of each boy's face is painted like a grotesque monster. Their mouths are surrounded by giant snarls. Huge, drawn-on eyebrows swoop down into scowls. The skin is painted red and patchy, as if burned and twisted. The result is something like Two-Face from Batman. It still looks pretty good, despite the smearing from their obvious attempts to scrub it off. Their costume designer has quite the talent.

I wanted to show the world that Isaiah and his friends are liars and hypocrites. That they, like me, have a rotten side, they're just able to hide theirs a little better than I. But not anymore. I hope the symbolism isn't lost on them.

Then I added the drawing of pursed lips – a kiss – right on the center of their throats. A threat, so they know I can get to them anytime I want.

And lastly, Armand shaved their eyebrows and filled their shoes with Kool-Aid powder, so their feet will turn purple once they sweat. No symbolism there, we just thought it was funny.

There's a long shocked silence. Then a choked snort.

Then the entire cafeteria bursts into laughter.

A comedy, this.

Isaiah's furious scowl lands on me. "YOU!" he

screams, right on cue. The cafeteria turns en masse to enjoy my false innocence. My victims march across the cafeteria – the entire length of the long, long cafeteria, so the entire audience can get a good look – to stop in front of me.

It's almost like someone planned it. Teehee. Dance puppets!

"You did this!"

I bat harmless, innocent lashes. "Who, me?"

I must not be a very good actress. Isaiah lunges, but Omar slaps an arm across his chest to hold him back. "Not now," he murmurs.

"I'll kill you!" Isaiah screams.

I narrow my eyes. "You're welcome to try," I purr. Then I lower my voice and cock my head, casting a look at the kiss, centered on his tender, beating throat. His Adam's apple bobs, lifting my artwork, and the un-painted side of his face turns red enough to match the other. He moves again towards me.

"Mr. Hooper," says the headmaster from his table across the cafeteria. Ah, some audience participation! The headmaster pushes from the table he shares with the visiting Northerners, and tosses his napkin onto the table. He strides down the aisle.

That snaps Isaiah out of his rage a little, and he looks smug. "This was a mistake, Monster." He twists to face the headmaster, morphing into a dutiful little soldier. "I'm sorry, sir!" he says smartly. "But look at what she did!"

The headmaster's mouth twitches, but he recovers nicely. Who knew he had such a talent? *All the world's a stage and we are but actors in it.* "Miss Porter did this to you?" He addresses Isaiah, but looks to me for the answer.

I shake my head, looking shocked.

Ah, what a phenomenal actress! So believable, so endearing. She quite stole the show.

Isaiah's mouth thins. "Of course she did!"

The headmaster's voice hardens. "Of course, Mr. Hooper? And what proof do you have?"

This is not how Isaiah saw this going, I can tell. "But," he sputters. Never say, he forgot his lines! "She's a demon. She hates me. She just attacked me last week." He lists facts in a tone suggesting the headmaster to be stupid – a mistake. I could have told him that. Not that I would, of course. "She came into my room at night, while I was unprotected! She can go into anyone's room. She could kill us all in our sleep if she wanted–"

Suddenly, down in the pit, the band starts the ba-da-da-da-da-da theme-music for the Wicked Witch of the West. I look up and see Graff, already in his spiffy suit at this early hour, striding down the aisle to join us. His costume designer, while unimaginative, has clearly been busy. Pleats that crisp take time.

"The boy has a point, Gordon. She's allowed to move too freely among the grounds."

"Sorry, Arthur, but he doesn't," the headmaster

responds, placidly.

"You have a half-demon running loose in this school, practically unsupervised," Graff says, calm, emotionless. "You can't blame the boy for being anxious."

"I can, if he throws out baseless accusations."

Hope blooms in Isaiah's eyes. "They're not baseless."

"Do you have proof they're not?" the headmaster asks.

Graff cuts in smoothly. "Do you have proof they are?"

"I do, actually." The headmaster taps gnarled fingers against his stomach and looks around the room until he finds who he's looking for. "Miss Beauregard?" We all turn to where Jo sits across the cafeteria. "Come here."

"Yessir," Jo says, and hops gracelessly to her feet and limps over to us, her face carefully blank.

"Did you lock Miss Melange in her room last night?"

That juicy bit of gossip pulls a gasp from our already-breathless audience. The headmaster doesn't turn to face Jo as she answers, confident in her answer. Instead he faces Graff with a raised-eyebrow-you're-wrong look that I'm intimately familiar with.

"Yessir," Jo answers.

"Did you unlock her door this morning to let her out?"

"Yessir."

"Did you let her out anytime in between?"

"No, sir."

"Did you lose sight of your key anytime in the night?"

Jo reaches under the neck of her T-shirt and holds up the key, from where it hangs from a chain around her neck. "No."

Isaiah, nearly forgotten, cuts in, "She lies!"

The headmaster, out of patience, smacks Isaiah with a look that shuts him up. He turns back to Graff and says dryly, "We're a school full of teens, this is hardly the first prank," he raises an eyebrow, "or the last, I daresay – that has been perpetrated here. I'm not in the habit of crucifying students for harmless jokes." Then he gives all the gathered students a gimlet glare – lest we get any ideas. "At least, not unless they get caught." There are gulps all around.

He turns back to Isaiah & Co. "Why don't the lot of you head to the infirmary and see if they've anything to take that off, hmmm?" Then his placid expression is replaced with something much harder. "Then report to my office." His cold eyes lift to the rest of the room. "And we'll all finish our breakfast." Forgotten flatware suddenly clinks against dishes as everyone does as ordered. The headmaster turns and heads back up the aisle. Graff doesn't leave right away, but stays a moment longer. He eyes me, his expression cool and flat, then Isaiah. His dead-fish eyes give nothing away.

Then, he turns and strides up the aisle in his too-stiff walk.

Isaiah's forced to settle on an evil look that promises revenge before slinking off after them.

Just let him try.

His posse follows suit.

I take a bow.

Then my eyes come to rest on the one person remaining next to me. Jo. But she's not looking at me. Her eyes are on Graff's retreating back. She looks worried.

Then she feels me watching her and turns. "Meda," she murmurs shooting a glance around to make sure no one can hear. "Did you?" She suspects. Of course she does. She knows me.

But I know you too, Jo.

My mouth twists. "Why ask, when you won't believe my answer? We both know you're going to check on me tonight, so why bother?"

She pulls back. "Of course I'm not going to check on you," she says stiffly. She gives me one long look, then walks away.

Not anymore, is what she means.

Dance, puppet!

***

Predictably, jokes about my prisoner status are added to the kindergarten jokes. It's regrettable that it had to come out, but worth it. Because even with the additional fodder, I've had to endure fewer taunts than in any day the previous week. It simply can't compete with painted faces and shaved eyebrows.

Surprisingly, kindergarten has become my favorite class. Most of the little kids don't get why it's funny I'm stuck in their class or locked up at night, and the few that do are easily distracted with be-tailed portraits and fart jokes – heretofore undiscovered skills at which I excel. It's a nice break from the rest of the day. Still, I can barely pull my eyes away from the clock.

I scarf down dinner, and am back at my room by six. I force myself to sleep. Force my eyes to close and my breathing to slow. I'm a child on Christmas Eve, or rather, a prisoner the night before her probation kicks in. But I need to sleep, so I do.

I sleep through Jo locking me.

I don't sleep through Armand letting me out.

And, like Christmas, Armand has brought gifts. But he is no fat, sweet Santa Claus who rewards the nice; he is the Lord of Misrule, the Abbot of Unreason in charge of scandalous fun. After a brief and giddy celebration, we're off again. Clothes are coated with itching powder, shampoo bottles are filled with hair remover. Homework escapes, hidden stashes of contraband disappear and reappear in hiding places all over school. We start with Isaiah and his friends, or at least the ones who were foolish enough to let themselves sleep, but it's over too soon and we expand our circle to anyone who taunted me, then to anyone who laughed too hard or too loudly.

Then grey taints the pitch black of the sky, and I have to return to my cell. It's hard to be quiet, drunk as I am on so much fun. Armand takes exaggerated sneaking steps, his knees coming almost to his chest as he tip-toes. I smother a giggle and he shushes me as seriously as if we were hunting wabbits.

He unlocks my door and opens it with an elaborate bow. I curtsy, playing Lady Misrule to his Lord. He starts to close the door, but stops. Instead of closing the door, he stands there looking at where the knob rests in his hand. When the door closes, our night is over.

Drunk on repressed laughs, I lean against the door frame for support, my hands behind me. He looks up from the doorknob, and his too-pretty eye-traps rest on me. Less than a foot separates us. My eyes slide up and down his frame, admiring the way his shirt fits and his lips curve. I wonder if his mouth would taste like he smells, rich and dark, or if it would taste forbidden and toxic, neon-orange. He's everything I wish I could be, has everything I wish I could have. He's free, not chained with the relentless weight of a conscience. Although I seem to have left mine behind somewhere. Like a toddler, consciences, burdensome and likely to wander off the instant you forget to pay attention.

My eyes traipse up to his and see in them a breathless excitement that says he knows exactly what

I'm thinking. I wonder if, once he's gone, that will ever happen again.

There're probably only a dozen creatures in the world who have a chance of understanding us, he told me back in Colton's backyard. *It'd be a pity to waste one.*

A pity. I can't think about that. It'll come to that when it does. Not tonight. Tonight there's him and there's me and there's air filled with secrets and laughter and darkness. There are eyes filled with heat, and boys that smell of spice. It's all going to end, but not tonight.

The moment stretches longer and gets hotter and heavier. He moves slowly, deliberately, achingly slowly, and slides his hand up my arm. My skin prickles with goose bumps and my breath comes too fast. Then gently, so gently, he wraps his big palm around the side of my neck, his thumb tracing along my jaw. Our eyes hold and—

Don't ever… give yourself to someone you don't trust, Meda. The words cut into the moment like the scream of an angry infant. *Whether you know it or not, you give them a little piece of you they can break.*

I close my eyes and give my head a little shake. To expel the voice of my mom, or shake off the spell of the moment, I'm not sure.

"Meda?" he asks softly in the rumbly, shivery voice of his. His hands slide back down to pull mine into his.

Meda.

Nothing like your mom's voice to totally ruin the

moment.

I haul my conscious back in as if it's attached to one of those kiddie leashes. It comes, but with an impish little smile. Even my good side has a bad one.

I allow myself a sway in his direction, an inhale of spicy boy scent, a minute in demon dark eyes.

Then I shut the door in his face.

Eighteen

THE PRANKS HIT the next day, and by lunch everyone's abuzz about it. Some students are angry, but many more think it's hilarious – Crusader schools have a long, proud tradition of pranking. Something that'd been forgotten in the wake of the tragedy in March.

Everyone, of course, wants to know who's to blame. Accusations fly around the cafeteria like missiles, occasionally blowing up friendships. Some accusations head my way, but not many. After all, I'm locked in my room each night.

The Lord and Lady of Misrule may need to take a night off. Something tells me the halls are going to be teeming with activity this evening as my classmates creep around for revenge. Of course, none can get me – my door has a lock on it.

Hehe.

I stifle my yawn so as to not give myself away and trudge up the stairs to change for my second-to-last class of the day. I'm actually dreading S and C for once. I haven't been getting near enough sleep to look forward to physical exertion. I already dread the day when I have to skip a night's freedom to sleep.

Or you could just feed again. The dark thought slips through my mind like a snake through water.

A clearing throat pulls me away from the appealing thought. Jo's planted solidly in front of my door, arms crossed, already dressed for gym. Except for her face – that's dressed for war.

"We need to talk."

"About you not locking me in my room?" I ask sweetly.

"No."

"Then there's nothing to talk about." I turn sharply on my heel.

"We can either do it in your room, now, or we can bawl it out in front of the whole school," she threatens. "Either way, we're going to talk."

I shrug and keep going. I hear her uneven gait as she comes after me.

"Meda, wait!"

I don't.

"Dammit, Meda. I know it's you pulling those pranks."

I shrug.

"Meda, you have to stop! They're going to catch you."

I shrug again.

She stops walking but I keep going.

"Meda, I'm sorry," she says, and her voice cracks a little.

I stop and turn abruptly to face her. I raise my eyebrows and wait for her to talk.

"Meda, I'm not doing it to hurt you, I promise."

"Then why are you doing it?" I snarl. "You're supposed to be my best friend, Jo. Friends don't lock friends in prison. If anything, they pretend to, just so they can get the key and let them out." Or they steal a key. I barely know Armand and he figured that out. Already he's a better friend than Jo.

"I'm trying to help," she says between gritted teeth.

"Please, don't put yourself out."

She gets a hold of herself, and she's back to pleading. "Meda, just trust me."

"Like you trust me?" I smile mirthlessly. "Sure, Jo. No problem." I turn on my heel and walk away.

I make it about ten paces before the sirens begin to wail. My breath catches.

Armand.

I hold still, counting down the minutes until the beeping starts. Please, not long-short-short, the alarm for an intruder. Please, not long-short-short.

Then it comes. Long.

Short.

I can't breathe.

Long.

Thank God. My breath gusts out – then it hits me. It's not an intruder.

It's worse.

It's the wail calling the back-up medical staff to the infirmary. There's been a demon attack – a big one.

"Chi," I say looking at Jo.

She shakes her head sharply. "No, he got in last night. And Zee." Still she wears the look of sick dread that always accompanies this particular alarm. It's a given that whoever is injured will at least be an acquaintance, if not a friend. It won't be her family – the siren sounded for them years ago. But it probably will be for some of the students.

Jo swallows and makes for the stairs. The students gather outside the infirmary, holding vigil even before the wounded arrive. The half-demon in their midst will be the last thing the students want to see. I return to my room and watch from my window. Class will be cancelled.

It's not long before the gleam of cars racing into the valley appear in the distance. Three oversized kidnapper vans come first, followed by a beat-up blue pick-up and half-a-dozen motorcycles. Outside the bunker the students stand in a ring, far enough back so as to not be in the way, and the medical staff stand with gurneys, ready to go. I make out Crusader Helva, a middle-aged woman who can assemble bones like puzzle pieces, and Zee and Mags, but I can't make out Jo or Chi.

The makeshift ambulances slam to a halt outside the hospital, spraying gravel. Immediately the doors open to disgorge their mangled passengers. I'm too far away to see details, but the splashes of red are hard to miss. I push away from the window and flop on the bed.

I exhale and close my eyes, praying none of the victims are tied to my friends or not-enemies. Everybody but Jo has parents still living. Chi's got an army of siblings. Zee comes from a family of four. Mags probably has family besides her little brother, though I can't remember specifics. I barely get through the list before I hear Jo's uneven gait, moving quick, coming up the stairs.

This doesn't bode well. I jerk up on the bed. If Jo's running, it's someone she knows. Shit, shit, shit. She wouldn't cry in public.

So much for my prayers. As always, thanks, He-Who-Does-Not-Listen.

But then Jo runs right past her door, and slams mine open with a bang. I jump to my feet. Why would she come to me?

Then it hits me. Hits me hard, right between the eyes.

I forgot that I know someone in the field. One single person, out of all the Crusaders fighting demons, is mine.

No.

Jo's face is a stark pattern of red on white. "Meda,

it's Luke."

I squeeze my eyes shut. *No, please don't say it.*

But she does. "He's been hurt."

I was unfair to you, God, for accusing you of not listening. I prayed for my friends, but I forgot to pray for myself. The oversight is mine.

But don't expect me to apologize.

NINETEEN

THE THOUGHT OF losing Luke, one of my very few friends, almost a step-father, registers a bit like a donkey kick to the gut. No, worse than that, because at least I could kick the donkey back.

How is he? I want to ask, but the words won't come out.

But Jo knows. Her face answers my question before her mouth gets a chance. Her eyes are huge and too-shiny for good news. "Not good, Meda." Her mouth trembles. "They crushed his skull."

I sink to the floor.

"They were on their way to deliver..." she trails off. "He's still alive, and they've tried to piece it back together. They're digging out all the bone shards, but..."

You can't unscramble an egg.

"They don't know if he'll wake up."

I nod, but it's a distant motion. I don't feel attached to it. I feel alone, isolated in a bubble of... I don't know. Not denial because, in my life, death is too common to bother wasting energy on denial. I feel separated. It's here and it's happening, but I'm stuck, unable to react. Unable to speak. But what is there to say?

Jo doesn't seem to know, either, and doesn't say anything. Instead she sits down on the dirty, rotten floor with me. We don't touch and we don't talk. For all practical purposes, she might as well not be here. It makes no sense that it, alone, should help. But she is, and it does.

"I want to see him," I say hoarsely.

She nods and stands. "OK."

We start down the stairs and I'm itching to get there, now, to get news, but I stay at Jo's slower pace.

Jo senses my impatience. "Go ahead."

My feet fly down the stairs and over the grass to the infirmary. I don't know how long we sat on that floor. Half an hour? An eternity? The students are no longer gathered outside. I halt when I reach the door. Posted outside is a tall redheaded Corp. I think her name is Sarah. I nod and expect her to step aside.

She doesn't.

It's not because she doesn't recognize me. I'm kinda a celebrity around here – even if it is in a Lindsay Lohan kind of way. There's no way the higher-ups can be in a meeting right now. As fascinating as I am, in the wake of a big attack I doubt they're talking about me right now.

"Sorry, Miss Melange," she says, in a flat way that makes me think she isn't. "No visiting allowed."

"How can there be no visitors in the hospital?" The students aren't waiting outside anymore, because half of them are probably now inside, sitting with their injured friends or waiting for reports. Like I want to be. Then it dawns on me and my eyes narrow. I don't need this shit right now. "No visitors? Or just no *me*."

"Just following orders," she says, not looking at me but scanning the trees.

I notice she didn't answer my question. "I've always been allowed in before."

"There are new rules. You're not allowed in the main building unless summoned."

"What the hell? What did I do?"

"You'll need to discuss it with the Sergeant."

"Fine. Let me in and I'll talk to her right now," I growl.

She smiles faintly. "Nice try."

"I'm feeling anything but nice right now," I snarl. She stands unmoved. "Look, I promise not to do anything. I just want to see my friend. Please."

She frowns. "I'm sorry." She seems like she means it this time. "You can talk to the Sergeant once things are under control."

"Luke might be dead by then!"

Her frown deepens, but she doesn't say anything.

My fists clench and my head gets hot. "You've got to be shitting me!" I scream at her. The only thing that could make me feel better is to hurt them as much as they hurt me. Hurt her.

"I'm sorry, Meda." She sounds sincere. But still, her hand moves to her knife.

"You're sorry? *Sorry?*"

"Meda!" I hear a shout from behind me. Jo. I twist to see her horrified expression. She starts running toward us.

And I run away.

My feet pound over the school grounds, faster than Jo could possibly follow. I tear into the woods. I can't go too far or I'll run into the perimeter guards, but I've mapped their placement diligently enough, I know the blind spots – far enough so I can get out of range of the school, but not far enough to be seen.

The place I'm looking for is a low spot beside the river. On either side rise rock cliffs cut by the river, blocking this place from view, but here is a muddy bank strewn with boulders. When I come to a stop, I'm too worked up to sit. I pace. I kick the ground. I swallow screams. Late afternoon sun filters through the leaves to sparkle on the river. It's beautiful here, and peaceful.

I want to destroy it.

I grab a boulder the size of a basketball and hurl it into the river. Then grab a bigger one and do the same. I throw bigger and bigger rocks, seeing how violently I can make them splash.

Crashing steps sound in the woods behind me, loud enough that I can hear them over the sound of my destruction. Jo, no doubt, coming after me. I heave another stone. This time I overthrow and it flies across the river to explode against a boulder on the other side. I delight in the deafening crash of rock on rock.

Jo follows the sound of my boulder-on-boulder battle, and I hear the crack and shush of breaking twigs and rustling leaves until she comes to a halt somewhere behind me. I probably look insane – possessed. At the thought, I let out a howl of almost-laughter. My chest heaves at the exertion, not only at throwing boulders, but at limiting myself to only boulders. What I really want to hurl onto rocks are Crusaders.

They, who treat me worse and worse, yet expect me to act better and better.

Jo still doesn't say anything, so I start. "Here to talk me back from the edge?"

There's a pause, and the voice that answers isn't Jo's. "Nope. Here to shove you off it."

I turn. There's no Jo. Instead, Isaiah, and a half dozen of his sycophants stand in a line on the edge of the clearing. They're spread out, their knees slightly splayed and bent. The expressions on their faces are set. Determined.

I get the impression the cliff they want to shove me off isn't a figurative one.

TWENTY

SEVEN ON ONE, and I put myself out of range of any Crusaders. Brilliant, Meda.

"Are you happy now, Monster?" Isaiah asks.

"I'm about to get jumped. So… no?"

"This is your fault." I get the impression he's not referring to the aforementioned jumping.

"Ha," I bark. "I wish." I sneer. It isn't true, but I don't care. I'm spoiling for a fight. "But I'm afraid I can't take the credit. You Crusaders have been getting your asses handed to you for years before I came on the scene."

"Not like this."

"Exactly like this."

"You don't know anything!"

"I know you're a cowardly little asswipe. How's that for something?" Not particularly clever, but it has the desired effect. He leaps at me. I dodge out of the way and bring my elbow down hard on Isaiah's back as he goes flying past. He slams into the ground with a grunt. I don't have time to enjoy it, because the other six jump me. Eli comes in low, at my knees, and I'm able to jump over him, but while I'm in mid-air Abel, a thick black kid whose sister was slaughtered by demons just six months ago, comes in over the top and slams into me. We go flying backwards and he lands on top. I kick him in the nuts. He grunts and pulls back, I'm able to get both my feet on his stomach, and send him flying. There's a splash as he lands in the river.

Looks like I get to hurl a few Crusaders after all.

I'm still smiling when I take a fist to the face and I feel my lip split against my teeth. I ignore it to jump a sweeping foot, and dodge another swing to the head. I snap out a foot and kick Micah in the knee. He goes down in front of me as I'm tackled from behind, and I land on top of him. He flails back with his elbow and gets me hard, right in the middle of my forehead. I feel the skin tear, and hot blood floods into my eyes, blinding me. I flail wildly behind me with sharp elbows and hear a grunt. The weight's lifted off me, but before I can climb to my feet someone grabs my arm, and someone else grabs the other. I tense waiting for the snap of my arms, but it doesn't come. Nothing comes, and I furiously blink the blood from my eyes.

Isaiah's in front of me, his eye blackened again. I smile to see it, and I can taste the blood in my mouth. I can picture how it's running between my teeth, giving me a grotesque monster's grin. Isaiah's lips tighten.

"What do you want, Isaiah?" I ask.

"I want you imprisoned," he says simply. "Or gone."

"I belong here, asshole. I'm as much Crusader as demon," I say sweetly. "Those are just facts."

"No, your mom abandoned the Crusaders. She gave up the Inheritance. She was barely a Crusader, and you're not one at all."

"Don't talk about my mother."

"Never say the thing has feelings."

"What the hell have I ever done to you? Other than be born, which, I think you'll agree, was not my fault."

"What have you done?" He laughs, a harsh sound. "Everything. You've ruined everything."

"Like what?" I growl.

"You destroyed the school."

"The demons destroyed the school."

"Because of you."

"How the hell was I supposed to know?"

He jabs me in the chest, a wildness in his eyes. "You got Uri killed. God, he was just a *kid*."

Ouch. "The demons killed him." I say it through my teeth.

He doesn't bother to correct me this time. "*You* started a war."

I snort. "There's been a war for centuries."

"No, there hasn't. You started the war." Again with the jabbing finger. I swear to God, if he does it again I am going to bite it off.

"What are you talking about?"

He laughs again, that ugly, manic laugh. "You expect me to believe you don't know?"

"No, I'm pretending for shits and giggles." I roll my eyes. "Humor me."

His lips tighten. "Crusaders and demons aren't allowed to fight each other directly – or at least, we *weren't*. We're supposed to fight over souls."

"I know that. So?"

"So when we rescued you from demon headquarters, we broke the rule." He explains in exaggerated slowness. "Now the demons can attack us in return."

But… "That doesn't make any sense," I argue. "The demons broke the rule first – they invaded the school to get me."

He shakes his head in disbelief at my stupidity. "No, when they invaded the school you were just a halfling. A neutral soul. They were allowed to come after you."

Understanding dawns. I put it together, before he even says it.

"When we rescued you from headquarters, you'd accepted the Inheritance. You were a Crusader."

"But the Crusaders didn't know that."

"That doesn't matter. The demons outnumber us three-to-one, they've been looking for an opportunity to attack us for centuries. *Centuries*. And you delivered it right into their hands." His eyes show the depths of his horror. "We're going to be wiped out. The world will be destroyed." He narrows his eyes, blasting me with hate. "And it's all your fault."

When he punches me in the gut, I'm too shocked to block him.

As I gasp for breath, he comes in close. His brilliant blue eyes are electric. "In the three months since you've arrived, you've been responsible for the destruction of Mountain Park and the deaths of hundreds of Crusaders, and will be for thousands more. You gave the demons the opportunity they've been looking for for centuries. You expect me to believe, *honestly believe*, that you did all that by accident?"

Put that way, it *does* sound a little unlikely.

He pulls back to punch me again, but this time I jump, using my captors to swing my feet forward to double-kick Isaiah in the chest. My unexpected kick sends him flying and my captors are pulled off their feet and we land in a heap.

Just because I can understand their point of view doesn't mean I'm going to let them beat the crap out of me. Hell, even if I *agreed* with his point of view, I wouldn't let them beat the crap out of me. I'm not the martyring kind.

And, besides, I'm innocent. For once, I'm actually, honestly innocent. I didn't mean any of those things to happen; I didn't know enough to foresee any of these outcomes. It might be my fault, but I'm not to blame. And honestly, am I supposed to be sorry they rescued me?

As I said, I'm not the martyring kind.

An alien form of rage pumps through my blood – the righteous kind. The rage of the falsely accused, and again I'm smacked with the unfairness of the Crusaders. Reviled, imprisoned, forbidden to see Luke.

Luke.

Sergeant Graff might be off limits, but I've got seven assholes right here I can take to pieces.

I jerk Micah's arm forward and pop him on the tricep with the other, dislocating his shoulder. He screams and I scramble to my feet. I'm tackled again, this time by Abel, I use our momentum to flip us a few times, away from the others. I rotate so I end up on top and get a few hard punches in before I'm taken off by another flying boy, Omar. He sits on my chest and slams his fist into my face. Brilliant lights dance across my vision, and he slams his other fist against my cheek. Before he can swing again, I knee him hard in the back, sending him flying over my head.

I scramble to my feet, and put my back to the river.

I'm out-matched; there are too many of them. At least, not unless I'm willing to take it to the next level and do some serious damage. Those are my options: take a savage beating or give one.

Yeah, I bet you can guess which way I'm leaning. I snarl.

A movement behind the boys, in the treeline,

catches my eye. A dark shape against darker shadows. A boy with an expression of such fury it takes my breath away. Ugly rage made beautiful because it's on my behalf.

Armand.

My heart instantly lifts — seven on two. But then it comes crashing down. He can't reveal himself. If he does, I'll be busted for consorting with the enemy — that won't go over real well with the Crusaders. If I kill the kids so they can't tell on Armand…

Well, I don't think that would go over any better than plan A.

And that's when it dawns on me. Isaiah's plan.

What do you want, Isaiah? I had asked.

You imprisoned, or gone.

There are other things that could get me locked up, besides being caught with Armand. If I give these students a savage beating, breaking arms, ripping open body parts, the headmaster won't be able to look the other way. It would be the proof Graff needs to show I'm dangerous, that I can't be trusted. Isaiah would get what he wants — me, out of the Crusaders. These assholes are setting me up. This isn't just a fight, it's a trap.

One I have to escape.

My bloodthirsty heart howls at the thought of retreat, but the rational part of my brain knows it's the only option. The realization distracted me from Armand, and he stalks from the treeline, his entire body clenched so tightly he appears to vibrate. I shake my head furiously at him.

While I'm distracted by our silent argument, three of the guys jump me. We go down in a flurry of strikes. A fist hammers me in the face, blinding me temporarily, and I roll wildly trying to get out of the way. I scramble to my feet but am tackled from behind. We land painfully on the rocks that line the river.

I look up in time to see Armand storm from the woods again. "No!" I scream, thrashing my head wildly. Again he stops, but his rhythmically clenching hands give away the effort it takes. Isaiah lands a vicious punch on my cheek, and though I'm blinded by the brilliant exploding red of pain, I know Armand's coming forward again.

"No!" I scream at him. He halts, angrier at me now than at the boys, I think. Finally, he turns and storms back into the woods, out of sight, unwilling to watch.

I'm grateful, because I haven't an ounce of attention to spare him. I take another kick to the ribs that flips me onto my back, into the river shallows. I grab the foot and jerk the boy off his feet. I scramble, but the rocks are slippery, and it's too easy for Eli to catch me, before I can gain my feet.

They aren't pulling any punches, and I start to wonder why I am. The fury builds under my skin, pulsing under my many bruises. It swells until I can't bear it, and when I snap my elbow back, it's with enough force to crack ribs. There's a gasp as the weight comes off me.

I jump to my feet and duck another punch, this time from Jacob, on the other side. Isaiah sweeps for my feet. I jump over his leg and tackle him onto the rocky river bank. I land on top and we skid a few feet. We come to a halt and there's a rock the size of a small basketball next to his head. I snatch it up and hold it over his head.

I could crush his skull.

I hear a shout and shuffle of feet as his comrades run to his rescue, but Isaiah's hand goes up subtly, just a few inches, small enough that I almost missed it. There's a noise of denial behind me, but no one attacks.

Isaiah's brilliant blue and bitter eyes look almost… relieved. Victorious.

Horror dawns.

He's willing to let me kill him, to get rid of me.

He's so sure I'm evil that he's willing to die rather than risk trusting me. His hate is such that he would die rather than live with me.

It's easy to hate someone enough that you wish they were dead. It's even easy enough to hate some enough to actually kill them. There's a whole legal defense built around the idea that you can hate someone enough that it's actually *okay* to kill them – temporary insanity.

But to hate someone enough that you would kill *yourself*… even I, an expert at hate, am amazed.

But it's all there, in his eyes. He wants me worse than dead. He wants me imprisoned with the other demons. To be used, to be experimented on. To be possessed. I am not a person, I am just another weapon in their endless battle. Isaiah's hatred of me knows no bounds.

And suddenly mine for him knows none either. For one precious second, rock clutched in my hand, I consider giving in. Because in that moment, him dead is what we both want.

Victorious blue meets malevolent black as the moment hangs like a body from a noose.

I slam the rock down as hard as I can and he squeezes his eyes shut, bracing for impact.

The rock buries itself harmlessly in the sand by his head.

His eyes open and I lean down.

"I won't kill you, Isaiah," I growl. Then I pause, and smile, all sharp teeth and sharper words. "At least, not at *your* convenience." I shove off him and face the rest of them. Their faces are a mixed bag of relief and anger. I give them a look of absolute disgust, and turn my back on them.

It was a mistake.

There's an angry scream from behind, and a quick crunch of leaves. I spin to see Eli, his face twisted in rage, jumping right at me, a holy blade clutched in his hand. I try to dive to the side, but I forgot about Isaiah at my feet. He grabs my leg, jerking me off-balance. I fall, helpless, as Eli and his knife descend.

I want you imprisoned, Isaiah had said, but that wasn't all.

Or gone.

TWENTY-ONE

I ONLY HAVE one hope – Armand. My life with the
Templars will be over, but that's better than the alternative: my life over, period. I let out a strangled scream
as I go down. I meant it to be a "help", but it's more a
terrified squawk.

I pray Armand got the message anyway. I pray he's
still near enough to hear it.

I land hard on my arm and it twists under me,
shooting fire. The knife, a dagger as long as my hand
comes down to cut the life out of me. I snap my other
hand around and grab Eli's wrist, stopping the descent
of the blade just six inches from my throat. Eli bears
down throwing his weight into it, I try to jerk my other
arm around to help, but Isaiah grabs it. I jerk so furiously to get it free that I pull Isaiah off the ground, but
I can't get it free.

Where the hell is Armand?

The knife gets closer, and with a furious grunt I

muster as much strength as I can and shove it back a couple of inches. I'm stronger than Eli, but he's got his whole weight pressed into it, while I'm pinned awkwardly and can't get any leverage. I struggle ferociously, trying to get my other arm free, but only end up pulling Isaiah further onto me. He throws his legs over mine, and now Jacob has joined Eli, shoving down on that blade. My whole world has focused on the shiny blade. It eats up my vision, it eats up my world.

I force myself to shove yet harder, arching my back, trying to buy a few more inches, a few more millimeters. I catch a movement in the woods, straight behind me. A black-dressed blur.

Armand. He's coming, running toward me, his face a mask of rage.

But then he snaps his head to the right and stops. *He stops.*

He turns back toward me and jerks his head to the right before diving backwards, away from me. *Away from me.*

Fucking demons. My rage comes out as a strangled scream. My scream merges with an enraged shout from the woods. There's a flurry of motion. I jerk my head around in time to see Chi's big form as he comes charging at us like an enraged rhino.

The blade disappears. Jacob jumps back and Eli attempts to climb off me as Chi slams into him, sending them over backwards. Jo emerges from the woods behind him, a wild-eyed, wild-haired lunatic. The other boys are holding up their hands like mobsters caught in a sting. Eli lies unresponsive under Chi, his arms out to the side. Chi has him by the front of his shirt and looks like he'd like to pound him into the dirt.

Jo's expression says she'd like him to. "What's going on here?" she demands, coming to halt in front of us.

"She attacked us," they say, at the same time I say, "They attacked me." We look at each other and snarl.

Jo stomps her foot. Chi climbs off the unresisting Eli and offers me a hand up.

"Having fun without me?" he asks me, as he hauls me to my feet.

"Sorry, man. There wasn't time to get out an invitation."

I stand beside Jo, but Chi stays between us and the boys. Jo checks me over for permanent damage. I feel a little tender in places, but nothing that won't finish patching itself up within a few hours. I spit the taste of blood out of my mouth. It's not usually a taste I dislike – but then, it's not usually my own.

The boys start pleading their case, talking over each other, but I sit back smugly.

Jo puts her fists on her hips and her expression is truly terrifying. The Jo the school has seen recently is a pale shadow of the Jo standing before them now. They thought she was weak and ridiculous. But this Fury is the Jo I know. The one who faced down demons with me. Hell, the one who faced down *me* when I was planning to eat her.

What? I changed my mind!

"Shut up!" she roars. They instantly silence.

I grin. Get em Jo!

"If I see any of you near her again," she jabs
a finger in their direction, and I get ready for vivid
descriptions of disembowelment. "I'm going to tell the
headmaster."

What? My grin freezes and I jerk to face her. They
almost killed me, and she'll *tell the headmaster* if they do
it *again*?

No, please, dear God, anything but that.

Jo doesn't look at me. "Are we clear?"

They all nod.

"Come on, Meda," Jo says, and with one more
hard glare at them she turns and walks away.

I stand there stupidly for a minute, still somehow
waiting for the climactic finish where she goes all cra-
zy-Jo on some A-holes. But it doesn't happen.

She just leaves.

My rage switches focus. I jog after her.

Chi stays behind with the guys, wanting to give us
a head start, just in case. I manage to wait until we're far
enough away where they can't hear us. Until I can speak
without screaming.

"You'll tell the headmaster on them? That's it?" I
hiss, the words squeezed out of a tight throat. "*If* they
do it *again*? Nearly killing me once isn't enough?"

"Don't be melodramatic," she snaps, not bothering to turn to face me. "You could take them." Her shoulders are stiff.

"I punch one of them *once* and I'm busted down to kindergarten – they jump me seven on one, and they get a warning?"

"It's your word against theirs," she says flatly.

"They're lying," I shout.

She jerks to a stop and whirls on me. "Even if that's true–"

"*If* it's true?" My voice raises a notch. "You think I'm lying? You think I jumped the seven of them?"

"Yeah, Meda. *If* it's true." She matches me, anger for anger. She jabs a finger back toward the school. "I saw how pissed you were when you stormed off–"

"I stormed off so I–" wouldn't kill the stupid guard, but Jo doesn't let me finish.

"You were in a rage, Meda. I saw you. Half the damn school saw you. Then you stormed off to where there were no witnesses. You think that looks good? You think that was smart?" She jabs her temple.

"I did not attack them," I say resolutely.

"Who cares? Who do you think they're going to believe?" Her hands punch the air in her anger. "You attacked Isaiah in the middle of class not last week. How is anyone supposed to believe you didn't again?"

Because it's true. Because you're my best friend. But I don't say either of those things. "So this is my fault?" I demand instead. "They jump me, and it's my fault?"

Jo narrows her eyes at me. "Can you stand there

and tell me you didn't bait them? That you weren't positively itching for a fight when you took off into those woods."

She sees the truth on my face, and hers twists in disgust. "Meda, can't you find the tiniest shred of compassion for them? Just the smallest scrap of understanding?" She pinches her fingers together in my face. "Do you know what it's like growing up to be a Crusader? It's not easy to kill."

I open my mouth to tell her it is. And how easy it seemed for Eli just moments ago, but she holds up her hand.

"Oh, I know you love it. You revel in the blood and the brains and the power." She waves her arms around and her voice has a hysterical edge. "But I don't. *We* don't." She points back the way we came. "Those are teenage boys, practically children, and they are asked to murder. To cut demons open and rip out their lives, fake or not. And they have to risk their lives to do it. Take one second out of your precious self-centeredness and think what that's like for them. And this isn't some hypothetical in the future, either – Isaiah and Abel just found out this week that they've been drafted. They could be called any day now, *any day*, to go out and fight for their lives.

"Do you know how they manage it? Dedication. Because they know what's at stake. Because they've been raised their entire lives with one central tenet – that demons must be stopped, no matter what." Her voice cracks, but she patches it together to continue. "To pay that price requires dedication to the point of blindness, and I won't apologize for it. They need that blindness in order to do what they do, and then get up the next morning and do it again."

I don't even bother trying to say anything anymore. The runaway train of her rant is too strong for me to halt.

"It's worse for those boys in particular. I know you know Isaiah's sister was recently killed, but did you know he'd already lost his parents? Did you know Omar's little brother was snatched on his way to visit their grandparents? Omar was escorting him. Eli lost both his sisters defending the school." She pauses, then levels her eyes at me. "Because of you.

"You lost who to the demons? Uri, who you knew for what, a week? Luke, who may even survive? And you get to go all bat-shit crazy. Well, all of those boys have lost most of their families, many of their friends. They hate demons. And can you really blame them? Demons have taken everything, *everything* from them. And maybe it's wrong to hate." Her chin jerks forward. "But maybe it's right. Maybe hate is what keeps them going, in the face of everything."

"And you, Jo?" I ask softly. "Do you hate them?"

She looks away and doesn't say anything. But it doesn't matter. I already know.

"You treat living here like a joke." She hasn't turned back to me. "You float along, barely civil, and act like they owe you. You act like they should be grateful the Great Meda Melange didn't kill them today. You want them to treat you like a Crusader?" Now she does look at me. "Then stop acting like a demon."

Their screwed up upbringing isn't my fault. None of this is my fault. They don't get a free pass to kill me; I'm not their demonic whipping girl. "I *am* a demon, Jo. In case you've forgotten." My words are slick and sharp. "As equal parts one as the other." I step forward, invading her space. "Maybe the problem is, Jo, that I'm not meant to be a Crusader. I'm not meant to be 'good.'" I make quotation marks with my fingers. See how she likes them. "A hammer isn't broken because it won't saw wood." My lips curve, but not into a smile, for all it has the look. "Or bone in my case. It's just the wrong tool for the job."

She doesn't back down, not one inch. "You're right Meda; you may not be a Crusader." She glares. "But you certainly are a tool."

I growl and she glares right back.

"You *are* meant to be good. You're a *Beacon*, Meda. Do you realize what that means? It means you have potential to do good, so much good that you will change the course of the world. So no, I won't believe you if you say you're trying if *this* is trying." She waves back toward the river again.

Still I don't speak. She expects an apology but, believe me, that is *not* what's on the tip of my tongue. So instead I stand, stiff, and refuse to say a word.

She can't stand to look at me and turns with a disgusted sigh to stomp toward the school. "Just stay away from them," she says, but she doesn't turn around.

"*They* attacked *me*," I shout at her retreating back. I punched Isaiah because he incited me, and I get punished. He attacks me, and I still get punished. I don't even mention the knife. What would be the point? I slam my fist into a tree. The wood cracks, as do my knuckles, I'm pretty sure.

Not even Jo takes my side anymore. What am I doing here?

You have options. Even the memory of Armand's voice is seductive.

As if the thought called him, he steps from the woods. "Are you alright?" he asks. His voice is stiff with fury, but, unlike Jo, it's not directed at me. "They're still in the woods, Meda, let's get them." The words come whipping out, thick with French accent and violence. "Say the word, Meda, and I – no, *we*," he knows I'd never miss the fun. I appreciate the consideration, though I haven't the power to smile, "Will rip the life out of them, piece by bloody piece."

"Then I'd have to leave," the words fumble out, weak.

His eyebrows shoot up. "You can't mean to stay?"

I don't answer. I don't know what I mean.

"Meda, no. They'll kill you." His voice is harsh and he grabs my hands, wrapping his around mine. "Please, Meda. Come away with me." I don't respond, but my eyes go to the trees between which Jo disappeared. It's just an empty space now, where she used to be.

"Forget them, Meda. Forget her." He reaches up and puts his hand on the side of my face, tugging it toward him. "I like you as you are. Good, evil, whatever. All I care about is that you're *alive*. Please, Meda." His hand on my cheek slides backwards, through my hair and he tugs me forward, touching his forehead to mine. His voice is hoarse. "Please, just come with me. Where you'll be safe."

His words beat on my ears, but my eyes stray toward the gap in the trees. *Good. Bad. Alive. Safe. Forget her.*

"Meda, please. It's killing me to see you this way," he says softly. His thumb traces lightly across my cheek, across a bruise that has not yet faded.

"What way?" I ask dimly. *Good. Bad. Alive.*

His lips tighten. "Leashed."

Leashed. Locked in my pen at night. Fed at their convenience. A pet monster.

You can't understand them, not even a little bit? Jo had accused. But when she said *them*, what she meant was *us*. Because she is one of them and I am one of me.

"Hey," Armand says, gently, and I look back into his eyes. Demon-dark, hungry, angry, and yet with the tiniest bit of softness. Eyes that can see me for what I am, can accept me for what I am. Because he's like me.

Together we make an us.

And it's us versus them.

They don't want me here, I don't want to be here. I tried to be good. But I'm an addict, addicted to bad, and they keep waving it under my nose. They try to pull me in with it, then punish me when my rehab fails.

But they do not have a monopoly on my future. I have options, and one is right in front of me. Freedom, escape, sin, danger, violence, all rendered beautifully on his too-perfect face. He's offering everything they deny me.

If they won't give me my freedom, I will take it.

Heat pumps through my body, my hand tingles in his, and fire follows the tender slide of his thumb over my cheek. The power that comes with freedom electrifies my nerve endings, and that dark part, cramped from being penned in its cage, springs to the surface.

For too long, I've let them dictate my worth, let them decide what I should be. I may not be a Crusader but I am not nothing. I am everything. I am valuable. I had forgotten, I let them make me forget, swallowing their "should" pills like a good little psych patient. But I am not sick, or crazy, or broken.

I am Meda Melange, demon-saint monster girl. I make full-grown men scream in terror. I break bones and drain blood. I turn nightmares into reality.

I am the most powerful creature on earth. I do not wear a leash.

The darkness seethes under my skin. I blink and the world is a new place.

Armand senses the exact moment I flip. His teeth

come out in a smile, and he wraps his large hands on either side of my face. Our foreheads touch again, and I know he would kiss me if I let him, but I am not in a kissing mood.

I put my hands against his hard chest and grab fistfuls of shirt. I can smell his breath, feel the softness of the fabric crushed in my hands. I can count his every pore, see every dark-on-dark fleck in his eyes. The world around us pulses with life and brightness and energy.

"Come for me tonight," I whisper, staring at his mouth too long. "I have some things to take care of."

So I act like a monster, do I?

I'll show them monstrous.

TWENTY-TWO

CONTRARY TO WHAT you might expect, I don't go on a murderous rampage.

A real monster is too clever for that. A real monster shakes the hands of elderly couples as he invests their life's savings in his Ponzi scheme; he kisses babies and runs for political office; he waits until she's in love. A real monster knows that an attack hurts; but a betrayal scars.

So I return to my room. And, later, when The Sarge tells me to come, I don't argue. When she tells me to sit, I sit. *There's a good girl, Meda!*

She feeds me excuses disguised as explanations. She pretends to care that it's unfair; she pretends to apologize.

I pretend to believe her.

I, too, pretend to care.

But my other ears are now open, and in her words I hear all the things she doesn't say. The real reason I can't visit Luke. The real reason I'm locked in my room. The real reason Graff was allowed to possess me.

I read once about miners who took canaries into coal mines. I can see them, little dots of singing sunshine, desperately out of place in the dark. Although they kept the miners company, cheerfully noisy things that they are, they weren't pets. If the miners hit a pocket of poisonous gas the canary, with its small, delicate body, would die long before the miner, letting him know it's unsafe.

That's what I am to the Crusaders; what The Sarge won't say. I'm useful but inhuman. I'm not worth what they are. She looks me in my young-girl face and doesn't want to admit I'm expendable.

Some things, terrible things, are better left unsaid, I suppose.

To that end I won't tell you about how, after I leave The Sarge, I go back to my room and plot my revenge. I won't say how the *thunk* of the key locking my door no longer feels like a slap. How it now feels like a challenge, a call to come out and play. It's a reminder and a tease and taunt, but no longer a slap. Its sting is gone.

I won't say how I wait while the old building goes to sleep, but how I have never felt more awake. I won't talk about the ferocious look on a monster-boy's face when he lets me out of my room. I won't tell you about following the delicious shape of a bad-boy's back up to the attic, then leaving him and my belongings there, while I have my revenge.

I won't talk about how I scale a certain building to a certain hidden window with a broken latch. How Jo showed me the building's only weakness.

I won't say how that thought makes me laugh.

I won't tell you how I search for a certain map, or how I know it's here somewhere because Jo used it against me. I won't tell you that I find it.

And I certainly won't tell you that I steal it.

I won't tell you that I know what it means to the world if the Crusaders lose it. I won't tell you that I know what will happen if the demons ever manage to get a hold of it. No, I won't tell you any of that.

Because some things, terrible things, are better left unsaid.

As I move through the hallways of the school to meet Armand in the attic, the thing I won't tell you I stole stuffed in one of those nylon-and-string triangular sports bags. I trot up stairs until I reach my hall. I pause, listening, but it's silent. I slide around the corner and slither down the dark hallway. My feet move over the creak-happy boards so softly, they barely sigh. I move by Jo's door, then mine with its despicable lock, but I don't spare it a glance. It was never truly mine. A person doesn't belong to her dog, the master doesn't belong to her slave, and a cell doesn't belong to its prisoner. The one with the power is the one who owns. But I don't belong to that room anymore. The world belongs to me.

I slip down the hallway, but just as I reach the stairs up to the attic, I hear a metallic scrape behind me. I duck inside the entry to the stairs, sinking into the shadows.

Jo's door opens and she slips out into the hallway. She's in her pajamas, a white tank top and sweats, lumpy over her leg brace, but it doesn't look like she's been sleeping. Her eyes are swollen. The key hangs on its long chain around her neck. It gleams in the light flooding from her open door.

Never say Saint Jo is breaking the rules.

She steps silently into the hallway, but slowly, as if she isn't sure of herself. She pauses at the door and her fingers slide up to fiddle with my room key. My stomach flips.

No, Jo. No. Don't go to my room. Trust Jo to ruin my plans. If she finds me missing, I haven't the slightest doubt that after what happened today, she'll call the Crusaders down on me in a heartbeat, the traitor. My legs coil on the stairs as I consider options. They aren't great. Run, but I doubt even I could escape fast enough that the Crusaders couldn't catch me. And if they catch me with the Beacon Map...

But that only leaves one other option: stopping her.

I would have to silence her so fast, she couldn't call for help. There could be no betraying tussle, no thud as I tackled her. I'm stronger and faster than she is, but all she has to do is make a noise and I'm caught.

Despite her pathetic showings in S and C, the girl's a natural at ass-kicking. She must be... silenced, before she even becomes aware I'm here.

Don't go in my room, Jo.

But the girl was born to be contrary. She walks the ten paces to my door. Armand locked it to give us the greatest head start, but that helps not at all when the one person who comes to check on me has a key. She pauses outside my door and I hold my breath. She raises her thin arm, white in the darkness, to knock, but pauses to wipe her cheeks, then she lowers it again without ever rapping. She stares at my door, and I Jedi-mind-trick the hell out of her.

Go away, go away, go away.

Because she lives to piss me off, she instantly lifts her arm again, quick this time, as if she wants to get it done before she can change her mind again, and raps softly on the door.

No one answers.

Go away. Actually, no, this is Jo. *Please, do come in,* I think instead. Can you reverse Jedi-mind trick some-one?

She knocks again. "Meda," she says softly. "Meda, please talk to me." She presses her forehead and hands against the door. She looks pale and thin. Thinner than me, now, maybe. She looks like she's had every ounce of fight sucked right out her. It occurs to me, in the cold vacuum in my chest, that not only did I start a war, a war that potentially means the death of everyone and everything she believes in, I made her help me do it. Jo turned me into a Crusader in the demon headquarters. I didn't ruin the world alone, she helped me.

How that must feel to someone with a conscience.

"Meda," she says again, then adds a few taps with her knuckle. When my reply doesn't come, her jaw sets. She swipes her hand across her face. "We're friends, dammit," she snaps. "Now open the door."

I wince. If she keeps up making noise like that, I'll be caught anyway.

Fortunately she takes a breath, and when she continues she's calmer and quieter. "Look, I'm sorry about how I acted today. I know I should have trusted you." She trails off, frustrated at talking to wood. She makes a quiet growling sound in her throat, then hisses, "Open the damn door!" Ah, a classic Jo apology.

But I can't open the door, no matter what she has to say. And she can't be allowed to, either. She says she trusts me now, but it's too late. Her trust is misplaced. I'm ten feet away in the wrong direction, mid-nefarious plan. Ah, Jo. As Armand always says, you should never trust a demon.

But she's lying too, anyway. Actions speak louder than words, Jo, and you don't trust someone you lock in a cage.

As if she heard my thoughts, her hand reaches for the hated key gleaming against her chest. Fed up, apparently, she whips it off in a quick jerk.

She's going to do it. She's going to let herself in.

She'll sound the alarm and I'll be caught stealing the Beacon Map and it'll be over. The hated existence I've lived until now will seem like a dream in comparison.

Jo would never forgive me. Even Chi would be hard-pressed to justify my theft. I'd finally prove to them that I am what they've always feared.

This is it: I'm caught or she's dead. Those are my choices. Her or me. But hasn't that always been the case? Mom or me. Jo or me. We butt heads, we battle. And in the end we always come to this point. Her or me.

I crouch in the darkness, a monster prepared to pounce. A wicked thing, incapable of letting anything get between It and what It wants. *She doesn't care about you,* I tell myself. *She'll pick the Crusaders every time. She's not your friend. She's your enemy.*

Jo looks at the key in her hand, the symbol of her control over me.

Now. I have to do it *now.* I bend, I curve, I pretend away all those things I wish weren't there. I force a silent snarl to my lips. I'm ready.

And yet, when she slides the key in the lock and twists, I stand in my dark doorway and watch, unable to move. My impending destruction curves over me like a breaking wave, and I'm frozen, waiting for it to crush me. Drown me. Pull me under and swallow me.

I deflate. Wasted adrenaline and shame combine to make me shake jerkily. Shame because of what I almost did or shame because of what I couldn't do, I don't even know.

I can't be good, but apparently I can't be bad either. I'm a wasted half of everything. I won't kill Jo. I smother a silent bark of laughter that I ever thought I could. Kill her. I couldn't even hurt her. Furious as she makes me, she's... *Jo.*

Jo pulls the key from the lock, and I wait, helplessly, for her to open the door and sound the alarm. I don't even run. I lean against the wall quivering. Pathetic.

She still doesn't open the door, but rather contemplates the key in her hand. But it doesn't matter how long it takes for the inevitable to occur. The stressful part is the decision-making. Do I stop her, or do I not?

My best friend, worst enemy, and certain destruction, and yet, somehow the answer is "no."

Then, as I watch, Jo closes her hand around the key into a fist and drops to the floor. I stand in shock as, with a smooth swing of her arm, she sends the key skittering under my door.

She rises to her feet as smoothly as her bum leg will allow and sticks her chin slightly in the air. She looks as relaxed as I've seen her in weeks.

It's always the decision-making that's the worst part.

"I'll be waiting for you," she says to the door. "Whenever you're ready to talk." She waits one more moment, then turns and pads back to her room. Right before she closes the door, she adds, "*Doctor.*" Then closes the door with a quiet snick.

Doctor. It's what I told her to call me when we were in the demon headquarters and I wanted her to finish casting the spell. She knew what I meant was "trust me" and, despite everything, all rationality, she did.

And now she's saying it again. After I almost…

But some things, terrible things, are better left unspoken.

I twist and take the steps two, three at a time. I run across the beam over the rotten floor until I reach the window, still open from Armand's exit. I lean against the frame and try to breathe. After I get some air I shove my fist into my mouth and scream silently into my knuckles. Then I punch the air, swinging wildly, so frustrated, so *torn*. I push my hands into my eyes, grinding my palms into them and drop to the ground.

Jo always has a way of ruining my plans. Just rarely in the way I expect.

Suddenly there are strong hands on my arms. "Hey, hey, what's wrong?" Armand tugs my hands from my eyes. He looks slightly panicked and his eyes fly over me searching for injury.

I look back at him, sick, and just shake my head. I don't even know what I'm saying "no" to.

He pulls from my expression the problem, and for one brief moment he looks as sick as I feel. As if he can feel my shame. And maybe he can, in a way. Only he can understand the pull of the darkness but capacity for light. He's given up the fight, but that doesn't mean he doesn't remember the battle.

The battle he eventually lost. We haven't the capacity to win. How could a girl who plots the– But no. That will remain unsaid.

Armand strokes my arms with a gentleness I wouldn't expect from him. "Come, Meda. You can't stay here." His eyes ache. "They're tearing you apart."

That's exactly what it feels like, being pulled in different directions until the flesh tears. I needed to get away, to take a break. To breathe.

I close my eyes. A break. I open my eyes again, and Armand senses the change that's come over me and rocks back slightly on his heels.

"You're right," I say, hoarse and slow. Then I cast my eyes around my little retreat. The one I used to share with Jo and Chi. I close my eyes again and take another breath, and make a decision. My eyes open, and I'm calmer still. "Just give me a minute, will you? I need…" I wave my hands uselessly, letting him conclude what he will.

He looks like he thinks it's a bad idea. His lips tighten a hair, and again I can't miss that unexpected look of concern in his eyes. But "no" is not really an answer I would accept anyway, and he knows. He climbs to his feet, and with one more look at me, slips out the window.

Once he's gone, I move quickly. I reach into my pack and pull out the Beacon Map, and stare at the skull as it sits, glowing, in my palm. I can't take it, not when I know how it will hurt Jo. I don't know what I am, hopeless or hopeful, but if I steal the Beacon Map the decision will be made. I grab a blanket from the cubby where Jo, Chi, and I stashed it months ago, and fold it around the map and thrust it back in the hiding spot.

Jo trusts me. After she gets over her shock and hurt, she'll know I didn't steal it, and she'll guess where I hid it. She'll find it, and then she'll find me, but meanwhile I'll have my break. The Crusaders will be furious but once the map resurfaces, surely (*surely*) the punishment won't be as severe – the difference between a misbehaving teen and traitor. I wince. I don't actually know what they *will* do, but that's a worry for another day.

I exhale, take one last look around the school, and climb out the window to meet Armand.

Thirty-seven days, eighteen hours, and twenty-two-ish minutes later… but who's counting?

TWENTY-THREE

I WAKE WITH a luxurious stretch. A patch of afternoon sunlight brightens the far wall. It makes a striped pattern but, unlike at the school, these lines are horizontal, signifying the freedom to pull the blinds and sleep all day, rather than a symbol of my captivity.

Time with Armand has passed in a red-grey haze. Bloody nights fuzzy with soul-drunk. Hot hazy days slept away waiting to do it again. We've murdered dozens since my escape. I still stick to Mom's dictum to only slaughter the wicked, but that definition has become more fluid. I still get vengeance for the ghosts, mostly because they won't let me not, the pesky things, but for once in my life their demands can't keep up with the Hunger's. For the first time in my life, I can kill as many as I want.

And I want a lot.

So we pluck victims from the pages of newspapers, chasing headlines of brutal murders, missing

children, and the like. On slow nights, or if we're
feeling lazy, I'll simply stand around looking helpless
in a bad part of town. It's entrapment, I know. These
scumbags may go their whole lives without ever hurting
a girl, were such a ripe opportunity not placed into their
sweaty palms.

And yet, I somehow fail to feel sorry for them.

The uptick in murders is so drastic, it couldn't
go unnoticed, but as our victims were, for the most
part, known scumbags, no one cares. Oh, a few of our
victims were mistaken for upstanding citizens, but few
enough of those to raise alarm. And we can clean up
our messes. When we want to.

A few bloggers have put it together – the death of
all these dirtbags – and speculate that Gotham has its
very own Batman.

Crazy conspiracy-theorists.

Armand doesn't mind my rules. He finds it funny
that he should be considered a hero.

I shove out of bed and pad into the living room,
in search of my unlikely hero. Armand's flat is elegant
and expensive, if a bit cold. Cool grey walls, modern
furniture, chrome, glass, a wall of windows overlook-
ing the skyline. But every inch of the dull grey interior
plays the backdrop to a brilliant memory. Memories
I've socked away.

Armand thinks returning to the Crusaders is a
choice I have to make. Every day to him is another
victory, another day I've decided to stay. But every day

isn't a victory, but one more burnt and gone as the clock winds down to Jo's eventual arrival. And so I pack up each memory carefully, like Christmas ornaments, to preserve when the holiday season is over.

"Are these yours?" I ask of a clustering of family portraits, incredulous.

"Who? Muffy and Buffy?" He laughs. "Not hardly. It's a prop. Welcome to my stage." He swings his arms expansively. "Ever read Les Liaisons Dangereuses?"

"No."

"Me neither," he confides with a wicked smile. "But I watched the movie adaptation when my boss explained my part. I play Sebastian the wealthy, wicked boy, who is not truly bad, just really waiting for his one true love to change him." He smiles darkly. "All of them."

"Isn't that a bit over-complicating things? Why don't you just seduce them?"

"Because getting someone to sleep with you is easy. Getting them to sell their soul for you? That requires so much more."

The way he says it makes the darkness flutter.

"It has to be just a little bit hard." He holds his fingers up in a little pinch. "They studied the phenomenon at Harvard."

"They studied soul-stealing at Harvard?"

"What else do you think they do in business

school? In any case, it's called the Ikea effect."

"As in furniture?"

"They discovered that people are disproportionately pleased with things they build themselves. Like self-assembled furniture. It doesn't matter how truly crappy the final product is, people are willing to pay more for it if they made it themselves." His face shutters, and his accent thickens. "Much, much more."

I don't say anything and he finally looks at me, his eyes shadowed.

"I just realized something," I say softly, studying him.

He looks almost worried, but defiant. Like he's testing me, waiting to see what I think of his confession.

"You are a total nerd."

Not what he's expecting, the darkness wiped away by a startled laugh. "What?"

"Why else would you possibly know that?" I say it like I'm piecing together a puzzle – and I'm appalled by the picture it's making. "You're a nerd. A complete nerd. You nerdified sex. That just happened."

He laughs. "Ha, fine," he says when he finally catches his breath. "I won't show you my notes on the Kama Sutra."

The faux-family portraits are now haphazardly piled in a corner and the wall is decorated with drawings we've done ourselves. Most of them are of us

– it is a portrait gallery after all. Armand's are mostly pencil, drawn with quick, fluid lines, as if the energy that vibrates through his body flows out of his pencil and into his subject matter. Mine are done in color; the vibrant colors I adore look especially vivid against the grey walls, lit from above by can lights. In my favorite, we're both decked out like superheroes with our chests stuck out and our hands on our hips.

"What do you think?" I hold out the drawing for his inspection.

"Oh, it's… ah." He scratches the back of his head. "Nice."

"Thanks," I grunt with satisfaction and tape it to the dry wall.

"Um."

"Yes?"

"Errr, I just…" He doesn't seem quite sure how to put it. "Don't you think I look a little… cold?" he finally asks.

"No. See? I gave you a cape." I point.

"I see. But… why exactly am I in a thong?"

"I wanted a break from the usual gender stereotypes."

He laughs. "And my…" he clears his throat and points. "It seems unnaturally large."

"Of course," I nod, eyeing my drawing with satisfaction. "The male equivalent of quadruple-Ds."

"Is that a thing?"

"Only in comic books."

"I see."

"Improving gender-equality one sketch at a time," I say piously.

"So you're saying you drew me in a thong for the good of mankind."

"Exactly," I grin wickedly. "I keep telling you I'm one of the good guys."

The squishy couch covered by its rumpled blankets, where we've ended more nights than I can count, the sweat from dancing and the stink of underground clubs, where they don't care about things like smoking regulations or fire marshals, lingering on our skin. Barely-touches and almost-kisses; Venus eye-traps and breath that comes too quick; laughter that fades to silence. Silence that stretches and stretches and stretches.

"Do you know why a girl would risk falling for a bad boy?" I ask him when the silence is too full to stay that way. We are lying on the couch together, squished into the tiny space. He is on his side, pressed against the back, his arm thrown over me. His finger traces swirling designs on my arm. He pretends they were idly done, absently even, and I pretend to believe it.

"Because she's bad herself?" he asks hopefully.

I laugh. "Nice try. I'm good, remember?"

"Ah, yes, that's right."

"There are a few possibilities," I say, trying to keep my mind on what I'm saying and not on what he is doing. "One," I hold up a finger. "She thinks he's not really bad."

He looks up at me from beneath his eyelashes.

"And I don't believe that about you."

He smiles his dark little smile.

"Another possibility is that she thinks he can change," I reason. I shake my head. "I don't think you can change, Armand."

I feel a quiet laugh against my neck and shiver.

"That leaves only one option." I slide my hand up to his shoulder and push him back, so we are face to face. "She's a fool."

"Meda." He sighs it more than says it.

"I'm not a fool, Armand." It comes out almost as an apology, then I push him gently but firmly back, then slide away from him and to my feet.

"There is one other option." He grabs my hand before I can get out of reach. "Sometimes people are together because they can't help it," he says urgently. "They don't have a choice."

"There's always a choice. That's the point," I laugh, though it's not the least bit funny. "Of everything." I pull my hand free and he lets it go with a groan.

Meh. I think I'll leave that memory behind. I have a dozen other, more fun ones, on that couch.

I wander to the bathroom to take care of the necessities, and consider changing out of my jammies into real clothes, but decide not to bother. It's already evening, and we'll need to get ready soon for tonight's adventures.

A shiver of anticipation ripples under my skin at the thought of tonight, and I shove my head under the sink to cool myself back down. Tonight's victim is… special.

I flip my hair back, briskly rub it with a towel so it's not dripping, and carefully blot the water drops off my arm. Armand gave me a sharpie tattoo-sleeve on my left arm and I don't want it to smear. Dragons and snakes and fire curl from my wrist to my shoulder.

I climb up the metal rungs bolted into the wall of the condo and onto the roof. Eventually the roof is to be made into a garden for the top-floor folks to enjoy, but the safety regulations have apparently made the transition temporarily insurmountable. It works for us though, as it means no one uses the roof but us. My guess is that's where Armand is now.

Sure enough, he stands on the edge of the roof, one arm crossed over his chest with the other elbow resting upon it and his hand covering his lower face. He lacks his usual buzz of edgy energy, instead he looks deep in thought.

Mwah-ha-ha!

I ease the trap door closed, making not a sound. Then I spin, softly on bare feet, and creep up behind him, easing from tip-toe to tip-toe. He doesn't move, contemplating the beautiful city skyline. It could be a poster, or a billboard, advertising jeans or cologne – handsome boy, pretty city. Lots of seemingly deep thoughts.

When I'm about ten feet away, I leap. "GRAAAAAAAAAAAAAAAAAAAH!" I bellow.

He starts, spinning into attack position. His lips curl back in a snarl, and his eyes...

I consider the possibility that this was a mistake – surprise-attacking a murderous monster.

But there's not a lot I can do mid-air. Fortunately, recognition registers right as I slam into him. He relaxes into the hit, so it's more catch than anything, and we go rolling across the roof in a laughing tangle of limbs.

Then we roll right off the ledge.

My arm snaps out and catches the edge of the roof. We swing into the wall of the building, and Armand hits it back-first, letting out a soft "oof", as the air is shoved out of his lungs. I don't let go of the ledge, and swing my other arm to grab it as well. Armand doesn't let go of me. His arms are wrapped just below my armpits, and he pulls up his legs and wraps them around mine. His face is inches from mine. He looks like he showered recently, or at least stuck his head under the faucet as I did, and his tangly dark hair is damp.

"Good morning," I say, cheerily, and he groans then laughs.

"Good morning, *Mademoiselle*," he says, casually, as if we weren't suspended from the roof , tangled around each other like a pair of monkeys. He always whips out the French when he's trying to be cute. Or obnoxious.

I wait a minute, but he still makes no move to climb up. "Well? Climb up."

He smiles wickedly and squeezes me a little tighter. "I'm fine where I am."

I smile angelically – long enough to let him get nervous – then heave myself up toward the roof. Since he's hanging in front of me, he whacks his head on the overhang with a yelp and lets go of me to grab the ledge. I grin as I finish hauling myself back up.

The roof is made of light colored cement and is flat but for the jut of air conditioner units and chimney spouts. There are vertical posts around the outer ring of the roof, the skeleton for a fence that never happened, and I spin and sit next to one, leaving my feet to dangle over the side. Armand hauls himself up next to me.

"That's what I get for playing with fire," he grumbles, rubbing his head. It can't hurt too badly – his head is far too hard.

"And here I always thought *I* was the one playing with fire. You being the bad boy."

"Nope," he says, dropping down beside me. "The one playing with fire is the one most likely to get burned."

"Ah, well, that settles it. You were only bumped not burned."

A pause. "Maybe today."

I don't respond. It'd only encourage him.

Philadelphia's skyline is slowly fading to grey as it is swallowed by darkness. It's hot on the roof, but heat, like cold, barely bothers me when I'm well-fed. It doesn't bother Armand either. When I asked him about this, he laughed and asked what kind of demon would he be if he couldn't stand a little heat?

The creeping darkness serves to add to my creeping excitement. It starts at the base of the buildings and slides up their walls. Soon it will swallow them completely, leaving only shadows upon shadows. Places where monsters can slip and slide, snatching unwary victims.

And tonight's dish is something special. Something that's been weeks in the making.

Peter Phearson is one of the city's wealthiest inhabitants. Popular, successful, good looking for an old man, and, of course, a generous philanthropist. He also happens to be a serial killer, and the finest psychopath Philadelphia has had to offer since the Frankford Slasher. When Phearson was arrested, the dear citizens of Philadelphia didn't want to believe it.

But then the evidence came out. Then more evidence. Photographs, bodies in his house. It was irrefutably true. He had done it. The city was ready to lynch him. Of course they didn't. Decent people that they are, they waited for the courts to deliver justice.

How grown adults can still manage such naivety is shocking.

Phearson is a clever beast. He knew this day was coming and planned for it; set his dominos in place carefully to fall in a grotesque pattern when the time came. He made powerful friends – the close kind of friends who whisper their darkest secrets. Secrets that could get them arrested were they ever uncovered.

A clerk "accidentally" ruined the chain of custody of the murder weapon; a police officer "forgot" what he saw at the scene of the crime; the DA bungled the case, missing court deadlines left and right; the judge constantly ruled in the defense's favor – the list goes on.

The world was forced to watch in horror as the judge signed an acquittal. The country watched in silence as a gleeful Phearson tripped down the court-house stairs. He wore a brilliant red shirt, as if waving a flag in front of the bull of the city. You could feel the creeping hopelessness of a nation realizing for the millionth time that life is not fair.

The most fascinating part of Phearson isn't his technique (though I admit, the man has style), but his response to the whole affair. He doesn't bother to hide his guilt. The mask has come off, and he laughs in the face of the city, sneers his contempt, and delights at their helpless rage. He didn't just plan for the day of his capture, he looked forward to it.

But we aren't all helpless, Mr Phearson.

For the past several weeks Armand and I have been toying with him. A special piece of work like Phearson deserves some special work of our own. I want him to feel the thump-thump of terror. Live under the grind of chronic fear. I wanted him to know we were coming. I want him to know he can't stop us.

We flicked his dominos one at a time. *Thump*: the corrupt police officer disappeared. (Well, most of him at least. Pieces were found.) *Thump*: the not-so-honorable judge's indiscretions were revealed to the world – in his suicide note. *Thump*: the world learned that the district attorney, rotten beast, benefitted off some lovely insider trading tips on Phearson, Inc. One by one, each mistake was revealed for the corruption it was. *Thump, thump, thump.*

It's enough for a mistrial, of course. But I credit Phearson with enough cleverness to get to the court of appeals before the case does. That is, if he has the time.

He doesn't.

And all through this Phearson's been watching. At first telling himself it's a coincidence; then growing more and more terrified as he realizes it can't possibly be. He can't miss the message, he's far too clever:

We're coming for you.

On an estate as large as Phearson's, it was an easy thing for Armand and I to slip onto his property and leave things where they ought not to be. Red things.

Red like the shirt he wore to his acquittal. Red like the blood of his victims; red like my rage. Red like the pieces of him I will pull off and not put back.

Red flowers from the judge's garden appeared on his kitchen table. A red apple from the police officer's lunch lands in his dining room, a toothy white bite taken out of it.

More guards! More cameras!

A red pillowcase on his fanatically white bed.

More locks on the doors!

A wall of his bathroom painted red.

He replaced all his guards, then replaced his security company altogether. Still the gifts appeared. At the urging of his baffled guards, he relocated to his downtown condo. It has few windows and fewer doors, not to mention it's forty-eight stories off the ground.

Now, he thinks, *now, I am safe.*

Tonight we show him that he is not.

My thoughts move happily through a red-splashed daydream, and I let out a little contented sigh. At the sound, I see Armand's mouth stretch into a soft smile. He's watching me.

"What are you thinking?" he asks.

"Peter Phearson," I answer, and shiver a little at the sound of his name. "Why? What were you thinking about?" I ask him, because, really, what else is there to think about mere hours before the event? It's like expecting a kid to think of anything other than presents on Christmas Eve.

There's the briefest pause. "Same."

TWENTY-FOUR

PETER PHEARSON'S CONDO is the entire penthouse floor of a highrise in downtown Philidelphia. It employs doormen and parking attendants and security cameras. The elevators require a key. Phearson attempted to fill the lobby with armed guards upon his arrival, but not even a serial killer can compete with the determined viciousness of a homeowner's association. His guards were sent packing.

Instead, Phearson filled the hallway outside his condo with a good half-dozen burly men, and has four more stationed inside his condo. Three walk rounds, and one follows Phearson wherever he goes, including the toilet. Even for number two. Given what I know he's capable of, I suppose I shouldn't be quite so horrified by this, but I am. Even we serial killers should have some standards of decency.

The guards are armed, well-trained, and well-paid but they are also, unfortunately, only human.

Night falls and deepens. It's only 11 and this part of downtown is busy on a Friday night, with people returning from late dinners and drinks with work buddies, or on their way out for more determined night-living.

Or lounging in the shadows, preparing for a little homicide.

Armand and I dressed for the occasion. He looks like a Calvin Klein model in a narrowly cut grey suit, tie, and a rakish little hat. I'm in a red dress that looks like a stylized version of a man's dress shirt. It buttons up the front from hem to neckline, and is cinched in the middle by a thin belt. It's short, justifying my black leggings. On my feet are expensive black heels with red bottoms, and an enormous expensive handbag hangs from my arm. We stand in the shadows, and I rest against the wall behind me as Armand leans over, his arms braced on either side of my head. We look for all the world like an overly-wealthy couple coming home from a date.

Armand presses in, his permanent smile playing on his mouth, and when he breathes I smell peppermint. The look in his eyes makes my breath come a little faster. He slides in a little closer, crowding me, surrounding me with his scent. I tip my face up, just a hair, so our lips are in line. Sensing an opportunity he bends towards me, but just as our lips are about to touch, I stop him with a question.

"How much longer?" Then I lift a brow to let him

know I was screwing with him.

Some might call me a "tease", but don't believe it. "Tease" implies that I owe him something, that I should feel guilty. As if my flirtation is forced on him and he merely tolerates it for an eventual pay-out. That's bullshit. We both have goals in our little game; why should his goal (sex) take priority over mine (to mess with his head)? Is it because he's a man?

In that case I must object on principle. Superhero Meda establishing gender-equality one almost-kiss at a time!

He presses his forehead against the brick wall behind me and groans before glancing at his watch. "Two minutes." When the new guard arrives he goes through a routine of getting settled before he really focuses on his job. He makes coffee, goes to the bathroom, sets up his iPod, chitchats with the guy leaving. We know because of the camera we planted in his office.

Armand pulls his phone from his breast pocket, and opens the app streaming the footage from the office. He starts. "He's early." Armand shoves away from the wall. "Who shows up to work early?" His tone is full of disgust. "Come on," he says, reaching out his hand for mine, and the young-couple-not-quite-in-love stroll around the corner.

My fingers are twined through Armand's and I sway into him as we walk up the street, looking harmless and a little tipsy. We stroll past the opening to the parking garage with the attendant sitting in his

little air-conditioned booth. A black metal fence rings
the parking garage, but there's a locked gate to allow
residents in on the far side. As we near it, Armand
pulls his phone from his breast pocket and watches the
surveillance footage. He tugs at my hand, slowing our
pace, then speeds up again a few seconds later. The
guard is distracted. We reach the gate and with a quick
jerk of my wrist I break the lock. There's a loud metallic screech-and-snap that catches a few eyes. If I had
a crowbar it would look suspicious, or if I were big,
manly, and poor. But a small, expensive girl with only
her bare hands is never anything to fear.

I smile as if the noise embarrassed me, and pull
Armand through the gate. We stumble into the elevator, entwined. We don't have keys, so can't actually go
anywhere, but the door still closes for several seconds
while it waits for us to make our floor selection. When
we don't slide a key card into the slot the doors open
again to disgorge the disappointed passengers, but by
then we are already up through the ceiling and into
the elevator shaft. Armand checks on the guard while
I strip out of my dress, revealing a black tank-top. I
shove the dress and shoes into my purse and pull out
my sneakers. Armand strips down to his bogeyman
gear – black fitted pants, black tee. I pass him his shoes.
I leave the bag in the elevator shaft to grab on our way
out.

Then we climb the cables forty-eight stories to the
penthouse, and past it. There's an access door set above

the elevator's machinery to allow for repairs and we pull ourselves out onto the roof. The wind blows gustily and the lights of the city spread out below.

But we are not here for the view.

We slip across the roof, then drop down onto the patio outside of Phearson's condo. The patio is large, and covered with enough exotic plants to qualify as a botanical garden. There are two sets of French doors. One set leads into the bedroom and another into the living room. A guard stands in the living room, his back to the patio. He's a large black man and must weigh at least two hundred and fifty pounds. He holds the classic secret-service pose, feet spread hip-width apart, arms loosely crossed in front of him. We head to the bedroom doors instead.

The bedroom is decorated entirely in white, like the one at his house. It's dimly lit by a lamp on the nightstand, though there's no one in the room.

Afraid of the dark, are we, Phearson?

I look to Armand, who crouches on the patio next to me. He's lit by the light shining from the bedroom, and lit from within with a giddy excitement. My heart pounds in response, because it's finally time. Once I jerk this patio door open the fun begins. I wrap my fingers around the cool metal handle, and my skin feels hotter in comparison. I smile and bite my lip, revelling in the feel of flesh on teeth, even though it's my own. For now.

The handle cracking under my hand brings a rush

that makes me gasp.

Armand and I coordinate without planning and without words. We glide through the silent apartment, taking out the first guard, then the second, laying the now-still mountains of men on plush carpet. We don't kill them. My rule – Armand lobbied hard for the alternative.

Men who willingly take orders from evil men should be tarred with the same brush, he argued. But for the complicity of their servants, the world's worst monsters would never have succeeded. Where would Hitler have been without his SS? Or Stalin without his NKVD?

It's a solid argument, and it's hard to remember my counter-argument as the second-to-last guard flails under my chokehold. I feel his carotid artery throb against my restraining arm as I deny his blood its path to his brain. I could squeeze too hard, I could twist with a snap, I could pull with a wet plop and all the life flooding through those veins could be mine. It would billow through me, beautiful as a rainbow, bubbling like champagne.

Armand holds the guard still, keeping his struggles silent. Armand's mouth is slightly open, showing his teeth, as he breathes in the guard's terror. Our eyes meet, and I know with the slightest nod of my head, he would go for it. He's dying to do it. The call that pulls me pulls him just as strongly, but he hasn't anything holding him back.

Blessedly, the guard stills and I haul my self-control back.

We bind and gag him, leaving him limp on the floor. Only Phearson and the guard at his side remain in the apartment. We decided to leave the six outside the apartment alone. It's funny, the thought of them guarding the door of a dead man. In the morning, they'll scratch their heads as CSI's cameras flash, wondering how such a thing could have happened.

Light pours from a mostly-closed door at the end of the dim hallway, splashing on the wall. Anticipation builds, dragging up our pace with it. I already know what I'm going to say, what words I'm going to string together into a noose. It's not that I rehearse – a natural needn't. Rather I daydream, enjoying the pleasure as long as possible. I imagine the pleading, the terrified look as reality strikes.

At the door Armand and I share one last bloodthirsty look. I press my hand to the door and peek in the crack.

And stop.

Phearson sits in a wing chair, his knuckles white as he grips the arms of the chair. He already looks terrified – but he's not looking at us. He's not alone. *What the hell?*

Someone got here first. The Hunger screams its denial.

He's mine. I bite back a snarl. I shoot a glance at Armand, who has pressed himself to the wall at my left, so he, too, can peer in the room. His face has the same monstrous denial. Our blood is running too hot, our Hunger running too free. We behaved with the guards; we deserve our reward.

Whoever it is, they will give him up or I will add their body to his.

I bite back the rage and force myself to ease the door open. Phearson doesn't spare it a glance. Fair enough, as the opening door reveals the barrel of a silencer, attached to a handgun, which is held in a black-gloved hand, attached to the end of a black-clad arm – which is attached to the entire person of Crusader-in-Training Joanna Ruins-Everything-Fun Beauregard.

Her pissy eyes meet my shocked ones. "Took you long enough."

Twenty-Five

Typical damn Jo, come to stop the monster from taking another human life. She could have picked any time to "catch" me, but no, she would choose now, just like with damned Annabel. I try to pull the red rage from the world. To calm myself. I wanted her to find me.

But not right now! the Hunger roars.

"I could say the same to you," I retort, trying to bite back the beast.

Jo's eyes widen slightly at my accusation, but trust her for an instant comeback. "Yeah, well, you forgot to leave a forwarding address," she says sourly. "Are you coming in?" She waves the gun, motioning me into the room, but not in a threatening way. At least not to me – Phearson goes even paler.

Jo hasn't seen Armand, as he was pressed against the wall behind me as I pushed the door open. I decide now's probably not the best time to reintroduce Jo to my evil friend. I flick a finger for him to stay put before

I step into the room.

"How'd you get in here anyway?" I ask, still trying to calm my hot Hunger. The final guard is tied and gagged in the corner of the room. He whimpers and writhes and it's all I can do to keep myself in check. Jo sees my discomfort and bends to whack him on the side of the head with her gun. He goes limp.

"Once I found out where he was moving to," she nods toward Phearson, "I stole a key off a maid and have been hiding here, waiting for him – and you – to show up."

Clever, classic Jo. Sneak in before the place is guarded. She's ruining the kill I've been planning for weeks – classic Jo again. My tone is ferocious. "A little convoluted, no? But of course, no challenge is too great to stop me from taking the life of an 'innocent.'" I wave at the sleazebag.

She draws back at the accusation. "That has nothing to do with it."

But I barely hear her. The soft *pant, pant* of Peter's breath seems screamingly loud. A harsh little sound; it's like I can hear each air molecule as it's dragged into his throat. It tugs at my attention, pulls it, drags it. Kidnaps it. My prey sits in his chair pumping the smell of terror into the room and the scents, the sounds, the expression on his face is mesmerizing.

Jo claps her hands and I start.

"Really, Jo? I'm supposed to believe you thought this was the most convenient time?" I wave around the heavily guarded apartment, to the three-hundred-pound man lying bound in the corner, the serial-killer rigidly stiff in the wing chair. "It's like you sit around coming up with ways to thwart me."

"Are you expecting me to apologize?" she asks in amazement.

I snort. "I'll come back with you, Jo, but things are going to be different. I'm not going to let you or them boss me around." I turn a feral face on Phearson, and his terror makes my shrivelled heart swell. "I eat when I want and not you – or anyone – can stop me."

"Meda, that's not why I'm here." Jo waves the gun in her exasperation and Phearson cowers.

"I'm not the Crusader's pet. I'll work *with* them, but not *for* them." My eyes are on Phearson, and my head weaves a little, side-to-side, in that snake-like way it does when the Hunger takes over. "You can't save him, Jo," I whisper, but it's more for Phearson's sake than Jo's. For my sake, really, so that sweet scent of fear ratchets up until it's all I smell.

"Dammit Meda, I'm not here to save Phearson," Jo snaps, frustrated.

I lick my teeth, glass-smooth and sharp and Phearson screams behind his gag. "Prove it," I say taking a sliding, creeping step towards him.

Jo lifts her arm and shoots Phearson three times in the chest.

Holy shit!

He jerks, and lets out a startled, strangled scream

that ends in a gurgle. I can only imagine the look on my face when I turn to Jo. It must be spectacular, because even recent homicide doesn't stop her from snorting when she sees it. She lowers the gun and, if it weren't for the smog of gunsmoke burning my nose, I wouldn't believe what I'd just seen.

No, scratch that. I still don't believe it. I'm too shocked to even leap for the soul as it pours from his carcass.

"Now that you're paying attention," she says, sharply-sweet. "Maybe you'll listen. I didn't come here to save him."

I can't… I don't… I nod.

Jo's tone becomes deadly serious. "I came to save you."

"What the hell are you talking about?" I sputter.

Her words come quickly. "If you turn yourself in, we can convince the Crusaders to not punish you as harshly. It's the only way."

The Crusaders. Of course. I snort. "Lower my prison sentence for good behavior?"

"Prison sentence?"

"Yeah. You can't say the Crusaders are real happy with me right now."

"Meda, they aren't going to put you in prison." Her words come out slowly, as if they are almost gagging her.

"Nice try, Jo. I hardly bet they'll hail me as the prodigal daughter."

Jo's eyes are enormous in her drawn face. "No, no Meda." Her words pour out quickly, and the panic in her face finally sinks in. Her words stumble over themselves, and they don't really make sense. "Meda, the Corporates… Meda, they've been looking for an excuse for months. I couldn't tell you, I should have, I know now, but I didn't then… I'm so sorry… and when you stole the Beacon Map and ran away, you gave them what they were looking for."

The hair on the back of my neck rises. I've never seen Jo like this. "Jo, calm down, you're not talking sense."

Her runaway train of words comes to a ragged halt. She swallows.

"Meda," her voice is forced-calm. "You're to be killed on sight."

TWENTY-SIX

I'VE HAD MY share of surprises in life. Discovering my need to eat people. Learning my father is, literally, the embodiment of evil. Finding out Mom was some kind of superhero, and, only slightly less shocking, that she had a secret, long-distance boyfriend.

And yet, they all suddenly fade compared to this new knowledge that I'm being hunted by the very people I thought would keep me safe – the good guys, the elite society I still somehow thought I would become a member of. My response is as eloquent as I can manage under the circumstances.

"Gah-huh?" Try not to judge.

Jo sounds calmer, but I can't focus on her face. Panic has made the room go fuzzy. "They haven't followed me," she says, her hands out-stretched like she's calming a wild animal. "They don't know I know."

"Gaaaaah?" I might be sick.

She talks rapidly, probably trying to get it all out

before I faint. "You're a threat, Meda. The Corps have always thought so – they've wanted to take you out from the start. And with how badly the war is going…" She makes a frustrated sound. "It's not *fair*. The demons just get reborn if we don't purify them and, in these battles, there's just not time. We lose more and more people each week, while they–" she waves her hand in the air, off topic. "Anyway, when they saw what you could do magically – and that you couldn't be controlled through possession – the Corps started to convince the other chapters that you're too dangerous to let live."

My mouth just dangles open.

"The Sarge has been standing up for you, but once you ran away… And the Beacon Map, Meda? You stole the Beacon Map! What the hell were you thinking?"

The Corps wanted to take you out from the start. My brain is catching up. "Wait," I cut her off. "How long have you known the Corps wanted to kill me? Since before I left?"

Her compressed lips are all the answer I need.

"Why didn't you tell me?" The implications of what she's saying are becoming clear. Panic is making my mind whirl. They have the Beacon Map, they want to kill me, I'm going to die, I'm going to die, I'm going to die. "You don't think I should have been told that they were planning to execute me?"

"I begged you to behave, Meda. Why do you think

I was all over you? Like I care if you punch the crap out of Isaiah. They were all watching you, looking for any justification–"

"I thought I'd be sent to detention, not the guillotine!"

Jo's mouth tightens. "I should have told you. I see that now."

"You think?"

She sticks her chin up. "I'd planned to, the night you left."

When she came to my room and left the key. This all could have been avoided if I'd just stayed put and listened to her. I want to punch myself in the face. Her, too.

And every bloody-damn Crusader on the whole bloody-damn planet.

"And I'll tell you everything from now on." Her tone is solemn. An oath. "I promise. Perfect honesty."

"But why didn't you tell me?"

She doesn't like what she's about to say, but she did just promise honesty. "I wasn't sure how you'd react."

"What's that supposed to mean?" It hits me. "You doubted my loyalty? Not three months ago *I almost died for you.*"

"No," she says quickly. "I don't doubt your loyalty – to me. But your loyalty to the Templars?" She sticks up her chin, unafraid, as always. "Yes, I was worried. Can you honestly, *honestly* say for sure that you're loyal to the Crusaders? That you wouldn't have freaked out, run away or taken some kind of revenge if you'd known they were considering your... elimination?"

Seeing as I ran away, stole the Beacon Map, almost killed Jo, and now stand over the body of a planned homicide, a believable defense isn't quick to appear on my tongue.

And, besides, that's only the half of it.

Fortunately she keeps talking. "Look, I know how they treated you, I saw it, and you had a hard enough time dealing with it. Would it have made it easier if you had known that even those in charge didn't want you there? That, in fact, some of them wanted you dead? I don't like everyone who's a Crusader, and I certainly can't say we never make mistakes. But our mission is important, vitally important. Despite all their flaws—"

Which currently include wanting me dead.

"—the alternative isn't an option." She finally takes a breath. "Giving up and letting the demons win."

She finally pauses and I open my mouth, then shut it. Perfect honesty, she'd said. I think of my state of mind when I left. I think about what I almost did. "I don't know," I finally say.

She has no idea what I'm talking about.

I clear my throat. "Whether I'm loyal to the Crusaders. I don't know."

She smiles slightly. "I do. You are, Meda. You'd never hurt us, hurt *me*, like that."

I think now about her constant strain. Her weight

loss. Her reaction when I made that joke about being tired of everyone trying to kill me. The tightrope she walked for weeks trying to keep me alive. And I did everything I could to make it as hard as possible for her. She pleaded with me to behave, but I couldn't be bothered. She asked me a hundred times.

What do I say? What is there to say?

"How do you know all this, anyway?" The best I can come up with.

"I've been spying on their meetings for months," she says.

I blink. "Months?" I manage. How could she have been spying on them for months and I not know about it? I was there. The building was heavily guarded whenever they were in session – not to mention it was held on the fourth floor. It's not that I don't think Jo's a badass, but *I* got caught, and let's be honest – the girl's only got one working leg, and wasn't exactly tearing it up in S and C.

"I've been faking it." She must think that's some sort of answer. "My leg," she clarifies. "I've been faking it so I'd be allowed constant access to the infirmary. And so they wouldn't suspect me of being capable of scaling the building to spy on them."

"What?"

"My leg's fine, Meda," she snorts. "Well maybe not *fine*, fine, but no worse than it ever was. A little better, actually, I think. From all the physical therapy I had to do to keep up my cover." She shrugs like what she's saying isn't completely shocking. "Once I was in the building, I could leave out that third story window. Even I can climb a dozen or so feet, especially with that gutter..." She trails off, waiting for my reaction.

The truth explodes, highlighting the dark corners of my rotten brain with brilliant light. I thought she met up with Chi every evening – because that's what she wanted me to think – but instead she was going to the infirmary. Her failures in S and C were famous, so it seemed natural that she would need to go to the infirmary for treatment. Jo's a cripple, incapable of climbing a rope for pity's sake; they would never suspect her of climbing out a small window in a second-story stairwell, scaling the side of the building, and hanging outside of the fourth floor windows to spy on them. It's absolutely brilliant.

And utterly heart breaking.

I think of her humiliation in S and C. I think of the rope climb and how I ordered her up that rope and was so horrified when she gave up. The bullying from the other students because they thought she'd get Chi killed, the constant lectures from the faculty, being sent to the headmaster's office.

Being thrown out of the Crusaders.

And she did it all for me.

How did I ever get a friend like Jo? Not because I deserve her. I'm like a lazy man who won the lottery: completely and utterly undeserving, and yet without the grace to give the prize back.

My mom was able to pull the same trick somehow – catch me being bad and somehow make me want to be good. What is it about love, whether it be motherly love, or friendly love, that has the ability to devastate and uplift all at the same time? I don't think I've ever felt quite so small and so large all at the same time.

But I don't say any of these things to Jo. I don't know the words to give her, and she wouldn't know how to accept them anyway. It'd just embarrass us both.

So instead of demonstrating my change in words, I do it in action. Complete honesty she said, the least I can do is give her the same. And that means not sneaking around with the enemy.

Without a word, I reach out and swing the door completely open, revealing my monstrous compatriot. They're both completely taken by surprise, the expressions on their faces almost exact mirrors of shock.

Jo reacts first. Before I can even think to stop her, she swings up the gun and shoots twice, *pop pop*, dead-center of a shocked and frozen Armand.

As I stand there, mouth open, it occurs to me that, in hindsight, maybe I should have used a *few* words.

Twenty-Seven

I DIVE AT Jo, catching her around the middle, and tackle her to the floor before she gets any more bright ideas. She's not expecting it and yelps as we go down. I grab the gun and wrench it out of her hand.

"Demon!" she shouts.

"No shit! He's with me." Which she no doubt would have realized had she taken a minute to think before shooting. I keep her pinned and twist to check on Armand.

Please, please, please.

He's still standing in the doorway, which I take as a good sign, staring curiously at his chest and prodding it with his fingers. There's no blood, or smoking holes. Also good signs.

He looks up. "Appears I'm the kind of half-demon that can't be hurt by guns." He's amazingly calm. Then he adds, "Good to know."

I snort, then laugh. He laughs too. Apparently his

humor can't be shot dead either.

"I'm glad you two think this is so funny," Jo says, and gives me a big shove. I don't budge, and don't plan to, until I'm sure she's not gonna go homicidal on Armand again. "Get off!"

"Not till you promise you won't kill him."

She glares at me. I shift my weight so I'm sitting on her chest, forcing her air out with a whoosh. She growls – or would have if I'd left her any air.

"Promise me, Jo." I bounce up and down a little.

"Fine," she expels on a gasp. "I won't kill him." Then, because she can't resist, she adds, "For now."

Fair enough. Hadn't I only promised myself the same thing? I climb to my feet and offer her a hand up.

"Do you know what would happen if the Crusaders learned you were consorting with evil halflings?"

"Gee, I dunno," I say dryly. "They'd try to kill me?"

Jo winces. "Good point. But Meda–" Her eyes are worried.

"Give off, Jo," I roll my eyes. "He's a friend, alright?"

"Some friend," she eyes him nastily. He gives her a happy little wave, just to irritate her. "So this is what you've been doing? Going on a murder spree with this, this…" she hunts for a word, "spawn of Satan." An idea occurs to her. "He's the one who let you out!" She's triumphant at having answered a question that obviously bugged her. Then horrified: "He's been on school grounds. *In the school.* Meda!"

"That about covers it," Armand cuts in easily.

Not helping.

"Jo, calm down. It's fine. No harm done," I say, before her head can really explode. "He's on vacation," I add in explanation.

She looks at me like I'm an idiot.

"He's my friend," I repeat. I hold her eyes, and let her see what she will there. It seems to mollify her somewhat because she backs down a smidge.

She eyes him. "He looks like a creep."

I shrug. "He *is* a creep."

"Hey!"

I wink at him and they both roll their eyes.

"So what do we do now?" I ask to change the subject.

Jo's still eyeing Armand distrustfully. "*We* need to talk."

"Really Jo, he's already heard everything."

That was not the thing to say to get her cooperation. Her eyes spit fire. I give in with a graceless "fine" and wave off Armand. His lips thin, but he doesn't argue. "And shut the door," Jo shouts after him, just to be annoying. Jo isn't the only one who looks homicidal now, but he closes the door anyway, with a too-polite smile and a sharp click.

Once he's gone, Jo relaxes a bit. "Meda, you can't be friends with him after we go back – you can't even talk to him. He's the enemy – you know that right?"

She asks the last bit very slowly.

I do.

Really.

I nod.

She eyes me sharply, but seems satisfied enough. For now. "Well, I've got some good news. I think we can undo the damage your leaving caused. If you turn yourself in, and we show that you just ran away and didn't have anything nefarious in mind, they won't kill you."

"How can you be so sure? I mean, no offense, but they were willing to kill me before I ran away."

"We'll negotiate it as a condition of your surrender. If they won't accept your – our – terms, you threaten to go to the demons and take the Beacon Map with you. They can't risk the demons getting their hands on it. The Crusaders won't break their word once they give it," she finishes, matter-of-fact, as if negotiating against her own people, her purpose in life, is no big deal. I'm struck again by the weight of her friendship. "Don't worry, Meda, we'll fix this – but we need to do it fast, before…" She trails off, probably not wanting to remind me that the Crusaders are currently trying to kill me. As if it's something I'd forget.

So that's it then. Bye to my freedom, bye to Armand. Back to school, back to the cumbersome weight of being good.

But back to Jo, too.

"OK," I say. There's no point fighting it. I must

play for one team or the other; I don't get to be a neu-tral piece. "What do we do?"

"Well, first we retrieve the Beacon Map."

Easy enough. "Why didn't you bring it with you?"

Jo stiffens. "What do you mean?" she asks very slowly.

"Why didn't you bring it with you?" I reply, just as slowly.

"No, Meda." Her voice is too controlled, like she's trying to keep hysteria out of it. "Why would I have it?"

"Then how did you find me?"

"I followed the rumors of a mysterious superhe-ro murdering all the bad guys of Philadelphia." The hysteria has definitely crept in, and she flails her hands a bit wildly. "Next time you run away, you might want to try to make yourself a little less famous. Once I figured out you were in Philadelphia, I started scouring the news and heard about him." She jerks a thumb at Phearson's red-soaked corpse. In all the excitement I'd almost forgotten about him. "I knew you wouldn't be able to resist. I've been stuck to his side for almost a week, now."

Turns out I don't know Jo as well as I thought. I was sure she'd check the cubby. Fortunately, she knows me a lot better than I realized.

"But Meda, you thought I had the map… does that mean you don't?" The end of her question squeaks.

"No, I don't, but relax." I say the last part quickly, before she can have a meltdown. "I left it hidden at the school for you to find."

She does relax, the tension floods from her, leaving her limp. She actually almost smiles. "I thought you might have – I knew you wouldn't take the map off school grounds." The confidence in her tone makes me squirm. Jo takes another deep breath, still recovering. "So where is it?"

"Wrapped in the blanket in our attic cubby."

The color leaves Jo's face so fast I'm worried she might faint. "You're sure?" she chokes out.

"Yeah, Jo, of course I'm sure. I'm not likely to forget where I hid the world-endangering artifact."

Jo grips my hands like a vice. Her mouth opens and closes.

"Jo, what is it?" Now it's my turn to try to keep the hysteria out of my voice.

"Meda, that's the first place I looked."

No, no, no, no.

Don't say it, Jo. Don't say it. I squeeze my eyes closed, as if that will stop the words from coming.

But she says it. Of course she does.

"It's gone."

Twenty-Eight

Jo sits on the floor. Actually, she collapses. Fair enough. My own knees are a little weak, but I've got two of them. I remain standing, my knees trembling but locked. My breath comes out in wheezy gasps. I'm actually hyperventilating. I look to Jo. Last time she told me the Crusaders were out to kill me – you know, like five minutes ago – she was a calm reassuring presence.

It's not so bad, it's not so bad, it's not so bad.

She looks back at me, eyes monstrously huge. Then she vomits on the carpet.

That does it. I go ahead and collapse on the carpet next to her, put my head between my knees, and breathe.

I scrunch my eyes closed and pull my head from my knees, trying to think clearly. The Crusaders, an army of trained warriors, are out to slaughter me. Oh, and all of Hell, too, let's not forget.

Yeah. It's not so bad. Really.

Hey, I promised complete honesty to Jo, not myself.

Jo's making little rocking motions. "Oh, God. This means the demons must have it." She shakes her head, in rhythm to her rocking. "It's the end of the world. They're going to destroy the world."

"It doesn't. Someone in the school must have found it—"

She shakes her head harder. "I've been spying on them, Meda, I would know."

"Maybe not. Maybe they just didn't—"

"—mention that they found the most important Crusader artifact stuffed in the attic? It just slipped their minds?"

"Ah, no, but…" I stutter, hoping my brain will come up with a brilliant explanation for why the destruction of the world (and of course, me) is not my fault.

"Meda, if the Crusaders have it, where are they?" She looks around as if expecting The Sarge to pop out from behind the curtains. "If they had it, you'd already be captured."

"But if the demons have it they'd be here, too—"

"They don't know you're a Beacon, do they?" She shoots a horrified look at the door Armand left through. "Do they?" It ends on a panicked screech.

"No!" I wave my hands for her to keep it down and she takes a few breaths.

"So, as far as they know, that spot on the map is

just another Beacon. One of hundreds they want to take out." She's not really talking to me anymore. "That buys us time." Her rocking has ceased and she's in full-on scheme mode.

"Time for what?" I ask. Come on Jo, time for one of those brilliant plans you're famous for.

Any minute.

Come on…

Now!

Still nothing. My head goes back between my knees for more gasping.

What the hell am I going to do?

As if Jo heard my question, she grips my hand and answers.

Finally.

"We just have to get it back." Her voice is firm, with only the slightest betraying tremble. I pull my head from my knees to find her hazel eyes staring back at me. *We.*

"Jo, they can't track you. You need to get away from me before they come." The words come out without thinking. After I say them, I think about what they mean. I don't stand a chance without her. But with her, I still don't stand much of a chance, and she'll most likely die. I'd rather risk more of myself than risk Jo.

Mom would be proud, I think. Of course, why can't I prove my blossoming conscience in situations other than the life-threatening kind?

I still can't help but be a tiny bit relieved when

she snorts. "Really, Meda. Don't be self-sacrificing. It doesn't suit you."

"Jo—"

"Meda, I don't have a choice, anyway. When I snuck out, I became a traitor. The Crusaders won't take me back either, without the map." She closes her eyes. "Oh God, the demons… It will be the Hemoclysm all over again."

I'm worried she might vomit again. Instead she puts her palms to her eyes and presses them in. When she pulls her hands away she has the panic back under control. "OK. We just need to find the Beacon Map." She shoots me a look. "Before they find you."

There are so many "they"s after me, I almost ask which one. Then I realize it doesn't matter.

"Or destroy the world," she adds absently, then runs her fingers through her wild hair. "All right. So how do we figure out where they're keeping it? Then how do we get to it?" she mutters to herself. "It's got to be the DC headquarters — surely they wouldn't take it to a minor base…" She bites her lip.

And no wonder. She's suggesting we go into the demon headquarters, steal the Beacon Map, which I doubt is sitting somewhere obvious, and presumably make it out alive. Yeah, I'd say a lip-bite was appropriate. I'd go so far as to say it's an understatement. I remember the enormous maze of twisting tunnels, Armand's stories of the secret passages and hidden rooms he used in his pranks, the—

Armand. Armand, Armand, Armand!

"What is it, Meda?"

"Armand!" I squawk. "He can get us in!"

"Armand," she repeats, lunging awkwardly to her feet. "*That son of a bitch.*"

"Whoa!"

She rounds on me. "How do you think the demons got the map in the first place?"

"He wouldn't!"

She gives me *that look*. "Of course he would."

She's right. He totally would. The truth hits me like a sledgehammer, though it really shouldn't. The whole beauty of his and my friendship was its lack of expectations.

In the face of his betrayal, it doesn't seem quite so beautiful.

When Jo lunges for the door, I let her, and follow. When I make it to the living room, Jo's already laying into Armand. She's not a foot away from him, screaming into his face. For his part, he lounges against the back of the chair, pretending to be nonchalant. His white-knuckled grip on the couch gives him away.

"–and now, thanks to you, the Crusaders are going to murder Meda. They were her only hope of living in safety–"

"Not her only hope," he murmurs indolently, baiting her.

"–but you ruined it. You understand they're going to kill her, right?"

He snorts, and eyes her small, crippled frame contemptuously. "And you're supposed to be the smart one?"

She growls low in her throat.

"What reason would I have to steal it? I'd have had to turn myself in in order for it to do any good." He waves at himself as if to point out that he's still here.

She makes a disgusted sound. "You could be keeping it somewhere, hiding it for when you're ready."

Armand turns expressionless eyes on me, sensing my arrival, though I've said nothing. "And you? Do you think I did this?"

"Of course she does—" Jo speaks for me.

"If I wanted you to speak, I'd wave a treat in front of your nose."

"You mother-f—"

"Yes, actually, I am. All part of the job." His words are whiplash sharp and fast, delivered without sparing her a glance. His dark, unreadable eyes are on me. "Do you?"

"She—"

"Jo!" I cut her off, and she turns sharply. When she sees my expression, she bites back whatever she was going to say.

"Do you?" He asks again.

"I think you would do anything to get what you want." I want him to deny it.

"I've never lied to you about who I am." He says

it almost gently. Gently, but his eyes glitter.

"You'd lie," I say it like a challenge.

He agrees easily. "Yes."

"Cheat." I take a step closer. Then another, and another until I'm striding across the room.

"Yes."

"Steal," I snarl, more angry at myself than him.

"Yes."

"Murder." I hiss it. He agrees again. Then I clarify. "Or set someone up to die." Set *me* up to die.

He doesn't back down under my accusations. Instead he leans in, his big frame curving over me like a wave. "I would do all that and more." His tone betrays a carefully restrained ferocity, and I see in him, shifting and fluttering, behind his eyes the monster I've always known is there. It makes my breath catch, the beautiful horror of it. He doesn't try to hide it, if anything he leans in closer, filling my vision until he fills the world. Him and his dark devil's eyes.

He holds my eyes trapped in his. His long-fingered hand slides to my jaw, as if to keep me from looking away. "There is no limit to what I would do to get what I want."

I shake his hand off, shake him off, with a jerk of my head. "Then how could I possibly believe you wouldn't steal it?" It's just a question, just a rational question. Not a plea; I'm not begging. I am not that girl. "You said yourself; you'll need some kind of leverage to avoid being punished when you return to the demons. The Beacon Map would be just the ticket, wouldn't it?" I sneer.

He doesn't answer right away, but watches me with a hungry patience. Finally, softly. "How could you possibly think my safety is the thing I want most?"

I hear Jo gasp in the background, but I'm eye-trapped. I can't turn away.

"I know what it would mean if the Crusaders thought you stole it. *I've* never had any illusions as to what you mean to them."

I blink, breaking his hold, and look away so I can't be caught again.

"Do you really think I value my boss's good graces over your life?" It's just a question. Just a rational question. Not a plea; he's not begging. He isn't the type.

I don't answer, so he does for me.

"I don't," he breathes into my ear, the words just for me, though I've no doubt Jo heard them. "My motives are entirely selfish. You are absolutely correct; I haven't an innocent bone in my body." And there it is again, the dangerous violence, the monster behind his eyes, filling his voice with all the darkness of which I know him capable. "But I know what I want – and it's not you dead."

Our eyes meet. The moment hangs long. Finally Jo invades it.

"Meda, no." But it's weak. "How can you trust him?"

"I don't trust him," I say. Then I pause, searching

his face for answers. "But I do believe him."

"It has to be him," she says hopelessly. "Who else is there?"

He doesn't break his gaze away from me right away. Finally, he says, "Plenty. The woods were crawling with demons when we left. It was only a matter of time before someone found their way in."

"*What?*" Jo demands.

"You don't think they knew who Luke was? Your mom made a whole library of videos addressed to him. Attacking him was a trap, to find his home base. To find you."

"Why didn't you tell me?" Me this time.

"I care only what happens to you. Not your," he runs a sneering look over Jo, "friends."

"I don't care what happens to you either," she returns just as nastily. "Just so we know where we stand."

"Just so."

"Well I care." But neither of them look at me.

Great. Just great.

TWENTY-NINE

THEY LISTEN TO me long enough to admit that we should maybe not continue a loud, screaming argument at the scene of a homicide with a dozen or so guards at the door. We head back to Armand's place. Upon arrival Jo drags me into Armand's bedroom, leaving him exiled in the living room. It would have made more sense to use my room, but Jo's mama-bear rage doesn't allow her to stop and ask for directions in her mission to separate him and me.

Jo left Chi back at the school. He didn't want to stay, but agreed it would be better to have someone keeping an eye on events there in case I, or the map, were found. Now that she has found me, there isn't any reason for him not to join us. That is, reasons other than his almost-certain death, but that's never really bothered Chi. Besides, Jo and he have a pact where they're not allowed to exclude each other from dangerous situations. They made the agreement so Chi wouldn't baby Jo because of her leg, and I know Chi loves being able to turn it around on her. Jo, on the other hand, is not so happy. Her knuckles are white where they wrap around the cheap little burner phone. She clicks it closed.

"He's only a few hours away. I texted him when I realized you were making your move."

"Texted. Wow, Jo, you sound almost modern."

She wrinkles her nose. Then her face gets serious and she sits next to me on the bed. There's a long pause. Long enough for me to get nervous. "Meda, there's something I need to tell you." Her almost-gentle tone tells me what she's going to say before she gets the chance. My heart seizes painfully in my chest. "It's about Luke. He…" She doesn't finish the sentence, just lets it trail to a quiet death. She, too, must know the rule of leaving terrible things unspoken.

Terrible things left unspoken, like creeping through a dark hospital, the weight of my betrayal heavy in my hands, and yet unable to stop myself from approaching a friend's hospital bed. Terrible things, like standing in the shadows listening to the *k-shhh, k-shhh* of the machine that helps him breathe and looking upon a damaged face, sickly green in the glow of a monitor. Standing there for one minute, then two. Then creeping off, rage filling the tattered hole where other things used to be.

Terrible things like not getting to say goodbye, because your friend's soul is already gone.

Yes, all that is better left unspoken. Even to one's self.

I look out the window, but the black night offers no distraction from my memories. With Armand, I could hide in the blood and the guts, expend my rage on wicked creatures in dark street corners. I could bury my loss under a pile of frantically stacked bodies, steal some of Armand's contagious glee to patch over the hole in my own smile.

But Jo knows. And her wordless sympathy pulls liquid from my eyes like some kind of sadness-absorbing sponge.

"It's not goodbye, Meda," she says softly. "Crusaders never say 'goodbye'. Did I ever tell you that? Only 'see you later' because it's never goodbye. Not forever. Not for us."

We sit silently, pretending not to hear all the things we don't say.

Finally she clears her throat. "I'm sorry, but we can't leave him," she jerks her head towards the living room, rising, "alone. We don't know what he could be plotting."

I stay seated. "Jo, he's not our enemy." She gives me a disbelieving look, but I can tell she's as relieved by the topic change as I am. We're both more comfortable arguing. "At least, not in this. Besides, we need him. Armand's lived in the DC headquarters since he was thirteen. He knows his way around; he'll know where they'd keep it."

Jo shakes her head. "Meda, we can't tell him what we're planning."

"But–"

"We can't trust a demon!"

"We have no choice!" I snap, just as harshly. "What's our other option? Stroll through demon headquarters? Knock on doors? Ask for directions, perhaps?"

She glares at me.

"You don't think they'll notice when a Beacon walks right into their lair? It might take them some time to find me on the Beacon Map, but I'm pretty sure I'll catch their eye when we waltz right into headquarters," I add.

Her face loses color. "You're right, you can't come with me."

"No, Jo. I can." I say it in a totally faked calm. Absolutely, completely faked. "I'll be the diversion. But we need a plan – one to get us in and out with the map before they catch me."

She opens her mouth to argue, but closes it. She's nothing if not practical, and a diversion makes sense. The plan's already impossible enough.

And as for me, what do I have to lose? If we don't get the Beacon Map, I'm dead anyway.

"Jo," I say, sensing her weakness. "We need his help."

When she doesn't immediately deny it, I walk towards the door. Jo stands slowly after me and then, as if something occurred to her, she casts a look at the rumpled bed and all the male-things scattered around the room. "Meda, just how close are you guys?"

"What do you mean?" I stop with my hand on the knob.

"I mean, did you guys… ah…?"

"'Ah' what?"

Jo blushes. *Blushes.* "You *know.*"

A suspicion creeps its way into my mind. "Jo, are you trying to girl-talk with me?"

She gives me the evil eye.

"You are; you're trying to girl-talk."

"I just wanted to… get a better understanding of the situation," she says, too polite.

"A 'better understanding'?"

"Alright, fine," she admits grumpily. "I'm worried about the hold that… creep has over you. If you want to talk about it, I just want you to know I would listen. But never mind, forget I said anything."

"No, no, let's girl-talk," I release the doorknob, and grin evilly. Really not the time, but who knows when I'll get another window like this? "You first."

"This isn't about me. It's about you and that… thing."

"Na-ah." I shake my head. "Sharing goes both ways. You first."

"First what?" she asks sourly.

I wiggle my eyebrows.

She rolls her eyes, but she really must be worried

about Armand and me because she actually answers. "You know we haven't."

"But why?" I lean in like a giddy gossip.

"Not until marriage," she says primly, sitting far too stiffly.

"So get married."

"Don't be ridiculous, we're seventeen." She pauses, then quietly, "What if we change our minds, later?"

I shrug. "So get divorced."

"Ugh, Meda, really? And, anyway, Crusaders can't get divorced. Don't give me that look. I mean it literally. Because marriage turns someone into a Crusader, it's not something to be taken lightly – so it can't be. There are even limits to how far you can be separated from each other and for how long. Even if you end up hating the person." She shudders. "You're trapped with them forever."

I shrug again. "So then we'll just kill him."

"Meda!"

"Kidding, kidding." I tap my chin. "I bet God already has that escape-route covered, anyway."

She winces. "He does, actually. It's not… pretty."

I don't ask for details. I don't think I want to know. "Are there any booby traps to pre-marital sex?"

She narrows her eyes at me. "I should tell you there are. But no."

"Then why wait?"

"I am not talking about this anymore." She cuts me a look. "So did you?"

"No," I say shortly.

Her mouth falls open. "Unbelievable!"

"What, you wish I had?" I dig my elbow into her ribs, then pull it back before she tries to break it.

"Of course not! I just can't believe you tricked me like–" but she cuts herself off. Of course she believes it. And anyway she looks relieved that he and I haven't gotten that close. "But why?" She mocks me.

"Armand is one of my many arch-enemies. It seemed like a bad idea," I answer easily.

"Oh good, it's nice to know you still think some things through."

Now I roll my eyes. "I do, Jo. And it's that same thinking thing that's telling me we need his help if we're to break in to the Acheron and steal the map."

She whinges but doesn't disagree. Taking advantage of her weakness, I call Armand in. His gaze goes first to where Jo's hand still grips mine and his lips thin. Jo sticks up her chin and grips harder as if to prove a point. Armand's eyes narrow, and I tug – jerk – my hand out of Jo's and take a step away from her – just in case she decides to pee on me next.

She seems to have a hard time remembering that we need Armand's help.

Of course, when I step away, Armand smirks as if he won. Better not get too close to him either, especially as boys have much better range.

"Hey, guys," I say. They ignore me, too engaged in a staring contest. Jo's face radiates a blistering hatred, while Armand smugly smirks.

"Yo," I try again. Nothing.

I can't help but wonder who would win if I let them at it. Jo's meaner, but Armand has an obvious size and leg advantage. He's quite clever as well, and fairly sneaky, but I think Jo has a more developed killer instinct, at least where demons are concerned. She already shot him, after all. Armand kills for fun – he's more of a hobbyist. It's a tough call, really.

"Fighting out of the red corner, standing six feet tall and weighing in at one hundred and ninety pounds, this man is a half-demon known for disarming his victim with a single, blinding smile. From Washington DC: Armand 'I-Eat-People' Delacroix!"

Big breath. "Aaaaaaaaaaaand…"

"Fighting out of the left corner, standing at five feet nine inches and weighing in at one hundred and forty pounds, this woman is a black-belt in kicking ass and taking names. The reigning, defending, champion of the wooooooooorld: Jo 'Don't-Mess-with-Me' Beau-re-gaaaaaard."

I've daydreamed too long; they've crept in a few feet and are now actively snarling in each other's faces.

"Hey!" I say and clap my hands. They turn in sync. "Focus!" I step forward and shove myself in between them. When they still don't part, I lose my patience.

You want to know what has two thumbs and would win if a fight breaks out? THIS GIRL.

I elbow Jo hard enough to make her grunt and when Armand's smile widens at her discomfort, I give him a hard shove and he stumbles backwards, landing on a chair behind him.

"We have important things to discuss," I say now that I have their attention.

I fill Armand in on everything – hiding the Beacon Map, the fact that I am a Beacon (the look on his face is priceless. Apparently he didn't have me figured for a saint).

I wrap up with our plan – and his part in it. It's not like I was expecting a relaxed shrug and a "sure, we can do that," but his outright laughter is a bit too far in the opposite direction.

I glare at him until he gets himself under control. "You're insane," he says when he can catch his breath around his hysterical laugh.

"I don't have a choice, Armand. I can't fight off both the Crusaders and the demons. Not forever."

"You have a better plan?" Jo snaps.

Armand gets a calculating expression and, I'm not gonna lie, I get a little excited at the thought of another option. He opens his mouth, but then his eyes go to Jo and he shuts it. Armand looks to me and his eyebrows raise a hair, *I do, actually*, they say. He holds my gaze until I get it. It's the light in his eye, a gleam, that finally tips me off.

Hope shrivels and dies.

Join the demons. I can't fight both demons and Crusaders, and the Crusaders no longer want me.

The demons, Armand's eyes say, *do*. The victory in

them is almost painful. But then it fades, drains away like blood from a mauled corpse, as my eyes hold his. Maybe as recently as an hour ago I would have agreed with him, accepted it as inevitable. But things have changed. I've changed.

Jo changed me.

And Armand is now realizing it. "No!" he snarls, leaping to his feet, leaping at Jo. I'm faster and slide between the two of them, my hand on his chest, shoving him back.

"Armand, no."

"You can't be serious!" He shouts into my face. "The demons will kill you! And for what? The Crusaders? *They want to kill you, too!*"

"Be quiet!" I snap.

"I won't be quiet," but his tone drops a few decibels. "Not while you make plans to kill yourself. I won't sit back and watch."

"I don't want you to." I force a half smile. "I want you to help."

He jerks back and pulls at his hair, with a sharp barking laugh. Then he stomps the ground with a garbled swear and another crazed laugh. "Why?" He looks at me. "Why?"

But how can I explain it? Or rather, how do I explain it in a way he'd understand? I'm barely human enough to understand and I've had humanity spoon-fed to me all my life. Hell, who am I kidding – ever since I met Jo, I've been beaten over the head with it.

For all the things I have in common with Armand, this isn't one of them. Sacrifice, loyalty, love are all emotions on a part of the spectrum his dark soul can't reach.

I'm going to die, and yet I find I pity him.

"You can't mean it. You'll never make it," he says, but it's weak.

"I'm hurt, Armand," I say. "I thought you'd have more faith in my abilities."

"This isn't funny," he growls.

"You either laugh or you cry."

"Then you ought to cry," he snaps.

"I'm not the crying kind." I tilt my head. "Are you?" My tone is cold. There's a limit to the amount of histrionics I'm willing to tolerate.

He makes a noise of disgust.

"You don't get to make my choices for me; you can only make your own. Are you going to help me, or not?" I say it hard, like I don't care, but I definitely do. Without him, we're doomed. Or rather, more doomed, if that's even a thing.

He glares at me, and the thoughts fly behind his eyes. He's not loyal to the demons, not in the same way I'm loyal to Jo or in the way that she's loyal to the Crusaders. That involves an element of heart I'm not sure he has. But he is loyal to himself, and helping us is not exactly risk-free. If the demons ever find out he helped us, the repercussions would be deadly. It shouldn't surprise me if he decided against it. He is a bad guy, after all.

And still I wait, holding his gaze, and wonder at the things I see there. The moment grows long, and the emotion hangs in the air like a fog.

Jo cuts through it with a sneer. "He won't, Meda. What do you expect from a demon? He's not your friend; he doesn't even know the meaning of the word."

But I raise a hand and silence her.

"You're sure this is what you want?" he asks me.

"Yes."

"Then I'll do it."

"A loyal demon? Who knew," Jo jeers, and I want to hit her.

"No," Armand's voice lashes out. "It's predictably selfish."

"Yeah? What's in it for you?"

He doesn't answer, but his eyes are heavy on me.

THIRTY

JO CAN'T STAND Armand, but she doesn't trust him either, so we have to stay in the same room while we wait for Chi to arrive. Three. Long. Hours. The living room is filled with as much hate and as many barbs as one containing a teenager forced to endure a family night.

Armand keeps giving me Significant Looks and trying to talk to me alone, while Jo does her best to thwart him. I let her. She doesn't trust him; I don't trust myself.

Finally (finally!) the doorbell rings.

"Why don't you get that?" Armand suggests slyly to Jo.

"Why don't you?" Jo responds sweetly.

"You'd let me?"

"No."

Oh, for freak's sake. "I guess I'll get it then." Neither of them answer and I leave, muttering about idiots and bigger problems.

I check the peephole before pulling the door open. "Meda!" I'm yanked into a giant bear hug.

"Mmmooooff."

"Where's Jo?"

"Goooofmfi-key." I shove the gorilla off. "Good to see you too Chi," I say, but when he just looks at me expectantly, I jerk a thumb toward the room behind me. It occurs to me that this is probably the longest they've been apart since they started dating. Maybe the longest they've been apart ever.

He claps me on the shoulder and I lead him into the battleground.

The insults must have picked up again once the referee left, because they're both on their feet when we enter, engaged in the world's nastiest glaring contest. I make a note to see if the Guinness Book of World Records offers any prize money to its title-holders – I feel like we could have a contender.

When Jo doesn't turn at our entrance Chi wraps his big arms around her from behind. The first time he did that she head-butted his nose and crunched his instep before she realized who it was (which happened as he soared over her hip), but Chi's persistent and fearless, so she's used to it now and relaxes slightly against him. "Hi, Jo," he says into her ear. She keeps her death-glare trained on Armand, but it's ruined by the fact that the rest of her has gone limp.

Chi regards Armand, a little wrinkle on his forehead, then recognition dawns. "Armand." He releases

Jo with one arm and reaches around her to stick out a hand. "Good to see you again, man."

"No, it's not," Jo says frostily.

She speaks too late and Armand is already shaking Chi's hand with a sardonic smile.

Chi looks at Jo. "It's not?"

"No."

My sigh could blow a careless piggy's house down. "Welcome to the party."

"Meda," Armand finally looks away from Jo. His eye-traps are in full effect. "Why don't we give them some privacy, hmmmm? Jo can get Chi all caught up." His eyes bore into mine.

Chi's mid-agreement as Jo says, "Not a chance."

"Err, ah," I say, ever the clever conversationalist. "We should stay and, ah, help." I drop onto the couch, as immovable as a boulder.

Armand sweeps in to sit next to me. "Coward," he murmurs, but it doesn't bother me. Bravery has never struck me as a particularly desirable quality. "You can't avoid me forever."

He must have forgotten about my almost-certain imminent death. Just goes to show there's a silver lining to everything.

Jo takes the lead explaining (as expected), while Armand offers unhelpful side commentary (also as expected). I manage not to bash either of their heads in (unexpected!).

Chi listens, digesting the information, and accepts

our plan to use Armand's information to invade the demon headquarters with the lack of panic of a true optimist. Brave and suicidal missions are sort of his thing.

By the time Jo wraps up, the sun's starting to creep up the horizon. We all stand, and it's decided (by Jo, again as expected), that she and I'll take my room, while Chi bunks on the couch. Before we break, Chi gives Armand and me a *look*. "Hey guys, could we," he nods towards Jo, "get a little alone time?"

"Happy to," Armand responds instantly and tugs at my elbow. I throw on the brakes.

"Chi," Jo hisses and gives a pointed look at the two of us. "We can't leave them alone." Yet even as she says it she sways towards him.

"Just a few minutes. Five… no ten…" He slides her a look. "Make that twenty minutes." Then back up to me.

I don't want to, but Chi has this entreating look, all big eyes and charming adorable-ness. I have no idea how Jo has held onto her reserve. I hear myself answering before I make the decision. "Fine." Chi smiles like it's Christmas.

"Chi!" Jo tries again. "We can't trust him with her!" If she didn't want *him* and *her* to hear, she failed miserably.

"Jo – what do you think we're going to do?" I ask. "Spider-Man-climb down the side of the building?"

She gives me A Look. Fair enough, the idea does

have potential.

I groan like a child. "I promise I won't go any-where. I'll be right out here when you're done." She makes a face at the suggestive way I say "done", but doesn't have time to push her argument before Armand sweeps me onto the balcony, sliding the door closed with a *schhht*.

I lean against the bannister. "Ahhh, nice and quiet out here."

"Meda."

"Hate to spoil it with a lot of talk. Silence is gold-en, or so they say–"

"Meda."

"So how about you and me get rich?"

He snorts. "We need to talk."

I accept the inevitable with ill-grace.

"How can you possibly think to go through with this? You have to join the demons. *Her*," he spits the word, as if it's the nicest way he can force himself to address her, "plan is insane."

"Because I love her," I say simply.

He starts.

"You're surprised? It's sweet that you think I'm altruistic enough to risk my life because it's the right thing to do, but I'm afraid I'm much more selfish than that." I pause. "She's my best friend."

"So you think half-demons are capable of love?" he asks, expressionless. "Or even full demons for that matter?"

"A little, I think," I answer thoughtfully. "But not like real people."

"You loved your mother, no?"

"Yeah," I smile mirthlessly. "Right up until I ripped her open and ate her." I catch his wince out of the corner of my eye. "My mom gave and gave and gave until there was nothing left. My 'love' was a pale reflection of hers; she blasted me with it and I sent her a fun-house mirrored version back. Same with Jo. She's given up everything for me." I shrug. "The least I can do is try to get it back."

"And that's not love?"

"Jo says love is about giving; that she gives everything she has to Chi, but she doesn't miss it, because he's giving everything he has to her. Demons, or halflings, could never love like that. We're takers by nature."

His voice is carefully bland. "Maybe the problem is that demons belong with demons. Because they're both takers. One takes from the other but she doesn't miss it because she's taking just as much from him. Like children with straws in each other's milkshakes." He pauses. "They would be as sneaky and mean in love as they are in everything else; but they'd also both be full and happy."

The air is heavy. I force a laugh to stir it up a bit. "I don't think that's love."

He doesn't return my laugh, but instead smiles wryly. When he speaks his characteristic lightness is back, though a little forced. "Sure it is. Why do you think it's called 'stealing a heart'?"

I snort. "Is that really what you called me out here for, Romeo? To talk about love and watch the sunrise?" I bat my eyes.

His mood sours. "I wish, but no."

"Somehow I didn't think so," I say with a sigh.

He glowers. "Astute of you."

I tip my head.

He launches in. "You can't seriously be thinking of waltzing into the Acheron, can you?"

"It's a good plan."

"No, it's a horrible plan."

"Fine. How about, it's the only plan?"

"It's not."

"Armand, I'm not going to join the demons. Not without at least trying to fix this. I'm a—"

"Good guy?" he smiles grimly.

"Yes," I say firmly. "And Jo and Chi are traitors, thanks to me. They can never go back to the Crusaders. At least not without the map. What are they supposed to do?"

"I don't *care*." He slams his palms on the bannister. "Whatever normal people do. Grow old." He laughs without humor. "Get fat. Have babies. Retire off their kids' inevitable success as professional athletes."

I'm horrified. "Just what kind of monster do you think I am? That I'd do *that* to the world?"

"What?"

I shudder. "Unleash Jo on it as a soccer mom."

That forces a reluctant smile. "You're right. That offends even my non-existent morals." Then his smile dries up. "The point is, they'll be fine. And you'll be *alive*."

"It always comes back to that with you, doesn't it? Nag, nag, nag."

He rolls his eyes. "I'm being serious."

"It doesn't suit you."

"Aaaaaaaaarg." He puts his head on the bannister and takes a minute before lifting it swiftly to look at me. "And what if they're wrong?"

"Who's wrong how?"

"What if the demons didn't take the map?" he says each word carefully.

That has my attention.

"As you pointed out, the demons aren't the only ones who want you dead."

I cock my head. "Yes, but the Crusaders want me dead because I stole the Beacon Map. It doesn't make sense for them to steal it."

"Doesn't it?" he asks, softly.

He waits, and I get it. Of course I do. Diabolical schemes are kinda my thing.

He keeps talking. "Some Crusaders have always wanted you dead, but they couldn't get the others on their side. Not until the map disappeared."

I close my eyes. It doesn't keep the words out, but I don't have ear-lids.

"How convenient for them. You're found missing, the map's gone, and they're proven right – it was foolish to leave you alive." His silky voice has a hard little edge. "There would have been a search of the school grounds. It would be an easy thing to find the map and not report it. Then, once you're out of the picture, 'Surprise! Look what I found!'"

I hate to admit it, but it makes sense. As much sense as the demons having it. Still, I shake my head.

"They'd do it, you know they would," he pushes.

"Whoever found it knows I didn't take it. They'd know I could have, but that I didn't. That has to count for something." Doesn't it?

He hears my unasked question. "You tell me."

There's no way to know. So it comes down to this: faith. Faith that the Crusaders wouldn't go that far, that they managed to find that slippery line between right and wrong. That their hate isn't personal; that it is, in fact, bigger than me.

And anyway, I don't have any choice – there's no way I'm telling Jo I'm siding with Armand. As I said, bravery has never been my thing.

He sees the decision on my face. He curses and grips the railing and shoves against it hard enough for me to pull back from it – just in case. Then he bends over, putting his head to it and takes a few deep breaths. He stands back up. In a tone that's half-anger, half-resignation and all sulk, he says, "Then I'm coming with you."

I'd expected him to share information, not to actually come with me. "It's suicide."

"Isn't that my line?" he says with a twisted approximation of a smile. Then even that sad thing dies. "But you're leaving me no choice." He barks a laugh and slaps the bannister again, like he finds what he's about to say is *that funny*. "Invade the Acheron." He shakes his head. "You understand it's a maze, right? Literally a maze. Where do you think your precious Crusaders got the idea?

"It's called 'the Devil's Anthill' – twisting hallways, tunnels, secret passages." He barks another laugh. "Secret passages that are constantly changing, by the way, and walls designed to appear like they curve when you're walking straight and vice versa. I can't possibly teach you the layout. Jo and Chi may make it, since they're going from point A to point B, but your options are limitless. And if–" I don't miss the emphasis he puts on *if*, "–you're right and the demons have the Beacon Map, the only chance you have to survive is if you know it better than you know your own hand. It's impossible." Then he leans against the bannister, facing me. "Impossible, that is, without me."

I don't know what to say. I expect it from Jo. I accept it from her; her nature basically requires it. If I wasn't involved at all, she would still do it, to save the Beacon Map from the demons.

Not so Armand.

"Don't worry Meda, I wouldn't be doing this if it

wasn't in my best interests. You can trust me for that, at least," he says, and I see in his eyes he's referring to our earlier conversation, where I accused him of setting me up to die. Then a wry smile. "And I'm not going to die for you. I'm not the kind. It's those two clowns you need to worry about."

"Why?" I whisper the word.

"I have no choice." His eyes hold mine and I know what he's thinking.

Do you know why good girls fall for bad boys?

Sometimes people are together because they can't help it. They don't have a choice.

"There's always a choice," I say.

His lips bend up but, again, it's not really a smile. "You don't have one. Not this time. Letting me come with you is the only chance you have to make it out alive."

I let out a shaky laugh. "That again." I stick my elbow into his ribs. "Nag."

"Lunatic," he says, and I hear a real smile in his voice.

"Look who's talking."

"Touché."

It takes waaaaay longer than twenty minutes before Jo and Chi come get us, but I don't mind.

THIRTY-ONE

WE SPEND THE next three days grilling Armand and be-ing grilled in turn. Chi and Jo memorize every possible route to the Beacon Map, and every possible way out – at least as far as Armand can describe it. In my role as a distraction, the number of routes I could take are limitless, more dictated by where the demons chase me rather than by anything else, so Armand focuses on the major tunnels and general layout, using the few places I've been before as reference points. He'll do his best to keep us along them as much as possible in case he… in case we become separated so I have a chance to escape.

Places to avoid – the dungeons. Just the thought of going back there makes me shudder, but it's also filled with anti-Crusader magic. Red doors are also a no-no.

"What's on the other side?" challenges Jo. "Some-thing the Crusaders aren't meant to see?"

"The gates of Hell."

That shuts her up.

"Literally. You won't be able to get through. At least not without a demon escort. They take humans Below to sell their souls. So unless you have plans...?" He raises his eyebrows at her.

Jo flips him off.

"The Gates are another layer of caves and tunnels, bigger even than the one we'll be in. It connects all the headquarters. The whole world, really, to Hell. So keep in mind that red doors equal more demons. They can travel through them. You can't."

I wince.

"You won't be able to use cell phones once we're below, obviously, but Crusader communication spells work—assuming you know how to cast them." He looks at us expectantly, but we shake our heads. His expression sours. "Zi's can speak directly into the heads of demons and some halflings." He looks at me in question and I shrug. How would I know? "Including me. So until they realize I'm with you I should be able to hear them communicating once things start going down."

I thought getting in was going to be the hard part. Not so.

"The Acheron was built to let demons out; they never had to worry about Crusaders getting in thanks to the interdict on direct attacks. Of course, that's changed, but even so, I doubt they blocked everything off." He smiles grimly. "Getting in is easy."

And here we are. Three days later, walking through a brick tunnel underneath a townhouse in Washington DC. Teleportation, I learned, works the same for demons and Crusaders, and they can use each other's portals. That's why the Crusaders never put them directly in their communities, even before the interdict was broken. The demons can't eliminate the teleportation spots even if they wanted to, however, as there are no physical entrances into the Acheron.

Chi and Jo fall back a bit and I hear the rumble of his voice and soft whisper of hers. I pick up the pace until I'm next to Armand, giving them some privacy. I wave at the brick tunnel around us. "Where did this come from?"

Armand flicks a look around the tunnel. "The demons possessed a guy oh, about a hundred years ago, and had him dig a ton of these." It's just wide enough for us to walk side by side and about six feet tall, with arched ceilings. "There are tunnels like this all over the city. A couple were discovered, but the rest are still open."

"Discovered by who? The Templars?"

"Well, them too. But, no, I meant them." He jabs a finger upward. "The world. A truck fell through one once, way-back when." Armand laughs. "They interviewed the Body," Body and Rider, I know now, is how they describe the possessed and the demon doing the possessing, "about why he did it."

"What did he say?"

"That he 'liked the exercise.'"

"You're kidding."

"Nope. But what else could he say? That he was possessed? That'd hardly make him seem saner. Besides, I think he'd already used that one when he was charged with bigamy." He makes a thoughtful noise. "Or maybe that came later."

"A tunnel-building bigamist? Where do you find these people?"

"Not me. It was like a hundred years ago. I wasn't even close to born yet." He reaches the end of the tunnel and pauses in his story to climb down a ladder that leads into another tunnel. "In any case, he was neither tunneler nor bigamist when Chaucy – that's his Rider – met him, but he was as good as anyone for building tunnels. He even had a bit of a flair for it." Armand runs his hands across a decorative row of white enamelled bricks. "But it took years to make them all and his Rider got bored."

"So he got married?"

Armand shrugs. "This was before cable. Or so he tells it."

I do a double-take. But of course the demon's still around. Why wouldn't he be? I reach up as we pass under an arched doorway and run a finger across the peak. "Was the… Body… an architect?"

Armand snorts. "Nope, an entomologist. At the Smithsonian."

I laugh. "A tunneling, bigamist, bug-studier?"

Then something occurs to me. "The Devil's Anthill?"

"It was his design."

"Chaucy's or…" I don't know the Body's name.

"Eddison's design," Armand supplies. "They became friends after a while. He even ended up divorcing his own wife so he could live full-time with Chaucy's."

"What happened to Eddison? Did he…" I point downward.

"Sell his soul? Nah. He actually became very spiritual." Wry smile. "Nothing makes you hope for the existence of God quite like meeting the devil."

We draw up to a dead end, a wall that appears solid but isn't. This is it, I know, without him even saying it.

Jo and Chi catch up, and I hear her snort. She points to an inscription in the wall. *Facilis Descensus Averno*. She translates: "The way down to the lower world is easy."

"So is turning back," Armand murmurs, but his tone is wistful. He knows I'm not going to change my mind.

Armand sighs, then slips through the wall to check whether the entrance is guarded, leaving Chi, Jo, and I to wait.

And to say goodbye.

Armand and I will be entering elsewhere. The only place I'm not going to go in the devil headquarters is anywhere near the two of them.

We all stand around awkwardly for a minute. I

hate goodbyes.

Finally Chi grabs me into one of his giant hugs. "Oooof." Seriously, bears have nothing on this guy.

"Good luck, Meda!" he says, obnoxiously cheerful.

"Mamdnsdff!"

"What was that?" he asks innocently as I jerk out of his arms.

I get back on my feet and straighten my shirt. "One day when you do that, you're gonna find a knife in your gut," I growl.

"No, I'm not," he grins, blissfully unafraid. "You don't use knives." Behind me Jo laughs.

Armand chooses that moment to pop out of the wall. "It's clear."

Jo asks Armand something and I murmur to Chi. "Take care of her."

"Always. And you take care of you."

I grin. "Always," I say and he laughs.

"You ready?" Armand asks.

Chi swings an arm over Armand's shoulder and pulls him around a little bit to give Jo and I a moment of privacy. We regard each other, neither one of us having the slightest idea what to say. There's too much. Too much between us, too much about to happen, too much at risk. If you know it's the last time you will probably see your best friend alive, where do you start? And once you start, how can you possibly stop?

"Well," I say, the best I can come up with.

"Well," Jo says just as awkwardly.

I clear my throat. "What do you say to a friend when standing at the gates of Hell?" I ask lightly.

"They're only the gates to the gates of Hell," she points out.

I force a laugh and she forces a smile. "Know-it-all. But good point. What was I worried about?" We trail off into silence again. I jerk my head towards Chi. "Take care of him."

"*Always*," she says in a way that lets me know she heard Chi and me just moments earlier. Then she clears her throat and sticks out her hand. "Well, good luck."

I grab it and give it a shake. "Good luck to you, too." Then, screw it, I jerk her into a Chi-hug. She yelps as she goes off balance.

"Mmmmasdf!"

"What was that?" I ask, just as innocently as Chi moments ago.

She shoves out of my hug. "I said, I *do* use knives."

I laugh, and she grins.

"Ladies, we need to get moving," Armand interrupts, thin-lipped.

"Right." But seriously, what do you say to your best friend when you stand at the gates of the gates of Hell?

Nothing. If it's your best friend, she already knows.

"Bye Jo. Chi." I turn my back. I hate goodbyes.

"Meda, no." Jo grabs my arm. She doesn't let go

of it when I turn. Instead she gives it a squeeze. Her eyes hold onto mine. "See you later."

I don't cry. I'm not the type.

"See you later, Jo."

It's a long, quiet drive across town. And we repeat the routine. Into another vacant apartment in the basement of a renovated row house, then down through the brick tunnels beneath. Armand tries to break the silence, but I'm not interested. We wait in silence, Armand's outrageously nice watch counting down the minutes.

Finally he turns and looks at me. "It's time."

It's time.

I turn and walk into the gates to the gates of Hell.

THIRTY-TWO

THE PROBLEM WITH desperate plans is they always sound better when you're in an expensive high-rise plotting with your friends. When you're sitting around a kitchen table, clapping each other on the shoulder and telling yourselves how brave you are, they sound brilliant.

When you're exhausted from running for miles and miles underground through the gates to the Gates of Hell, bumping into danger at every turn, they seem decidedly less brilliant.

When your partner turns and tells you that your one advantage, that he can hear your enemy's plans in his head, no longer exists, the plan sounds downright stupid.

It didn't take long for the demons to realize we'd invaded, but then, in our role as a distraction, we weren't exactly trying to be sneaky. Ever since, they've been hot on our tail, the moments of respite few and far between. Too few and too far between.

We dive through another doorway and pound down the hall. Armand's mouth is compressed, a slash across his determined face. He leans forward, over his feet, putting as much speed into his stride as possible. He knows he's holding me back; I'm far faster than he is. But without him, I don't stand a chance.

Judging by how close the demons are on our tail, it looks like I don't stand much of a chance with him either.

We cut around a corner and hit a twisted staircase. The steps are all at different heights, so I can't get a steady stride – damn demons love to be difficult. I have to watch my feet, leaping from one step to another like a billy goat.

We hit the landing and run down a curving hall. Armand pants softly next to me, his mouth now open as his breathing becomes labored. From what I've seen, he's as fast as any demon, but each group of demons is fresh while we've been running for what feels like hours. He catches me watching him and lifts his chin, trying to hide his weakness.

"Left, go left," he pants, and I see a gleam of satisfaction on his face, despite his exhaustion. "Tunnel," pant, "secret." I cut hard down a snaky offshoot, and Armand gains a sudden burst of speed and pushes past me. He suddenly dodges to the left, hitting a heavy wood door at full speed and shoving it open. It gives and he staggers to regain his footing. The footsteps are even louder behind us, and he doesn't bother shutting the door.

We're in a large library. The walls are round and spiral upward, at least three stories. A ramp with a wrought iron bannister wraps around the walls. Ancient books pack the shelves messily, with slips of paper sticking out here and there. The main section of the room is divided by more shelves and filled with tables and uncomfortable-looking chairs elaborately carved from black stone.

It's strange to think of demons studying, but Armand demonstrated his geekiness often enough, I really shouldn't be surprised.

There's another door across the room but Armand doesn't run for it. Instead he cuts around a set of shelves into a darkened nook. He reaches a shelf and starts tugging at books, frantically shoving them back when nothing happens.

"Tunnel," he gasps, still breathless. "Haven't used it in years. Let's hope…"

He's searching for a switch, just like in the movies. I start jerking on books as well, our hands blur as we frantically work down the shelf. The pounding of the demons' hard-soled shoes on marble grows louder as they approach the library.

"Come on, come on," Armand mutters.

We're completely cornered. There's no way we can make it out into the hallway now. I shoot Armand a frantic look, and suddenly he jerks a dark blue volume. The bookcase lurches forward, and a manic grin splits

Armand's face and I hiccup on a happy cry. Armand digs his fingers into the edge and hauls the bookcase open, revealing a staircase into a pitch black hole. There's a bang as somewhere behind us a door bounces off a wall. Armand doesn't hesitate, shoving me in and jumping down behind me. He's barely caught his balance before he spins to wrench a lever on the wall, swinging the bookcase closed. The little room falls into pitch darkness.

Armand's gasps sound smothered, and I hear him half stumble a step or two down the stairs. I wish we could rest, catch our breaths, but we can't. They have the Beacon Map – like sharks, if we stop moving, we're dead.

As if Armand heard my thoughts, he starts forward again, more cautiously. "Follow me," he breathes. I move down the steps after him, carefully sliding my foot out until I feel the edge of the step, then cautiously to the one below. "Bottom," Armand whispers in front of me, his breathing now under better control. Sure enough as I slide my foot out again, I don't feel the edge of a step. Armand moves forward, I can't see him but his feet move more confidently. I pick up the pace behind him.

"This leads to–" Armand comes to a sudden halt and I slam into the back of him in the dark. I hear his breathing pick up again and the shush-shush of hands running over stone.

Something's wrong, something's really wrong.

I slide around him, reaching out my hand, blindly groping in the dark and I feel a stone wall in front of us. Armand sidesteps, his arms moving even faster as he feels the wall in front of us. He then moves further to the right.

Please, no, please, no.

"No," Armand breathes. "No," he says again and feels along the wall, and I feel with him, our hands moving so furiously in the dark we bump into each other. The wall's only about six feet across from corner to corner, so it doesn't take long before we're forced to accept the inevitable.

"It's sealed," Armand whispers, and I can hear my own horror in his voice.

No, no, no.

Armand jerks and I hear the fleshy impact of his hand hitting the wall. "We're trapped." I feel him spin beside me. "We're trapped." His voice gets lower as he slides down the wall, defeat pulling him down.

I turn and lean back against the wall, needing the support. I squeeze my eyes closed, not that it makes any difference in the dark, but it makes me feel better. It makes me feel like I'm separate from everything. Like I'm not here, like this can't be happening. There has to be a way out. There has to be another option. I fling my arms out to either side, as if to double-check if the wall is still there.

Yeah, it is.

The demons move briskly around above us,

searching the library. It's hard to tell exactly how many there are, muffled as the sounds are by the stone ceiling, but it's obvious there's a large crowd. Over a dozen, easy. With the Beacon Map, it's only a matter of time before someone realizes where we are. Honestly, it's a surprise they haven't already. Then it's over. I can't fight them all. We are well and truly trapped.

I slide down the wall next to Armand.

It's fitting that the room is pitch black and cold, for it is a tomb. I can't see my hand in front of my face and I can't see Armand. No light leaks down the staircase from the door above. There's nothing but the harsh sound of Armand's breathing, his warmth at my side, and the pounding steps of our impending doom above us.

There's no escape, and we both know it.

I make a sound, one of frustration and defeat and anger and push my palms into my eye sockets, hard. Armand's strong arm reaches out in the dark, wrapping around me, enfolding me like a wing.

"I'm sorry, Meda." The words are soft, a hoarse rumble that I feel more than I see. But it's not his fault. I'm the one responsible for *his* doom, for being unwilling to accept the inevitable. This harebrained scheme was mine; I dragged him into it.

I wonder what the demons will do to him, once we're caught. Torture him for sure. Kill him, possibly.

But I don't apologize. Instead, I shake those thoughts away entirely. I haven't time for regret. It's my last few minutes alive, and I won't waste them on blame, even my own. Especially my own.

They say when you're about to die, your life flashes before your eyes, but mine doesn't. What a waste that would be; why think of all the things I've already done? Good or bad, they're already mine. Instead, I think of the things I want, the memories I've yet to make. As the minutes in our pitch black hole creep and sprint, simultaneously lightning fast and terrifyingly slow, I think of the adventures I'll never have. I think of birthdays I'll never reach, jokes I'll never hear. I think of growing old. I think of wheelchair races with Jo in the nursing home sixty years from now. I think of Armand.

When your wallet's stolen, do you think of the good things you already bought? No, you think of things you would have had. But unlike money, once someone's stolen your life, you can't get more.

I remember jeering when Chi announced to Jo, in the midst of demon-fighting hell, that he'd loved her all his life. But now I suddenly get it. When your life is shortened to mere minutes, it has a way of focusing your priorities. You're in the burning house of your life – what's that one item you're going to grab?

For me, it's Armand's hand.

His breath catches as my hand finds his in the dark. For a moment he does nothing, then he exhales and wraps his fingers around mine. It's warm, his hand, in the cold dark. Palm to palm, we're connected, and I imagine I can feel his heartbeat pulsing in time with my own.

I mentally laughed at my mom for her euphemism when she warned me never to "give myself" to someone I can't trust. But as usual, I'm an idiot. It wasn't a euphemism. She wasn't talking about sex – or at least not only sex. Turns out there's a lot of ways to give yourself to someone.

I've given a part to Armand. If he dies a part of me will go with him. It's almost fortunate, then, that the rest of me will soon follow.

But, still, I don't want to think of that now. I don't have the luxury. Instead, I pretend the world away. We're back on the roof of the school, sitting under the stars and daydreaming of blood and shadows.

The demons are still pounding around the room upstairs. I don't know how they still haven't found us though I can't help but be grateful. Each minute is a gift.

There's a long silent moment. "I'm sorry," Armand says again, but this time it feels different. There's an aching heaviness to it, a depth of pain and sorrow, and a mess of other things I can't even begin to decipher. I turn to him, wishing I could search his face, but of course I can see nothing.

I wonder if he, too, is thinking of our futures, and what we'll miss. We've always been alike, he and I.

I feel his breath on my face and know he's facing me. We're close, so close, and I think of another thing

I've never done. Not really. I lean in, and now I'm sure
I can hear his heart, hammering in his chest. Or maybe
it's my own. Or it's both.

Thump.

The sound from above makes us jump apart. The
demons are at the entrance to our hiding space. They'll
be on us any minute.

In sync we squeeze each other's hands, then
scramble to our feet. We work our way toward the
stairs, careful in the dark, and I press myself against
the wall. Our best bet is to jump the first one down the
stairs before he can make a noise, then get out of the
tunnel. We may find a way to run. Unlikely, but it's our
only shot.

And really, I kinda wanna kill some folks – my
other dying wish.

The fire comes, flooding over me. All tiredness is
forgotten, sadness and sentimentality swallowed, as the
violent Hunger crawls through my system, begging for
the red.

I will bathe in it.

My predator's eyes are on the ceiling, not that it
does any good, and they track the footsteps toward the
entrance.

You may find us, but you will regret it.

The footsteps come into the cubby and I crouch
as they move around the shelves. They reach the wall.

Any minute now, any minute.

There's a low rumble, a growl coming from my

throat. My eyes are fixed where I know the door to be. I will rip out his throat.

But then the boots suddenly turn away, and take a few steps in the other direction. *What? How can they not find us?* I turn my face toward where I think Armand is, hoping he'll answer, but he stays silent.

Then there's another loud rumble, but this one isn't from me. It grows louder and louder, and closer. More demons coming?

God, no, not more.

Angry shouting erupts overhead, but I can't make out their words. It's loud enough, I risk speaking. "What's happening?"

"I don't know," Armand whispers back. "Reinforcements?"

Damn.

There's an explosive bang above and I duck as the whole room vibrates, and dust rains down on me. *What the hell?*

Then there's no mistaking the sounds that follow: the sounds of battle.

"It's not reinforcements." I breathe. I can't believe it.

It's Crusaders.

THIRTY-THREE

I MANAGE TO contain my euphoric dance to a few fist-pumps and a tiny bit of tappy-tap running in place.

Armand doesn't say or do anything. I know he and the Crusaders aren't exactly BFFs, but this is good news. Maybe he doesn't get it. "Armand, the Crusaders are here!" I hiss.

He stays quiet a moment longer. When he finally does speak, it's slow and cautious. "But why are they here?"

"Who the hell cares?"

Armand, apparently. He still uses the soft and careful tones of a horse-whisperer. "Meda, the demons couldn't find us."

"So what? Armand, this is good news."

"Meda, if the demons couldn't find us, it means they don't have the map."

"Yeah. Still good news. Spit it out, Armand."

But he doesn't. He waits a beat, and in his growing

pause the crash and screams of battle rain down along with bits of dust and stone. A battle with Crusaders. In the demon headquarters.

Oh.

No.

I shake my head, not wanting to believe it. Armand can't see the horrible realization hitting me, so he continues. "If the demons don't have the map…" He doesn't want to finish and I can't blame him after the way I bit his head off the last time he brought it up. But he doesn't need to. I finish it for him. If the demons don't have the map…

Then the Crusaders do.

Why else would they attack the demon headquarters? They're badly outnumbered and can't afford the loss of manpower an attack on the Acheron would cost them. At least, not unless they have a really, really good reason.

Like, say, the last time – when a Beacon popped up in the middle of headquarters.

This time they know it's me, and they're not here to save me. Whoever has the map must have seen me in the headquarters and assumed I was siding with the demons. Why else would I come here? And they couldn't risk me joining the demons.

They didn't come to rescue me. They came to stop me.

And that means Armand's been right all along. The Crusaders betrayed me.

The Crusaders, whether it's Isaiah or the Northerners or both, or maybe other enemies I'm not even aware of, stole the map and hid it. They framed me, set me up to die. I risked my life and the lives of all my friends to help them, and they're not six feet above my head fighting for the right to kill me.

I'm not sure who I'm more angry at: them for lying, or myself for believing in them. No lie is more dangerous than one you want to believe; nothing burns quite so painfully, or shamefully, as misplaced trust.

Red spots enter the black of the room, and I realize I'm gasping for air. Armand stumbles over, groping in the dark until he finds me. I focus on the feel of his hands on my arms, his voice in the dark. "I'm sorry, Meda." He sounds like he really means it, but for what? Again, this is all my fault.

"I should have listened to you," I whisper. About so many things: that the Crusaders stole the map; that they wanted me dead; that it was impossible for me to be one of them. If I'd listened to him, I wouldn't have put us in the impossible situation. Now I sit in the dark waiting to see which side has the honor of killing us.

And it was all for nothing.

Oh, God. Jo and Chi are upstairs this very minute chasing a wild goose.

A creeping hotness builds under my skin, crawls into my head, burns along my fingertips. Hot, hot rage. Jo and Chi always accepted that they would die for the Crusaders, but I doubt they ever thought they'd die *by* them. They would do anything for the Crusaders, but did they ever believe it would come to this? That the Crusaders would betray them? The Crusaders have to know Jo and Chi believe I'm innocent and came to help me; whoever had the map has to know Jo and Chi are right. They also know Jo and Chi are now seen as traitors and will be caught in the crossfire. They could have stopped it.

They didn't.

I hope the Crusaders win the battle with the demons upstairs. I hope, because I want to rip them to shreds.

The noises above us grow louder and more wildly violent. The little room swells with the screams of the dying, the magical explosions, the cries of agony, and I feel a part of it. I swallow those sounds, swell with them. I pulse with hatred. I can't wait to join them, to show them what I think of them all. I pull myself back, forcing myself to wait. I will let them kill each other first, increasing my chances of survival. I need to save Jo and Chi.

There's another explosion from above, and this one was close enough that I feel the vibrations all around, even under my feet. I brace myself against the wall. The explosion dies down, but there's a rumbling, grinding sound that continues, and it sounds close. I curse the dark, because I can't see the new threat. The ceiling could be collapsing and I wouldn't know it. But the sound is not from above, it's from beside us.

Beside us, where the wall is sealed.

"Meda," Armand hisses, but I'm way ahead of him. I stumble toward the stone wall, my hands in front of me. I stretch, reaching for the stone wall.

It's not there. The wall has slid away.

The tunnel is open.

Giddiness swallows up the rage. Bloody revenge is all well and good, but it can't quite compete with survival.

Besides, my revenge will keep.

"Armand!" I barely get his name out before he stumbles into the back of me. He runs his hand down my arm until he finds my hand, and I let him take the lead, since he's been here before. I hear his other hand slide against the wall, and I slide my feet along the floor, as this part of the tunnel's as dark as the part we just left. We walk for probably ten minutes, but we haven't gone far as I can still hear the sound of the battle behind us, though it's a way off now. Armand moves slower and I can tell he's waving his hand out in front of him. He comes to a complete stop and feels the wall to our right. Then he draws back and slaps something.

The light, when the wall swings open, is blinding.

I blink, then squint into the room. Another library, this one is like something from England a hundred years ago: small, cluttered, and with lots of wood paneling. We're in a corner hidden by bookcases so I can't see the entire room. We pause, listening for anyone nearby. I release Armand's hand. There's a pretty good chance we'll need them free to defend ourselves.

When we don't hear anything Armand shoves the door – which I assume is another bookcase on the other side – open until it's wide enough for us to scramble through. Armand leads the way still, moving quickly and quietly. He looks around the shelves and must not see anyone because he moves forward, and I after him. The door is about thirty feet away, and Armand picks up the pace, running now. I dive after him – and crash into his back as he's come to a sudden halt.

That's soooo not good.

He shoves me backward with the back of his arm and takes a step back himself. I can't see around him to identify the problem, but I don't really need to. There's enough to let me know it's bad. I twist and take a leaping step toward the other exit.

"One more step, and I call down my minions," a voice calmly states. A familiar voice.

I stop in my tracks, though not at his words. Well, partially because of his words – I'm not exactly eager to have an army of demons called down. I stop because I know that voice.

I shouldn't be surprised. The way this day is going, I really shouldn't.

I force my eyes back open and rotate on the balls of my feet, until I'm facing our captor, who leans languidly against a heavily-carved table in another shelved nook.

"Hello, Meda," he says.

I sigh, then put on my most disrespectful face. "Hiya, Pops."

THIRTY-FOUR

"I WAS HOPING I'd get a chance to talk to you," he says pleasantly, for all as if we bumped into each other at a park – and hadn't tried to kill each other, oh say, four months previous.

"Weird. *I* was kinda hoping you were dead," I say, just as pleasantly. I sidestep Armand so I've got a clear shot at my father. There's no reason I can't make my dream a reality. He's only a single demon. I may not be able to run, but I can kill him before he summons the others. Or at least try. I don't have a whole lot to lose.

"No, Meda," Armand warns sharply. "Flare line." He nods toward a ring drawn around the table where zi-Hilo leans. I don't know what that means, but can guess from context. "He's a zi, he's got powers other demons don't," Armand adds in explanation.

So we can't kill him, and we can't run. Crap, we need a plan C.

Plan C, plan C, plan C. I casually glance around the

room and come up with nothing. Judging from Armand's resigned expression he hasn't either.

That leaves negotiation, and there's only one thing the demons want from me. "Let me guess," I drop my voice into the mockery of a man's, "'Join us or die!'"

My father's compressed lips curve into a thin smile. "And? Which would it be? You *are* caught."

Instinctively, I open my mouth to tell him off, but then stop.

The Crusaders betrayed you.

And worse, they betrayed Jo and Chi. Am I still really willing to die for them?

The answer is no. I'm not.

But I can't join the demons either. My mother. Always, there's my mother.

She sacrificed everything she loved for me, she sacrificed *herself* for me. She spent her life keeping me away from the demons, keeping me away from him. Despite my fury at the Crusaders, I can't side with my mother's enemy.

But that means… I swallow hard and feel sticky sweat prickle. It means I'll die, but not right away. They'll try to change my mind first, and they'll ask hard. And I don't know if I'll have the strength to say no. Moral fortitude has never been my strong suit.

But where does that leave me?

I feel Armand watching me, waiting for my answer, willing it to be the right one. He'll suffer right alongside me.

It occurs to me that, were I to side with the demons, Armand could play it off like this was his plan all along. He could say he befriended me, convinced me to come to demon headquarters, knowing I'd get caught… my mind runs away, playing the story in my head.

"Well?" my dad's voice intrudes, and I blink. I'll cave in in the end, my flimsy morals will collapse like a sandcastle under the wave of pain I know the demons are capable of delivering.

But I won't side with my mother's enemy without a fight. I can give her that much.

Armand's expression gives my father the answer before I can; he saw my decision in my eyes. He shakes his head like he can't believe it. "Meda, no. The Crusaders betrayed you–"

But I shake my head and stick up my chin. I fill my face with contempt and sneer at my father. "That's not it," I say. "I won't side with *him*." If that means a slow and painful death…

But I'd rather not think about that. Soon enough I'm sure it will be all I can think about.

"This is about your mom, isn't it?" Armand realizes. Damn how he gets me.

I'm gonna miss that.

"Meda…" Armand starts, but he doesn't know what to say. It's not like reason will work – my decision is hardly rational. I look at him and I hope he can read the apology I won't say out loud. I'm sorry I've dragged him down with me, but I can't do any differently. I can only hope he can figure his way out of here.

I won't die for you, he'd said. *You can trust me for that.*

I can only hope he'll keep his promise. "You promised," I mouth. I want him to do what it takes. I'm lost, but maybe he can work the situation to his advantage.

His mouth twists, he blinks hard, shakes his head and turns away.

"Your mother," my father says, and something in his tone turns my head. His face is tipped down and he's rubbing the bridge of his nose. He doesn't look like his usual Cold Magnificence. He appears, well, disappointed.

I can't say it bothers me.

"I think we need to talk about what really happened with Mary."

"Not a chance."

His jaw flexes, and he matches my snotty tone. I guess I know where I got that from. "In a rush? You do realize the longer we talk, the longer you live, right? I know a clever girl like you is probably working on a dozen different scenarios on how to escape." He stirs the air with his hand. "Surely staying alive – longer at least," a sharp smile, "is a crucial part of each of those?"

I don't like the man, but he does have a point. I cross my arms over my chest. "Ah, please continue. But maybe we should start with your childhood. Your mother didn't love you enough and all that." I raise my eyebrows and tip my head to the side.

There's a spark in his eyes. Humor, maybe. "When you do that, you look just like your mother."

My eyebrows slam back down, threats written all over my face.

"I *will* talk about Mary, and you will listen, or you will die."

I glare at him, but again, the man makes a compelling argument.

"Haven't you ever wondered how she escaped?" he asks.

My ears perk. I have wondered, but Luke refused to talk about it. Still, I shrug, pretending indifference. "I knew I had to inherit my awesomeness from somewhere."

"I let her go."

"Sure you did."

He narrows his eyes. "I did."

"Absolutely. Whatever you say."

"I did," he snarls.

"Why would I believe you?"

"Because he did, Meda." This softly spoken from Armand. I jerk towards him.

He glances at my father who responds with a wave and a mocking, "Pray, do continue."

"It's not a secret. When she escaped, everyone involved was… questioned. Remember what I said about memories being pulled from people in Hell? Demons, or halflings even, can't hide the truth Below."

"How do you know?" I demand.

"Everyone knows." He starts to raise his hands but stops and shoots another glance at my father. Armand clearly understands he only continues to survive on sufferance. "Once you were sighted, you were all anyone could talk about."

"Why didn't you tell me?"

His shoulder lifts slightly. "Would you have wanted to hear?"

My head spins. Zi-Hilo helped my mother escape? But why? I can't help it, I look to the one person who has the answers. "Why?"

"Because I was stupid, and young," he says, sardonically. "I helped her and she betrayed me. She was supposed to wait for me, but she…" He waves his hand in front of his face, as if chasing memories. "I am not the monster you think I am," he smiles his evil smile. "Or rather I am. But not to her. So if that's what's holding you back, it shouldn't."

It's a convincing act, but then, so was the last one when he tried to turn me against my mother. I cross my arms, a study in skepticism.

He lets out a long-suffering sigh, as if relaying the story is merely an irritation. "I was assigned to guard Mary, while she was our… guest. She needed constant watching, as she wasn't put in a cell."

I tip my head curiously. He obliges. "They wanted her to access her magic. To heal."

"Why?" I ask, but I don't think I want to know

the answer.

He regards me with dead eyes. "So they could try, again and again, to break her."

Break her. My stomach roils. I don't want to think about what they did to her. What, I realize, they're going to do to me.

"But Mary wouldn't break."

"And let me guess, you fell in love with her courage. Or was it love at first sight?" I sneer, the bile in my soul boils out my mouth.

"Ha," he barks. "Not hardly. I spent every day for seven months with her, and I swear she tortured me worse than they tortured her. She taunted me, ridiculed me, made me laugh." He says the three like they're the same thing. "And she'd talk, sometimes until I wanted to strangle her." He curls his fingers as if they could wrap around her neck. "She'd tell me…" He shakes his head. "Then sometimes she'd face the wall and not spare me a word. For days."

He brings himself back under control. "But no matter what they did to her, she wouldn't break." His voice is soft again, but not a gentle soft. An eerie, creepy soft. "She couldn't hold out forever. Or rather, I actually believe she could, but her body could not. She wasted away, starving. Dying."

He looks at me. Not in apology, never that. "I wasn't ready for her to go." He says it coldly, nonchalantly, with the non-sadness of a cat pawing the dead body of a vole it'd been chasing and pouncing upon for the past hour, still wanting to play. "So I fed her."

He laughs. "The expression on her face…" There's a flicker of something in his face, then it hardens. "And I took over her… questioning. I was nicer than they were." He snorts. "She wasn't grateful.

"It was her and me, alone together. And she played me like a bloody violin. Or maybe it'd be more appropriate to say she beat me like a drum." His expression turns vicious. "She made me beg for her words, for her attention. Until I couldn't think of anything else. Then they decided to kill her." He turns tortured eyes on me. "What was I supposed to do?"

Holy shit.

Never give yourself to someone you don't trust. Whether you mean to or not, whether you know it or not, you give them a piece of you they can break. The uncomfortable expression on her face I couldn't place. It wasn't embarrassment. It was guilt.

He didn't break my mother's heart. She broke his.

Don't think you're immune just because you're different.

Holy shit. She would bloody damn well know, wouldn't she?

"*She* seduced *me*." He holds up his hand, as if I were going to argue. I wasn't. I'm too horrified/shocked/flabbergasted – and all right, a little impressed by Mom – to do anything but stand there gaping. "She did. I thought it was…" He goes rigid. "But it was all a damned trick, to convince me to help her." The twisted smile returns. "I fell for it. She was supposed to wait for me." He shakes his head. "She left me to be interrogated, tortured. Humiliated. But I showed them. I showed every single one of them – and her. Before I was no one, a nobody. A fool." He smiles his razor-sharp smile. "I am a fool no longer." He waves expansively at his kingdom.

"Why are you telling me this?"

He steeples his fingers. "Because I want you to join us."

"And this is, what? Supposed to make me feel sorry for you?"

"No," he snaps. "It's because I know the kind of hold that woman has over you." He spits *that woman*. "Probably no one understands as well as I do." His mouth twists. "And I know you would never side with her abuser."

I don't know what to do with all this information. My head is swimming in it – no, drowning in it. The Crusaders betrayed me, but I couldn't side with my father because of what he did to my mother.

But what if he didn't.

Where does that leave me?

Once again, only Jo stands between me and my evil. Can I betray her? *Again?*

That was answered the day she dangled like a fool on that rope in front of the entire school. I can't. At least, not without a fight.

There's a crash from across the room and then muffled shouts. The tunnel.

My father cocks his head. "Crusaders," he offers,

with no sense of urgency. "They've found the tunnel."

"Coming to rescue me," I bluff, forcing a smile. "You'd better get going."

He snorts.

Eh, it was worth a shot.

He taps his chin. "What *do* you think they will do to you when they get here?"

Kill me, but I don't say so. For starters, because I get the feeling he already knows. "What do you think they'll do when they find *you*?" I ask sweetly, instead.

He ignores my question. "And what do you think they'll do to him?" He nods toward Armand, who stands stoic, his face carefully blank.

Kill him too. But again I say nothing.

"Do you really think you can escape? From me, from them, from the rest of the demons searching for you this very moment?"

My eyes dart to the tunnel where the voices have gotten louder. Something slams into the bookcase. "It's looking increasingly unlikely," I say, mimicking his blasé tone.

"And if you somehow made it past the hundreds of demons and Crusaders searching for you, what then?" He looks genuinely curious. "Do you think you can go back to them? Or do you just plan to somehow evade all of us, forever?"

I wince. He doesn't even know how impossible evading them would be, with me being a Beacon.

"I'm offering you an escape. The only escape."

A row of books fall from the shelf with a crash.

"Why should I believe you? How do I know any of this is true?" The look on my mother's face in the car that day says it's true, but is that enough? Or is that just what I want to believe so I can side with the demons instead of being tortured to death? There's no reason to believe my subconscious is any less of a liar than the rest of me.

"Your friend already told you I set her free."

"But the rest of it?"

"You think I would make up this, this…" he waves his hand. "I'm not the sort to brag on my failures."

"That argument only works if I believe you have shame." I aim for flippant, but it sounds a bit weak.

"Ha, no. I have no shame. But I do have pride."

I study his artificially-perfect profile. *That* I believe.

"I'm supposed to believe you set her free from the goodness of your heart?"

"No. It wasn't from 'the goodness of my heart'. It was purely selfish. I didn't want her dead, so I saved her. And before you ask, this isn't selfless either. I don't want you dead. You're mine." He sharp-smiles. "And you're still the most unique weapon the world has ever seen."

But I'd sorta focused in on the *I don't want you dead* part. "This *what* isn't selfless either?" My breath hitches as I say it. Hope clogging my throat.

"I'm not going to kill you."

I can safely say I did not see this coming. My head might explode from relief. I'm giddy to the point of fainting.

"Instead, I propose a little experiment. I let you live, and we see how long you last at the tender mercies of your Crusader friends." He then shoves off the table and leisurely strolls toward the door. "When you realize who your real friends are, just say the word." He smiles wolfishly. "We'd be happy to defend one of our own, but until then, daughter dear, I'd be wary. The other demons don't share my fatherly affections."

So we're still caught between the two armies, but, hey, we aren't dead yet. The Crusader's mantra floats through my head: *Dum spire spero*. In life, hope.

My father slides through the open door and a wicked smile bends his lips. "Let's start now, shall we?" With that he snaps the door closed and I hear the lock slam into place – trapping us in a room with an invading Crusader army.

So much for fatherly affection.

THIRTY-FIVE

I DIVE AT the door and rip at it for all I'm worth. But of course, dear daddy would have prepared for that, and it doesn't budge. "Armand, where's another exit?"

Armand's only answer is to slam his body into the door.

A massive explosion nails the bookcase across the room. I can't see it from where I stand, but I do see books soar across the room from the force of the explosion.

"Armand, this isn't working!" Panic makes my voice crack. "They're going to be here–"

As if to prove me right, there's another crash.

"We have to hide." He spins, frantically searching the room.

As for me, I'm paralyzed – not with indecision, never that, but with futility. "We can't hide, they have the map."

Breathe, Meda. *Think*.

Armand ignores me, still searching for a place to hide. Suddenly he freezes and takes off, hauling me with him. His plan to hide sucks, but I don't have any better ideas.

At least not until I realize the idiot is taking us *toward* the Crusaders. I slam on the brakes, but he jerks a finger upward, toward the shadowy gap between the top of the shelves and the ceiling. Not a hiding spot, an ambush.

Armand lets go and I scramble up the shelves. Another explosion almost shakes me loose but I manage to stay on and haul myself the rest of the way. I reach the top, and slide into the skinny place on my belly. I get myself turned around just as another explosion hits the wall and I hear Armand grunt. I lean over to see that he's lost some ground. Another explosion, and suddenly the Templars' voices are no longer muffled.

Armand's legs are tucked up under his chin and he's pressed as flat as possible to the shelving. On the ground below is a pile of books and debris.

The Crusaders have broken through – and the hole is right where Armand's feet were. His expression is filled with profanity.

I slide over the side and stick my hand down as far as I can reach just as another explosion hits the wall and more of it collapses. Armand reaches up, but there are still several feet between our hands. The first Crusader, one I don't recognize, charges from the hole and Armand leaps. I catch him and haul him up into the gap with me.

Armand's and my eyes are huge as we look at each other. We're wedged into the tiny space in a tangle of arms and legs. Below us, Crusaders barrel out of the tunnel.

We don't have much time before they realize where we are. If we want the element of surprise we need to move fast, before whoever has the Beacon Map informs them we're right there. I think I could take two, possibly three before they realize they're under attack. Armand might be good for two, but it's unlikely. There's not enough space in the nook below for many Crusaders to be within striking distance before we lose the element of surprise.

On the bright side, that means there won't be much room for a large group to manoeuvre, they'll have to come at us only a few at a time. Armand and I have been killing together for months, we're perfect partners. If there aren't too many, maybe we have a chance.

I listen carefully, trying to gauge when the last one leaves the tunnel. The last thing we want is to be surrounded once we start our attack. Fortunately the Crusaders aren't bothering with stealth. It'd be pointless after the explosions they used to get free of the tunnel. I hear the words, the voices, but I try not to. I don't want to recognize any.

What if it's Chi's sister?
Or The Sarge. She's got to be here somewhere.

 I shake my head. *They betrayed you.*

I call the rage, the blind Hunger.

The desperation.

I have no choice. It's our only hope.

I ease away from Armand, careful not to let any part of me drift out into the open. I lay flat on my belly, my head near his. Still I hear footsteps in the tunnel. Bad for so many reasons. They're going to figure out we're here.

And there are a lot of them.

I slide a little closer to the edge. The wait is killing me, crushing me. Finally, *finally*, I don't hear more steps from below. I can't be sure, not without looking and risking my position. I tense, preparing to launch head first into the fray. The first thing that moves, dies. A quick anonymous kill.

Think of what they're here to do, Meda. It's you or them. Armand or them.

Jo and Chi.

Betrayal.

The world reddens. The heat creeps out under my skin.

Still, I hear no more footsteps from the tunnel.

It's time. I lunge.

Armand's hand on my arm jerks me back. I growl at him, low, in my throat. It's nothing to him, killing Crusaders, but I need to ride this heat. He jerks a finger to his mouth in a "shhhh" and points at his ear. "Listen," he mouths.

"Get us through this door. Now," a Crusader says, and there's an explosion from the door my father sealed.

"Sarge says to circle back. Raider squad is pressed." Another one clips.

It's not about us; they still don't realize we're here.

I look at Armand, and he gives a tiny shrug.

I'm too shocked to move, but then it's all I can think about. I don't know how we were saved, but we are. I don't stop to think about it – I haven't the time to waste looking this gift horse in the mouth. Besides, it sounds like a good way to get bit.

I stick my head over the edge. A Crusader guards the tunnel, but his back is to us – and the tunnel – as they watch the activity at the door.

"It's magical. Our blasts aren't making a dent," someone says.

I look at Armand and point down to the tunnel. "Let's go."

He gives an urgent little shake of his head.

Yeah, it's not exactly risk-free, but I don't know how long our good fortune – and the Crusader's incompetence – will last. We can't just sit here. I don't argue with him; I silently slide a leg over the side and start down without him. The last thing I see as I duck over the side is him frantically shaking his head.

Without me, there's no reason he couldn't remain hiding indefinitely, so when I see his boot stick out over the side, I almost breathe a sigh of relief.

Almost. There are, after all, about twenty Crusaders standing not thirty feet away.

I ease onto the floor, carefully picking spots clear of noisy debris, and slide silently into the tunnel, sinking into the shadows. I creep down the stairs, then wait, breath bated, until Armand appears at the top of the stairs.

When he reaches the bottom a grin cracks across his face.

I cannot believe we pulled that off.

I use the celebratory energy boost to start running again. We still have two hostile armies between us and escape, but, hey, you gotta celebrate the little victories, right? And the demons' not having the map helps us, as it looks like even with the map the Crusaders somehow still have a hard time finding us.

I jerk to a halt.

The demons don't have the map.

Armand turns at my stop, confusion all over his face.

The demons don't have the map, but Jo doesn't know that. When it's not where it's supposed to be, she'll keep looking. She won't accept failure, not with so much at stake: the Beacon Map. My life.

Jo will never give up on me, and I can't give up on her. I have no choice.

I turn to Armand. "We have to find Jo and Chi."

THIRTY-SIX

ARMAND SERIOUSLY CONSIDERS knocking me unconscious and carrying me out over his shoulder, but he knows I know what he's thinking, and he knows I can kick his ass. He opens and closes his mouth a few times, a futile gasping like a fish on dry land, then shakes his head in a few frustrated jerks. He looks like he's about to explode from all the things he wants to shout.

He manages a growled, "We don't even know where they are by now."

I shrug. "We'll start with where you told them the map would be, and take it from there." What else can we do?

"They could be dead for all we know!"

True. But what else can we do?

He shakes his head again. I should tell him to save himself, that I can do it on my own. I'm not entirely sure where I am, but I do know the part of the map that Jo and Chi had to memorize. I'm not completely hopeless.

But I'm pretty damn close.

If I were talking to Jo or Chi I would probably propose that they leave and save themselves. I still wouldn't mean it of course, but offering would be the right thing to do. They would be too good to accept, even if they wanted to, and would come with me anyway. But I don't have to say the right things to Armand. I want him with me; my chances are better with him. And he doesn't need my permission to leave. If he doesn't want to help me, no honor will keep him at my side.

He wouldn't be here with me, if he didn't want to be.

"There!" someone shouts and Armand and I twist at the same time.

Crusaders, in the tunnel.

"Dammit," I curse, more at myself than at anything else, and take off running, Armand at my side. We underestimated the Crusaders incompetence – they must have been unable to unseal the door. Why the hell did we stop running to argue? Like I can't argue and run at the same damn time?

A holy water globe explodes against the wall to our left, and this time Armand curses. Another holy water globe comes whizzing by, right past my head and explodes on the floor ahead of us. I leap over the spill. We cut around another bend and I'm grateful that, at least for now, we're out of sight of any missiles.

We reach the stairs up to the black library and practically leap up them, then across the library and back out into the hallway, the Crusaders hot on our heels. We're faster, and at several turns they hesitate, listening to figure out which way we've gone.

We start to put a tiny bit of space between us. Then we hit a straightaway, and suddenly the holy globes start flying again. We duck and weave, trying to become harder targets. A globe explodes on our left and Armand yelps. I shoot a look at him over my shoulder. His face is tight with pain and he cradles his arm in front of him. It's blistered, raw and bleeding profusely as, acid-like, the water eats through his skin.

Our eyes meet, but he says nothing, just keeps running.

Fortunately, the hall starts to snake again and we get a reprieve from the globes, though not from the pounding of their feet behind us.

Armand grunts something, but I can't make it out. I slow a half-step. "What?"

"I can't keep up much longer."

"Yes, you can." We turn hard.

"Maybe, just maybe, I could get us out of here." He grunts as we hit a staircase and start down its uneven surface, each step jarring. He loses his balance and rocks into the wall, leaving a bloody smear. "But I can't…"

He's panting too hard to speak. Before he can catch his breath we come around a bend and hear the sounds of battle in front of us. We backpedal then turn to slide down a rounded tunnel, more like a chute, really. We slide on our butts and shove off with our arms. At least I do, he's handicapped by his injury.

Voices echo in the tunnel behind us. Damn. I was hoping they'd be distracted by the battle sounds.

I hit the bottom and hold out my hand. He grabs it with his good one and I haul him out of the tunnel. He pauses, just for a second and looks at me. He doesn't say what we're both thinking. That he's slowing me down. That he's a liability.

That he needs my help if he's to escape.

That I have to choose between rescuing him or Jo and Chi.

He doesn't say any of that, and I don't say it either. But he knows. He releases my hand. "I can get you to the arena. At least you'll know where you are, then." He takes a breath, tucks his injured arm against his chest and starts moving again.

"You're coming with me if I have to drag you." It's not hyperbole. It may come to that.

He doesn't argue, but saves his breath for running. Blood loss makes him dizzy and I have to support him, which slows us both. He pulls off his shirt and wraps it around his arm, but it soaks through, leaving a trail of blood for our pursuers. Rescuing Chi and Jo is becoming a pipe dream. I'm not going to be in a position to save anyone soon.

Finally a grey-faced Armand smiles grimly. "The

arena." He nods ahead towards a beautiful set of arched doors, carved and painted in beautiful jewel-tones. We both pick up our pace, hope making us faster. We explode through the doors.

It's like running back into my worst nightmare. It's just as I remember it, down to the stone posts where Chi and Jo were chained, though there's only one this time. The sight makes me stumble. I wonder how recently a Crusader was chained there and tortured.

I wonder if it was someone I knew.

Armand gasps beside me. "Demons."

"What? Where?" I twist.

He shakes his head, bent over his arm and gasping. "The post. Demons are chained there too, for punishment. A lot more often than Crusaders." Armand doesn't wait for my reaction, but twists and slams one of the doors we just came through. I shake off my stupidity and leap for the other. He moves to the side and starts, one-handed, pulling down a heavy gate.

"No, go." He grunts. "You're faster – check to make sure it's clear."

"No," I say. "You're coming with me." As slow as he is, if anyone needs a head start, it's him. I reach to pull down the gate, but he shoves me off.

"I need a chance to catch my breath," he pauses, gasping, as if to make his point. "Let me do this, while you check–"

I don't make him finish. I didn't want to see it, but it's obvious. He can't keep running. He's right.

I curse hard, but do as he suggests. I know from his description that there's only one other exit from the arena – the tunnel I came through the last time I was here. It's sealed with a steel door this time – to keep the participants from having anywhere to hide, probably – and I jerk it out of the way and take off down the tunnel.

I don't know how much further Armand can go. He might be better off without me – without a Beacon leading the Crusaders right to him. If the demons catch him, he'll be punished. I can't think of what that would mean, what it would entail, him at their mercy. They do have a rule against killing their own, only I don't know how absolute that rule is. Still, Armand is smooth and clever. Maybe he'll be able to talk himself out of a death sentence. At least without me, he could hide from the Crusaders. At the Crusader's mercy he would have no chance.

The Crusaders couldn't find you before, maybe they won't again, a hopeful little part of me whispers, the part that can't face leaving Armand behind. But the rational part of me knows I can't bank on being that miraculously lucky again. My mind whirls furiously, seeking options, seeking escape like a rat trapped on a sinking ship. *Maybe, we'll get lucky again. Armand seemed confident we could continue hiding from them in the library.*

I reach the end of the little hallway and jerk the door open.

Then stop, frozen in horror.

No, no. It can't be.

Please, no.

I slam the door closed, and race back down the tunnel. Back to Armand. He pushes off the wall he's slumped against as I enter. "Demons!" I shout. "Demons coming the other way!"

I am sick. Sick to death as I say it. "We're surrounded."

THIRTY-SEVEN

I SPIN AND slam the door, locking it. Before I even turn back around, the room echoes with the sound of the Crusaders slamming into Armand's door. There's no exit back that way. Not that I deceived myself into thinking there was. The gate's in place, so once they break through the doors they'll have to get through it as well. But it only buys time, nothing more. They'll get through eventually, I know.

Armand knows it too. "You have to join the demons, Meda. It's the only way."

I shake my head, but it's not so much in response to him as it is to the truths attacking me now.

"Meda, please." He strides forward and grasps my hands, ignoring his injury in his urgency. "The demons are our only hope. If the Crusaders break through first, we'll die." He makes to move past me to the door I just closed, but my hands tighten convulsively on his, stopping him. I'm not ready.

I feel dazed, like I can't choke down this reality. I know I need to accept it, work with it. Keep moving, keep fighting. Accept what's happening and go with it. Make some goddamn lemonade. That's always been my way.

But right now, I can't. I feel like I've lost, even as I try to convince myself the game's not over.

"Meda, please." The pain in his voice pulls me to him. My eyes meet his, and I read so much there. Layers and depths, hopes and nightmares. He wraps his hands on either side of my face, and I feel the slick warmth of his blood on my cheek. He's determined to save me – no, save *us*, I can see it in every agonized line on his face, the flex of his jaw. "I know it's not what you wanted, but you have to." His words are fierce. "Please. It's the only way."

He never understood my reasons, but he understands my pain.

My heart aches. It bleeds and throbs. It breaks, as was always inevitable. I put myself in this impossible situation, torn between two worlds. I wanted all of it; Armand and freedom, Jo and the light. But that was never a tenable situation. Something had to give. I waited too long to make the decision myself. I was greedy; I took it all, and all, and all. Telling myself I would deal with it tomorrow, tomorrow, tomorrow. But I'm out of time, and the decision has been taken from me.

There's only one choice I can make. Only one left.

I look into Armand's eyes, and he reads me as

only he can, and he knows I've made a decision. But I don't want him to ask. I don't want to say.

So instead, I kiss him.

I take everything I'm feeling. The fear, the rage, the desperation. All the good and all the bad. What could have been, what *I* could have been. Everything I've ever wanted with Armand, but knew better than to admit, even to myself. Especially to myself. I take all these emotions and I shove them into that kiss. My world is on fire with feeling. He takes them all as he kisses me back, his lips as hot on mine, and I feel like I am being devoured, like I am devouring him. And I know it's the end, the end of all of this, so I put every ounce of everything in that kiss. I drain out all the softer emotions I have.

Because I don't want them. I can't have them, where I'm about to go.

The force of it, of *me*, because I am a force, shoves him backwards. He pushes back. Our kiss is like us, heat and violence and greed. But I'm stronger than he is, of course I am, and he stumbles backwards, until he fetches up against the pole behind him, the one where Hell punishes those under its control. The chains of the manacles clink; with the battle sounds, it's a perfect soundtrack.

Armand's hands thrust through my hair, and my own clutch his shoulders. I pull him down, roll up on my toes, try to get closer, try to crawl into his skin, try to swallow this moment as if I could keep it, as if it could live inside me.

It's real. This.

Everything will change, but I have this.

We break apart and he presses his forehead against mine and I close my eyes. I'm breathing in his heavy breath, and there's a catch in the way the air leaves my lungs, but it's not a sob. I'm not that girl and this is not the time. Later, there will be time.

His fingers trace lightly down the side of my face, filled with a tenderness at odds with our very natures, and he tips up my chin. I meet his dark eyes, filled with the shadows that haunt us both, that bind us. The shadows that make our fate inevitable.

"It will be OK, I promise," he whispers. "We'll be together."

I can't bear to listen, and I shake my head as if to scatter the words away, like crows.

This is not a happy ending.

I break eye contact, looking down and breathing deeply. I want to scream, to sob, to hit him, to hit the world. Instead, I gather my tattered courage, trading it for the remnants of foolish, greedy, broken dreams. Then I look back up into the eyes of the only person who can accept me no matter the horrible things I'm capable of. Those eyes.

I'm making the right decision. But it hurts. God, it hurts.

I reach up and take his good hand, tugging it down and twining my fingers with his. I wrap my arms around him, taking his hand with me.

It's time. I can face it.

I have no choice.

With a quick tug, I snap the manacle on his wrist.

THIRTY-EIGHT

IN THE MOMENT it takes Armand to realize what I've done, I pull out of range. His expression goes from shock to horror. He jerks his wrist and looks back at me. "What are you doing?" When I make no move, he jerks harder, his gaze shooting to the door. "We have to – the demons–"

I take the moment of his inattention to swallow the softness. I slaughter the affection; I brutalize my foolishness. I blink away tears. They had their moment, but it's passed. There's no room for them in what comes next.

A human probably couldn't do what I'm about to do, feeling as I feel. Even a saint could kill her enemy; it takes a monster to kill a friend.

That I'm destroying my humanity as I work to save it is not lost on me, but the irony does not make me smile. I told Armand once, a thousand years ago, that I was not a girl for moonlit daydreams. I am a ruthless monster, capable of doing what she must for what she wants.

When he twists back to me once more, my eyes are filled with an iciness few have survived. Armand won't be one of them.

"The demons aren't coming, Armand. I lied."

He moves his lips but no words leave them.

"I know it was you, Armand." The frost in my eyes seeps into my blood and turns my tone frigid.

He shakes his head, not wanting to believe.

"You set me up. You stole the Beacon Map. The demons couldn't find us, so the Crusaders must have it. You said so yourself." I shake my head. "But then the Crusaders couldn't find us either and *you knew*. You knew we could hide." I laugh, but it's not a happy sound. "I'm embarrassed I didn't figure it out sooner."

I know how devious our kind can be. He even told me – how many times? – that demons always have ulterior motives. But I know why I didn't see it sooner. Because I didn't want to. Because I knew what I'd lose. Because I lie to myself as much as I lie to anyone.

But I'm not really being fair to myself. I didn't know the specifics, but I always knew that it would come to this: me versus him. The specifics don't really matter, only the outcome: that I win.

The best part is he never lied. Not about wanting me dead, at least. He didn't; he was after a bigger fish. He was after my soul.

It makes me laugh, almost.

I look at him. I *look* at him and I *see* him.

The lies dance on his lips, his own rat-like nature begging him to scramble, to deny. I hold his eyes and the rats still, as does his frantic jerking on the chain. We know each other too well for that.

In that minute a thousand expressions play on his face; he lets me see them all. Then he finally speaks. "It was the only way."

My tiny heart gasps at the cold spreading through me. I ignore it. I knew, *I already knew*, but hope is a silly, irrational thing.

"It was the only way for us to be together." His voice is filled with a depth I don't care to hear. "I can never be a Crusader, Meda, but you, you can be one of us. If I could choose, I would. I would choose you." He jerks on his chain. "Please Meda, choose me." His dark eyes beg for me to understand.

And I do understand. I understand everything. Finally.

But as he tries to connect, I withdraw. This heart isn't the bleeding kind. Not in that way, at least.

My voice is all violent business. There are things I need to know before he dies. "You told the Crusaders I was here, to make me think they had the map. That's why they're here, isn't it?"

"Meda–" he starts, but I slice him with my eyes and his jaw tightens. "Yes." The apology, the pleading, is gone. "Your *friends* were already so eager to kill you I merely had to let them know where you were."

"And that little scene with my father, it was planned, wasn't it? So I would hear what I needed to in order to side with them. With you." I laugh, harsh and bitter. "It's so obvious; such a coincidence." I match a cold smile to that laugh. "I can only say in my defense that I was a little preoccupied."

"Everything he said was true."

I snarl.

"But, yes, it was planned."

Horrible realization strikes. "Jo and Chi–" They're upstairs, they don't know Armand's a traitor.

"It's not a trap," he swears. He twists his face in disgust. "I would never… I know how you feel about them. It's no more dangerous than it ever was. Less even, as there aren't even any demons monitoring the map." He looks at me like I'm capable of forgiveness. "They don't know it's here."

There's a cracking sound at the door and both our heads turn as if we can see through steel.

"So the map really is here?" I ask, calling him back.

"Yes. Meda, please, I wouldn't hurt them, because I know it would hurt you. And I never wanted to hurt you. I just wanted to–"

"What, Armand?" I snarl. "You wanted to *what?*"

He is unafraid, unapologetic. "Keep you," he finishes.

"You should have learned, Armand, as the Crusaders did, that I'm no one's pet." Stinging and soft.

His lips curve, just slightly, and he says just as softly, "You don't think I know that? Don't pretend to misunderstand, Meda; we are far too alike for that."

I look away and ask my next questions without turning back. "How far does this go back? When you tracked me to Colton's?"

"Further." He admits without hesitation. "The day we met in the dungeons. Zi-Hilo offered a reward to anyone who turned you. I planted myself in that cell to convince you to join the demons before you were taken upstairs."

"Uri." It's an accusation.

"No, Meda, that wasn't part of the plan. And I was truly locked in. There was nothing I could do."

"I'm supposed to take you at your word?"

"No, though I wish you would," he snaps. "But it wouldn't make any sense for zi-Hilo – or me – to want him dead. The last thing we wanted was to piss you off. The plan was to convince you to join us."

"And zi-Hilo thought you'd be in a position to gain my trust, after our shared prison time," I hypothesize. "He sent you after me."

"No. I suggested it," Armand says, as if it makes a difference.

"It was all a lie," I say this to myself, not him.

"No it wasn't." His reply is harsh. His expression is twisted, as ugly as his artificially-perfect face can allow. "Oh, yes, I did lie about a lot of things. And in the beginning, no, it wasn't about you, and, yes, I've always had other motives." His smile is bitter. "I'm a monster, Meda. I've never claimed to be good; I've never claimed to be anything other than what I am. I'm selfish and evil and greedy, I want many, many things, most of which I shouldn't have." His eyes glitter. "One of those things I want is you, and what kills me is that you are one thing that I should have. We belong together. They," he waves his free arm, "demons, Crusaders, they want to pick little pieces of you; I would have you all. Unlike your *friends*, I can delight in the darkest recesses of your soul just as I can the other parts."

A series of booms rock the room.

He moves suddenly, flying away from the post until his chain is fully stretched. He's only a foot or so away from me. "I wanted to be with you, and the only way for that to ever happen is for you to join the demons." Rage twists his face. "Maybe you can go both ways, Meda, but I can't. I'm trapped. The Crusaders would never accept me, even if they could. If you chose them, we could never be together. It wasn't betrayal; it was expediency. You may not like my methods, but I did it all for you."

"How could I ever believe–"

"Because you know it's true," he spits. It's an attack, not a seduction. "Oh, it started out as a mission to win you for the demons, I won't lie." He barks a laugh and jangles the chain at his wrist. "Not now. But it ended with me trying to win you for myself. And to keep you alive. No matter what you say, you know the Crusaders don't accept you either. They were fighting for the right to kill you long before I ever became involved. But more than that, they're outnumbered, and losing. If you join them it's only a matter of time before the demons kill you."

He laughs again. "What I don't understand, is why you're willing to let them. The Crusaders *hate* you and *still* you're determined to sacrifice yourself for their hopeless cause." He jerks his free hand through his hair. "I wasn't willing to accept that." He gets quiet, taking deep breaths as he gets himself under control. He stands silent for a moment, and there's another loud slam against the door behind him. He doesn't turn this time. Instead he looks at me.

When he speaks again, the anger has drained away. "I'm still not willing to accept it." He moves as if to come closer, but the chain holds him back. "I know you're mad – understatement, I know – but please Meda, don't kill yourself for people who don't give a damn about you." His lips quirk in a half-smile, the one I know so well. "Don't kill *me* for them." He reaches for me with his unchained hand, but he can't quite reach. "I'll do whatever you want, Meda." His voice is rough. "But pick me."

His eyes hold mine, and God, I want to. Our friendship was real, as real as is possible between two monsters. He betrayed our friendship *for* our friendship. We're selfish beasts. He wanted me, so he went after me. I wanted him, so I ignored all the reasons why it was wrong. Each step I took down the path of Meda-and-Armand flickered red with flags I chose to ignore, because something in him called to something in me. My head knew all along it was a mistake, but my heart refused to listen. It's only fair that it now writhes in pain, punishment for its stupidity. What a foolish thing, the human heart, being both fragile and reckless. No wonder we spend such an inordinate amount of time in pain.

Even now, it wants to take his outstretched hand and set him free. To leave this hellish place full of hateful lies and even more hateful truths.

But life doesn't work that way, I can't forget his betrayal, or forgive it. You can love a monster, it can even love you back, but that doesn't change its nature. This isn't *Beauty and the Beast* where my kiss would transform the monster to a prince. If anything, it's *Shrek*, and his kiss brings out the ogre in me.

I understand why he did it; that's the problem, isn't it? How well we understand each other. But just because I understand, doesn't stop me from hating him.

Just as that hate won't stop me from missing him.

My eyes burn and blur, and I'm grateful, because I don't want to see him anymore. Because I won't pick him, I won't let him live. I can't, no matter how my heart screams in its cage. I'm not that girl. I'm too clever, too practical, too *ruthless* to let him live.

And I am a monster.

My pathetic heart screams from its prison to stop

it, that the damned stupid little piece I gave him is going to die with him. That he's our friend, our companion.

That he's the only one in the world who has a chance of ever understanding me.

Seems a pity to waste one. I hear his voice in my head. But I shake it away, I shake him away.

He lets his hand drop, without me having to say a word.

In our silence, the room echoes with the Crusaders' attack on the door. "They're going to kill me," he says softly.

"I know," I say, keeping my voice emotionless. "I'm counting on it."

"Coward," he says, but there's no malice in the accusation.

"Always," I agree. "I told you, I warned you, that it would end this way."

"You did."

"I won't apologize."

He shakes his head, but his eyes never leave mine. "Neither will I."

There's an extra loud bang, and the door holding the Crusaders back collapses. I turn to see the Crusaders working to haul it out of the way so they can get to the gate.

"She's here!" I hear one of them shout.

My time is up. I turn my back on Armand, but I ask one more question before I go. "What did they offer you, Armand? The reward if I joined the demons?"

"My soul," he says simply. "I'm not a halfling. Not anymore."

Thirty-Nine

I CAN'T THINK about Armand. I can't think about his admission and what it means. Not now. Later I can let my little chest-creature out to whine and moan and make its painful fuss. But not now. Now I have more important things to do. Like undo this disaster I've caused, rescue the Beacon Map (and incidentally, mankind) and my friends. My true friends, I remind myself, the ones who didn't try to side-deal my soul to the devil. To do that, I need the Crusaders' help.

And to get their help I have to trust them.

"Stop!" I shout, running to the gate's lever. "I'm turning myself in."

The Crusaders still and I eye them in all their armed, bristling, demon-hunting fury.

"Errr, promise you won't kill me," I add hastily. "Get me The Sarge and I'll turn myself in." Hey, I'm still trusting them to keep their word. Baby steps.

There's a quick conference, and I'd bet anything

someone in the back is communicating with headquarters. "Fine," says a bulky, scarred black woman, who I deduce is the squad leader.

"Promise you won't kill me first," I push.

"Done," she clips and I appreciate her sense of urgency.

"Meda–" Armand makes one last plea, but it's pointless; that part's over. With a quick jerk, I pull the lever, and as soon as the door lifts, Crusaders swarm into the room.

I'm surrounded, and I have to force myself not to struggle as my arms are cuffed behind me. Even after I'm restrained, a Crusader takes each of my arms at the elbow. The squad leader, who I learn is called Gabo, stands in front of me and directs the rest to search and secure the room.

"There's only one other door," I volunteer. I can't move my arms, so I nod toward the vault-like door I'd shut earlier. She ignores me. "Where's The Sarge?"

"On the way."

"Who's this?" shouts a Crusader behind me.

The squad leader looks to me for explanation. "Friend of yours?"

"No," I say, without turning around.

She doesn't blink. "Kill him."

It's what I wanted.

Thankfully there's a commotion from the hallway that pulls my attention away from what is happening behind us. The Sarge must have arrived, and not a minute too soon. I can't see, the squad leader standing in front of me, but I hear a curt "Sergeant," and I sigh in relief.

I sighed too soon.

"Miss Melange," the Sergeant says in fat satisfaction.

I close my eyes and think lots of profanity. When I open them, the squad leader has stepped to the side.

"Hello, Sergeant Graff."

I really should have been more specific.

"I need to speak to Sergeant *Reinhardt*," I demand.

His attention is already elsewhere. "Sound the retreat," he orders.

"Chi and Jo, they're out then?" I ask.

No one answers. Several Crusaders mutter the communication spells and body-less Crusader-heads start popping in-and-out of existence, and the word "retreat" repeats down the line. The Crusaders in the room start moving, my escort pulling me towards the door, Graff walking with us.

"Chi and Jo are out, aren't they?" Graff doesn't answer, but the way squad leader Gabo won't meet my eyes says it all. I ask again anyway, even though I already know the answer. "Aren't they?"

"Crusader Gabo, leave half your people behind to work clean up," he jerks his head back towards where we came from, "and the other half to scout ahead." he orders. She motions people down the tunnel ahead of us. Sergeant Graff nods to another Crusader working the communication spell. "Tell the Rhinos they're on back-up. Get them on our tail." Graff turns back as a Crusader says something to him about Red Squad being pinned down. "Tell them we're sending reinforcements, then find Rhys and see if you can get him over there. Everyone else able to retreat?"

"Yessir."

"But Jo and Chi – you can't retreat." No one listens as we march into the tunnel. "Wait! You can't retreat!" I jerk free and throw myself at Graff, slamming into him. We don't fall, but I certainly have his attention.

"Chi and Jo are still in here. You have to get them!"

His eyes are cold and dead. "No."

"What do you mean, *no*?"

"Get her out of here." I'm seized from behind, by the squad leader herself this time.

"How can you call the retreat? They're still in there!" I thrash in her arms, and one of my previous guards jumps back into the fray. "You can't call the retreat!" I shout, pulling against the restraining arms. "Jo and Chi are still in there!" He doesn't pay me any attention and I fight for all I'm worth. "Let me go! I'll do it myself!"

Crusader Gabo looks sincerely, genuinely sorry as she forcefully drags me down the tunnel.

"No!" I scream and keep screaming. I smash my head into Gabo's nose and lash out with my legs to slam another one in the gut, but it's to no avail. More just pin me down. Why did I let them cuff me? *Why?*

"The Beacon Map!" I scream, frantic. "I can get you the Beacon Map." That gets a glance, just barely a glance from Sergeant Graff, and I hold my breath.

He turns his back.

I lunge at him. I get nowhere, but I can't stop myself. "You heartless son of a bitch. Don't you care about them?"

He stiffens, and turns slowly. His face is a mask of fury. "I'm heartless?" He hisses. "*I'm* heartless?" The restraining arms stay around me, but they no longer try to drag me away. "Do you have any idea how many people have died today *because of you*?" It's a low, vicious growl.

I flinch, but I won't back down. "You never liked me," I accuse. "But don't punish Chi and Jo for it."

"Punish them? *Punish* them?" He laughs. *Laughs.* "You petty, stupid *child*." He bites off each word slowly and hatefully. "I don't pick who lives and who dies based on whether I *like* them — I don't have that luxury." The look of absolute disgust he gives me says I wouldn't be there if he did. "It's a balancing act. I can't risk more lives — *dozens* more lives — to *try* to save two. Two who could be anywhere, who might already be dead." He slams a hand over his eyes and breathes deep, getting himself under control. When he pulls his hand down, the rigid, icy mask is back. "It's not personal, Miss Melange. It's math."

"You won't have to risk dozens," I jump in. "I know where they are, I can lead you to them. I just need a few people to help me, eight… no, six, even. Please."

He doesn't say anything for a heartbeat and I realize I'm mouthing the word "please" over and over again. But then he shakes his head. "I can't risk it. We can't trust you. Not after this." He waves and the restraining arms start pulling me away.

"No! No!" But no one listens. "If they die, it's on you!" I scream.

He turns. "No, Miss Melange," he says, and I see beneath his mask. "I have a lot that I am responsible for, but this? This one," he pauses, looking almost sorry as he says it, "this one is on you."

And he is absolutely, completely right, and the realization leaves me stunned. It was my friendship with Armand; it was my running away; it was my stealing the Beacon Map. It was my plan to invade the Acheron; it was me who involved Jo and Chi. It is utterly and completely my fault, every stupid, stupid mistake.

"Sergeant," someone calls from behind him. I watch wordlessly as he turns away, his movements somehow both heavy and quick.

"Yes?"

"Red Squad is on their way out."

Graff raises his arm and whips it around his head. "Move out."

"No!" I scream, pointlessly. "No! You can't leave

them. You can't–"

But he can and he does. They start to move out.
A few sympathetic looks are cast my way. They love
Chi, they love Jo, but they agree with Graff. They can't
risk it, can't risk taking me at my word and risking their
friends' lives. They can't trust me, and it's going to cost
Chi and Jo their lives. Because this is all my fault.

Because I am not trustworthy.

"Please," I'm mouthing the word again, but
everyone looks away. "I was wrong. I made a mistake.
I'm sorry, just please…" I beg, sobbing. But they can't.
They're too smart for that. Words are hollow, hollow
things.

Trust is earned, Jo told me once. *Trust is earned*, and I
hadn't earned it. Graff made mistakes, true. Possessing
me by force was wrong, of course it was. But at least
his motives had been pure. Not mine. It has always
been about me. How the other students treated me,
how I didn't get to play with magic, how I didn't get to
eat when I wanted. Sneaking out, playing the pranks,
Ar– but I can't finish the name.

Graff was right. I am a stupid, petty child.

Jo was right. This war isn't about me. But of
course, Jo was always right.

No, *is*. Jo *is* always right.

Jo.

Trust is earned.

And I know what I have to do. There's only one
way to prove that I'm one of them – one of the Cru-

saders. To teach them where Jo and Chi and the Beacon Map are without wasting the days it had taken us to learn all the different routes. The only way to save my friends. The only way to save the Beacon Map.

The only way to earn the Crusaders' trust.

"Sergeant Graff," I say. The formality, the *deference* in my tone catches his attention better than a thousand screams would have. "I know how we can save them." He spares me one almost-curious glance before turning his back. My next words stop him before he can walk away.

"Possess me."

FORTY

IF I'D HOPED that the mere noble offer would be enough to convince them of my trustworthiness, I would have been severely disappointed. As it was, I barely had time to suggest such a thing before Sergeant Graff was bent over, breathing into my face.

The transition is smoother, faster, this time. I don't fight him, but slide into my corner, making space for his swollen redness. Once in, he instantly clambers to Our feet, and with a few quick stretches and light bouncing, like a fighter about to enter the ring, he's ready.

"Where are they?" He asks me out loud, but he doesn't need to. I'm not blocking him out and I feel the words before he says them, like little ripples through the amorphous liquid that is Us.

I let the information flood back: the lessons with the demon boy, the Beacon Map's location, what I know about the Acheron. The sudden rush of information sends Us to Our knees.

"Easy!" he shouts at me, again unnecessarily out loud, and I slow the flood of information to a steady stream. The squad leader grabs Our arm, and I see the Crusader who cast the spell striding forward. We hold up a hand to let the others know We're fine, and get back to Our feet.

I can feel his concentration as I feed him the information, and I can follow the clear-cut paths his thoughts make as he connects dots, calculates odds, and debates and discards options before they are even fully formed. His mind is rigidly, beautifully organized; his thoughts are a constantly running algorithm that combines his knowledge with potential actions and calculates their probable outcomes – and all of these are weighed against each other in a rapidly adjusting equation I can barely follow.

He doesn't have a mind so much as a calculator of fates.

I hear his conclusions as he makes them and I know each of his moves before he gives the orders. The Royce Rollers are already near where we think Jo and Chi are, so we'll meet up with them, freeing the present company to take Graff's limp body to the surface. We'll take two of our current squad with us in case We run into trouble on the way. The Rollers have lost three of their squad, so that brings us to eleven for the rescue mission. Ten-and-a-half, really, as one of the Rollers is only a rookie.

He debates bringing more, but favors speed and stealth over numbers. It's better to call as little attention to ourselves as possible because even if we called every Crusader here to go with us, we still wouldn't have enough to face the demons head on in a battle.

Not anymore.

But he can't think about that. Not now. There's too much to be done. There will be time for that. Later.

We'll order a final push from the retreating army, draw the demons into battle there. They don't know about the Beacon Map, so they won't be anticipating a retrieval mission.

It's fluid, this information transfer; our thoughts and feelings mingle without a wall thrown up to block them. I'm not digging into his mind, attacking, as I did the last time, so I'm not getting the vivid images of memories stolen, but every thought is in some way the result of emotion and experience, and little bits of those leak into the pool of our shared information.

I wonder what he gets from me. What he feels when I think of Jo and Chi. When I think of the Crusaders. When I think of—

But I stop myself from saying his name. It is now one of those things that is better left unspoken.

Crusaders Chan and Jones flank us as we set off after Chi and Jo. We pause at intersections as We try to get our bearings, trying to recall the routes the demon boy sketched on scratch paper. We picture the kitchen, the table, the curving snake-like lines of tunnels, dark eyes–

Left. We go left.

Eventually we hear the sound of battle. It's got to be Royce Rollers, and we pick up our pace, racing toward the battle. We come around the corner, just as there's an explosion and we hit the deck and rubble flies over us, pelting down like rain. We look up cautiously and see an enormous hall, the ceiling held up by a forest of columns meant to look like trees from some wicked wood. Cut down the middle winds a narrow path, widening at the end to make it appear as if the room beyond is a clearing in the forest. Blocking the way, however, is a huge barricade of stacked furniture that looks like it was cut from stone, behind which waits an army of demons. Nearby are a couple of the Rollers using the "trees" as cover as they hurl magic and holy water grenades at the demons' barricade. We wave Jones and Chan forward and bear-crawl forward to join a Crusader I don't recognize, a middle-aged man, sitting on the floor with his back pressed against a column. In his arms is the limp form of a young woman.

"Dupaynes and Beauregard are somewhere in there, but they can't get to us," he says without preamble. "There are demons in the woods, with more flinging magic from the barricade. Anytime we try to move forward, they blast the crap out of us." He looks down at the woman in his arms. "We're down to six," he adds grimly. "And my leg…" We notice now the ground-meat condition of his left shin. Five. They're down to five.

Graff is unflappable. "Now we're back up to eight." We press Ourself as close as possible to the column and peer into the room to take stock. The other five remaining Crusaders are behind columns of their own, spread out across the room as if planning to flank the demons with their pathetically tiny army. Crusaders Janus, Teague, and Hudson I recognize from school, and another is a Corp who looks familiar, but I never learned her name. The fifth I know far, far too well.

Isaiah.

Not exactly my first choice to protect my back.

He glances back as if he feels Our eyes on him. He doesn't look surprised to see me, but then, he would have known I – or rather We – were coming. For once I'm glad I don't have control of my body; he'd enjoy my horrified expression far too much.

A cloud of black fire comes rolling our way, and we duck back into hiding.

Graff's busy using the cold abacus of his mind to consider options. "We'll need to strike them again," We finally say, "before they realize reinforcements have arrived. Use what little element of surprise we have to distract them and give Beauregard and Dupaynes a chance to get to us."

The other Crusader's eyes flicker. He knows how dangerous that is, but, like all of us, has no better plan.

"But first, we need to get closer. Make them concentrate their forces close to the barricade, clearing up the woods for the students to escape." We look again at the Crusader's leg, and I feel an abacus bead slide. Graff orders him to get himself and the woman back to the others and out of the Acheron. The Crusader looks like he wants to argue but is too well-trained.

Quickly the others are informed of the plan. We'll try to rush the field, trying to make it at least half-way across the room, before taking cover and reevaluating – hopefully to do it again, then again, until we focus the demons on the far side of the room.

At Our signal, we go. I barely have time to brace myself before We're dodging among the trees and flinging magic with all the fury We contain. It's not boundless, the magical energy, and I can feel Graff's impatience as he waits the seconds it takes for the energy to reload. The demons cackle and fire back, and a column to my left crumbles and I hear a scream that ends too abruptly. We dive over another pile of rubble, and send a bolt of white fire zinging towards the demons. There's not even the length of a football field to our planned rendezvous point, but it feels far, far longer as we dodge death with every step. I see another Crusader ahead of us miscalculate and go down, screaming, encased in a black cloud of gnat-like particles.

Jones. It was Jones.

We reach the rendezvous point first and duck behind a tree. Isaiah comes running up next, and as he gets close, We duck out from behind the tree and lash out with Our magic. This time it snakes like a whip, and with a terrific *crack* rips down an entire tree, crushing the demons caught beneath. We swing around to face another one coming up over the barricade. She pulls back her hands, as if to throw magic, then she freezes mid-motion. We recover and launch a lightning bolt, but she drops behind the barrier, and it flies harmlessly into the room behind. We duck back behind Our tree, Isaiah safely behind one of his own to the left.

Once We're able, We duck out to launch another attack, protecting the female Corp, then Teague and Hudson as they get close. This time, however, the demons don't fight back.

I feel Graff's uneasiness. *Why aren't they fighting Us?* He ducks out and launches another bolt toward the barricade. Still no response. *Every time they see Us, they stop.*

What? Are you disappointed?

He starts as if he forgot I was there. He doesn't bother to respond, but I get the general feeling of someone waving a mosquito away.

I pause, thinking. The demons have never used magic against me, the whole time I've been in the Acheron. I can't fight back; I'd be dead if they did. *They aren't using magic because they aren't supposed to kill me.*

I feel his confusion.

This whole thing was a show, a set-up by Armand and my dad, to get me to side with Hell. They still think I might join them. I pour the information at him. *They know you came to kill me*. If I was hoping for some denial from him, I'm disappointed. I continue, *and they think your attempt to murder me will cause me to throw myself on the demons'... mercy*, I say for lack of a better word. *They don't realize the game's changed, that I've sided with the Crusaders. Until then – they're not supposed to kill me.*

Only one person knew I was a lost cause, and I didn't really leave him in a position to tell.

Focus, Graff barks. *So you're saying they've orders not to kill you?*

Not until they figure out I've sided with the Crusaders.

I feel his wolfish delight. *Well that changes things, now doesn't it?*

Before I can respond, We leap from our hiding space and stride down the path, despite my frantic attempts to stop Us. The demons hesitate, unclear what to do. That hesitation is all We need – with my super-amped demon-Crusader abilities, We are among them before they make a decision, flinging the whip-like lightening left and right. This close to the barricade, We can see the demons behind their trees and slash them down, bringing down entire columns in the process. Two more bounds and We're on the top of the barricade. On the other side of the barricade are even more demons than Graff anticipated. I don't know how many – I'm not really in a position to stop and count.

The demons' hesitation ends, and they attack.

I think they figured it out! I yelp, as We dive back over

the barricade.

Thank God Isaiah and the three other surviving Crusaders are waiting to give us back up. With the protection of the barricade, we're now at a stand-off with the demons.

Isaiah suddenly jerks right and, not having magic, launches a holy water globe at a demon lunging from the wood. It explodes in the demon's face, and Isaiah leaps forward to cut his throat. He drops the demon then spins to confront another movement to his left.

It's Jo, staggering from the wood, half-dragging a blood-soaked Chi.

FORTY-ONE

A SURPRISED ISAIAH grabs Chi just as Jo's knees give out. We jump forward and she collapses in Our arms. All the blood makes her slippery, and We lower her to the ground carefully, then drag her back toward the barricade. Isaiah does the same with Chi, where Crusader Chan tries to assess his wounds.

Jo looks dazed, and her pupils don't match. Suddenly she jerks and twists trying to find Chi. "Chi, he's—"

Dying. She doesn't need to say it. The gaping wound across his stomach and Crusader Chan's horrified expression say it all.

"Sergeant—" Chan says.

Graff doesn't need to hear anymore. "Get him up top, Chan. Now."

Jones rips off the remains of Chi's shirt and cinches it across his belly, then heaves him into his arms. We've turned back to Jo before he's made it out of the room.

"The Beacon Map," We demand. "Where's the map?"

"Hid it," she gasps. "Didn't know you were coming, didn't want them to find it on us…"

"Where?" We demand, but she's already holding up a trembling arm. She points over the barricade, into the other room – the room currently filled with demons. "On a balcony." Her words slur together. We leave her with Isaiah to scramble up the barricade.

The round room on the other side is pitted with balconies, dozens of them. It looks like a drunk architect decided to fill a room with ornately carved opera boxes. We slide back down and drag her back up with Us. She points to one about thirty feet up.

"There're carvings in it. Dozens." She still can't catch her breath, still can't quite focus. "A gargoyle. Big eyes. Big, watching eyes." She opens her hands with a weak "pop" in front of her own eyes, which then roll back in her head.

We shake her but she doesn't regain consciousness. I feel Graff's assurance that she's still alive, but his thoughts are already elsewhere, already calculating the odds. There are at least twenty demons between us and the balcony. Hudson, Teague, and Ellie – that's how Graff thinks of the woman Crusader – are holding them back. If they could provide Us with enough cover to get through, We could throw the map down to them. They could escape, the map would be safe.

I screech an instinctual *no* and he flinches.

We might be able to make it out. He says with an unbelievable off-handedness. *In our limited acquaintance, Miss Melange, I've never known you to lack for confidence.*

I'm too terrified to snort.

His redness grows serious. *You know how important the Beacon Map is, and I think you know we can't leave it behind. I'm sorry, he thinks at me solemnly, that you'll die with me. I don't force people into suicide missions, but in this case, I have no choice.*

I don't want to. Holy shit, do I not want to, but I can't come up with a better plan. We can't leave it.

And the part of me that's capable of shame knows that it's right that this duty falls to me. Chi, Jo, the dead Crusaders littering the halls of the Acheron – all of it's my fault.

Karma, as I told Colton all those weeks ago, is indeed a bitch.

But I don't say any of that to him. *Suicide mission?* I, too, try to sound off-hand, but as the guy's literally in my head, I'm pretty sure he knows I'm glad I'm not currently in control of my bladder. *Come now, Sergeant Graff, we may make it out alive. In all our limited acquaintance, I've never known you to lack for confidence.*

Graff's satisfaction and…pride, maybe, swell around me, but he doesn't respond with words. We scramble back down and relay the plan to the others, who resist instantly.

"No sir," Ellie says immediately. "Let me," she

waves at the others. "Or any of us. You – and her – are too important."

I feel no surprise from Graff at Ellie's offer. Graff knew she would, but, as he said, he doesn't force others into suicide missions.

Well, you could have told me.

I feel his mental shrug.

Isaiah stands from where he was kneeling by Jo. "No. Let me."

Well, color me surprised.

He looks at Ellie. "I don't have the magical abilities to provide any cover." He turns back to us. "And you have the best chance of getting out of here with the others."

There isn't a chance he'll make it out alive. He knows; I can see in his electric blue eyes the same burning commitment I saw weeks ago when he tried to get rid of me.

If he goes, he will die.

"You think you can retrieve it?" We ask Isaiah.

"Yes, sir," he replies, smartly, not looking towards the hordes of demons between us and the Beacon map. "And if I can't…" He trails off. If he can't, then someone else can take their turn. In the pause, an explosive blast hits a column behind us.

"Permission granted, Crusader Hooper." None of the sadness I feel in Graff, none of his memories of Isaiah as the small boy he was just a few years ago, bleed into his words. But I see it. I see it all.

Isaiah's not doing it for me, I tell myself. He's doing it for the cause. He's dying in my place, but not *for* me.

But he looks in his enemy's face when he says it. It's his enemy's head that tilted in assent, sending him to his death.

Isaiah nods and turns to the barricade where the others launch our defense. He looks solemn, his face carefully blank, but I see his hand, where he places it on the leg of an overturned table, trembles slightly. He looks back at Us.

"Sergeant."

"Yes."

"You can hear her thoughts, can't you?"

"To an extent, yes."

"And she's with us, right? Really *with us*."

We nod.

He licks dry lips. "Can she hear me?" he asks, and again We nod. Isaiah peers closely, searching for something in Our face. "It was never about you, the things we – *I* – did." He waits as if for a response but I don't have the voice to give him one.

You can, Graff says. I feel his redness, shifting, sliding out of the way until there's a path to Our vocal cords.

Before I can use them, Isaiah forces a twisted smile. "Don't get me wrong, I still don't *like* you, Monster."

"Ha, good," I say, my throat tight. If he's surprised it's me talking, he doesn't let it show. "For a second I was worried you were going to hug me or something."

Isaiah's too anxious to laugh, but manages a snort.

"And you know I'd have to gut you if you tried, because *I* don't like *you*, either."

That does get a laugh, if a short, tense one. "No, you wouldn't," he says. We hold eyes for a moment, then his sharp smile is back. "It'd ruin your escape."

"You're right, I wouldn't," I agree.

He straightens sharply with a salute. "Sergeant," he says, and turns to Ellie, "Crusader," then turns to me. "Monster," he says, and I return his salute with a one-fingered one of my own.

Then, with a glittering smile, Isaiah is up and over the barricade. We provide cover as best we can, launching magical attack after magical attack. At one point I climb over to draw the demons' attention to me. Isaiah's scrambling up the carved gargoyles when he takes the first hit. It rocks him to the side, but I don't hear him make a sound. He grimly continues, up, up, up, until he reaches the target balcony and hurls himself over the bannister. He disappears from view.

The demons swarm up the wall after him, like ants after a sweet. We give him the best cover we can, but we need to keep them off us as well. There are too many, and it's only a few minutes before the first demon makes it over the bannister after him. Then another.

Isaiah doesn't reappear.

Then suddenly, suddenly he's there. With a terrific yell he hurls the package in our direction as hard as he can, just as the demons swarm over the bannister, dragging him down. The package flies over Our head and We lunge for it. We catch it, land hard, and roll. Ellie hurls one last blast of magic, then goes racing by, the unconscious Jo slung over her shoulder, while the others cover our retreat. Graff and I overtake Ellie, to lead us out of there. We don't need to turn around to know the demons are behind us.

We don't need to turn around to know that Isaiah no longer is.

EPILOGUE

ONCE AGAIN Jo, Chi, and I are in the back of a big kidnapper-van, bumping over twisting mountain roads on our way back home. I'm in much better shape than last time, but Chi and Jo are mummified up and passed out on painkillers. Jo's next to me on the first row of passenger seats, and Chi in the row behind us.

The van's windows are covered in black paper, but I stare as if I can see out anyway, thinking about the nature of friends and enemies.

I don't know what happened to Armand, and I don't ask. Jo says it's better this way, probably because she knows he's dead. But I'm not afraid to ask because I don't want to hear he's dead; I don't ask because it doesn't matter. He's dead to me, what we had is dead, regardless. I'd be more afraid to hear he's still alive.

"Meda, what's wrong?" Jo's groggy voice next to me.

"Nothing," I say, hoarsely.

"It's *him*, isn't it?" Her voice is a little more awake, a little sharper. She hasn't said Armand's name since I told her what happened. I hear the springs creak as she pulls herself upright on the bench next to me. "Meda, you should *hate* him. He *betrayed* you." She tries to sound calm and rational, but her fury pops through, emphasizing almost every other word. "He almost got you *killed*. He *stole* the *Beacon Map*. You *know* what that would *mean*. He—"

I turn and look at her. I just look. I don't say a word, but whatever she sees in my face makes her stop. This isn't something she can fix, nothing she can explain away. It's not that I don't understand the facts; it's that my human heart doesn't care. My monstrousness could kill Armand, but my humanity can't escape mourning him.

"Tomorrow, OK, Jo?" I exhale, and it aches. "I'll hate him tomorrow."

She gingerly takes my hand. "OK, Meda. Tomorrow."

We ride in silence for a few more minutes, the air tense with my misery.

"It's Chi," Jo says out of nowhere.

"What's Chi?" I ask, absently.

"It's Chi," she repeats, in a weird way that gets my attention. She shoots a look at where he's still sleeping. "Who won't."

"Won't what?"

She makes a face and a circular *you know* motion

with her hand.

"Jo, I have no idea what the hell you're talking about."

She makes a frustrated sound and says through her teeth, "Why we haven't *you know*."

"No, I don't know." I don't know why she's the frustrated one. "Use your words, Jo."

"Jesus, Meda!" She throws her hands in the air. "You've been pestering me for months, I finally tell you, and you don't–"

Oh my God, she can't mean–

"'But why?'" she mocks my tone from earlier this week.

OH MY GOD SHE DOES!

"Chi? Chi?" I squeal.

"Shhhhhhhh!" She twists, making sure he's still asleep. She's still embarrassed, but can't resist a little smirk at my shock.

Me, I'm stuck on repeat. "Chi? Chi?" So much for Superhero Meda, bending gender roles – it didn't even occur to me it could be Chi. Mind. Blown.

Jo forces nonchalance. "Yeah. I figure, the way things are going, we could die any day. Might as well…" She shrugs. "But you know him–"

Apparently not.

"–always the optimist. He's convinced we're going to make it to a ripe old age."

Suddenly, as if to prove Chi an idiot, there's an explosion.

It's so close by that the van rocks, and instinctively I grab the passenger seat in front of me. The driver shouts and brakes so hard we spin sideways on the gravel and Chi slams onto the back of our seat. He scrambles up just as Jo rips the paper from the window.

Spread out below is the flaming rubble that was once Mountain Park II.

The Crusader in the passenger seat is yelling at us to buckle up and simultaneously casting the communication spell, while the driver works to U-turn on the narrow gravel road. Other vans, filled with wounded, are trying to turn around, while motorcycles zip around and head into the valley.

As for me, I have an overwhelming, entirely inappropriate urge to laugh.

"Seatbelt, Meda!" Jo snaps hers into place, and pulls the sling off her arm, wanting it free. "Seatbelt! What the hell is wrong with you?"

"'He's convinced we're going to make it to a ripe old age' – those would have been some terrific last words. So close." I hold my fingers in a little pinch.

"Seriously, Meda?"

"Look on the bright side, Jo – maybe this will help convince him." I wave at the flaming wreckage.

"Oh for freak's sake! She's lost it." Jo jerks my seatbelt out of my hand and slams it home just as the driver guns it back down the mountain.

Maybe I have lost it. Maybe there's just so much crazy a person can take. I should be worried, scared, freaking out. I know that. But I'm not thinking about the flaming school, yet another near-death encounter, or where the hell we're going to hide next.

No, I'm still thinking about last words, about the last thing Armand said – that Hell would give him back his soul if he convinced me to join them.

It means that selling a soul isn't permanent. The demons can give them back.

Or we could take them.

Acknowledgments

First, a huge thank you to my husband, Adam, and my daughter Madeleine. Thank you for making my hardest year also my best. I love you both.

I'd like to thank all my critique partners, but especially Mónica and Reg for being willing to hop on the crazy train for another ride. I couldn't have done it without you—or your devil-faces, Mónica!

I would like to also thank my agent, Victoria Marini, and my editor at Penguin India, Ameya Nagarajan, for their excellent guidance, and the rest of the Penguin India team for their hard work. And thanks to Dominic Harman for my kick-ass cover.

I would also like to thank the folks at Strange Chemistry, particularly my former editor Amanda Rutter and PR-person extraordinaire Caroline Lamb. It was an awesome ride--I just wish it could have lasted a bit longer.

And last but not least, an enormous thank you to my fans. It was your massive roar of support when Strange Chemistry went under that convinced me to do whatever it took to get this bad boy out there. I love making you laugh, cry, and hurl things against the wall. This one's for you.

About the Author

Eliza Crewe always thought she'd be a lawyer, and even went so far as to complete law school. But as they say, you are what you eat, and considering the number of books Eliza has devoured since childhood, it was inevitable she'd end up in the literary world. She abandoned the lawyer-plan to instead become a librarian and now a writer.

While she's been filling notebooks with random scenes for years, Eliza didn't seriously commit to writing an entire novel until the spring of 2011, when she and her husband bought a house. With that house came a half-hour commute, during which Eliza decided she needed something to think about other than her road-rage. Is it any surprise she wrote a book about a blood-thirsty, people-eating monster?

Eliza has lived in Illinois, Edinburgh, and Las Vegas, and now lives in North Carolina with her husband, daughter, hens, an angry, talking, stuffed dwarf giraffe, and a sweet, mute, pantomiming bear. She likes to partially-complete craft projects, free-range her hens, and take long walks. The Soul Eaters is her first series.

She is represented by Victoria Marini of Gelfman Schneider Literary Agents, Inc.

Connect with Eliza

Website:
www.ElizaCrewe.com

Twitter:
www.twitter.com/ElizaCrewe

Goodreads:
www.goodreads.com/author/show/6559113.Eliza_Crewe

Other Books by Eliza Crewe

Cracked (Soul-Eater Series #1)

17648030R00242